Silver Winner for General Fiction
Foreword Reviews' 2014 INDIEFAB Book of the Year Awards

Winner of the 2015 Adirondack Literary Award for Best Novel
and
Winner of the 2015 People's Choice Award
presented by the Adirondack Center for Writing

Praise for *The Truth and Legend of Lily Martindale*

"...the strength of the writing in *The Truth and Legend of Lily Martindale* made it a pleasure to read."
— *North Country Public Radio*

"Shartle has written a rich novel. She captures the 'otherness' of the Adirondack camp, with its family and seasonal rituals, and its solitude. She has created a troubled character who finally puts the pieces of her life into a whole. And she creates the story within the larger context of bits of prayers people have sung for centuries."
— *Adirondack Daily Enterprise*

"Mary Sanders Shartle paints a strong portrait of New York's rugged Adirondack region in her debut novel, *The Truth and Legend of Lily Martindale*. It's an atmospheric tale about a great tragedy that devastates two little girls. One refashions her life, finding love, faith, and a rewarding career, while the other struggles for many years to forge herself anew ... Shartle's memorable novel will find a ready audience with readers who are already fond of the Adirondacks, but it is so studded with rich detail and scenery that others will want to transport themselves to this wild, dangerous, yet achingly lovely place."
— *Foreword Reviews*

D0813437

The Truth and Legend of
LILY MARTINDALE

The Truth and Legend of
LILY MARTINDALE

—— An Adirondack Novel ——

MARY SANDERS SHARTLE

excelsior editions

State University of New York Press
Albany, New York

Cover art: Painting by Laura Von Rosk: *Whiteface Landing*, oil on wood, 12" x 10", 2009

Published by State University of New York Press, Albany

Excelsior Editions is an imprint of State University of New York Press

For information, contact State University of New York Press, Albany, NY
www.sunypress.edu

Production by Eileen Nizer
Marketing by Fran Keneston

Library of Congress Cataloging-in-Publication Data

Shartle, Mary Sanders
    The truth and legend of Lily Martindale : an Adirondack novel / Mary Sanders Shartle.
        pages cm. — (Excelsior editions)
    ISBN 978-1-4384-5018-6 (pbk. : alk. paper)   1. Women hermits—Fiction.
2. Adirondack Mountains (N.Y.)—Fiction.   I. Title.

    PS3619.H35666T78 2014
    813'.6—dc23   2013014431

10 9 8 7 6 5 4 3 2 1

For Geneva Henderson, my daughter,
who still sings in the choir

Love wants to reach out and manhandle us,
Break all our teacup talk of God.

—From "Tired of Speaking Sweetly," by Hafez

Hermit Song 1

Come to me caution
mild as sleep
sipping at my limbs
like the lakes' tiny fish
until I'm lazy and care
is a caress and less
I've lived too long
in the wilderness
of my possessive self
my hands furled
in fist so long
I've been driven
by turnings and tides
the willful moon
shut me down
to a moan of myself
a whisper a still life

—Marilyn McCabe

The winds blow as they list,
And love goes where it will,
And I would go where my heart is
And sit on a lonely hill—

—Jeanne Robert Foster (from *Rock Flower*)

Chapter One

"As pants the hart for cooling springs
When heated in the chase . . ."

"Martyrdom" (orig. "Fenwick" or "Drumclog"), #450, Episcopal Hymnal, 1940

Tune: Hugh Wilson, c. 1800, harmony by Robert A. Smith, 1825

Text: Tate and Brady, 1696, based on Psalm 42

The snows are not eternal, but she is. Snows are driven, she is not. She drags through the landscape inside out: not a pretty sight. She is given to sighs that rival winds and winds that rival the roar of the blow down, bursting rages that hurl crashing like water down a flume. She is rain and wind together, blessed by neither. She does not walk; she rumbles along like a storm. Overhead a raven calls. Together they are the stuff of legend. Animals follow her. She smells of them. People say she talks to them.

A slow-moving part of the landscape of trees and hills, she is brown and gray like a slow-rolling glacial erratic. She is layered and sturdy as corn husks but part feather, part fur, part skin and horn. The only incongruous part of her, the part that identifies her as more human than elemental yet nonetheless elemental, is a pair of snowshoes. Older than she, they are as venerable as the landscape—ash, willow and the tendons of a long-fallen creature. The bindings are kept loose by rubbings of mink oil, replaced here and there by new joins fashioned of wood, cloth, twine, wire and duct tape.

When the snow melts, she sheds layers of felt and wool, fleece and leather. But she is thick today with the fat of clothes like blubber on a whale. Underneath she is quite lean, though pained and achy. Her body, though not young, is taut, wiry, strong and stubborn. Outside it can be thirty below, but inside her tent of clothing she is just breaking a sweat. Her face is covered but her eyes show. They are balsam green and keen as the needles of the white pine. She is pausing, mid-rumble, to look both at the sky and at the landscape. There at the crest of an escarpment where a large open meadow meets the woods, there's a kettle pond of good size. Two sturdy birches and a scrub of alder and witch hazel line one side, but the bushes are so covered with snow they form little mounds of six or seven feet in mockery of the mountains to the east and south—the High Peaks of the Adirondacks.

She trudges to the clumps of alder and snow where like a badger she has hollowed out a temporary shelter. Around her chest—the barrel of fabric and fur—is a rope. Behind her the rope pulls taut to an ancient ten-seat toboggan with a pile of something under a tarp; behind that, at a respectful distance, are twelve deer. From her hands she pulls off the outer layer of boiled wool, matted felt, and leather mittens: great paws carefully batted, stitched, and mended. Underneath that are wool gloves and underneath those are dainty silk liners. She leaves the silk and wool on. She turns slowly so as not to startle her gathering herd, unleashes herself from the rope, and begins to loose the oiled canvas tarp from the toboggan. From some deep recess in the folds of clothing she pulls a pair of sturdy wire cutters and snips the baling wire around three bales of hay. Huffing and puffing, she rolls each one off the toboggan. Then she pulls the toboggan along toward her shelter to let the deer come forward and feed.

She carries a pack basket, and from its black ash depths she draws out a thermos packed in batting and an insulated bag with some nuts, chocolate and raisins, and several slices of buttered toast. She sits on a snow-covered rock beside the pond with the pack basket and thermos. The clip-on thermometer on the basket shows twenty-eight degrees below zero. The sun has risen and is warming things up a bit. It will soon be between minus ten and zero as the sun climbs the peaks in the east over Lake Placid and Saranac Lake, fifty miles away. It's seven o'clock on Sunday morning, February second, Groundhog Day and Candlemas.

She sniffs the heat of the tea from the thermos and deems it too hot to swill from the lip. She pours a bit into the metal cup top, wrapping her woolly hands about the cup and waiting a few seconds only. It will chill too soon and then freeze. She sips eagerly until the cup is drained, but already it is cold.

The deer are dainty in their approach to the hay—early July hay cut from this very field on a sunny, warm day full of brass bees and sunbeams. It was a day she remembers now as being one of the few, the last, when she had known a tiny, vestigial moment of peace and contentment, the beginnings of some stirring of a whole, new self. That was all to change with the seasons, the currents of the mountain streams, the movement of fish and deer, and the infernal intrusion of people. The dry, biting cold has replaced the warm sun. Now there is steam from all breath. The vapor drifts a few inches and seems to shatter in the cold and drop. The air is too dry to sustain moisture of any kind. The snow aches and squeals. Only the path she walks with the toboggan is packed enough for somewhat easy passage, at least until the next snowfall. It's only February.

She opens the bag of nuts and chocolate bits and tips it into her mouth, uncovered briefly to allow the passage of food and tea, then rapidly recovered. All these years she's never been frostbitten. Never. It's a matter of care.

Glad to rest and catch her breath, she now needs to move and soon, so she stands outside the snow shelter. But she picks up a noise in the distance. She looks west and sees them—high and silver in formation, fast, loud and furious. The deer, too, hear the noise and quiver, but the pull of the hay is too strong for the moment. The jets turn north. Good, she thinks, they're heading toward the border, possibly patrolling. But they bank in a circle, turn east and south.

They are coming so fast she is startled. Three of them, still at cloud level; but they are dropping and directly overhead in a short breath. One peels away, heads west, then north, then east and then south in a tight sinking circle. She doesn't like this. The jet is too low, a threat. The deer bolt toward the woods at the far edge of the field, away from the noise of the jets. She reaches under the tarp and pulls out an old rifle—a single shot over-and-under with .16 gauge on top and a .22 on the bottom. She snaps off the safety. The deer are in full panic now and stampede into the woods. She waves the rifle at the jet far above her.

"God dammit!" She stands and fires randomly just as the jet roars overhead too far, too fast. Her ears ring and the air pressure pounds waves around her. The jet banks again and circles. She has already reloaded. Once again, she aims and fires, reloads. One glove is gripped hard between her teeth. The jet comes back a third time, the other two following. She fires again, ducks back into her shelter under the alders. The noise is fearsome. "Shit!" She covers her ears. "*Shit!*"

She stays put for thirty minutes, her back and knees aching like crazy and her heart going into its jazzy double backbeat. The jets are gone. Will they come back? In her mind she plays out the old scenario—the press, the microphones. She sees explosions of flashbulbs again, and everyone hollering.

"Shit."

She grabs her pack basket, her ruined breakfast, and hastily retreats back along the path she came. She'll come back later for the toboggan. The raven, she notices, has disappeared along with the deer.

Jim Porter, ranger and guide, gets up late as usual of a Sunday when he's not on call or ushering at the Methodist church. He was awakened earlier by the sound of jets flying overhead, too low again, he thought; but he rolled over and went back to sleep. About ten-thirty he gets up, pulls his pants over his long, lean legs, a turtleneck and a wool sweater over his head, and walks into the kitchen to stoke the wood stove. He makes his coffee in the automatic outfit Eleanor Winslow Livingston gave him a bunch of Christmases ago. He breaks two eggs in a pan and starts four strips of bacon between two paper towels for two minutes, in the microwave oven Eleanor gave him the Christmas before that.

Jim's tidy little cedar-shingled house, formerly his parents' house, sits just off the main highway into Winslow Station. The old place consists of an upstairs and down, the upstairs mainly a loft-like room with a dormer window, but he shuts that off, seals it up tight to conserve heat in the winter. The only time the upstairs is open is in July and August, when he needs the air circulation, or when he has the company of stranded hikers or flatlanders he's agreed to take out fishing.

Jim has North Country Public Radio on, waiting for the twelve o'clock news when the phone rings. "M'lo? Yeah? Yeah? No shit. Where was this at? Oh Jeez. Yeah, I know who it is. You bet I do. That's private land, you know—Winslow's. Yeah? Sure. S'not a problem. I mean, she's no threat to anybody. Well yeah, those flyovers piss everybody off. I heard 'em this mornin' yet. They piss me off, too. Whaddya want me to do, go up and have a word? Sure. No need to do that. No I mean it. She's been up there a long time, you know, maybe twelve years. She's been good lately, but she does have a temper on her like a bull moose. She's Eleanor Winslow's, I mean, Missus Livingston's, well you know, old friends and so forth. Yeah, that's the one, but you don't dare call her that to her face. Yessir, I understand. I'll be happy to talk to her. No I ain't gonna take her gun away from her. I know that old gun. For God's sake, she's a good shot but she ain't that good of a shot and it ain't that good of a gun. I can't believe she hit the damn Warthog, and I don't know what they're gettin' so riled up about. She's almost as old as I am and I'm fifty-two. She ain't no terrorist, if that's what they're thinkin'. Any damage? Yeah. Don't sound too bad. Yeah, sure. I'll go up and talk to her. You know me. Don't worry; I'll take care of it. I'll call Eleanor, too. Yeah, see ya. I'll call when I've been up there, but I'm havin' my coffee now and God dammit, it's gettin' cold."

Jim hangs up and rubs his cheeks and chin with both hands. How he hates having to shave on a free Sunday, but he's got to if he's going up to check on Lily. He sighs with a great exhalation of many, many years of Lily. A lot of time wasted, a lot of time crazy, a lot of time sad, and just when things are getting serious with this nice woman he's been seeing down to Paul Smiths, here comes Lily again to mess it all up in his mind. Jim shakes his head, sighs again, sits down with his coffee, and picks up the phone.

The fire crackles in the living room fireplace on East 86th Street. A stack of unread *Wall Street Journals*, *New Yorkers*, and *New York Times Sunday Magazines* are gathered at the side of Eleanor Winslow Livingston, still in her church clothes. Colin, her husband, has brought in tea and her favorite almond scones fresh out of the oven, placed on the butler's table between them. Aside from having to glance at some papers she's brought back from the Nairobi AIDS conference, Eleanor is looking forward to a day of rare leisure with her husband. Every time she comes back from a trip abroad, she looks in the mirror, sees the changes in her face—a bit more wrinkle here, a sag of chin there, more white than the former classic, past-shoulder blond hair inherited from her mother, an aristocratic English beauty. There's a bit of a stoop of the shoulders in the tall frame bequeathed her by her handsome father. And Colin—she sees him aging, too, and worries for both of them. He's changed into his loose trousers and an Irish flannel grandfather's shirt—a far cry from the trim young man in starched bib and tucker she met at a ball in New York twenty-seven years ago. He only lacks a monocle to set off his ruddy cheeks, Brit complexion. If she were casting *The Scarlet Pimpernel* for the screen, she would choose him over Leslie Howard. He'd be an admirable Lord Peter Wimsey, too. He was the only man of her own age back then who could match her in stature, and yet be so different in temperament. He is the serene yet elegant domestic male with a penchant for cooking exquisite food and taking her to the opera and ballet. He reads constantly, travels little, loves New York second only to her. He sits across from her on the overstuffed sofa covered in rose red brushed cotton. Colin has today's *Times,* picked up as usual on their walk home from St. Bart's on this bright, chilly Candlemas Day. He methodically separates the sections of newspaper on his lap and discards the advertisements, real estate and sports sections, and settles back against the bolster to read the news.

Eleanor, still a little jet-lagged, has kicked off her shoes and stretched out her long legs on the ottoman. She takes a sip of tea and a bit of scone, tasting both as appreciatively as the Eucharist this morning, glad to be home with a relatively free week ahead, except for a debriefing at the UN on her discussions with the doctors she met in Nairobi. In her mind, the Anglican Rite One post-Communion prayer plays again: ". . . and so to assist us with Thy grace to do all such good works as Thou hast prepared for us to walk in." The odd phraseology makes her wonder what kinds of works are possible to walk in—like a brewery or a steel mill full of large, loud machinery? She remembers walking through the "Upper Works" at Tahawus, the MacIntyre iron foundry way up in the Adirondacks, where nothing was left but the huge old stone furnace, silent since the 1830s but such a strong testimony to man and Nature. The forests they cut down more than two hundred years ago have all grown back, cooling the stones that once burned so hot when smelting the iron ore dug from the surrounding denuded hills.

"I have wandered enough in the works," she thinks. Now the present fire, the communion tea and scones with Colin bring a feeling of immense contentment and relief. These are the last days before she retires from all those works. Only two more weeks, then no more long trips, no more jet lag, conferences, terrorism worries. No more orphanages or hospices full of sick men, women and children. She has seen, heard enough to grieve for the world for the rest of her life. She will in good conscience pass on the mantle to her younger associates in Anglican Relief. Two more weeks.

"I think more and more of someplace warm with a nice beach. You know—eco-touristy. I'd like to snorkel," she says to her husband.

"All right," replies Colin, and he tosses her the travel section. "I'm for that."

"I can stand just two more weeks of meetings, if I can have a month of turquoise blue waters full of jewelly fish, a white sand beach and a pile of good books. Everybody else leaves the city in the winter. Marbella, Côte d'Azure."

"But no theater," he cautions. "No opera. No dance."

"One month, no more, no less. When was the last time you and I had a full month free and clear, just the two of us?"

"You'll get antsy."

"Try me."

"Your restless legs," he says, waving a hand at her feet, which are waggling as usual.

"I know," she says, willing her feet to stop, stretching them out before her—long, strong legs still. "I see them growing fins. I'd like to study marine biology . . . or something."

"More tea?" Colin asks.

"Please. And thank you. The scones are delicious."

"You're welcome. No scones either. Not like these," he states emphatically. "Not in the Caribbean."

"I can't imagine what life will be like for us, can you?"

"You mean on beaches and things?"

Eleanor takes a bite of scone and mumbles through the crumbs. "More than that. I don't know. Self-indulgence, sybaritism."

"For once in your life."

"Maybe if I found something local and light—with an *i-t-e*. Literacy volunteers, perhaps."

"Here we go. Less than one minute ago you were snorkeling. Now you have a future of yet more taking charge before the local library or whoever knows what's happening to them. Let it go, Ellie, for today anyway. Let's just take one day towards retirement at a time. No plans yet. Just read and relax. Nap later. Dinner out. That's my girl."

Eleanor stretches out her legs again. She idly picks up the travel section and just as idly casts it aside for later. Just feeling the warmth of the fire on her stocking feet is enough for now. Colin is right. Restless legs indeed. She just wants to sleep a bit. How delicious—scones, fire, tea, no more works to walk in, just a big yawn; stretch out those legs.

"What I really want more than anything, I think, is a dog," she remarks.

"Really?"

"I've always wanted a dog."

Colin puts the paper down, giving her his full attention. Perhaps this is a better answer than yet another trip. He's been struggling to think of something to get her for her birthday in April. Something to anchor her down, yet give her restless legs a reason to keep moving, work off their combustive energy. "What kind of dog?" he asks.

"Nothing too large and lumbering, but nothing small and yappy. A calm dog. And one that doesn't shed."

"I'd fancy a Corgi," he says, "a Pembroke Corgi." Again, he envisions the two of them walking the dog, or perhaps two, to Central Park, stopping to talk to other people with dogs. It would be nice, just the two of them together with a dog (or two). No more days by himself pottering around in the old brownstone, cooking for no one but himself, going out to movies and the ballet alone. No more anxious long distance calls from East Timor or from airports where the alert level is red or luggage has gone missing, or some riot or civil war is going on. No more ghastly embassy parties.

"Yes a Corgi, or a golden retriever," Eleanor adds.

"Corgi. Pembroke."

Eleanor starts to close her eyes and drift off. "Lily always wanted a dog, too. I've always wondered if they were bringing us one back from Montreal. I wonder if that's why Lily never got a dog after we were older. But," Eleanor yawns again, "I asked her once and she said she was having a difficult enough life without having to care about something else. And really, I don't know how we would have managed it, she and I, along with everything else. So now she has a faithful old raven. Fancy." And with that Eleanor dozes off.

Colin helps himself to another scone and finishes three sections of the *Times,* before the phone rings. "Shit," he says and lifts the receiver. Eleanor stirs across from him. "It's Jim."

"What in the world?" She takes the cordless from her husband. Eleanor's brow creases deeper and deeper as she listens.

"Oh no," she says into the receiver. "Yes, I understand that. Did you talk to them? Did you explain the situation to . . . ? Oh." There is a long pause while Eleanor listens, her feet waggling more and more. "Yes, well . . . did she really? She always was the best shot. I can't say as I blame her. I hate those flyovers, it's totally against . . . Yes, I understand the military takes these things seriously, especially since that van blew up at the World Trade . . . All right! All right! But it's February, is the road plowed out? Has she at least done that? Christ! I'll call you back when we know what we're doing here. Will you call us when you talk to her?" (Waggle, waggle.) "Of course I'm worried about her. We all worry about her. Yes, of course we'll come. Yes, I can't wait to see you either." She listens for a few more minutes and then begs off.

"Dare I ask?" Colin asks, as she returns the handset.

"Lily," she replies sullenly.

"Oh, I'm *so* sorry I did."

It wasn't but a couple of weeks before this when Tom Aiken stood mopping down the old oak top of the bar at Aiken's Tap Room in Winslow Station, carrying on as he did. His audience of four was a group of college kids from St. Lawrence University in Canton—cross-country skiers on their way down to run the Jack Rabbit Trail and stopping off for a burger and a beer. He was telling them about the time he was hunting over on the other side of the lake.

". . . and I come upon Lily Martindale bein' mauled by a big black bear, oh, maybe two hundred'n fifty pounds and she, a little slip of a thing. Poor girl, to face a fate like that, but you take your chances bein' a woman and livin' alone in the woods," he said.

He told these boys about how he tried to get a shot lined up but couldn't without killing Lily too: so he waited until he had a clean sightline. It was then he realized, he told the boys, that Lily wasn't being mauled by the bear. They were dancing; she was teaching the brute to dance.

Tom threw his thumb over his shoulder at the picture that hung on the wall behind the bar, the ubiquitous rendering of black bears dancing in an Adirondack woodland clearing. That old picture hangs in every store, every B&B, every library, every school up there. Tom Aiken complained that his Uncle Jack always had the pinups from the Stihl saw calendar above the mirror behind the bar—healthy Alpine maidens dressed in barely stitched together scraps of denim and calico. But after Uncle Jack died, Tom's wife, a churchgoing woman, made Tom take them all down, and hung the dancing bears there instead.

"So about this woman, who is this woman you're talking about?" asked one of the boys.

"Oh you don't know 'bout Lily Martindale, ol' Cinder-Lily?" Tom seemed amazed.

The boys looked at each other and shook their heads.

Tom mopped in circles with his terrycloth towel, talking as he worked, but never quite finishing either his task or the story. "Well, isn't that somethin', now," he said. "Seems like there wasn't a day not so very long ago, but before your time, when you couldn't pick up a newspaper or turn on a TV station without seein' a picture of Lily Martindale and Eleanor Winslow, whose family named this town, this lake. They were both America's little sweethearts, both of 'em, but especially Lily. Six years old and cute as a button. Terrible time it was, for them, for all of us here. But those two little girls. Well, you can't imagine. Poor things. They had everything and nothing."

The boys were drinking their second Saranac Pale Ale. Tom's wife, Mary Lou, brought out an extra order of fries for them on the house. Tom said, "I was just tellin' these boys about Lily and Eleanor."

"Lily and Eleanor? Them two. Yeah. Quite the story."

The boys from SLU were dividing up the French fries and talking among themselves, except for the one on the end who asked Tom, "Who are these two girls?"

"Oh not girls now, not by a long shot. This was many years ago," Mary Lou explained as she picked up one of their glass mugs to refill. "A long time ago, it was."

Tom picked up the next twig of the branching tree of a story that would never grow to blossom in this hour at this bar with these customers. "Little hellion she was, was Lily. Come in here when she was a teenager and sing and dance and carry on. Nice girl, but a little, you know, carried away at times. Not no more. Twelve years alone in the woods will drive you to dance with bears. She's teachin' the bears to dance, by God; she's dancin' with bears."

Chapter Two

"Hush my dear, lie still and slumber;
Holy angels guard thy bed . . ."

"Cradle Hymn," #242, Episcopal Hymnal, 1940

Tune: Harmonia Sacra, 1753, harmony by Leo Sowerby, 1940

Text, Isaac Watts, 1715

Eleanor Winslow was five years old when Lily was born. She remembers it vividly, because the event was so wrapped in secrecy, yet the folks at the camp had talked of nothing else for the preceding three months. There was a plan to return to New York early so that the mother-to-be, Mariette, the French cook, could have access to a hospital. Eleanor liked the city and would not have been sorry to go along for the excitement, but in a way, this was more interesting. She wouldn't have been allowed to go to the hospital and watch anyway. This way, she felt a part of it, and had her little chores and responsibilities assigned either by her mother, or Mabel, or even Mariette, who was up and walking about a good deal of the time just like any other day; she pooh-poohed her husband's admonitions to take it easy, lie down, rest.

Mariette had grown up in a small village in Provence, the daughter of a shop owner and baker. Her experience with home births had prepared her for all contingencies. She'd served as a nurse's assistant before the war in France. Mrs. Winslow had also had nurses' training in England before her marriage to Charles during the war, and Mabel, the caretaker's wife, had seen her share of wilderness births. Nobody seemed to be too concerned if, like Eleanor, this baby chose to come when they were all in camp. And everyone knew and trusted Doc Burton to be there when they needed him. They just didn't expect that Lily would come almost two weeks early and right in the middle of the August season, interrupting the Winslows' plans to drive to Saratoga for the races that weekend.

When Mariette started labor early one cool August morning, Mack, Mabel's husband, phoned Doc Burton's, but he was out on call. Then Mack phoned down to Pop Finn at Mom and Pop's General Store to alert them, and sure enough, Doc was standing right there having a cup of coffee after seeing a child with the croup. Doc headed around the lake road to The Hill and managed to get there in plenty of time. Lily's birth, in spite of being a bit on the early side, posed no complications, and she was born in time for Doc to get home for a hot supper, a fact of which, until he died, he reminded her often over the years and which left him eternally in her debt for being so thoughtful to a country MD.

After the baby was washed, swaddled, and handed back to Mariette, her husband, Robert Martindale, and Mack, the caretaker, came in for the first look at the new addition to the camp. Eleanor came in not far behind. Charles Winslow, her father, pushed her forward so that she could have a good look.

"We'll teach her how to canoe and fish," he said to his daughter.

Eleanor nodded and then looked up at her father and asked, "How long will that take?"

"Oh, by the time you're about ten or eleven. Then she'll be big enough for the Wee Lassie."

Eleanor looked at him again and asked, "But what can she do *now*?"

"Well," said Mariette, "Why don't you hold your finger to her cheek?"

Eleanor looked at her mother, who nodded. The little girl laid her finger gently against the baby's cheek. Lily turned her head in response, as if in a kiss. Eleanor beamed.

Later, Charles set up the Hassleblad for a commemorative photograph. In it, Mariette lies abed with baby Lily, Emily Winslow and Doc Burton standing close. Robert gazes down at his newborn daughter, his dark, handsome face softened with what appears to be the beginning of an emotional moment held manfully in. Eleanor sits off on the other side, her fingers loosely grasping the baby's tiny fist. Eleanor is as radiant with joy as the parents themselves.

This 1946 photograph tells volumes, as many do, but especially in contrast with other photographs to come. Years later, this childbed portrait will be spliced side by side in the newspapers with the picture of Eleanor, age eleven at last, tightly grasping Lily as Lily, age six, screams something tearfully to the exploding cameras, her little face twisted with fear and rage. These two photographs—the birth of Lily, with Eleanor standing protectively by, and the one taken at the end of their childhood happiness together—illustrated the context of their relationship all those years to come. Here, Eleanor's proud, beaming protection of the infant; there, young Eleanor bravely holding Lily in despair. Only the photograph of Lily's birth day appears in the butler's pantry in Doxology Lodge at camp. The other, the one the press took, was banished.

This side room at the lodge on The Hill was a butler's pantry in name only. Contrary to what the press insisted, there was never a butler in service at The Hill during any of the years the Winslows stayed there, not even in the time of Charles's parents, who certainly brought lots of help with them from Boston back in the twenties.

Robert Martindale was *never* a butler to the family. He was more like a close confidant and friend, the kind the war engendered between some soldiers and certainly some pilots such as Charles Winslow Junior and Robert. No. Robert Martindale was certainly *not* a butler. If there was a gathering of friends or townsfolk, Robert was between two places and everywhere else at once: helping Mariette in the kitchen, corralling the kids, showing some young person how to fly cast, hitching the Percherons up to the wagon for a hayride to the pond, or joining in the festivities and making sure everyone was having a good time.

So the butler's pantry was just something they called that little anteroom: an extension of the library where male guests often gathered to refill their glasses and smoke a cigar outside of the presence of the ladies. It was part efficiency kitchen, part bar, part club. The pictures that hung there on the wainscoting portrayed every special event, featuring any Winslow and any guest in attendance and often those who just helped—guides, kitchen staff, house help. There was no clear distinction between those on the payroll and those who belonged to the family, for the most part, at least not after young Charles took over. This was important to the people of Winslow Station. They never forgot how well, how like family, they were treated by young Charles.

Emily Winslow said once that it took a bit of getting used to after her old-school British rearing, where the upstairs and the downstairs were distinctly separate. But she was a bright, egalitarian spirit, much like her husband, and she dearly loved him and all those *he* loved. Not to make it sound like a great festival of good feeling all the time, but it pretty damn near was. They extended a veritable run of high spirits after the bloody war into the era of tea, cocktails and dressing for dinner at eight. There was a great deal of love and high feeling around those days when the two young families, Winslow and Martindale, settled in at The Hill.

The mood could not have been more different where Charles's parents were concerned. The photos taken in the Charles Winslow Senior days, the twenties, show the two parents stiffly seated and frowning, with young Charles poker-faced and staring straight ahead, his already long neck seemingly stretched even longer by the starched collar he wore. His was, even then, the handsome face that would become, years later, the most sought-after photograph in papers, magazines and celluloid. He was blonde and blue-eyed, with a calm demeanor, his hands relaxed at his sides and that penetrating, direct look reporters loved, women fell for, and politicians envied. But he was reserved, if not shy. Gregarious only with a few close friends and those with whom he served in the war, he had no interest in the high society his mother had courted in Boston. Charles, in this way, was a constant disappointment to his mother. Debutantes found him stiff and ill at ease. As a boy and as a man, his heart was in the Adirondack woods. His father, a sportsman, fashioned the camp out of the old Winslow Mills logging operation, though he didn't live long enough to enjoy it much. His wife was, at best, indifferent to it. No. She loathed the place.

From the 1920s on, the framed photographs seem to take on a life of their own—friends, mates in various postures, sometimes with guests in costumes, sometimes full evening dress, sometimes casual, their arms around each other, rarely a face missing, more often additions. Lily and Eleanor, at various stages of their growth, appear in the photographs prettily dressed in Christmas outfits bought for them by Eleanor's mother in London or New York or Boston. One of Eleanor's favorite pictures was the one taken when she was eight years old and Lily was about three. They are both sitting together cross-legged, Indian style, on the floor and Ellie has her arm around Lily. Lily's brown hair and Ellie's blonde are cut in similar styles. They are wearing Japanese silk robes that Julietta Pima, the actress, brought them from a film she was making. The photos are black and white, but Ellie remembers that her robe was emerald green with beautiful embroidered pink peonies. Lily's was blue with green leaves and red birds with long tails. The two robes were favorite dress-up costumes and remained for decades in the costume trunk upstairs in the top room off the nursery at the lodge. They were later cleaned and pressed and framed in two large display cases that still hang in Eleanor's old room at camp.

As grown women, they have spent long hours studying these photos, especially the last two—taken at the last two Christmases—before the chronology of photographs ends, when Lily was five and six. Some people visit cemeteries and gravesites, bringing flowers, tokens. These photographs are all the girls have of their parents. And the camp, of course. The Hill is its own monument to all that has passed. A long way down the road, that becomes part of the problem.

Chapter Three

"Fair are the meadows
Fairer still the woodlands,
Robed in the blooming garb of spring . . ."

"St. Elizabeth," #346, Episcopal Hymnal, 1940

Silesian Melody, pub. Leipzig, 1842; harmony by Tertius Noble, 1918

Text: Anonymous

Sometimes it seems that it's always winter—always been winter, will always be winter in the North Country. Spring is an event so far off in memory it seems like a dream. Then, when it does happen, it happens fast. But first there's February, which brings the Tantalus madness of slightly longer days—one minute, two minutes, maybe three minutes added to the length of the sun's low, slow stroll through the sky. Some days in February the temperature will spike over freezing and even over forty degrees, and occasionally to nearly fifty. The temptation to bust out the Bermuda shorts and T-shirts is excruciating folly. The sap starts running, and not just the kind that comes from sugar maples. Cold, hard freezing nights, warmer days—is it any wonder North Country babies are conceived in those last winter months of cabin fever?

Then comes March, and March is a trial of soul and spirit. Most folk of the North Country get out before the roads get bad in March and April. Schools close for a couple of weeks. Like dimwitted robins, their late trek south begins. Sue Ellen Finn and her husband and the

Aikens close up shop and head south to Florida, where they've rented a condo close to Disney World for the kids. The Guilbeaults leave the marina locked up and head to Myrtle Beach. Even Pastor Clara and Joe Finn leave for a week to visit old friends in Nashville and go to the Grand Ol' Opry.

Then there are those, like ranger Jim Porter, that stay, who face the demons of cabin fever, cold and the madness of hope that *this* warm day presages the coming of all warm days, knowing full well the next snowstorm in March will be the topper of the season. Those that stay look like the poor soil around them—sodden, iced-over, unprofitable, stuck between despair and hope.

But finally the day comes, when, back from Nashville and tired of splitting wood, Joe Finn goes outside in his shirtsleeves at forty-five degrees to see if the old barrel on the lake is listing a bit yet, and in the distance he hears the first call of the returning Canada geese, a sound that makes a body's heart cry aloud in response. Two weeks later, when the barrel has finally sunk through the mushy ice, the lucky bettor at the taproom collects his or her winnings, and the loons come back with their wailing laughter. Then the shadblow blossoms and the lady's slippers come and then, boom, they're gone, the swarms of bloodsucking black flies are back, then the deer flies. By June, the deer look a picture of misery molting and shivering with bites. In July and August, the tourists and summer campers and hikers appear like long-lost friends with money. Then they, too, dwindle down. The last Labor Day picnic is over, the last bookbag and pencil case are purchased at Mom and Pop's. The kids trundle back to the one-room school house in Winslow Station, or board the bus to the bigger school in St. Regis.

Fall, now, fall is so beautiful—no bugs, no mud. The relief is palpable everywhere. The trees put on a show with lights and costumes. But then it's winter, winter goes on forever, hard and beautiful and very, very cold. The people who stay the winter in the Adirondacks are a certain breed. The people who stay the winter off the grid in the Adirondacks are either so poor or so stubborn and strong they couldn't think of doing it any other way. To think that Lily Martindale had access to such comfort on The Hill—flush potties, hot and cold running water, electric lights, a kitchen, icehouse, refrigerator, full pantry and wine cellar—and yet chose to stay in her dad's little rustic cabin farther up on The Hill Next was a testimony to her stubbornness and sadness. But even more, it was something she had to cling to, like a storm-tossed, upturned canoe mid-lake, until help came.

Eleanor calls Jim back to tell him they will soon be on their way. She leaves a message on his answering machine when he doesn't pick up the phone. She returns to her efficient packing. After all the years traveling for the UN and Anglican Charities, she has it down to a science. Going north to camp in winter only means packing with a thought to layering, and there are certainly clothes there, packed away in cedar chests in the cedar attic at the lodge. Eleanor just needs something to wear for the long drive up and the first night and day until she has a chance to get some sweaters and things out of their winter storage. She can't remember when last she's been to camp in February. Probably when they were kids.

The old Subaru station wagon in the garage is used so rarely that Eleanor can't find her driver's license, and Colin never had one. It takes him most of the early afternoon to stock up. It is not in his nature to travel north without at least several days' supply of essentials in large coolers. Most of these, like frozen spring roll wrappers, are in the New York brownstone's capacious Sub Zero along with various good cuts of meat and poultry, flash-frozen shellfish and several bags of exquisite fruits and vegetables. From his favorite local purveyor he picks up a few things, such as cheeses. He does not have to worry too much about wine, since there is an excellent wine cellar where they're going, assuming Lily's still on the wagon, but he loads up on whites and some Spanish bubbly. Bread and pastry are his specific delight to make from scratch and there should already be some venison in place if Lily has been out hunting more than A-10s. After all, they have been going to camp summer and winter holidays for years now. How would February be any different than New Year's? He's never entertained anyone from the military police or the FBI before, but he presumes they have appetites just like everyone else.

Colin moves around fussing with his self-imposed chores, realizing he is doing far too much, but he senses in himself, as in Eleanor, a sort of excitement mixed with the anxiety. He does love The Hill, has loved the place ever since Eleanor brought him there for the first time before they were married—the sublime rustic architecture and warm interiors, the challenges of the old woodstove in the dining hall kitchen, the weather, the vastness of the place and its old buildings. With a few personal reservations, he loves the history of the place, the Winslows, the famous visitors over the years, their pictures hanging in Doxology Lodge in the butler's pantry. And Lily. Dear, maddening Lily, the BMW—Beloved Mountain Woman. They'd had such a stressful, unpleasant Christmas together and not a word from her since, not that that is unusual. Often they don't hear from her for months at a time. But this, this is a bad sign. What was she thinking? Of all people to draw attention to herself like that. Did she think those jets were attacking her? Has she finally gone completely round the bend?

"I will not have it. You have no right! This is private land. I'm caretaker here!" Lily says aloud as she sits by the woodstove in the cabin with the cold stone floor. Aside from the deer mice in the walls and rafters, she speaks to no one. Outside, the wind chimes are making sweet music in the wind off the lake.

"Are you back? Is that you? Who are you?" Lily listens for footsteps, but no one is there, just the wind. She settles back in the old rocker and pulls her old raccoon coat close about her. The fire is dying out and she needs to restock the wood box, but she is so tired and her joints ache and burn. Her heart is thumping again like the tail of an old dog at a firehouse when the alarm bell rings.

Lily's father designed this cabin as his retreat on his days off from work on The Hill. It was his, his and Mariette's little hunk of peace and quiet, where they would stay during days off or when the Winslows were not in camp and Rockingham Hall was shut down. The Hill Next, twenty acres of steep escarpment on the lake shore, was deeded to him by Charles Winslow, so it was Lily's now by right. Her dad would have been upset—terribly upset—at the jets and the noise—and him a pilot, too. Not like these hotshots today, flying so low, so recklessly invasive. This place is as close to sacred ground as you can get—private, personal.

"You have no right!"

The cabin is a one-room affair with bunk beds built into one side, built-in tables and cabinets of cedar, plenty of room for storage, a nice-sized wood cook and heating stove, a fireplace built of stones set with garnet and Herkimer diamonds, quartz crystal, really—a masterpiece of stonework all the way to the crawlspace below where it spreads out to support its own weight. There are triple-glazed windows all around, now sealed with frost and ice and a thick layer of snow against the outside walls. The foundation is four feet thick, keeping a storage area below at a constant forty degrees. An intricate system of pipes, long since burst and useless, runs underneath the now-cold floors. They connect to a clever heating element Robert designed that begins at the buried spring-fed cistern on the slope above, flows through a circulator in the wood stove and finally through the pipes in the floor. When functioning properly with the valves open it sends a continuous stream of warm gravity-fed water from the stove and underneath the slate slabs ordered from Granville that he laid so carefully, so ingeniously. That was the way her father was, why everyone loved him so, and why so often Lily struggles to pin down his face in the night to the wall of her dreams and memory. Her mother's face is as elusive as her father's, but her voice is always calling to her from the kitchen, "*Viens toi,* Lily Fleurette. We are making bread!" Her hands are covered with flour. She smells of yeast, but Lily cannot see her face any more, unless she is looking at one of those photographs in the lodge. Try as she might to memorize both of their faces, they seem to dissipate, melt away. Only the scents of pine pitch, woodsmoke, of flannel, tweed, of flour and chocolate remain with base notes of Chanel No. 5, Bay Rum and motor oil.

Lily sits in an old cane-bottomed rocker, one support of which is held together with duct tape and another bound with twine taken from a package. She is small, thin and strong like the iron coil of an old bedspring but also drawn and tired. Her face is pulled tight with pain and worry. Her hair is matted, filthy and starting to gray. She took a bath last week and meant to today, but she is so tired. Looking about she is very aware of how far she has fallen and how she will be judged. She hasn't even fed the raven today, but she knows at least Schwartz can take care of himself.

They will come. They will see she hasn't taken care of herself, nor of the cabin, nor even of The Hill. Her head is heavy and her body and heart so sore and ill-tempered, she just wants to sleep now. Somewhere phones are ringing, authorities alerted, forces mobilized—all against a small, middle-aged woman living alone in a cabin in the woods. A woman crazy and scared enough to fire an old rifle at a military flyover.

More than a decade ago, when Lily first came home to The Hill for good, she was this exhausted. It was her first holiday in the mountains by herself, the first winter of her retreat, New Year's Eve. She'd arrived just before Christmas with Eleanor and was just feeling her way around the camp after all these years and tenuously touching old, still raw and sore memories. After Christmas, Eleanor had gone off with Colin to some extravaganza in Paris. Lily, alone, felt the stillness of the woods, like a vacuum, begin to pull at her. She was aware that she was too much of a presence in the deep silence. Her lone voice rippled the air around her. She was an intruder, unwanted, unneeded, a further burden to the Adirondack wilderness, which had borne too much since the white man first arrived. Who was she to claim stewardship over this land? What kind of caretaker could she possibly be? She had nothing to offer anyone any more. She'd tossed her last Valium, drunk her last bottle of champagne. She was finished. Eleanor would understand. Eleanor should have foreseen this moment. She should have stayed with Lily.

Lily sat then where she sits now, in the old rocker, planning it out. She would walk into the woods, dig a little snow hole at the base of an enormous old growth white pine that had toppled over, roots and all. She would crawl in and dwindle down to sleep and death in the chill. No more holidays alone. No more heartache and rage. No more memories. No more regrets.

She did, in fact, walk out back then more than ten years ago, mark the territory, find the tree, and test the terrain for the depth of snow she would need to dig through, and the strength of her resolve as well. It was a crystal clear night, thirty below and the moon as bright as a New York City streetlight. She couldn't resist it. She went down to the lodge for the old Winslow Bible to see if she could read the print by the light of the moon. And she could. She flipped the book in the middle—Psalms. Perfect, she thought, lots of "scattering mine enemies" and "laying snares" and "jackals" and "hills and mountains" and all that stuff of the wilderness. Not #23—"The Lord is my Shepherd." How can a psalm become a cliché, or how had she become so jaded? Here was one: #42 (and she began out loud):

"As the hart panteth after the water brooks, so panteth my soul after thee,"

She looked around her and said out loud. "That's old Drumclog! We used to sing that at school. The cabin closest to the lodge." But she couldn't recall it except for the part about the deer drinking.

"Deep calleth unto deep at the noise of thy waterspouts: all thy waves and thy billows are gone over me . . . As with a sword in my bones, mine enemies reproach me . . ."

As if in response, the frozen lake moaned with the weight of ice and snow; the deep timbre, a guttural vibration, a humming groan unnerving to any who had not heard it before, but Lily had many times. She snapped the big book shut. *"Shit,"* she thought.

The moment, with the stilted arcane phraseology, lost her. Waterspouts, for God's sake. Religion for whales. Biblical text, church and any preaching had fallen off her like a sloughing of dead skin. It wasn't about words spoken in vaulted buildings, promises and confessions (even Anglican). It wasn't about scripture. It wasn't about prayer to the faceless one. Here was this silence, this utter solitude, the night itself in which she read the words aloud to the blue light on Lake Winslow, for she had waded out through the snow off the boat dock. And once again, she felt she had intruded, fucked up. The night was still, or she could not have stood long, warmly wrapped though she was. In the quiet she sensed her family around her—the Winslows, Mack and Mabel, and her own parents as well. She expected they would beckon to her, call her to join them, but instead they seemed to be cheering, laughing, and applauding as if she had performed some clever little dance for them, played a recital piece particularly well. She felt suddenly foolish standing in the moonlight, holding the Bible, reading aloud to ghosts and the shining moonlight of a bright winter night.

She had turned to go when she saw, standing very still at the edge of the lake, a large buck, the lights from the camp behind backlighting his form, watching her. He was so still that she became still as well and for a long time she held his gaze. He took several tentative steps closer to her, paused as if a sudden itch, a flea bite perhaps, distracted his progress. He bent his head and rubbed his nose against his foreleg, but for all the world, she thought, as if he was bowing. He advanced a few more steps toward her through the blue moonlit snow, sniffing the air trying to get some sense of her. Still she did not move, but the cold was penetrating all those layers of winter clothing. She did not know how much longer she could stand it, but neither could she move. Who was it, she thought, what saint, saw the crucifix alight in the antlers of a deer? There was no cross in this creature, thank God. She wasn't that crazy. Just a deer, just a magnificent buck. Soon he would smell her and run. But instead, quivering, he backed away, bowing his nose to his foreleg once more, rubbing there, and finally turning back to the shore, to the line of white pines and red cedar. He disappeared, but she could hear him and with him a sizeable harem of does seeking shelter, possibly in the very spot she had selected to die.

As she trudged back to the cabin on The Hill Next, she wondered whether, had she chosen the hole in the snow instead of the moonlight on the lake, the deer would have shared her rooty, white pine sarcophagus. Would they have nestled about her, kept her warm? What a thought! At any rate, that New Year's night, 1985, was not to be the night for her death. She could do with a cup of hot tea, another log or two on the fire and, perhaps, a good book to take her mind off herself. Not the Bible, though; enough of that for one night. She thought back once more on the image of her family cheering her out there on the lake, as if she was doing something right for once. And the buck, too, acknowledging her presence as if she belonged there.

Lily sits, still in the rocker, but she is in another world now, drifting down and back. She is yet wrapped in the old raccoon coat, yet in her boots, yet with her hat pulled down over her ears, her scarf wound up over her chin. Still, she is terribly cold and achy. But in the distance she sees her father leading the Percherons with the dray full of logs for the big fireplace at the lodge. She'll get up soon to help. She wants to tell him about shooting at the jet. He'll know what to do. She needs to write the story in her book. She ought to lay on another log. There is the bell for tea, the old bell, the signal to come to the main camp or that someone is coming to visit the cabin. Then there are the wind chimes again. *He's* back, the Beloved. Perhaps he's just outside, finally ready to meet her, to reveal himself. She should wash up, dress, go with him. She's tired of all this. She's ready. But first she has to tidy the cabin, so he will see she knows how to take care of things. He will want to meet her father. If she could just get up, she'd tell Papa first, so he's ready. She ought to run to meet him, but . . .

Chapter Four

"Come labor on. No time for rest till glows the western sky,
Till the long shadows o'er our pathway lie . . ."

"Ora Labora," #576, Episcopal Hymnal, 1940

Tune: T. Tertius Noble, 1918

Text: Jane Borthwick, 1859

Butch and Daisy, steam roiling from their muzzles, pulled the sledge full of logs with ease. Neck, shoulder and haunch, the matched Percherons had lived and worked at this camp since they were foals. Robert Martindale held the reins and kept one strong hand on the brake, but this was a well-rehearsed routine: uphill from the barn with the wagon, load after load of logs, whole and split, delivered to their destinations. First he stopped for his wife, Mariette, in the kitchen, to the west porch of the dining hall, and then a handful of oats and a shorter trek to the lodge and, if there were guests in camp, the outlying cottages—"Drumclog," "Rosa Mystica," "St. Dunstan's," "Picardy," "St. Elizabeth's"—then the old guides' housing used by the girls' tutor and her husband, and then all the way back to the caretaker's cottage and the barn.

The buildings bore the names of the Winslows' favorite hymns: "Doxology Lodge," "Rockingham Hall" (the kitchen and dining hall), "Ora Labora" (the guides' and laborers' housing, now the tutors' cottage), "Melita" (the Naval hymn for the boathouse). Even the huge old glacial erratic over on The Hill Next had a name—"Toplady" after "Rock of Ages, cleft for me," written by Augustus Toplady.

The outlying guest cabins each had a distinctive decor. The cabin called "Drumclog," named after a hymn from the psalm about the panting hart, had deer heads and pictures of deer and deer hunters on the walls and an antique rifle above the fireplace. (The hymn is more often called "Martyrdom," but the Winslows thought that was too depressing). "St. Dunstan's" was a large cabin with old pictures of Adirondack guides like Alvah Dunning and Ruben Carey—people who, as the old John Bunyan words suggested, were valiant men who served "'gainst all disaster" by taking care of so many travelers who came to the woods. There was also an old portrait of Charles Winslow and Robert Martindale in front of a P-51 Mustang at Old Catton U.S. base in England in 1943. "Rosa Mystica" had a more feminine interior design with rose chintz and prints of still lifes, a vague allusion to the Christmas carol, "I know a rose tree springing." There was a cabin called "Rest," favored among the single gentlemen who visited the camp. With the words of John Greenleaf Whittier in mind ("when all our strivings cease . . ."), the walls displayed a few pre-Raphaelite prints of nymphs and springs, felt by the first Mrs. Winslow, a devout Anglican, to be inappropriately risqué.

The naming of the buildings followed a common enough tradition from summer camps everywhere. Naming them after hymns was as much of their Episcopalian tradition as the Winslows chose to bring with them to the woods. Charles kept the tradition after his parents died. He named the caretaker's cabin "Hyfrydol." The words "Love divine all loves excelling" expressed his deep feelings for his caretakers who looked after him and the camp so well. He often said it was hymns he loved more than sermons and ceremony. Lily was fond of the hymns, too. Years later, just a light touch of melody would bring back the memory of something that had happened at the camp in one of the same-named buildings there.

The Hill was constructed in the traditional style of Adirondack Great Camps—as a series of structures meant to imitate the concept of camping without duplicating its discomforts. The multiple buildings—those for sleeping, one for eating, several for various kinds of work or recreation—were situated so that one had to walk outside to get from place to place. Nature, in this way, was engaged inside and out. The buildings seemed to rise out of the earth, entwined, shaded, beckoning. They were the same color as the trees, the soil, the pine needles—dark brown and gray logs, green trim on the windows, doors and rooflines. The building interiors were as rough-hewn as the exteriors—whole beams were made of red spruce, great stone fireplaces (in the lodge there was one inglenook large enough to walk into). Beds were made of small tree trunks. Bureaus and highboys were faced with designs of silver or yellow birch twigs. Gunracks and coatracks were made of upturned deer hooves. Animal heads and talented taxidermy posed throughout. Balconies with views of the lake sported railings decoratively twisted with intertwining twigs and branches.

Just walking outside in the woods or boating on the lake were novel concepts for wealthy city dwellers such as the Winslows, who were used to being fetched and carried. Mr. Winslow Senior hoped that his wife would get some much-needed exercise and fresh air to overcome her neurasthenia. He also hoped that his boy would resist his wife's pampering and grow to love the outdoors as he did. In the former case, the plan did not work at all. In the latter, it worked quite well.

At the base of The Hill was Lake Winslow. The lake was accessible down the steep slope by a switched-back stair of logs set into the face of The Hill. Farther down the slope as the dirt road traveled was a root cellar, icehouse, guides' housing, caretakers' place, boathouse, barn, greenhouse, henhouse, forge and carpentry shed—The Hill functioned like a small village, sufficient unto itself.

So close to Christmas, as it was now, and with the weather cold and getting colder, Robert's rounds were more or less a daily enterprise. Wood deliveries were interrupted by vehicle maintenance and tinkering with the furnace or the boiler in the lodge or Rockingham Hall. A self-sustaining estate such as this was only as self-sustaining as the efforts of Robert, Mariette, Mack and Mabel, who worked like four men between them to keep the place, the land and the livestock tidy and operational. And Charles and Emily pitched in when they weren't on business trips or on the campaign trail. It was a good, full life, a life made better these last few years by the addition of the two girls.

Lily was running toward her father. She wore an oversize wool coat (a hand-me-down from Eleanor), rubber boots with buckles and two pairs of Robert's old wool socks pulled up over her dungarees and folded down over her boots. There was a hand-knit hat stretched down over her ears and a scarf wound around her face with just her eyes showing. She was running toward him with her arms out, so he stopped and knelt to receive that onslaught of affection, which instead deflected to his right and straight onto the leg of the largest Percheron, Butch.

She wrapped herself around Butch's left foreleg and tried to shimmy up like a lineman up a telephone pole. She was small enough yet that her head didn't quite reach the base of the horse's shoulder, so there was just enough room to shimmy a little. Butch bent his head down more or less tolerantly to examine the creature attached to his leg and politely cocked his hoof to add a little support. He nuzzled around the seat of her pants, accustomed to finding oats there. Lily loosed her grip, sliding down far enough to land on her bottom; her legs, still folded Indian-style, hobbled around the massive hoof of the patient horse. She reached in her back pocket and withdrew a small quantity of moist, grubby, lint-ridden oats for the horse. Butch started to shuffle forward with the girl still attached.

"Whoa!" she shouted in tandem with her father, but she was giggling. Butch minded, but still tried to get her to move forward far enough on his foot that he could reach his snout down closer to the fist full of oats, the bend of his great neck twisting and writhing, pushing his head against her to loose her from his leg.

"Will you stop torturing that poor, hardworking beast?" Robert had locked the brake and moved forward to help the horse extricate himself from its tiny limpet. Lily allowed herself to be collared by the ruff of her coat and hauled to standing. "My child is a monster. Look at those great teeth!" And Lily obliged by showing her ferocious fangs, missing a one here and there as befitted her age. She proffered a mitten bestuck with oats in the back-arched palm, the way she'd been shown so as not to lose her mitten (or hand) to the great mouth of the Percheron.

"Ladies first," she said, offering her first full mitten to Daisy. Butch bumped her small back with his nose until Lily replenished her mitten, augmented with some oats her father carried in a feed bag hung off the side of the wagon. Then Lily raised up her arms to her father, who stood now between the tracings in case the horses took it into their minds to move forward dragging the load in spite of the brake and the small girl. He lifted her up in his arms.

"Go have lunch."

"Already had lunch."

"Then go help your mother. She's making bread."

" 'K."

"Say 'yes, Papa dear.' "

"Yes, Papa dear."

"Where's Eleanor?"

"In the lodge. She wants a fire."

"There isn't one?"

"The logs are there, but we're not allowed to light matches."

"I remember. I'm glad that *you* remember. Good girls."

"Eleanor's still studying, but I finished. Tell her to come to the kitchen when she's done. Please."

"I will. Then we're going to get the skating pond ready before tea. Mack and I worked all morning clearing off the snow."

"When are we decorating the tree, Papa?"

"After tea, for the 'leventy-'leventh time, after tea. High tea today, and late so we can finish the pond. As soon as I get the firewood done, I'll come to the kitchen door to pick you all up. Now scoot."

He returned her to the ground. Lily ran off in the direction of the kitchen in Rockingham Hall. Butch turned his lumbering head questioningly at the man, who clicked his tongue at the team, released the brake, and moved forward to continue his rounds. Robert took in the sights: horizon rippled by hills in the distance across the lake, and the sky, bright for now but with possible squalls off to the west. Flying to Montreal should be all right tomorrow. But he'd make sure the chains were in the Packard for the drive to the Malone airstrip, where the Winslows' six-seat Aero Commander was waiting in a hangar.

Robert and horses dragged the sledge toward the lodge. The lodge sported a large dumbwaiter, the sole purpose of which was to transport logs from the area beneath the porch stairs, where Robert loaded them on large, wheeled dollies. The logs were rolled onto the lift and then boosted by a counterweight system to the first and second floors. This was Robert's time-saving invention. Before he installed it, hoisting in the logs was a two- or a three-person job, in which he was usually abetted by Mack and Mabel and sometimes Charles.

While the horses stamped beside the porch steps, Robert finished unloading the last of the split logs and placed them on the dollies underneath the porch. He checked his watch, then took the steps slowly, one at a time, scattering a number of chickadees and nuthatches feeding at the large covered platform off the railing. On the porch, leaning against the wall, was an enormous cut balsam. All around, draped over the Adirondack chairs and the railings were ropes of balsam, white pine boughs and wreaths ready for the evening's decorating. Robert supported himself on the railing with a slight hitch off-gait on his left leg. He knocked on the great double doors and walked in.

Eleanor was reading. She was wrapped in a throw on one of the big velveteen-covered log settees. It was chilly in the room.

"Eleanor."

"Hello," she said, sitting up and putting her book down.

"I heard you needed a fire."

"Yes. Thank you. Where's Lily? I thought she'd be with you."

"I sent her to the kitchen to help Mariette make bread. She says for you to come over when you're ready. Don't forget we're going up to work on the skating pond before tea. Where are your parents?"

"Upstairs. Mum is napping and Dad's working on a speech."

"Mack and Mabel should be here soon. I'm a little early."

Robert bent uncomfortably to light the newspaper twists neatly laid beneath the logs.

"Would you like me to do that, now that you're here?"

"Sure. Thanks." Robert handed her the box of safety matches and rose with some difficulty, using a poker for support. She struck a match and lit the paper.

"How are you feeling today?" Eleanor asked, her face as serious as a nurse shaking down a thermometer in a doctor's office. Robert had grown used to such a wise face on such a young child.

"Fine, thank you, the leg is just aware of some possible weather coming. The eyes are on the sky and the mind is ready to fly. How about yourself?"

"Fine."

"Working hard?"

"Oh yes. Nothing stops the old homework for Miss Doris and Mister Tom. Not Christmas. Not anything."

Robert nodded sagely.

"I'll be glad when company starts to arrive," she continued. "Then we'll all be too busy for lessons."

"Do you need my help?"

"Well, I wish *you* were teaching us. It's much more fun to learn about engines and carpentry and bridges and things. Electricity and radio waves are all right, but after the third week of Mister Tom's demonstrations on the ham, it loses its fascination. I'd much rather learn how to drive the Packard and see how it runs."

"I'll teach you when you can see over the steering wheel and reach the pedals. And we'll likely start on the truck, not the Packard."

"I wish we had a Rolls. The Hensley-Phytes have a Rolls."

Robert turned to face her squarely. "Now, I would think you were someone other than Charles Winslow's daughter saying such an outrageous thing. Besides, the Hensley-Phytes are a bunch of hammock-snogging wastrels and good-for-nothings. That's what money without conscience leads you to—Rolls Royces and hammock snogging. Disgraceful."

"Hammock snogging? Oh you mean Mister Hensley-Phyte and that awful lady last summer? Wasn't she supposed to be in the movies?"

"Eyelashes like bat wings caught in spider webs."

Eleanor laughed. "And fangs," she said, remembering the woman's ruby lips and sparkling bright, prominent eyeteeth. "I hope she's not coming."

"She's not. 'Never again,' your wise mother said. Besides, the Hensley-Phytes are in Palm Beach. Sissies."

There were footsteps on the stairs both inside and out. Mack and Mabel entered the library first: Mack nodded to Robert and helped Mabel out of her coat.

"Well now, there you go old girl," Mack said.

Mabel, a sturdy Adirondack native of fifty-six years, had the ruddy cheeks of a woman used to the out-of-doors in cold winters, and the stoutness of someone who enjoyed her own simple cooking, although she enjoyed even more the sometimes exotic French touches that Mariette brought to the table in Rockingham Hall. The famous *buche de Noël* was only one example. She looked around the room as if scanning for dust and disorder. She also looked at her watch and then at Mack.

Charles Winslow came down the stairs, and directly behind him his wife Emily. Mabel would later remember, as did everyone who saw the couple, how wonderful they looked, how peaceful and carefree they were together, how handsome a couple they made.

"Well looky here!" Mack said. "Got the whole bunch of us. This won't take long 't all. C'mon Mabel. Get up the stairs. Charles, you boss the crew downstairs."

"Yessir," Charles said, stopping to give Mabel a squeeze. He was half again as tall, it seemed, as both Mabel and Mack. Eleanor on the couch had put her book down and watched the gathering quietly.

Mabel looked around and said, "Many hands make light work. You got your studies done today, young lady?"

"Not quite, but I'm working on it."

"Poor thing, they work you s'hard," she said, laughing.

Charles dressed in his winter coat and boots. Emily sat down on the couch next to her daughter and put her arm around her. Eleanor would remember that moment as well as all moments of that day and evening: her mother's grey cashmere sweater, a white shirt with a rounded collar, and camelhair slacks and slippers. She smelled a bit of woodsmoke and her eyes were sleepy. Eleanor leaned her head on her mother's shoulder and Emily nodded against her, still a little groggy after her nap. "Can I help?"

"Sure. Please explain to me the importance of the battle of Tippecanoe."

"Oh, dear. Why can't you be doing English history? I know ever so much about that. Here, let's see the book."

She settled back with Eleanor on the couch, reading together the pages of the United States history book, listening to the sounds of Charles and Robert loading the dolly of logs onto the lift downstairs beneath the porch, the fire spitting in the huge fireplace. Mabel came down and sat with them. She was a little flushed from her exertions. She leaned over to see what Eleanor and Emily were studying. "United States History was never my strong suit at school. Course, you're probably at high school level, and I just made it through sixth grade before my mother needed me to help out here at the camp kitchen cooking for the loggers. My boys, now, they did well in school."

"Are they coming for Christmas?"

"Maybe after, before New Year's. Problem with schooling is that they get too good to stay on up here and work. Someday, they all say, they'll come back here to retire. I can't imagine what they mean by that. I'd like to see anybody here retire and this camp still standing a day after."

Mack came downstairs, and the last logs were unloaded from the lift in the library. Charles and Robert came in, stamping the snow off their boots by the main door and talking about the weather and the flight tomorrow.

"Can't I go to Montreal, too? Me and Lily?" asked Eleanor.

"Lily and *I*, and no," her mother replied. "You two need to stay here and look after things for us."

Mabel stood up and walked to the fireplace. "We need you and Lily here, Eleanor. Lots of work to do before Santa comes."

Eleanor looked glum, and her mother kissed her. Charles came over and put his cold hands against both of their faces.

"Speaking of Santa, are you bringing a dog back for Lily? She so wants a dog."

"I tell you what, sweetie," Charles said as he turned to go back upstairs. "When we get settled someplace, oh, like Washington, we'll talk about a dog, but not as long as we have to be traveling. It's not fair to Mack and Mabel. I own they'd be doing most of the caring for an extra animal. And training a puppy? Whew."

"And this ain't the place for a dog other than a huntin' dog," Mack said, lighting his pipe, "and a huntin' dog ain't necessarily a plaything. You come talk to me when you want to start a-huntin' and we'll talk about a good hound for you and Lily."

"Mack's got a good point, Ellie," Charles responded as he climbed the stairs.

"Well, daylight's a wastin' and I got work to do in the barn, 'fore we go up t' the pond. You with me Mabel?"

"I'm coming." The two of them shouldered on their coats and left.

"I'll see you later, dear," Emily said, kissing her on her cheek. "Keep at it. I bet Robert knows a lot more about Tippecanoe than I or even Tyler himself."

Robert went to the settee and picked up some of the books in the pile beside her. One was on phonetics, one on geometry and one on United States history. Pretty dry stuff. She'd also been reading a volume of the *Books of Knowledge*, probably the reason she was late in finishing her lessons. Ah, the *Books of Knowledge*. He'd read them all as a kid back in Chicago. They were the only books in the tiny library at the orphan's home where he had lived. He recalled the 1911 version— what was known about the Everglades in Florida: "Where snakes and alligators and other unpleasant things are found." Or the illustration that showed how long you would travel by train to Mars (seventy-six years) and Venus (fifty years), if the train could travel a mile a minute and never stop for fuel.

He picked up a companion volume from the rough-hewn cedar bookshelf nearby. In purposeful childish handwriting inside the cover was written the name of his employer, Charles Harrison Winslow Jr. Robert flipped idly through the pages but was thinking of Charlie, of what his life might have been like back then, long before the war. What twisted streams had brought them together to serve in England, both pilots in the same outfit, wounded, decorated, and together still; and not just the two once-boys, but their wives, and now their daughters? His own painful wounds were made easier to bear just by thinking about how miraculous his new life was—as a part of this place in the woods, doing good work with good people.

When he looked up, Eleanor was staring at him with a calm discernment and a certain detectable admiration. He smiled, replaced the book on the shelf, and commented that it was time he should be getting back to work. He had yet to do Miss Doris and Mr. Tom's place, and unhitch the horses for the ride up to the kettle pond before tea. He told her he'd be done in half an hour and meet them, dressed warmly, please, by the kitchen door. Then he left her with her books.

Lily shed her boots in the mudroom off the kitchen as well as her coat, hat, scarf and soggy, oat-caked mittens. Her mother, Mariette, turned her head briefly to see who had come in, said hello to her daughter, and returned to the risen bread dough she was punching down. She instructed her daughter to wash her hands, put on the little apron that hung by the door, and pull the stool up to the bread table. There she broke off a fist-sized piece of dough for Lily to work with alongside her own. She reached underneath to one of the two twenty-pound flour bins hinged to the underside of the maple butcher block.

Mariette Martindale had the high flush and steamed complexion of someone who spends a great deal of time over open flames and very hot water. Her long, light brown hair was pulled back and enclosed in a net held with pins. In spite of the full apron she wore, her spruce green gabardine skirt was mottled with swipes of flour. She wore brown knit stockings and boiled wool mules with fleece lining.

Mariette and Lily sang as they worked, sometime carols in French, sometimes American songs. Sometimes Mariette made up silly words in

French or in English describing what they were going to have for tea, or what they had planned for afterward. But this afternoon she was describing Montreal to Lily: the size of the Queen Elizabeth Hotel, where they would be staying; the French restaurants where she and Robert would eat after shopping in the fine stores; the list of supplies and Christmas gifts she had a mind to buy for her husband and the Winslows.

"What are you getting Eleanor?" Lily asked.

"I think I'm going to make Eleanor that special *gateau* you both like, the chocolate one with almonds."

"But what about me?"

"I'll make each of you one."

"And the *buche de Noël*?"

"But of course! For everyone, that."

"Don't I get any toys?"

"Did you make the list for Père Noël?"

"I did," Lily said. "You want to see it?"

"But of course," replied her mother. And Lily produced a folded piece of yellow lined paper, torn from a pad, with three words written very large with a very thick, black pencil. "Puppy, puppy, puppy."

"Does this mean you want three puppies or one puppy very badly?"

"One puppy very badly."

"You know Père Noël often cannot do everything we ask. He thinks of everybody, of the Winslows, and of us because we travel with them so much, we could not always take a dog along. And it would not be fair to ask Mack and Mabel to take care of yet another animal when we can't. Père Noël must listen to everyone's wishes and decide himself."

"I know, but I really, really, really want a puppy."

"Well then, are you ready to send your wishes to the North Pole?"

"Yes, *maman*."

"Then let's go over here to the stove."

Mariette led her daughter to the big wood cookstove and opened the draft. She lifted her daughter, hesitated a moment, and said "I think we have forgotten something important. Come over here." Mariette found a pencil and handed it to Lily. "You forgot to write your name and to say please and thank you."

"I don't know how to write please and thank you."

"Well you know how to write your name, so I'll do the rest."

Lily labored, her tongue sticking out of the corner of her mouth, her head level with the paper and resting on the hand that held the paper firmly while she wrote. Then she handed the pencil to her mother, who wrote in "Please may I have" above the puppy request, "Thank you" below, and added "The Hill, Winslow Station, New York, USA." Back at the stove, she held Lily up high enough to shove the paper in the flue, where the draught sucked it along into the rush of rising hot air and off to the North Pole.

"That's done," said her mother. "Now let's put this bread to rise again and get the tea things ready, before you go up with Papa and Mack to the pond."

Robert was stacking wood against the porch wall of Ora Labora when Miss Doris stuck her head out of the door. She was tall and angular with dyed black hair and a sharp-featured face that had seen the worst of the London Blitz and come out the other side with a shrewd sense of her own English pride and a love for children (though she had none of her own) and books.

"When you have a minute," she said crisply. He finished stacking, took his hat off, wiped his feet carefully, and entered the main room with its woodstove and hooked rug. The interior of the cabin, once the old guides' housing, was as far removed from Adirondack rustic style as possible. Miss Doris had swathed everything in tatted cloth, bedecked with ceramic icons of her British heritage and pictures of the Queen Mother and Queen Elizabeth and Prince Phillip on the wall, with little Union Jacks set behind. Doris had been sitting in the rocker in front with her books. Her husband, Tom, a retired performer from the London music hall stage, was nearby fiddling with a part from his short wave radio. Emily Winslow had brought the couple over from England to look after Eleanor and Lily and provide them with some education. Doris taught the classics, history (both English and American) and opera. Tom taught science and math and added his agile voice and an endless selection of music hall songs to their evenings on The Hill by the lodge's upright piano.

The old guides' house had been furnished with a small kitchen and modernized bath so the couple could operate independently from the family, which they often chose to do, unless it was a special occasion. Doris found it odd—this tendency on the part of the "manor lords" to be so clubby with the servants. Tom found it amusing, and took great pride in the girls' adoration for his songs, such as "Proper Cup of Coffee," "Don't Dilly Dally on the Way" and "Who's Taking Care of the Caretaker's Daughter?" Doris, for her own part, maintained a formal British hauteur in her status as governess and tutor, which Robert found amusing. The girls adored Tom and Doris, as irksome as the lessons (and Doris's strictness) could be, especially this close to Christmas. But how many American children could say they had lessons only in the morning before lunch and the rest of the day free as chickadees in the pine forest around them, so long as they finished their lessons?

"Will you have some tea?" she asked Robert. "I couldn't wait 'til five. I've just made a pot for us."

"Thank you no. I can't stay. What can I do for you?"

"Would you mind picking up four cartons of Gauloises for me when you get to Montreal. I really can't abide these American cigarettes. Tom, is there anything you need? For the wireless?"

Tom answered from the back, his throaty voice rich with phlegm and Cockney, "I already put my list in. Robert has it. And he's bringing us some spirits, as well. Good bloke."

"Well, thank you very much, Robert. I only wish we could go with you. I'd love to get a bit of a holiday from this place."

"Yes, ma'am."

"Seems odd, doesn't it?"

"No ma'am."

"Well thank you again. What time do you leave?"

"Early, weather permitting."

"I have the girls working on recitations for the Yule dinner. They're making books of their lessons so far this fall. I think that will be a hit with everyone."

"Yes ma'am. Thank you ma'am."

"Yes. Well that will be all. See you at high tea."

Robert replaced his hat and turned to go. When he reached the porch and closed the door behind him, he shook his head at the strange upright wonder that was Doris and took a deep breath of cold fresh air. He returned to the team and began the last stretch of his rounds. His fingers were cold and his leg was beginning to ache again. He reached into the pocket of his thick plaid shirt and withdrew six buffered aspirin, which he popped in his mouth all at once and then, grimacing, swallowed.

Four days in Montreal, a nice hotel, great restaurants. He found he wasn't excited about the trip, apart from the thought of being at the controls of the plane again, but Mariette couldn't wait to be back in a French-speaking country, back among people who knew a *galantine* from a *ballotine*. And soon it would be Christmas, with a great tree in the lodge and one in Rockingham Hall, too, and all the presents fresh from Montreal, such a feast to behold, the guests and old friends from New York, Washington, Boston, Los Angeles. Impromptu theatricals, musical performances, readings from just-published books, Lily and Eleanor opening their presents on Christmas morning.

He looked up at the sky again. The squalls hung like drapery off to the west, but seemed to be moving north and away from them. Not bad. They'd flown through worse, he and Charles, much worse. Directly above, the sky was clear, cold blue—a good sign.

Next to elephants and dinosaurs, the Percherons were the largest land creatures a child could imagine, and Lily's greatest joy was riding with her father high above the ground astride one of those massive beasts. It was hard to imagine that such Brobdingnagian creatures could be so prudent and cautious with the small spawn of humans, but Lily had grown up with Butch and Daisy as her tolerant nannies. When Robert Martindale wasn't taking care of cars and planes for the Winslows, he helped Mack out in the barn. He had a tremendous love and respect for those horses, which he passed on to Lily.

Robert and Lily, Mack and Eleanor rode bareback on Butch and Daisy up to the pond, all with the admirable assignment of staying out of the way while Mabel and Mariette readied the lodge for holiday decking. The snow on the road was deep and light. There was still bright sunlight, and the snow sparkled like powdered crystals. Robert was smoking his pipe and Mack one of his precious Cuban cigars. When they reached the pond, Eleanor and Lily played at clearing snow while Mack and Robert augured a hole in the ice and siphoned up water to coat the pond and make a smooth skating surface. The girls gathered what wood they could find to add to the pile beside the lean-to, for a bonfire when the friends came. The horses were tied to a nearby tamarack, watching. The girls carried oats in their pockets and the beasts knew that, and Mack knew it too, so he hollered to Lily to shinny up the tree and let the pair go so they could follow the girls around and baby sit. Eleanor made it to the tree first. After two minutes of cold wrangling with the stiff leathers, and with Lily helping her, she got the two big horses free, and patted them off to the field beside the pond.

Butch and Daisy didn't want to go too far from the girls and the oats, so the girls started a parade, Eleanor with Daisy and Lily with Butch, marching around the field with the big creatures trailing along behind. Then they stopped, and the Percherons came up and bumped each girl on the back, pushing them into the snow, until they got up laughing and reached in their pockets for the oats. They repeated this game until Butch got tired of it after a while and lay down and started rolling in the snow, sending up great showers of diamond dust in the remaining daylight. Daisy soon followed suit, but Eleanor and Lily kept up the march around the field, wading sometimes hip-deep in the snow, making hearts and figure eights and snow angels until they were exhausted.

The horses rolled and rolled and Eleanor walked gently over to Daisy, approaching her at the head and shuffling around as she'd been taught with one hand in constant touch with the horse until she'd shuffled around to the back. She motioned Lily to come. Daisy lay there quietly while they patted her. Then the two girls flopped onto her flank and lay with their ears pressed to her side listening to the cavernous rumblings and the huge bellows of her lungs and the echo drum of her big old heart. They lay still, and Daisy would lift her head and turn it to look, as if they were foals and might want to nurse. She sighed an exhaustive, heaving breath of South Sea Island vapors, heavy with heat and moisture. Butch, who'd been rolling off to the side, stood and shook himself. He approached and leaned down his head, the size of the front grille of a John Deere tractor. He sniffed and wurffled around their heads and pockets, which set Lily to giggling.

Years later, the memory of those great guardians with their internal winds and rumblings, enveloping her in their own climate of warmth and smell and sound in the cold Adirondack winter, would send an ache so sharp, so acute, that Lily would draw a breath and have to lean on something, bowing her head. She would remember, more clearly than any photograph could have captured it, that day in the snow. Missing those horses was nearly as painful as the loss of everyone else together.

As they lay there, Eleanor and Lily were peacefully cared for, warm in the topography of the Percherons. Robert and Mack stood respectfully alongside them. "Oh, Mack," Robert said, "How I wish I'd brought a camera."

❦

During the hour before high tea, while the children were still at the pond, Mabel, Mariette and Emily Linstead Winslow cleared away chairs and ottomans, tables and heavy couches, to make room for the ten-foot balsam Christmas tree. Emily was a somewhat pale and fragile-looking English beauty raised in a stately home in Sussex, but she was no stranger to the wilderness. In spite of her fair skin and thin frame, she had a well-earned reputation for horsemanship, hunting and fishing. She was a fabled dancer at the balls in New York and London, and had been honored for her service as a nurse during the war. Right now, her arms were laden with balsam boughs brought in from the porch. She carried them to a corner of the main room of the lodge where, in a twenty-gallon pickle crock, they joined as many branches of winterberry.

"Let's let the boys carry the tree in," she said. "They should be back soon."

"Mack brought the ornaments and lights up from the cellar, did he? Yup, there they are." Mabel removed the top from one of the storage boxes. She hated to see things so untidy, but it couldn't be helped. Once everybody left tomorrow, she and Mack and the girls would put it all to rights again. Then they'd breathe easy until the friends started to arrive.

"This here is the best part of the season. Right now. Just us and the kids and the tree and decorations. I've always loved this night," Mabel said.

"Me, too," echoed Mariette.

"As do I," Emily said patting Mabel on the shoulder. "What time is it?"

"Ten 'til," said Mabel, looking at a cloisonné brooch watch pinned to her dress front, a Christmas gift from Charles and Emily.

"Well let's get the tea table ready."

The women moved into the adjoining library and dragged a large table closer to the fire, then placed eight chairs around it. Mariette had brought savory ham sandwiches made with the fresh baked bread. In a separate basket were scones, clotted cream and wild blueberry preserves put up over the summer. There was an electric teakettle on the boil in the butler's pantry off the library. Two pots were already steeping, which she brought from the pantry to set on the table, one covered by a quilted cozy in the shape of a barn, the other by a thick knitted effort in blue with a white pom-pom on the top, the handiwork of Miss Doris in her spare time. Mariette had kicked off her boots and slipped into a pair of brown pumps. Mabel was smoothing the tablecloth and setting out cups and plates. Mariette laid out the sandwiches on a platter and covered them with a fresh linen tea towel. Emily was clearing the mantelpieces in both the main lodge room and the library. Very soon Mack, Robert and the girls could be heard stomping on the porch, then giggling by the deer hoof coat rack. They ran in and stood in front of the fire. The glow of the fire added little to the bright red of their cheeks as they chattered to their mothers like squirrels. Mack and Robert brought in the tree and stood it in the corner on the stand in the main room. Mabel stood ready with a broom and dustpan. Emily, standing off to one side, nodded approval. "It's a wonderful tree," she said. "The best yet."

"Mother, you say that every year," Eleanor responded.

"I don't remember every year, but I think it's a fine tree," added Lily, sounding so much like her father that it made Mariette shiver with pride and Emily and Mabel smile.

As the balsam warmed up, its fragrance began to carry through the open room. Mack and Robert washed up in the butler's pantry, their faces red and merry. Robert brought in two boxes—one of lights and one of decorations. Doris and Tom arrived to help.

"Can I put one on?" Lily asked.

"After tea," Robert said, picking her up and holding her close to the tree where she breathed deeply the resinous perfume of the fir. Mariette walked over to stand by them and take in the smell for herself.

"Oh, it is so wonderful," she said. Lily reached out her arms to her, and Mariette held her briefly before putting her down. "*Tu as très faim, p'tite Fleurette?*"

"*Oui, maman.*"

"Time to make yourself clean. Eleanor, too, yes?" The girls ran upstairs to Eleanor's room. "And make your hair nice, please!"

Charles Winslow came down the stairs on the stroke of five, wearing an old wool hunting shirt over a turtleneck sweater, loose corduroy pants held up by red suspenders, and slippers with thick wool socks. Looking the picture of a backwoods worker, he could have been Mack and Mabel's son, something out of a Winslow Homer painting. His wife shook her head and smiled. She'd turned down requests from *Town and Country* for interviews and photographs so many times, and here was the very reason. Charles, the decorated combat pilot, one of the first in the country to caution Americans against embracing the rhetoric of Joe McCarthy, narrowly defeated for a Senate seat, and, many rumored, on his way to the White House in another eight years; here he was appearing for high tea dressed like a lumberjack. Together, he and Emily were one of the most celebrated and mysterious couples in social and political circles. Photogenic in a near-Hollywood style, they preferred the quiet snow deeps of the Adirondack forest preserve to the canyons of New York or the blue waters off Palm Beach. Emily looked at her husband and knew he was very happy.

"What?" he said looking at her as she smiled. "It's a clean shirt. You were expecting Brooks Brothers?"

"No, dear, no." Emily still smiling, hugged him. "You look fine."

The girls came tearing down the stairs, until they saw their mothers, then they slowed to a ludicrous tandem display of ladylike walking, their hands cocked out to the side, index fingers delicately pointing up, their hips sashaying in the rustle of pretend crinolines. Charles put his arm around his daughter in a mock chokehold, and did the same with Lily.

"How are my girls?"

"Fine," they chimed, and laughed.

"Ready for some Christmas cheer? Two cheers for Christmas. Hip hip . . ."

"Three cheers, father dear. Three," said Eleanor.

"Hip, hip . . ."

They cheered.

Everyone sat around the table in the library in no particular order—Mack, Mabel, Mariette, Robert, Charles, Doris, Tom, Emily and the girls. They joined hands in a sung blessing, the "Doxology" for which the lodge was named:

Praise God, from whom all blessings flow;
Praise him all creatures here below;
Praise him above ye heavenly host:
Praise Father, Son and Holy Ghost.

The girls' high, thin voices, more or less in key but enthusiastic with ritual, the men's voices, especially Tom, Robert and Charles, clear as horns, Emily's fluty soprano, Mabel's in a wobbling lower register. Mack was the only one who could not hold a tune in a gunny sack. He pursed his lips and nodded along.

All seated, they passed the sandwiches around. Mariette poured tea at one end of the table, Mabel at the other. The girls described helping Mack make smooth ice for skating. Emily talked to Mack and Mabel about the arrangements for the extra help. There were only ten days until Christmas, seven before the friends arrived. Doris repeated the plan for the recitations, and the girls showed off how much they had memorized already.

This would be the twelfth year of Charles's marriage to Emily and the fifteenth year he had celebrated Christmas at The Hill with his Friends Without Family, a gathering he had loosely organized while he was at Harvard and later Columbia, because it was too painful to go home to Boston after his father died. The routine and tradition were unvarying—close friends who had no family, welcoming or living, were invited for the holiday. No gifts were given except to the children, but donations were made to worthy causes and the neediest cases (which did not include political parties). Otherwise, they were fed sumptuous foods, spent late evenings of spectacular chat about new books and movies, and otherwise solved the problems of the world. By the twenty-seventh of December, Charles was on his way home to Boston to visit his mother in McLean Hospital, where, until she died of a stroke, she was more or less a permanent resident following bouts of alcoholism, delusions and suicide attempts. The Hill was his treasured, most lived-in retreat—a place of peace, privacy and family, of distance from reporters, flashbulbs and ringing phones. Charles watched and listened to the girls, grateful that the attention was off him and on the grand spectacle of Christmas.

The decorating of the tree followed the clearing of the dishes. Miss Doris and Mr. Tom produced a rum-soaked pound cake, a bottle of port and some hard-shelled walnuts they'd been saving. Mack brought out a stepladder. Eleanor's privilege was to place the star at the top of the tree. Lily's specialty, with assistance, was a grouping of hand-painted ceramic angels in real satin and net dresses, each angel playing a different instrument. These were placed below the star, from a perch on Robert's and Charles's shoulders. The girls had made a "mile long" paper chain out of brightly colored strips of sticky paper, an annual special order from one of the Winslow paper mills that specialized in gummed products such as sealing tape. Mariette went through the vast collection of long-playing records standing in the corner next to the Victrola and played some Edith Piaf and then Dick Haymes and Helen Forrest singing "It Had to be You," which prompted Emily and Mack, Charles and Mabel, Doris and Tom and the children to dance, with a lot of cutting in from one grouping to another. Lily danced standing on her father's, or Mack's or Tom's or Charles's feet.

Once the decorating was completed and the tree toasted with good champagne brought in from a snowbank outside, the Victrola was switched off. Emily sat at the upright Steinway and played a round of Christmas carols while everyone sang along in sometimes atrocious, giggling harmony. Then, from upstairs, Charles produced the Hasselblad on a tripod, which Robert helped him set up at a remove from the Christmas tree.

"All right now everyone," he called. "Can we possibly behave properly and in a dignified manner for one minute and just please, please, please *try* to pretend like we're having fun. You over there," he said, motioning to the girls who were sitting on either side of Emily at the piano banging away at "Heart and Soul," "No more hooliganism there, I say! Your Ladyship, round up those varmints! Everyone to the tree."

The pictures were taken at a distance by means of a long cord and a plunger operated by Charles. In the first, Lily squinted in anticipation of the flash she dreaded. Emily, in one, can be seen appraising Charles's appearance and reaching to brush something away from his cheek, which created a blur. Doris and Tom were kissing in one. Mack had his arm about Mabel in every shot. The girls stood front and center, Eleanor's arm congenially around Lily like a proper mate. Robert and Mariette stood close to each other, looking straight at the camera with comfortable smiles. Several more photos were taken before the Hasselblad was moved away with its precious plates.

Everyone returned to the library, and Tom and Doris poured out some port in snifters for those that wanted (Emily could not tolerate fortified wines). Charles sat on the big overstuffed Adirondack log frame couch with the girls on either side. He cradled an edition of Dickens's *A Christmas Carol,* from which he was picking up where he had left off the night before with the tale of the Fezziwigs' ball. Tom and Mack had lit pipes by the fireplace, then, at a glance from Emily, donned their jackets and went outside to smoke; Emily sat knitting; Doris perched at the table playing Patience; Mariette, with her lisled legs tucked underneath her, sat next to Lily on the couch. Lily began to drift off to the sound of Charles's voice; Mariette gently pulled her back against her own breast, and felt herself nodding as well. Robert quietly extracted a log from the dumbwaiter pile. He pulled aside the huge wire screen decorated with flying ducks and cattails and prodded the fire with an ancient wood and iron peavey preserved from the logging camp, abandoned before The Hill was built.

With Dickens's words drifting to an end-of-chapter finality, Charles closed the book and put his arm around Eleanor, and looked around the room to see who was left standing.

"Is Lily staying with you tonight?" he asked Eleanor.

"Is that all right?" Eleanor asked Mariette.

"Since we're leaving tomorrow, perhaps she should stay with us tonight."

"Please?"

"Well, we won't see her for four days. You'll get to see her all the time until we return."

"Please?"

"Robert," asked Mariette, "do *you* mind if Lily stays here tonight?"

"No, not at all. Just have to carry her upstairs instead of down the hill. Here . . ." and he lifted the sleeping child into his arms. Mariette, whose legs had fallen asleep, reached up to give Lily a kiss. "All right then," she said. She breathed deeply the wispy smell of small child and touched her very soft, fine brown hair. As Robert lifted her over his shoulder, she started to waken, looked briefly around under half-lidded eyes, and, seeing who was carrying her to bed, relaxed her head back onto Robert's shoulder. Lily also saw that Eleanor was walking up the stairs, holding onto Emily's hand. Lily reached her hand over to Emily's shoulder and let it rest there like a knight's tender offering of devotion. Emily, with her free hand, reached up to acknowledge the gift.

Mariette watched them disappear at the top of the stairs, and began to un-kink her own legs and rub the circulation back into her feet.

"Are you all packed and ready?" Charles asked.

"I've been packed and ready for days," replied Mariette.

"Well, morning comes early."

Doris was already putting on her coat. Sticking her head out the door, she saw that the lights were on in the kitchen, and she started off in that direction, presuming that Tom and Mack had gone down there to have their smoke. Mabel had fallen asleep in the window seat with an expression of profoundly deep peace.

"I hate to disturb her, she works so hard," Mariette said. She merely touched her shoulder lightly and Mabel was instantly on her feet brushing down her skirt.

"Must have been that wine," she said. "I'm not used to spirits so late in the evening, unless I've got the grippe. Well, morning comes early, Charles. It was a lovely evening—the loveliest yet for us all. The children were having so much fun. And, mind you, sir, if I don't get a copy of that photo, there'll be hell to pay in the caretaker's cottage."

Charles placed his arms about her and rocked her singing "Who'll take care of the caretaker's lady while the caretaker's busy taking care?" And Mabel started to laugh and slapped Charles on the arm.

"We'll be up to see you off in the morning, then. I'll have a thermos ready for you and some sandwiches for the trip."

"The thermos will be greatly appreciated by the pilots and crew," Charles said, "but we'll be in Montreal by lunchtime, eating some very fine French cooking, unlike the horrible hog slops we get here." This time Mariette punched him as he tried amiably to wind her into his arms.

Robert came halting down the stairs and Mariette ran to him crying "Hog slops! What is this hog slops he is telling me?"

"Do I have to defend your honor *and* your cooking?" Robert declared, smiling at Charles. "Duel with pistols at dawn by the boat house, you cad."

Robert helped the laughing Mariette into her overcoat and shook Charles's hand while she struggled with her socks and galoshes. "I think we'll all sleep tonight," he said.

Charles saw them out and down the lane to the kitchen quarters before he switched off the lights in the long room. Emily came down from tucking the girls in. Mabel had gathered up the last of the glasses and plumped up the couch and pillows before donning her own coat and hat.

"I'll walk you down," Charles said.

"Oh, don't be silly. Mack's on his way over. You all need to get to sleep. It's nearly midnight." She embraced Emily and Charles. "Goodbye you two," she said, "I'll see you in the morning." Mabel left them by the door. Mack was indeed waiting by the foot of the stairs, and took her arm. Together they walked out into the black Adirondack night, Mack's flashlight illuminating a ring of glistening white snow ahead of them.

Chapter Five

"Let all mortal flesh keep silence, and with fear and trembling stand"

"Picardy," #197, Episcopal Hymnal, 1940

Traditional French melody, 17th century

Text: Liturgy of St. James; Para. Gerard Moultrie, 1864

The sound of the bell, the ringing of the wind chimes, the crunch of boots outside of the cabin now barely registers with Lily, who still sits in the old rocker. She is somewhere in a very deep, only semiconscious, place, like a nap in which noises are still audible but feed odd and ancient dreams. Her teeth have stopped chattering. She's somewhat conscious of holding very, very still, so as not to make a sound, not to draw attention to herself any more than she already has. She's in a purposeful state, like the tonic immobility of a frog when the shadow of the heron looms overhead, or the squirrel that flattens against the trunk of the red spruce when the hawk's screeling cry is heard in the air above. If she is aware at all, she is aware of her breathing and her heartbeat—both irregular—and of the sharp aches in all her joints and connective tissue.

She has gone astray in her dreaming, lost in the past. The bell. Someone is coming; someone is coming to ask her advice, to see what she knows, to chide her for her foolishness, ask for her hand, play a tune on the wind chimes. This is the way it is with hermits. They think they can escape, but they are sought out.

As soon as Lily moved back to the cabin on The Hill Next, the ringing of the "visitors' bell" became predictable and old. The bell itself was antique—from the old days of the Winslow Station volunteer firehouse. By the time the Winslow Lake Lodge and Motor Hotel ("Lakeside Cabins, AAA") burned down, they had already advanced toward the more audible siren, which Lily could faintly hear from the other side of the lake. Robert Martindale purchased the bell, built the pole, mounted an old oxbow to hold it up at the foot of The Hill Next and attached a nylon cord with a cleat at the base. There was once a sign, long gone now, reading "Ring 2X for tea, 4X for visit, like hell for emergency."

The system worked passably well for Robert in his free days and afternoons in the cabin. As young children, Ellie and Lily at first abused it, until they realized that they'd be put to work at some chore, like hauling wood for the stove. Sometimes Charles would ring, and he and Robert would go off fishing or tramping, just the two of them, for two or three days at a time in the summers. For Robert and Mariette, it was their honeymoon cottage (they'd never had a proper honeymoon during the war). Between bouts of summer or winter guests when the Winslows were in camp, the young couple would take a little holiday of a weekday or two up at the cabin. Later, Mariette and Robert would leave Lily with Mack and Mabel and continue the tradition of time to themselves. Lily later wondered if she was conceived in the lower bunk bed.

Robert and Charles had an understanding about the land: it was Robert's property, deeded over to him and to Mariette at first on a hand-shake, but later—in fact one Christmas—formally as a gift. Now it was Lily's, now that everyone else was gone.

As soon as word got around the hamlet that Lily had taken over as caretaker, various deputations came to call. Finding the old caretaker's cottage empty and locked, they would notice tracks going up the hillside road that winter and the plow parked at the base of The Hill Next and snowshoe or ski trails mounting up toward the old cabin. If they knew the camp at all, they realized that Lily had gone to live in her father's place. Finding the bell, of course, they rang it. Some of them still remembered what the bell was for and even the protocol, because they'd worked at the camp in the old days with the crews that helped open and close the buildings and served during the busy season. They were the summer season help—teenagers and a little older back then, retired now if they were still around. Not many were, except Jim Porter and the Finns, who ran the general store, and the Guilbeaults, who owned the marina, and the Aikens from the Tap Room.

The first time she heard the bell that winter more than ten years ago, Lily knew it was Jim, from the gentle hesitancy of the ring. She watched for him. As an old local wag used to say, "When he comes over a rise, you see Jim's head about five minutes before you see his feet," and every door was a challenge for his height. He'd been dipping his head to come through the cabin door since he was fifteen, and that hadn't changed. He was dressed for the cold in his old anorak and a guide hat studded all over with rusty buttons saying things like "We Try Harder." His lean cheeks were rosy from the cold and exertion coming up The Hill Next on snowshoes. The fire of his cheeks set off the clear, ice blue of his eyes with their fur ruff lashes that had turned her head so many years ago. On his back was his old ash packbasket. He brought M&M's, which he knew she loved, and her favorite tea he'd ordered from Mom and Pop Finn's (actually now run by the daughter and son-in-law), some frozen burgers and hot dogs, which she stowed outside in a cooler inside an old metal box, locked to keep the critters out. She made them both a cup of the tea and sat down with him at the old pine table. He had started his nervous talking the moment he walked into the cabin, until he noticed Lily wince. He knew that look and guessed he was in for the usual tongue lashing, but Lily bowed her head, saying, "Jim. I'm going to stop this dead in its tracks right now, before we even get started. I've pitched the last of my Valium. Threw the damn stuff down the privy last night, and I pray to God I don't get desperate enough to try to retrieve it. I have no booze, no drugs up here, in case you were worried."

She raised her face to him. He could see how the corners of her mouth were drawn down. She'd taken the little diamond studs out of her pierced ears. Her face was completely unadorned, plain and still lovely to him. He could feel his heart constrict and burn. He hadn't quite expected this. He got this goofy look on his face after a moment, as though there was still some kind of hope. She hated that look most of all.

"I'm not going to church with you," Lily said. "No church, no AA meetings, no concerts, skating events or movies in Placid. I'm not dating you, sleeping with you. You're my friend and what we were once is over, if it ever was. You know that. I messed up and I'm sorry. I'm here to get myself together. I'm in charge of The Hill now, and I plan to do a good job all by myself. If I need help in any way, you'll be the first to know. Like, you can help me with the wood until I get the hang of the chainsaw."

"Lily, you been in the city a long time and it's dangerous, you alone . . ."

"Jim. This is the way it's going to be. You are going to leave me alone from now on. That's the deal."

Jim took a sip of tea and frowned. "Don't call us? We'll call you?"

"Exactly."

Jim started to speak, but she shushed him again. "Can you please just sit there and see how long you can be still and not say a word?"

He tried. He really tried. He lasted maybe two minutes, during which he gulped his tea. "I can't," he said quietly. "I've got too much to say, Lily. How I've missed you. How much I still feel for you. I really do. I should hate you. I've thought at times I did, but I just can't hate anybody. Never could. I thought maybe," but there was that hard Lily-look again. He nodded. He rose, put on his old ranger hat and jacket with the 46'er patches on the shoulder, and headed for the door. When he turned, she shook her head.

After he left, she paced around the cabin, agitated in a way that she had not been since the last gala at the Museum of Natural History in New York. She rifled through the duffel bag she had thrown together for the trip with Eleanor up to camp. She had barely begun to unpack, except for a couple of shirts and sweaters, and a couple of pairs of jeans. Her Dooney and Bourke bag had been stuffed inside the duffel, and all that it contained—wallet, makeup kit, Social Security card, credit cards—now useless and ridiculous. But there, there in the middle of it all was this photograph of her with a young volunteer at the benefit. She stared at it long and hard, and at the closed door that stood so firmly like all the lost years with Jim. She angrily smashed the picture back in the bag and shoved it all back in the drawer under the bunk for the mice to revel in.

She didn't see Jim again for five whole months, and then only when she called him to help her take the plow blade off the truck in May. Then she didn't see him until nearly Christmas. She figured the chainsaw out all by herself.

So the problem of visitors wasn't Jim so much. It was everybody else.

Now what do they want? What can anyone want of her now? She's tired and weak and sorry. Over the months and years here in the cabin she has come to believe that all the anger has drained from her as though oozing through the soles of her feet through the stone floor and into the ground beneath the cabin. She's like a battery seeping acid. It drips to the very roots of the mountains, down to the earth's core. There has been such a frightening amount of it flowing, surely the governor will declare The Hill a Superfund site when next he visits the camp. How little will be left of her once the anger is gone? For all these years, this rage is who she is—antiwar rage, political rage, rage on behalf of the disabled kids she represented, rage against her own history. Now she is a cipher, a nautilus with every chamber empty except the ones that beat with syncopation and an ache of loss and *that* seems to be fading. It resonates with something, a shred of memory not so long ago. The rhythm of the city, the stop and go of traffic up Madison Avenue, pneumatic drills on the sidewalk outside the flat in Murray Hill, applause of the audience after a lecture at the 92nd Street Y or Steinway Hall on a Sunday afternoon. The knock on the door, no, a drumbeat—the symphony playing at Carnegie Hall; no, a dance band playing swing music at the Museum of Natural History, the last gala before she disappeared.

"Lily? Lily, it's me, open up. Lily, are you all right?" Pounding.

The door? There's a drumbeat, horses' hooves. No. It's her heart.

In the old days, it was not unusual for the townsfolk of Winslow Station to be seen around camp. Many had business there, but there was also the good sense that any good neighbor checks in now and again to see that everything's copasetic. And they were always welcome. Doc Burton would come occasionally and have a drink with Charles and Robert, or a cup of coffee with Mack and Mabel. Pastor Dan, the preacher back then, would drop by just to chat. The schoolteacher and her husband often came to borrow books or return them to The Hill's capacious library. Any number of town ladies would come help Mabel with the spring cleaning of the camp—airing out the cabins and beeswaxing the furniture, Butcher's Waxing and polishing the floors, beams, and pine counters. They did the same with the closing up when the Winslows and Martindales went back to New York or off traveling.

So when Lily came back, it was not disturbing to have people drop by. If she was down working around the camp, it was good to have an extra hand with whatever she was doing or a break to make coffee or tea in the dining hall. There was Clara Finn, the new pastor at the Methodist Church in Winslow Station (and also one other small hamlet church that shared her ministry on Sunday mornings). Then it was Clara and her husband, Joe Finn. Then Clara and Sue Ellen Finn (Lily couldn't remember her married name, but she was Joe Finn's sister). Lily knew Sue Ellen's mom from the old days when she and Sue Ellen's dad ran Mom and Pop's before Pop died and Mom Finn moved to Florida in the winters. Sue Ellen and her second husband took over the store.

Clara now, well Pastor Clara Finn—Clara was something special, and of all the people recently come to Winslow Station since the old days, the new pastor (as she was still known even after fifteen years) was one of the few people whom Lily could expect to come for a visit at least three times a year. She was a feisty little artillery-loaded tank of a woman. She and her husband Joe, the handyman about the town, had met at Paul Smith's College some years back when he was studying forestry there and her family lived nearby in a ramshackle place up in the hills. Joe was a logger when he felt like it and a member of the volunteer fire department. They scraped by until their son, Phillip, was born, then Clara got The Call.

Joe Finn was one of the most congenial guys you could ever imagine meeting at Aiken's Tap Room, where he could be found of a Friday and Saturday over a slow beer and a shot. He was never drunk or disorderly. He was a big Nordic fellow who could collar-lift anybody who was out of line in Tom Aiken's normally quiet establishment. Joe was the one who picked Mike McCalanaugh out of the barbed wire fence the night he went out riding on his Polar Cat after too much to drink. Joe was the husband who took care of his little boy while his wife went off to school to get her divinity degree and when she had to write long papers late into the night. Joe was the kind of guy you called on when you were in a jam—whether your house was on fire or your car broke down or your driveway needed plowing, you hoped Joe would be around to help out. When the child was little, Joe would arrive at the scene of whatever disaster with his truck and the kid inside all bundled up in the car seat either quietly watching or asleep. The little guy never cried, never complained. They were quite a family, the Finns, tough as locust posts.

Pastor Clara and Joe were at the store when Jim came in and told Sue Ellen that Lily Martindale was back and going to take over The Hill as caretaker. Clara and Joe were there getting a coffee. What she knew of Lily would wad a shotgun, but she'd heard the old story of the tragedy and knew that the reappearance of this woman at The Hill was like having a movie star with a troubled past set up shop locally.

"I'd like to pay her a call," she said to Jim and Sue Ellen.

"Good luck," Sue Ellen said. "I haven't seen her in years, but she used to come in here when she was a girl, and she was usually so stoned, I couldn't understand anything she said."

Jim said quietly, "She ain't like that no more."

Sue Ellen and Clara waited for the flood of explanation that Jim was known for, but he was unnaturally quiet.

"Well Jim, if she's okay like you say, when you going to pop the question?"

"She ain't like that with me no more neither. I ain't poppin' no damn question, so just forget it." He looked so dark that Sue Ellen shut her mouth.

"Well, Jim," Clara said, "How do I present myself to Miss Lily Martindale, if I go up there?"

Jim explained about the bell and said he'd leave a note for her in the mail that the pastor would be visiting, so put the guns away.

Several days later, Clara headed up to the camp to pay a call. She took one of her special poppyseed cakes. Lily was out splitting wood when she heard the bell ring and Clara came up the path to the cabin. Lily set down the maul and took off her heavy work gloves and looked Clara over. In New York, Clara would have struck Lily as someone better suited to housekeeping than leading a parish, and this made her curious. She invited the woman in for a cup of tea and set the pot to boil on top of the woodstove. Clara looked around the cabin and noticed that it was orderly and clean and spare. Unlike her house, the parsonage, there wasn't a single gimcrack, gewgaw, family photograph or kid's class picture anywhere. There was, however, a large shelf piled with books. She unwrapped the poppyseed cake and put it on a plate that Lily brought out, a plate, Clara noticed, that looked like it had come from the bargain section of Monkey Ward's.

Clara gave Lily the once over. She had little of the attitude of the city about her. She wore no jewelry, her clothes were ordinary work clothes, not L.L. Bean or Eddie Whatsis (Clara got those catalogues just like everybody else). She wore no makeup, although Clara would see her take out a chapped-lip thing on occasion. Lily Martindale was drab and handsomely plain. The only mark of a refined life on her was her streaked hair, in a cut that wouldn't have come from anywhere around there, and which, if Lily had a mind, she'd have to go to Placid to get anything close to it. As Clara was soon to learn, Lily had no such mind, and the streaks and cut would grow long and unkempt before too long.

"Thanks for letting me come up. I just wanted you to know I'm around, if you need me. Me and Joe, my husband." Clara thought maybe Lily might like to come once in a while for coffee down to the parsonage if she wasn't church-minded, you know, just woman to woman, whenever she wanted company. Clara wanted her to know she was there if Lily needed to talk.

Lily listened as Clara mentioned the Bible Study group that met occasionally and sometimes did a potluck and always helped to host the Hunter's Banquet at the firehouse in October, and they *always* needed help. And of course there were the holiday food drives for the folks like the Mabbs and the Pecaults and the McCalanaughs and such that were on public assistance most of the time or laid up like McCalanaugh who was still trying to learn how to walk after his bust-up in the skimobile accident and needed all the help he could get, even though he wasn't a churchgoer, and if anything, was drinking more than he ever had before the accident, to tell the truth. And if she'd a mind Lily should know they were collecting for a few repairs to the church in Winslow Station and the organ was in a state, and by the way, Jim says hello, he told us you was up here all by yourself, and so on.

And Lily held her hand up, feeling as though she were back in New York at a first committee meeting for a benefit. She asked "Pastor Clara, what is that *you* really want. What do *you* really need?"

"Well, as I was saying, the repairs and the organ—"

Lily interrupted her. "You're speaking of the church, which I understand is a natural extension of you, of your faith and heart, but I'm speaking to you, as you say, woman to woman. What is it *you* need?"

For a moment Clara blustered and coughed. She was here to minister as always and suddenly here's this woman about her own age turning the tables on her. That was when Clara broke down. She told Lily about Phil, her nineteen-year-old son, who was joining the military, the Marines, for God's sake; and Joe, her husband, was so proud of him and all the folks in town kept hugging Phil and saying how proud they were, but she, Clara, supposedly with all this faith in God and Jesus and angels, was absolutely terrified that her little boy was going to end up somewhere in the Middle East as cannon fodder, and if she let on how she felt, people would say she was unpatriotic or something. Clara wept and told Lily that no one had ever come to her and asked her what *she* needed. Never. Her life was all about handling other people's problems and talking with them about Jesus and here her own life was falling apart and she hated to say it, but she was losing faith. And here was Lily holding her hand and letting her babble and cry, and inviting Joe to come up and talk and Phil, too, because Lily could help, maybe with old connections in Washington. She told Clara to remember that with the GI Bill he can come back after whatever and end up going to college, too, and she could talk to him about his options. But she wanted Clara to know that faith was the most important thing, the only thing that holds this frail tissue of life together and that it just takes time and patience for things to work themselves out. You just have to trust. Lily was saying all of this like she believed it herself. It was the City Lily. Sure we can pull this off. You want brass bands at the benefit? Movie stars? How many?

Well, when Clara left that day to go back down The Hill Next to her car and back to the parsonage, she told Joe: "I think Lily Martindale is like one of them people you read about that live on mountain tops that folks go to visit to ask the meaning of life. Whatever happened to her down in that city has changed her for some powerful good. She's so quiet and strong and different from all the stories I've heard people say."

"Lily Martindale? That little hellcat? She's the one that got Jim Porter so twisted around, the only way he could function was with a pint of vodka every four hours."

"Well, neither one of them is doin' that now. And he's not with her. She's all alone up there. We need to look out for her, Joe. Not pushy, you know. Just keep looking out."

And a week or two later, Sue Ellen came in for Sunday services saying she'd been up to the camp to see if there was anything she could do for Lily, and Lily showed her around and gave her tea. Tea, mind you. She drank coffee so much, it was nice to have a cup of tea for a change.

Sue Ellen was, of all the steady folk in Winslow Station, probably the steadiest. She ran the store, served as postmaster, and there was not much that escaped her attention. She was, next to her sister-in-law Clara Finn, the most reliable source of information in the hamlet. She was not a gossip. She was a resource. Sue Ellen had gone up to the camp not out of curiosity but out of practicality. Whoever was up there, she was going to need supplies, sometimes help, and possibly mail delivery. As her brother Joe, Clara's husband, was fond of saying, "You need anything, Sue Ellen's your man," which he emphasized with a dramatic grasp of his crotch. This infuriated Sue Ellen into near inarticulateness. But she told Clara after Sunday services that she'd taken a black metal mailbox and pressure treated pole, and a set of stick-on numbers and letters she had lying around and delivered all that to Lily Martindale up there at the camp, so she could receive her mail at the end of the camp road, if she wanted, rather than have to come all the way into town. Sue Ellen told her, she said, that this way, if she needed anything, she could leave a message, letters or orders in the mail box with the red flag up, and Sue Ellen or one of the boys would pick it up on the regular delivery schedule and make sure the things were dropped off, or people were informed, or services called in for. Sue Ellen said that Lily was quite polite and cordial and seemed to be happy with the situation.

"I've not seen that camp so slick-whistle since the old days," she told Clara. "I come away from there like I'd just been in a big old cathedral, and this girl I used to know just wasn't the spaced-out, pissed-off hippie that used to come into the store for cigarettes back in the seventies. She's not the same person at all."

Lily was never the kind of hermit that spent her days like the Desert Fathers or the monks of the Russian Sketes in contemplation of the sacred and holy, reading scripture, praying. There was the raven later on. Schwartz she called him, but Schwartz was more a fluke than a herald, omen or curse. He was imperfect company for her, but a personality in his own right. He cadged food, followed her like a dog when she got out her rod or rifle. Like Lily, he preferred the solitude of the cabin, although he'd be seen around the marina when fishermen came in. Most people just left him alone. He was wary, not even cleaving to his own kind, not belonging to an unkindness of ravens. Jim, who was fairly knowledgeable about such things, opined that Schwartz had probably been low bird in flock ranking and hounded out by superior males. He was a loner, like Lily, unattached.

Lily was a serviceable hermit, more like Noah John Rondeau, the hermit of Cold River in the thirties and forties. Noah John took care of himself, his land there, his traplines. He guided a bit, and befriended the hikers off the Northville-Lake Placid trail—the great 46'ers like Grace Hudowalski, Orra Phelps. They'd sit around the campfire at Noey's while his fiddle drew the deer in, and he reviled Roosevelt and the rangers who challenged his freedom to hunt, fish and trap on protected lands. His dad had been rough on him as a kid, and he never again took to anybody trying to tell him what to do or how to do it. There were fights with those who did try and trouble with the law. That's when he built his tiny cabin at Cold River and the odd piles of notched firewood stacked like teepees that he whittled down in the winter months to feed the fire in his woodstove. He devised a secret code to keep track of the weather, the location of traplines and buried stocks of supplies that sustained his long rambles in the woods. If the rangers ever got him, at least they'd never get his stuff. Self-educated for the most part, even building himself a working telescope, he was literate and articulate. But Noah John was too irascible for society, so he just removed himself from it. He was no holy man. He was just alone.

The Abenaki have a legend of a woman, Mannigebeskwas, who lives apart. She is pursued by men but will not be tied to them or their campfires. She prefers the company of wolves and deer. She will entertain lovers but leaves them by the morning light to return to the mountains, to the woods. Lily was more like that (without the lovers) or Noah than some moaning monk, suffering nun or railing prophet. More like a nun than Mannigebeskwas, if only in respect to her celibacy, but a nun in anticipation of the next part of her life: a time when, free of sorrow, she might either die or return to the world. She wasn't averse to the occasional company as long as she was forewarned by the bell. She didn't like surprises. But after the first or second year, she found herself in a state of expectancy. Someday someone would wander by, lost and alone, bringing along the moon and the stars behind him. She would know him by his calm voice and song. He was the Beloved. He could also be Death. He was coming for her, unheralded by bells, and not in any damn A-10 Warthog.

Public Affairs Officer Captain Jeff Edwards gets the message off the machine when he walks in the mudroom door after early Mass that Sunday. From what he can make out, some lady up in the St. Regis area has taken a couple of potshots at a flyover. The lead pilot saw the figure below and went in low to have a look-see. He saw a flash of metal, but didn't think it was a weapon. When he got back to the Air National Guard base at Barnes in Massachusetts, he found a single bullet entry point near the back of the Warthog. No danger to the craft or personnel; no real damage. Edwards returns the call to the base.

"Who is this person? No, I don't know. Why should I? Who?" While he listens, he sheds his overcoat and kicks off his galoshes. His wife is coming in behind him with their eighteen-month-old and the five-year-old not far behind. "I *know* who Mrs. Livingston is. Oh brother. That's going back some years. Before I was born. That's who that is? Martindale? How old is she? I mean is she senile or something?"

Jeff's wife takes his coat and hangs it up in a crowded closet and shoos the five-year-year-old into the kitchen. Still carrying the toddler, she switches on the coffeemaker. Jeff looks at his wife and shrugs his shoulders. She rolls her eyes back at him.

"Have you called them? No, I mean, it sounds pretty stupid to me to get everybody involved up there. Can't we keep this in the family? Sure, sure, I know. Why didn't she call the hotline if she was so pissed off? Oh. She did. Figgers. Hermits have phones, do they now? What's the name of the ranger? Wait a min—" He retrieves a pen and a scrap of paper and starts writing. "Got it. Yeah. I'll give him a call and head out. Sure seems like a nuisance issue to me. I know. I know. Catch you later."

His wife gets two mugs out of the cupboard and looks at him without saying anything.

"Make mine a double," he says.

Before he can finish his coffee, a peanut butter sandwich and a stick of celery, the local upstate newspapers and television stations have called and he is in uniform and on his way into the heart of the Adirondacks.

Chapter Six

"Most Holy Spirit, who didst brood
Upon the chaos dark and rude,
And bid its angry tumult cease,
And give, for wild confusion, peace . . ."

"Melita" (also known as the Naval Hymn) #512, Episcopal Hymnal,
1940

Tune: John B. Dykes, 1861; Text: William Whiting, 1860

Lily, the Lily who, before dancing with bears and talking to ravens, lived
in New York City and raised lots of money for charity, was not untypical
of the young twenty- to thirty-year-olds who worked for big corpora-
tions and law firms, riding the coattails of the women's movement in the
1970s and 1980s. Except that Lily was famous, irritatingly well known,
and often pursued by the press that hoped to keep her childhood story
alive enough to sell copy. They hoped to find her in some kind of *delicto,*
preferably *flagrante,* but Lily, since they gave her no peace, gave them no
satisfaction. She rarely dated, kept to herself except to show up at work,
at meetings, and for the huge benefit extravaganzas she deftly assembled.
She was quiet and focused on the outside and thought to be a masterful
organizer, for which she was well paid and honored. But that was on the
outside. On the inside she was an impoverished stew, a swamp, a bog
of pitiful sadness and boiling rage. It was only a matter of time before
all that had to come out. She knew that herself. She ran four miles a
day before work. She visited a well-known psychiatrist. She took Valium.

She drank. She pulled herself together to do what she had to do—serve children who somehow managed to be worse off than she ever was.

The last benefit she organized was held in the hall of the great sea creatures at the Museum of Natural History in New York. The preparation for the benefit had been stressful enough through the preceding weeks and months. The planning, like all benefits, was tedious and meticulous, going through every detail: which band to hire, which caterer and floral designer, which security service, and, of course, the guest list and seating arrangements. That was routine and complicated and the sort of thing she was able to do while still maintaining peace and order among the various committees and board members. But then things got very nasty and complicated.

Against Lily's wishes, the board met to decide how many and which of her severely disabled kids—cerebral palsy, congenital birth defects, multiple physical issues—might be deemed presentable enough to appear at the benefit. According to the other directors, they needed to be, "manageable and even picturesque, dressed up, of course" (with free clothes—Macys' marketing director was on the board). The kids chosen would be souped-up, "parked" as it were in wheelchairs, visible enough to remind the patrons why they happened to be attending that evening. The contingencies alone were problematic—transportation, timing, the comfort of the children, willingness and permission from their caretakers or parents to participate in the event at the museum. There was one board member who barked out that "at the ASPCA events, we always have the animals!"

Lily almost walked out. These deliberations were so egregiously patronizing that she would flee to a local bar after work every night for weeks before the event. There she would lob a shot of vodka down her throat with a skipper of Valium chasing after. She tried to make sense of the tennis match back and forth across the net of her brain—"All for a good cause," *thock, point.* "Exploitation," *thock, point.* "The money," *thock, point.* "The kids," *thock, point.* "The money," and so on.

In the end, it was the availability of free clothes, and even hairdos and makeup, for those who wished, that trumped Lily's expressed horror at the rude, unnecessary and frivolous display of suffering children. In the end, six kids attended—three girls and three boys, of which two were African Americans, one Latino. Those that couldn't or wouldn't attend still got lovely clothes and a makeover and had their duded-up pictures framed and displayed at the benefit. One of them was a cerebral palsy victim, age seventeen, named Susan, with whom Lily had grown especially close through her work at the Institute over the years. Susan was one of those remarkable young women, who, despite crippling disability, had an indomitable spirit, a great intelligence. She wore a fitted helmet most of the time, and loose restraints on her wheelchair to keep her from lurching forward in spasms. Abandoned as an infant in the hospital, Susan would never have had a chance had not the Institute doctors and Lily recognized that there was someone in there, some light in the eyes, some great spirit that needed to communicate but was encased in useless bone and flesh. It was a long haul, but Susan learned to make herself understood with blinks and hand squeezes, to read, to write, and to speak with the assistance of advanced technology.

Susan had already finished several college courses through the Institute's outreach services. She planned to go to law school. Like Lily, she had no family. Having her at the benefit was a small comfort. In her painful way, she could make Lily smile. Seeing Susan's face as the benefit got underway and the children were introduced had a somewhat calming effect on Lily. Susan said in her twisted drawling voice, strained by the fruitless effort she made to keep her head still enough to communicate, "Lily, dear, take off that mask; this isn't a Halloween party."

That night, Lily had her hands full with the kids, their parents and a couple of young volunteers and one registered nurse from the Institute. They aided Lily with basics—feeding those who could eat, making sure the straws stayed in the mouths of those who could drink. Even before the event started, Lily was exhausted and more tightly wound than ever.

She looked overhead. Hanging directly above all the festive partygoers in their gowns by Bill Blass, Yves St. Laurent, was the model of the great blue whale, stretching two hundred feet from one corner of the huge room to the other. The frothy cream of New York stood, shook hands, air-kissed, and danced, surrounded by extraordinary dioramas—glassed-in cases containing moments in the lives of sea creatures, frozen in simulation of their natural environment: penguins or seals on an ice floe with orcas attendant and ready to feast; great walruses, narwhals, polar bears. Above were mounted sharks of all sizes, including the great whale shark.

And here below were the kids, waggling, gurgling, waving their fin-like hands, rolling their great sea eyes at the gathering, their heads lolling less and less in time to the live music. Here they were with their crippled bodies and sometimes perfectly adequate brains trapped inside. Here she was with a perfectly adequate body and a crippled brain. And here were the members of the press, the photographers again, all over again circling, circling, whispering to each other, she knew, remarking how well or ill "Cinder-Lily" looked tonight at the ball. How she hated it. How she had to smile and graciously decline their questions—not that many bothered to ask any more, not the society ones anyway. But always at this time of year, the Christmas season, pictures came back, appeared in the papers and on the tube, requests for interviews, always politely declined. "So many years ago today . . ." And there they would be: Lily and Eleanor, America's darling, tragic children, clutching on to each other, Lily with her mouth open, screaming at the host of onlookers we cannot see, her eyes wide in fear; Eleanor holding on, trying to be brave, the good scout protecting her friend.

And here was Eleanor, in attendance that night as she was most of the nights she was in town for such affairs. Patron of the arts, president emerita of the Institute, she was wearing one of her gorgeous high-necked Mandarin silk dresses that accentuated her tallness, and which, she said, made her feel like a shiny tube of toothpaste. Ellie and Colin, sweet Colin in white tie, his round chipmunk cheeks and neat moustache like a proper English veteran of the colonial wars—back straight, solicitous of everyone, raconteur, ever with the ready joke. Over the years, Eleanor and later Colin had maintained such a close relationship with Lily that it could be said they were her only friends, the only ones she saw or talked to on a regular basis. They were the only ones tolerant of her late-night, rambling phone calls. They were the only ones patient enough to listen to her litany of complaints and bitterness. They cajoled her, inveigled her out of her apartment to go to movies, theater or ballet. They appeared at her apartment every Sunday morning to escort her to church at St. Bartholomew's. They believed that if she could only turn her life over to a higher authority, she'd someday find something to love about the world, about herself. Lily was one of those many troubled women who could never do enough, never do anything well enough to suit herself. Lily, for her own part, never found that solace at St. Bartholomew's. She went for the music, she said, and sometimes for the brunch afterward with Colin and Ellie.

One of the Institute volunteers brought over a tray of hors d'oeuvres and a bottle of champagne. She was young, maybe eighteen, and Lily thought she looked familiar, but so many people there that night were people she worked with, passed frequently in the halls of the Institute or the cathedral offices.

"Miss Martindale?" the young woman said, "would you mind terribly if I have my picture taken with you?"

Lily's face darkened. "As a matter of fact, yes, I would."

The young woman looked so dejected, Lily poured her a glass of champagne, and another for herself as well.

"Look . . ."

"Jenny."

"Jenny, I'm sorry. I don't mean to be rude, but, well actually, I do mean to be rude. I hate photographs."

"Oh, Miss Martindale, I'm a student at Stuyvesant and I'm documenting my volunteer work over the winter break. It would mean so much, but I understand—" She had her little Polaroid in her hand, having pulled it with some difficulty from a pouchy India print bag slung over her shoulder.

Eleanor and Colin were nearby talking with the wife of the bishop. Somehow Jenny and the bishop got Lily to relent and everyone to stand with her in the picture. Jenny stood next to Lily. Several pictures were taken, with Lily growing more and more uncomfortable. Being the smallest in the group, she seemed dwarfed both physically and in spirit. Even Jenny loomed over and had to bend to lean in next to Lily. Colin, who had taken the pictures, handed each to Jenny as it came out of the camera. Jenny kept the first, gave the second to Eleanor, and the last one she gave to Lily. Lily never even glanced at it, just stuffed it in her bag.

Lily wasn't sure if it was the champagne, the event or the awkwardness and closeness of the young volunteer, but she felt even more agitated and ill at ease. When Colin saw Lily take more than two glasses of champagne, he signaled Eleanor and both of them approached her, casually, so as not to draw attention, and flanked her, one on each arm. Gaily chatting, they walked her outside, out the back way through the service area, away from the press and society photographers.

It was three weeks before Christmas. There was a light, cold rain, which would later turn to a magical crystalline snow, dusting the city and then melting before noon on Sunday. Outside, on the edge of Central Park, Lily started to weep. They were the champagne-fueled tears of self-pity and regret.

"It's happening again," she said burying her head in Eleanor's shoulder.

"I know. How can I help?"

"I can't stay here."

"Lily, you are doing too much. You need a break."

"I need to go back inside. And the party after. I have to go."

"I know," Eleanor said.

"Let's all get some coffee," Colin added. "I know a place near Columbus." The trio marched off, Lily between her friends.

The fresh air helped. They sat at the counter of a small coffee shop between Columbus and Broadway, onlookers gawking at their evening gowns. A waitress poured them coffee. Eleanor began to speak.

"Let's go up to camp a little earlier this year. After tonight you're done anyway, Lily."

"Ellie, you know I can't. You know what happens after these things—the accounting, the report, the plans for next year . . ."

"Delegate that stuff. You can't do this forever and always, Lily. You should be training someone to assist you, take over at these times. You're doing too much, taking too much on. You need a helper." As always Eleanor's tone was firm, practical, full of good advice, of plans, of a brighter time ahead, if only Lily would ease up a bit. She needed to be gentle with herself—especially at this time of year. They all did. "How about that young girl with the camera?"

"Why?"

"Oh, I don't know. She seems keen, I guess."

"She's a teenager in school. And I thought that was awful and awkward and I didn't trust her, and yet I'm sure I've dealt with her at the Institute. I'm losing it, Ellie."

"I'm here, Lily. I'm here to help. So is Colin. Aren't you Colin?"

"Of course, dear, you know I am." He sounded just a tiny bit exasperated, rightfully so, when all his fifteen years of association with Eleanor Winslow and, by extension, to Lily, should have obviated the need for that question.

"So tell me, what can we do to help?"

"I'm trying so hard to make them all proud."

"Them?" Eleanor asked, "What them?"

"*Maman* and Papa, Charles and Emily, Mack and Mabel. Even Butch and Daisy."

"Oh, merciful heavens, they are proud, darling. Look at what you've done. You've done wonderful things. Look at all the money you've raised. Look at how well you've done for yourself. Look at dear, incredible Susan. I know they see you. I know they all still love you. We all do. We are all immensely proud."

"I feel like I'm such a bother. I've always been this way and I hate it."

"Lily, you're the only bother I've got. Just think. If they were still alive, they'd be elderly, infirm, cranky, intractable and awful. We'd both have our hands full taking care of them. This way we help other people, far needier people. Remember that, Lily."

"Ellie, I'm so tired. I hate this fucking board of directors so much I could kill somebody."

"We'll get through it, Lily," Colin said. "We'll get through it together, tonight and every night."

"And," Eleanor interjected, "We're going to have a wonderful Christmas at home on The Hill. Colin's going to make *buche de Noël*—your mama's recipe, remember? The Livingstons are coming, and Reggie—you like Reggie, don't you?"

"Yes."

"He's bringing his guitar."

"But not Jim. Please don't ask Jim."

"Oh honey, Jim is so lonely up there by himself, and you know we're his only family since his mom died. He's essential to Christmas. And he adores you."

"It's precisely because of Jim's adoration that I can't deal with him. He doesn't know when to shut up. He only gets quiet when we're on a trout stream or when . . . Can't we fix him up with somebody, anybody?"

Eleanor began to giggle. "Remember when Jim and I tried to baptize you in the lake? You were only about four."

"Oh that was awful."

"Jim pushed me away. You came up laughing. You were always laughing."

"I was? I don't remember," Lily said.

Within a moment they were all laughing, reaching that point in the escalation of exhaustion that there would only be a complete breakdown if no one could laugh.

The waitress was staring at them, Colin realized, and he sized up the situation immediately. She was an older woman, so she might have recognized Lily and Eleanor or heard them speak their names. If they did not move soon and quickly, the inevitable question would come. "Aren't you—?"

Colin gently held his watch out, "We'd better be getting back." He threw a few bills on the table, stood, and nodded graciously to the waitress, who was still staring at them.

"Are you okay now, Lily?" Eleanor asked.

"I'm better, thanks."

"Do you want to stay with us tonight?"

"No. I'll be all right. Can you give me a lift home after the afterparty?"

"Sure, dear. No problem."

Lily was able to get back to the benefit before the toasts and presentations, one for her for the strength and dedication she brought to the cause. The sterling silver tray from Tiffany's with her name and date engraved would later join its mates on a pile of such things in her apartment. There was also a lovely shawl from Hermès which she pulled around her shoulders, and smiled a practiced charming smile for the photographer from the *Times*. Eleanor and Colin's hired driver took them to the afterparty somewhere near Fifth Avenue. Jenny, the volunteer, was there. She thanked Lily again for the photographs and made idle chitchat about work, the Institute, the kids under her care and her studies at Stuyvesant, and asked Lily simple questions about her years at the job. Eleanor joined in the conversation and asked where the girl was from.

"Chelsea," Jenny replied.

The bishop's wife came over and gave Jenny a kiss on both cheeks. "Such a darling. We've known her parents for ages. You're very lucky to have her volunteering at the Institute, Lily."

But Lily was more and more agitated. She wandered away from the conversation and out to the chill of the penthouse terrace. It was snowing lightly now, and cold, but Lily was having trouble feeling anything. The balcony was twenty stories up and she idly considered jumping, but instead she drank, went home in the limo, and slept.

※

The phone. Like now, the noise in the distance outside the cabin is unreal, vague and undistinguishable. Like the shadow of a great blue whale rising from the sea depths, Lily is fighting her way toward some vague semblance of consciousness, but the weight is too great. She has no phone, she has wind chimes, and someone has been teasing her, playing music on them—real tunes she can almost make out, played by someone who is too shy to make his presence known. How she has dreamed for years that he will finally show himself. The Beloved. The Great Man.

And then there's that drumming. Not sharp and rapid like the pileated woodpecker. More muted and rhythmic than the ruffed grouse. More like the drum in the band at the party, but she has no band with a drum. It must be her heart. She is lapsing back.

There were two calls after the benefit that night back in New York, one in the middle of the night. Lily awoke feeling none too well, between a dry mouth, a headache, and an all-over numinous extrusion—the psychic corollary to a hernia. Her insides, she felt, were swelling out, her heart pounding, her eyes opening and closing with each tick of an overwound mantelpiece clock. She had slept little and very badly, interrupted frequently by dreams in which Jenny, the young volunteer, figured prominently, but she couldn't remember why. She answered the phone.

It was the hospital. Susan, her kid from the benefit, had suffered a grand mal seizure and gone into cardiac arrest. Lily, head banging, pulled herself together and took a cab from her apartment in Murray Hill to the hospital. Not Susan, she hoped, even prayed. Please don't take Susan. Anyone but Susan. Susan, with her amazingly articulate, muffled voice.

When Lily got to the hospital, Susan was in the Intensive Care Unit. She saw Lily, and lifted a tube-ridden, shaky hand in greeting. Lily knelt by the bed and pressed Susan's crimped hand to her face. And that was it. Suddenly, all those contracted muscles, all the rigidity, torsion and spasmodic jerking ceased. The nurse on duty jumped to attention hearing the heart monitor's long flat-line beep. Immediately, the room was full of people. Lily understood in an instant what they intended to do, and she threw herself across Susan's body. The nurses and one doctor tried to pull her off. She screamed for them to stop, but they pulled her away. She fought and struggled. "Leave her alone, you idiots! Let her go!" She screamed curses at them, until the nurses called security and had her forcibly removed.

All the frayed and tattered bands holding Lily together snapped at once. She started screaming, keening like a child. The good hospital folks had another patient on their hands. After an injection of something, she started to calm down, but also to fall apart again. The last thing she remembered was being hustled into a cab. She couldn't remember getting into her apartment. Someone must have come with her, someone from the hospital or the Institute. She was fully dressed with her shoes still on when the phone rang again at dawn. This time it was Eleanor, in a panic.

"Wha—?"

"This is it. This is the last straw," Ellie said.

The incident at the hospital? Something she said at the party?

"You are coming with me to camp, today. Colin's going to come up later with Reggie."

"Wha—?"

"Now! Pack your things. I've called the Institute and left a message. You're on an extended leave at my request."

"Wha—?"

"Are you packing yet? Get going. I'm coming to get you."

"Ell—"

"Jim called. McCalanaugh is gone. You have to move in, take over. You'd be perfect. I have a plan and darling, you're it."

". . . the caretaker . . ."

". . . went on a bender at the taproom, rode off in a skimobile and into a barbed wire fence. He's alive but he's in bad shape and by God, he's fired." Eleanor paused but briefly. "I want you to take over The Hill, Lily. I want you back home where you belong."

It took a moment for Lily to realize that Eleanor could have known nothing of the scene in the hospital. Nothing of Lily's own collapse. Eleanor was calling. Eleanor needed her. She needed her to go home and take care of The Hill. How could this be happening?

Lily called the hospital. She apologized; she asked about Susan. Susan had died in spite of their efforts. Susan, the last icon of Lily's devotion to a host of lost causes, and her own steady march down into the swamp. Eleanor wasn't the only one who'd called the offices at Anglican Charities. The hospital had called to complain of her interference. By Monday morning, everyone in New York would know, Lily thought. Once again, it would be news. Once again the questions. Once again the old photo in the paper. Only Susan was at peace, in spite of all their efforts to hold her back. One last wave and grasp to understanding human contact, one defeated champion in Lily. There was no more that Lily could give and no more she cared to.

Lily started to pack.

Growing up almost exclusively at The Hill, Lily and Eleanor had only each other amid the vast landscape around them. Usually in January and February, Emily Winslow took Eleanor and often Lily to warmer climes— sometimes Arizona, sometimes Florida, sometimes the Caribbean—where they stayed with friends or rented a house. When they rented a place, the whole contingent came along. Doris and Tom particularly relished those "vacations," as did Mariette. Robert was less enthusiastic, since he had no real role to play away from The Hill. He functioned sometimes as co-pilot or driver, sometimes as excursion planner, fetcher and carrier, most frequently as handyman if anything needed repair. But he was told to rest his aching body. The heat was wonderful for that. He and Mariette agreed that once they had saved a bit, they would buy a house in the desert West or on the Pacific Coast somewhere, put Lily in regular school with regular kids where she'd have a regular social life and some normalcy and structure. They could return to the cabin on The Hill Next in the summers, if they wanted.

Lily and Eleanor, however, thought that would be a terrible idea. They couldn't imagine life without each other, without Doris and Tom, without all of them together like a crazy quilt of a family. They loved tearing off in the deep winter for California to visit Irene, Julietta and everyone. They loved Washington, D.C., and New York, where they could see shows and movies with Charles's friend the writer Jack Bannister and Padre. But come right down to it, The Hill was home, and once the wandering ceased and the warm climates had been abandoned for the cool piney air, they returned to Mack and Mabel, to chores and horses and the sweet pleasures of the lake and woods. Other places were nice, but The Hill was heaven. It was The Hill where, at nearly her lowest ebb, Lily Martindale dragged her few comfortable clothes, her broken life, and gratefully embraced solitude for the next decade in the Adirondacks.

Lily Martindale became Eleanor's "ornamental hermit," as Ellie called it, six remote hours from her city, her apartment, her high-powered fundraising, her vodka and Valiums, her disabled kids, her nonexistent sex life, all those wonderful restaurants, and forever and for always the interfering press. All she packed to take with her was her craziness. If the Fates, she thought, were suddenly determined to provide her with this egress from her predicament, she would face it unencumbered by the frivolous objects saddling her poor excuse of a life. She left behind jewelry, plaques, gowns, heels, beaded bags, paintings, Limoges china, and all the attendant bills and bank statements. Eleanor had people, people who took care of things. Eleanor and the Institute would see to it all.

But Lily was ill. She felt ill in a way more than the champagne she drank the night before or the scene at the hospital could explain. She felt both physically and psychically aflame because of Susan and the way she was handled *in extremis* by the hospital staff, who should have known better. Lily was enraged at the mishandling of the kids at the benefit, enraged at her own stupidity for letting things get out of hand like that, enraged at everything she'd ever done wrong, things that haunted her—there was so much. Her head throbbed, her heart ached slightly. She thought, this will be easy. She said out loud to no one, "I will go back home to The Hill to die. That's why I'm going." Then she became confused. Eleanor needed her. She couldn't let Eleanor down after all these years.

Lily took a Valium. There were clothes at the camp, so she packed lightly. Eleanor drove up at precisely ten a.m. Lily tossed her bag in the back, waved goodbye to the doorman who helped her stumble in. She was asleep before they reached the George Washington Bridge. She didn't awaken until Kingston, two hours later.

Chapter Seven

"In the bleak midwinter
Frosty wind made moan,
Earth stood hard as iron
Water like a stone;
Snow had fallen snow on snow,
Snow on snow,
In the bleak midwinter,
Long ago."

"Cranham" #44, Episcopal Hymnal, 1940

Tune: Gustav Theodore Holst, 1906; Text: Christina Georgina Rossetti, c.1872

That December day when Lily and Eleanor journeyed north from New York City was the first day in many months that Lily noticed the sunshine, watched fascinated by the glitter of the bright winter sun glistening off the trees braced against the hillsides of the Catskills, then the Helderbergs, and finally the Adirondacks with shining snowbound lakes, hamlets and villages as quiet as the cold blue sky. Only an occasional stray Jeep full of skiers passed them heading north.

Winter in the Adirondacks, the long winter, was well under way with snow-covered hills and pines. Here and there lay the solitary family burial plots at the edges of North Country highways—graves of settlers, women and children who tried to survive the brutal winter climate, the rockiest fields and shortest growing season in the forty-eight contiguous states. Who was Lily? A creature of the city, of asphalt and towering structures of welded steel and glass. This land with all its sadness and ruggedness was something she'd abandoned. But now The Hill beckoned. The Hill did not only beckon, it grabbed and pulled with the strength of a Caterpillar tractor hauling a chained load of logs. Hard to believe, with everything that had happened, the pull could be so forceful after all these years.

Here was the Ausable, the flumes frozen tight on the opposite side of the stream. Here was Cascade Lake, with its silver birches clinging to the rock face of the cliffs as beautiful as anything she'd ever seen in Switzerland. And finally, passing all the tawdry faux Alpine structures of Lake Placid and Saranac Lake, they turned north past Paul Smiths, deep into the lakes and high hills toward Winslow Station and the long road into the camp. There the sledding hill that she and Ellie and Jim and others had packed down so tight with their toboggan that they'd go shooting out on the frozen lake a good two hundred yards or more, marking the distance each time. There the little island in Winslow Lake where she and Jim would camp during the summers home. There Melita, the boathouse with its neat stack of six canoes and now a couple of kayaks. There Rockingham Hall, the dining hall and kitchen where her mother had baked, stirred, basted, gutted, whipped and sautéed. The caretaker's cabin, Hyfrydol, where (had it been twenty years ago?) Mabel and Mack would appear at the window to see who was coming up the road. They would race out when they saw the girls and hold on to them tight. And finally the old lodge, the Doxology sign hanging crooked from one nail over the front porch, a five-foot-long broken white pine branch blown down on the unshoveled steps, but no windows broken, no door ajar. Tight as a fist, but ready to open, warm up again, and welcome all to its big stone, spruce and cedar heart.

Eleanor parked the car, trudged through the deep snow and up the stairs to open the door.

Lily had barely spoken on the drive up. She seemed agitated, twitchy, irritable. When Eleanor turned, Lily was still sitting in the car staring out at the lake below the base of the hill. Once the door was open, Eleanor stepped briefly inside the old room, took a deep breath, and shook her head, wondering if she'd done the right thing. But when she turned around again to check on Lily, Lily was out of the car, wading through the snow with their bags.

"First order of the day—shovel," Lily said.

"Can you get the power on?"

"Sure."

"I'll take care of the water. Where do you want to bunk?"

"I don't know," replied Lily. "I wonder what condition Mack and Mabel's is in?"

"Last time we came up to check in the fall, I warned McCalanaugh he'd better clean up the place by Christmas." Eleanor held the lodge door for Lily. "You can stay in the lodge if you want. I don't really care."

"Expensive. To heat, I mean—furnace, oil. You know better than I do."

"Well, like I said."

Lily dropped their bags on the floor and straightened to look around. In the dusk light, the empty vastness of the main room gaped before her, and she felt the silence and loss begin to advance on her in the absence of all the old voices, all the anticipation gone, all the frantic childhood games finished. Like Eleanor, she stood in the silence shaking her head, wondering if she'd done the right thing. One more breath, one more Valium extracted quietly from the bag over her shoulder. She turned to go back outside, swallowing the tablet as she floundered through the snow drifts, sometimes thigh deep, down to the electrical shed to check the mechanicals.

The key was right where it should have been above the outside light. Inside, she found the tags labeling the switches, and general instructions neatly lettered in her father's handwriting and sealed in a cracked glass cover—his handwriting faded but still clear. She switched on the power to the lodge and the dining hall. The caretaker's house had not been switched off in McCalanaugh's absence.

It was four o'clock and just starting to get dark in the east. There was a snow shovel outside Mack and Mabel's. Damn McCalanaugh, it would always be Mack and Mabel's house. Lily quickly put her back to it and cleared a path to Rockingham Hall and the lodge. By the time she'd finished only that much, it was dark. She shoveled the steps and a wider path to the great, heavy, double lodge doors with the iron work. She loved how they moved again in her hands. She remembered the triumph as a little girl when she was able to move them at all on her own. Now she pulled one open and walked into the main room, where Eleanor had lit a fire and turned on some lights. She could hear the pipes and radiators straining as the hot water from the enormous furnace and copper boiler began to course through at last, although her breath was still visible in the room.

Bubble baths. She was suddenly remembering the shared bubble baths with Eleanor when they were little, coming down the stairs afterward with towels turbaned around their heads to sit in the warmth by the fire while one of their mothers brushed and combed out their clean hair. Bubble baths. How preposterous. The Valium must be kicking in.

Eleanor stood before the fire poking a bit of kindling back under the stack of logs. The old dumbwaiter and dolly system was still in operation with a few improvements to discourage the mice and cold draughts. There was a nice pile of wood in the bin. "McCalanaugh at least had a fire laid and it doesn't look as though he partied hard in here."

"Did you check the wine cellar?"

"Not yet. Let's go down."

Eleanor parked the fire screen in front of the huge cavern, full of now-blazing logs. Then she and Ellie switched on the cellar lights and moved cautiously down the old stairs. The wine cellar was behind a false brick wall built back in the days of Prohibition, some said, by the same guys who built the false room under the 21 Club in New York City. Too many people knew about The Hill's replica these days, so they had to deface the outside of it by fastening a locking system in place to deter even some of their own guests (and in their day, Lily and Jim) from raiding the stores of good stock put down by Charles Winslow's father and later Charles and Emily, and now Colin. Once the lock was unfastened and the bolt lifted, a long thin piece of metal, which had been tucked above a rafter, could be inserted into a virtually invisible crevice, whereupon the wall would magically open on its hidden seams and hinges. The novelty never seemed to wear off, even for Lily. There stood revealed a substantial subterranean room containing many dust-encrusted bottles of fine clarets, Burgundies and brandies, as well as the more popular Scotches and vodkas and a vast assortment—a near museum—of liqueurs. Deep below the frost line, the room's temperature remained a cool fifty degrees. From the racks, Eleanor lifted a bottle of Cristal. Lily appreciatively ran her hands along some more of Colin's recent acquisitions.

"We'll fill in the gaps when we get to Paris after Christmas," Eleanor said. "Colin's very excited. You don't need anything else from here do you?"

"I don't think so. I'm feeling a little steadier, just being here."

"Me, too, Lily. But the winters are long. I may have been hasty asking you. You know I can find someone else . . ."

"Ellie, I've been thinking—"

"Let's go up and crack this beauty and then we'll both think."

Lily led the way upstairs and put another log on the fire while Eleanor stuck the Cristal in a snowbank outside the door, along with two flutes from the butler's pantry. Lily rejoined her in the pantry and stood beside her as they often had, looking at the pictures from long-ago seasons at the camp. Eleanor put her arm around Lily.

Lily said, "I liked what you said about, about what if they'd lived, they'd be old now and cranky and a big handful. I can't imagine them at any age except then. In my mind they are still so young and so handsome, so vital. How different our lives would have been with them present."

Eleanor said, squeezing her shoulder, "You know, those empty spaces on the wall should have been filled with our own photographs, our own family pictures."

Lily drew a sharp breath. "*There* be dragons. That is exactly what I'm talking about, El. My train went off the tracks way back. I haven't accomplished anything meaningful, meaningful to me in a way—having a love like theirs, having that breezy, nineteen-fifties postwar, heroic, cocktails-and-movie-stars life, trips to Keeneland and taking the Twentieth Century Limited to Los Angeles and fighting McCarthyism. It must have been so wonderful to be them . . . then."

"They would have hated the sixties—frumpy looking hippies."

"That was me, as you may recall . . ."

"Well, me too, only more subtle," Eleanor laughed. "Let's go see how the champagne is doing, shall we? Did you bring the cooler in?"

"No."

"Bring it in. I don't think there's much, since Colin's coming up in a few days."

Lily went back out into the snow. The cooler was one she recognized from the old days, often hauled up the hill to the pond in summer in the back of the buckboard. The heads of oxeye daisy, hawkweed, black-eyed Susan and Queen Ann's lace bowed as they passed through the days of summer, rocking side to side behind the swaying haunches of Butch and Daisy. Mack and Robert would fill a barn trough with ice, sodas and bottles of beer. There was a little shelter beside the pond back then—a lean-to made of cedar and old barn planks rough-sawn, the floor lined with fresh-cut balsam, and there they'd picnic with the Friends Without Family. She wondered what condition the lean-to was in all these years later. She realized she was smiling. That was new. That was a good sign. There would be lots of projects up here. She had a lot to do. She could be a good caretaker. How could she screw this up?

Lily grabbed the handles and hauled the cooler out of the back of Eleanor's old station wagon. (In the old days it would have been the Packard, and later one of many and various Willys Jeeps, including the one Jim and Mack taught her to drive.) The old cooler was pretty dented after all the years being flung around rocky islands and the backs of vehicles and boats. She remembered lugging it in the guide boat when she and Jim, teenagers then, went camping on the tiny island they called "The Zit." Jim carried the fly rods on one side, with his pack basket full of gear on his back. She, on the other end, carried the towels and bathing suits in her basket, and her little makeup kit with joints, tabs of acid and, if she remembered to bring it, her packet of Ortho-Novum.

The cooler was much heavier than she expected. Colin must have loaded it in the car himself, back in New York. "Not much?" she said out loud to herself. She had to take the steps up to the lodge one at a time. Once inside, her hands freezing, she dropped the cooler hard on the sisal carpet by the door, and, looking at Ellie, rolled her eyes.

"Goodness!" They dragged the cooler to the pantry. Eleanor lifted the latch and the lid. "Oh he was generous, wasn't he?" She pulled out a six-ounce tin of Beluga caviar. Lily peeled back the foil on the snow-chilled champagne, removed the wire, and slowly twisted out the cork. While Lily filled the flutes, Eleanor wiped a plate clean and lined it with Melba toast from a tin, a wedge of lemon, and from a drawer she extracted a small object.

"Look what I found," she said. In her hand was a tiny carved spoon.

"Oh my God! That little bone spoon Julietta brought your parents."

"Along with about ten tins of Russian Sevruga. That was the first time you and I had caviar. No one dared ask her how she got all that Russian caviar during the Cold War."

"Cuba," Lily said. "I wonder who she was sleeping with to get that haul." She held the second flute out to Eleanor. "To Julietta."

"To the Martindales and Winslows, who never had to face the shaggy sixties, the polyester seventies, and the AIDS of the eighties."

"To us . . . who did."

"May we never forget."

Lily helped herself to a slice of Melba rye toast with caviar and a squeeze of lemon and made one for Eleanor. Eleanor had dragged out salami, Cambozola, baby lettuces crisp in a plastic bag, fruit, and a loaf of Colin's homemade wholegrain and seeded bread baked in the hearth oven in their brownstone. She and Lily settled themselves in the chairs by the fire and feasted. Eleanor had her shoes off and her feet up on the ottoman close to the fire. Lily had at last shed her coat. The room was warming up, slowly, incrementally, but now over fifty degrees.

"I'm trying to imagine what it will be like," Lily said.

"Lily, I truly believe this is where you belong. This is your home. This is where we were born. What more can I say?"

"It's so bloody quiet. It's so peaceful and reassuring. I feel them. Sometimes I catch a shadow out of the side of my eyes and I get the shivers, but I feel protected here."

"So do I, but I need the city, too."

"I thought I did, too. But now it's different. There's something I haven't told you." Lily recounted the scene in the hospital over Susan's body.

Eleanor said "I knew it was bad, but I didn't know it was that bad."

Lily sipped her champagne; her long nails polished a deep coral, a simple gold and diamond band on her right hand, a gift from some long ago fellow patron of charitable causes in gratitude for some service rendered. "What the hell am I going to do with the apartment?"

"Just make sure I don't leave here without the key. You may want to return someday. Or, you may not. Who knows? Let's just take it one day at a time."

"I'm not looking back at all, Ellie. That part of my life is over. You can sell it if you want. Box everything up. Donate it. Auction it off. I won't be needing any of it."

"Good. You deserve to rest and just shed all of that madness. Let it all fall away. I'm sorry about Susan. She had such a great spirit."

"Susan was lucky. She might have been like the others, wasting away in a wheelchair, pissing and shitting in tubes and bags and never able to speak. She had years of richness and promise. If ever I could have been close to someone other than you, it was Susan. She had this weird little smile I thought was lovely. I will really miss her." Lily stood up and walked to the fireplace to give an assist to two bits of log that had fallen to the side. "What will happen to her body? Who will go to her funeral while I'm up here letting it all fall away? If I can do that, if I can let it all fall away, the job, the Susans, I'll be doing very well indeed." She took another cracker with caviar from Eleanor's hands. "Thanks," Lily said, helping herself to more champagne and topping off Eleanor's glass as well. Together they toasted again, this time to Susan.

"We'll check out Mack and Mabel's tomorrow, but I meant what I said: you can stay here in the lodge. You can stay wherever you like. Colin will be here in a day or two. We'll all be together. Just another Christmas."

"I wonder how my father's cabin has fared," Lily said, slicing off a bit of hard salami and some Cambozola to go with it, wrapping it all in a red lettuce leaf.

"Did you go up last summer?"

"No, but about a year ago, it seemed all right. I can ask Jim to help me with the heat and check the cistern. He's here, by the way."

Eleanor's hand stopped as it was lifting her glass. "Jim's here?"

"Yeah—he's been driving around the circle. Three times. I think he's trying to make his mind up whether to come in or leave us alone."

"Well of course, he needs to come in." Eleanor got up, moved to the door and looked outside. "You're absolutely right, as usual. How'd you know?"

"The hair stands up on the back of my neck."

"Oh, Lily. You're awful. Poor Jim."

Lily gave Eleanor a look and a small shake of the head. "And I heard the motor. Do we have any sodas for him?"

The sound of footsteps on the porch and a polite knock on the door came as Lily drained her second glass of Cristal. She took the flute and the bottle out to the pantry. Eleanor, smiling, opened the door, "C'mon in Jim!"

Jim ducked his head to come inside, took off his hat, set down a brown paper sack on the floor. He kicked off his boots and wrapped his long arms around Eleanor.

"I brought you some groceries. Just some eggs, bacon, milk, juice in there and a couple of sodas for me. Didn't know if you'd get to the store on the way. You'll tell me if you can't use them before you go back, and I'm sorry about McCalanaugh, but you know I'll be happy to . . ."

"You didn't have to do all that, Jim. You should see what Colin packed for us."

Jim sniffed and smiled wanly. "Where's Lily? That's her coat, ain— isn't it? Gosh. I haven't seen her since, well you know, last Christmas time. You all must be so busy down in New York there, workin' and such, you and Lily and your husband there . . ."

"She said something about soda for you." Eleanor took his heavy anorak and hung it on one of the deer hooves by the door.

"Good. She doesn't forget. Fifteen years now I been straight and sober. She'll see the change in me. Oh! See you got your heat on and a fire goin'. Everything okay? If you'da let me know, I'da come up and gotten everything started. You didn't have to come. I'm as happy to . . ."

"Well as you can imagine I was a bit upset and worried. Yes, everything's fine as can be. Come sit. I have some news." Eleanor took the bag of groceries into the pantry and added what she could of its contents to the cooler, and the rest in the little fridge. Lily was standing by the wall, looking at the photographs again. She had a can of ginger ale in one hand and a glass in the other, and she was crying. Eleanor silently handed her a cocktail napkin from the pile on the small pine counter. Lily set down the can and glass, mopped at her eyes, damped the napkin in the cold water, dabbed it first on one eye and then the other. She took a deep breath. Eleanor patted her on the back, and together they walked out to the main room. Jim was still standing by the door, looking around. "Greetings," he said, and smiled his biggest smile at Lily.

"Jim?" Eleanor began. "I'd like you to meet my new caretaker."

And as Lily handed him his soda, Jim, a little stunned, folded her in his arms and both of them wept. For a long time, nobody said anything.

That evening was the beginning of the end of this story, an end, how-ever, that went on for more than ten years and was to conclude, more or less, with the incident of the A-10s. Lily had forced her last smile, raised her last millions for charity, swallowed her last Valiums. She had exchanged her many business suits from Lord and Taylor for a series of three work shirts for summer (blue chambray cotton—JCPenney—men's small, which are huge on her), three flannel plaid shirts for winter (a gift from Eleanor), six pairs of Levi jeans, a couple of pairs of corduroy pants, and two pairs of thick trousers lined with wool for winter.

Leaving behind the high heels she'd worn to work every day of her life in New York City, she now had two pairs of hiking boots and a pair of really ratty sneakers that she could use for wading and summer fishing. She had one good jacket for cold weather (another gift from Eleanor), and an old raccoon coat that had once belonged to Charles Winslow, which covered her down to her ankles and was the warmest thing she owned. With a judicious number of layers underneath that, with wool hats and gloves and thermal underwear and lots of wool sweaters in different colors, she could walk about in sub-zero temperatures and be as warm as a kitten by a coal stove. She also had a hat that her father had purchased in Chicago from Abercrombie and Fitch, the venerable safari outfitters, which she later learned was now a clothing store for teenagers. The hat had a fine mesh bug net and was waterproof.

Dress-up in the Adirondacks has not aspired to formal since the days of Marjorie Merriweather Post and Great Camp Topridge, where dressing for dinner was expected. Nowadays, if you're clean and dry, you're welcome. For Lily, there were a couple of long India print skirts left over from the sixties, which sufficed for the two occasions during the year she was commanded to appear at Doxology Lodge. As far as hermits went, she was commendably well dressed and even fastidious. She washed her clothes once a month in The Hill's laundry room. When she was really on top of things, she washed her hair and bathed at the lodge, but in winter that meant firing up the boiler and waiting, then re-draining the pipes afterward. In the cold months, then, she relied on water from the buried cistern, the stream, heated to a boil on the top of the woodstove. Standing naked and shivering on a towel in front of the stove, she cleaned herself hastily with an old facecloth and a sliver of soap.

When there were guests in camp, she could be, like her old New York fundraising self, in charge, brisk, polite, even charming when she wanted to be, but she kept mainly to herself unless she was asked to guide a fishing or skiing expedition. Many of Eleanor's guests had no idea that this was the woman grown from the child they'd read so much about years ago in the fifties. In fact, over the years, the memory of Lily Martindale as Cinder-Lily faded in everyone's but Lily's mind. And

Lily's mind, as has been established, was a fertile bed of stress, regrets and sadness. Chief among her regrets was Jim Porter, her old boyfriend. She had to face him again as she did that night when she arrived with Eleanor. She had to make peace—the very slim vestiges of peace that would begin to filter down, pushing the pain and sorrow and guilt a little ahead of them, slowly over the coming years. It would take one more crucial Christmas, years later, to force the rest of her private and public crises to a head. Until then, there would always be the sense of a slow-sliding megaton of tragedy waiting poised. If she just held very, very still, not making a sound, it might not come crashing down on her all over again. It was all about gravity and a considerable amount of erosion. No way to escape it in the end.

For the next ten years or more, Lily was the best caretaker at The Hill since Mack and Mabel and her father, all put together. She kept the road plowed, the field mowed, the buildings in repair, and the generators working, the guide boats and canoes caulked, oars and paddles sanded and shellacked, the guns cleaned, oiled, and locked away, flies tied and fly lines dried and carefully stored. She scraped down the skis, and sharpened the skates on the old foot-pedal grinder in the workshop, just the way Mack showed her years ago. Every holiday season, she cleaned the fireplaces, stacked the wood, waxed the floors, and dusted. She made balsam wreaths studded with teasel she'd sprayed gold and pinecones sprayed silver just like her mother and Mabel used to do at that time of the year, and adding sprigs of winterberry for red, though she thought it a shame because it stands out so neon bright outside against the winter snow and grey stalks of the grasses and alders.

Mostly it was Lily doing all the work. Oh, there were the Guilbeaults from the marina and the Aikens at the taproom in Winslow Station, Joe Finn and the Finns from Mom and Pop's general store. These good people often helped with the heavy cutting, chimney sweeping and road grating in the time-honored Adirondack tradition of needing many serviceable skills to survive. She needed these people and their skills, and it became abundantly clear that they needed her as they had the Winslows and the work the big camp provided in the off-seasons. When Lily came back to The Hill, she didn't see any reason for that to change. Just like Mack and Mabel, she bossed the crews of helpers in spring and fall, but she opened and closed the camp all by herself. She minded any bills, sending them off to Eleanor, kept books on expenses, and ordered fuel and repairs she couldn't manage herself—not much.

It had been years since she'd fished and hunted—not since the days when Mack, Jim's dad and Jim were showing her the ropes with rod and gun, Teaching her to tie flies, to roll cast, to still-hunt for deer. Back then, as the sadness and depression grew, these kind men knew they could only try to take the place of a father, and they tried and they tried in the only way they knew. Teach her some survival skills. Teach her what they knew as much as they could, thinking it would cheer her up, help her find her way. And they succeeded to some degree—as long as she was in camp. Not much one could do with those talents in Manhattan, except for those she needed to be alert, aware of what was going on around her. Being mindful of one's surroundings is a good survival skill anywhere. But now it became more or less a part of her profession as caretaker, and the more she went out, the better she got at it, better than she had as a kid. She kept the "ice house" stocked with smoked trout and landlocked salmon. There was venison, geese, duck, partridge.

Occasionally she went fishing or hunting with Jim, but mostly they kept an awkward and apologetic distance. That he continued to hope for something more amazed everyone, and especially Lily, and she was careful never to let her guard down with him. She never invited him to stay over with her, fearing all that old stuff would come up and she'd get crazy with him again, lose the best and only real friend she'd ever had, save for Eleanor and Colin and Susan.

But the camp was closed after New Year's until July or August most years and from Labor Day until, usually, Christmas. During those stretches, Lily was alone. Colin didn't hunt, so fall was dead quiet except for Lily going out for her limit, dressing it, putting it up frozen, stewed or pemmican. After every season of visitors, she closed up the camp tight and spent her days and nights in the cabin or wandering the woods, but checking every day, every door, every window at The Hill. She had restored Mack and Mabel's house to the nearest memory of how it had been in the days when they had lived there—neat, polished, orderly— and the same for the barn, horseless now. Every single day, she made the rounds, taking special care.

But there was a large part of Lily's new life that was anything but life. She thought of death metaphorically, because much of this act of solitude was in fact a death—the death of her life as she had known it. No apartment, financial responsibilities, trafficking with foundations, lawyers and bankers, telephones and TVs. So to think about real death—abandoning the body—was a logical next step. She thought that was why she had arrived, alone, to wait. Life alone in the mountains was a constant and present risk: of venturing out in the snowstorm or blow-down, of falling through soft ice or getting careless with a chainsaw. Lily thought that, for her, death would be subtler. The lump, the chest pain—a dwindling into bed, to be found after someone realized the road in had not been plowed. Now, in view of the waste of what she had called her life, to be truly gone would just seem redundant.

In her new life, her purpose was to go on as long as she could, move light and fast. There had to be a way out of the darkness that could be found by seeking a new life without too much stuff. Not simple, because in each daily walk—spring, summer, fall or winter—there was too much to absorb, too much to register and proclaim. Everything from the white-tailed deer, black bear, osprey and owl to the tiniest newt, shiner and spring peeper. She was master of a range roughly the size of Manhattan, but which encompassed only fifteen buildings. The rest was trees, lake, pond and wild animals in four seasons as dramatic in their presentation as grand opera at the Met. This space, in all its fullness and emptiness, was all she could handle, more than she needed to know for the time being and still empty of the one thing she so missed in her life—someone to hold, someone to hold her in return. Yet she most assuredly had found the one place that both needed her and responded to her for all she gave. The camp and everything she touched there, flourished, shone.

Except for the few people closest to her and the good folk of Winslow Station, who felt a sense of protective custody of their resident orphan, no one knew what had happened to Lily Martindale. Rarely, some reporter would come to the hamlet asking questions in the taproom. Tom Aiken or Joe Finn and many of the others of the town took delight in busting on these people, making up all sorts of stories about her. They'd heard she'd gone off to India to meditate with some long-bearded guru. No, no, no, she was gone to India to work with Mother Theresa. Or was it China, to teach English? Certainly no one in *town* knew where she was or ever heard anything from her. Still, there were these legends of a white woman in the woods running with the deer, riding a moose, talking to ravens, dancing with bears.

Now, regular folks, folks everyone in Winslow Station knew, who came back year after year to fish and hike and hunt, knew something of the tales of Lily Martindale, but also knew to respect the private property boundaries on the maps. There was the occasional smartass that tried to push through and have a little look-see at the old camp but in Lily's ten-plus years there, she only confronted three or four, and it only took a few words or a random overhead shot fired, to send them back into town to the local ranger (Jim), who told them they had been trespassing and there was only a cantankerous caretaker up there who had long hair like a woman. They'd better stay off.

Eleanor gave out that Lily had moved abroad. For herself, Lily had never been more content, even considering her solitude and her thoughts of death, since her childhood on The Hill. That is, until the A-10 Warthogs flew overhead.

Jim, frustrated with his fruitless pounding, tries the door of the cabin again, as if now it will open, but the latch is fast and Lily, if she's in there, is not answering. He curses the fact that they ever agreed to put a lock on the door. He's in a fight against time. He got out of his own house as soon as he could after calling Eleanor. He knows that the military and the government are ramped up about this, and he's doing his level best to get to Lily before they do.

Jim has taken off his skis, and in just his boots he slogs the unshoveled way to the back, through the buried garden with its broken stalks of sunflowers and the upended, nearly buried bathtub with its sacred inhabitant. Five years ago on Christmas, Colin presented Lily with a statue of the Virgin Mary, arms outstretched, camo-painted and with a little toy rifle in one hand, a miniature fishing pole in the other, and a blue and white BMW hood ornament pasted onto the crown of one of Lily's ratty old guide hats—Colin called it the BMW, Blessed Mountain Woman. There was no clear resemblance, of course, but Lily thought it was funny and gave Colin a big hug, and he was moved.

Jim notices Lily's Gokey boot tracks to the outhouse, the most recent from that morning apparently, to his keen eyes. He moves back toward the front of the cabin and the side porch. From the porch looking out over the lake, the only signs that Lily has been up and about in the last day or two are her well-trod path to a nearly full bird feeder and its contingent of chickadees, nuthatches and titmice. There are the tracks of the raven she calls Schwartz, and the remnants of a hare she's likely snared for him. There are the tracks of the three-legged fox, rescued by Jim from an illegal trap. The fox liked to hang around Lily's bird feeder during winter because the abundant tunneling voles and deer mice were relatively easy pickings for him. There are ermine tracks, too, and a pine marten as well. All, Jim knows, have been recorded in Lily's little notebooks.

Jim rubs his sleeve against the outer windowpane. He can barely make out the interior of the cabin, but thinks he can see Lily's form seated in the rocking chair by the stove, her head resting on her chest in an awkward manner.

"Oh, Jeez. God dammit, Lily."

He raps harder on the window. He calls, furious and scared. Finally he smashes open the locked door with the sledgehammer and wedge she uses to split wood. The cabin is freezing, the stove long out, he notices when he touches it. Lily sits in the rocker in her old raccoon coat, hat, scarf and boots.

"Oh, Lily," he says, shaking her gently, "It's me, Jim. What happened?" He quickly removes his gloves and unwraps her scarf enough to feel for a carotid pulse. It's there, but he thinks it's weak. He tears up some cardboard, balls up a couple of pieces of old newspaper, and breaks up the little bit of kindling that's left in the woodbox.

"Lily," he asks, "when was the last time you pulled in some wood here? Lily, it's a beautiful day outside. I hear you've been huntin' big game! Lily! Eleanor and Colin are comin'. They'll be here soon. Surprise visit! We'll all have dinner at the lodge—just like Christmas, huh? Lily, please talk to your old friend, Jim."

He doesn't like her color, which may be just the cold, but he's not sure. Something's wrong. The kindling catches and he puts one of the only two split logs left on the top and opens the draught a bit to increase the air flow. The wood, at least, is nice and dry. As soon as he gets the fire going, he adds the other log. He warms his own hands and pulls Lily's rocker, with Lily in it, closer to the heat source.

"I'm gonna get you some more wood in here, then I'm gonna head down, get us some help up here. I wish you'd talk to me Lily. Can you hear me? Jeez I hate to leave you alone to do anythin'. At least the birds are fed. And you snared a big fat hare for your raven there. Good for you." He rubbed his hands together. "Boy that deck's held up nice hasn't it? Your dad was a good builder, and he let me fetch and carry. Build somethin' right the first time, it lasts. You hang on here. I've got this fire goin' real good now, but I got to get us some more wood."

He adjusts the damper on the stove and heads out to the shed. He grabs the snow shovel and digs his way out. He brings in an armload, then another and another until the wood box inside is full. Still, Lily hasn't moved.

"You got to admit, Lily. This cabin is chinked so tight it's like a thermos bottle. You could be in here twenty-four hours before it starts to get cold once the stove goes out, and I would guess you been here just about half of that. Thermometer says forty-five. Not too much longer and you'da been in trouble. Don't you worry, Lily. Come spring you 'n' me, we'll get the cistern workin' again, fix them pipes, get these floors to warm up. Yeah boy, it's been a slow winter. Can't remember havin' so little to do. I'da come up more, but I know you don't like that. You like your space, don't ya, Lily?"

He kneels beside her and takes off her gloves, though some part of him feels shy and a little forward to be touching her bare skin again after all these years. He chafes her hands. They are barely warm, but he notices no signs of frostbite. He does the same with her feet, then quickly replaces her socks and boots. He has a devil of a time getting her old raccoon coat off, but when he does, he grabs the sleeping bag off the bed and the couple of Hudson Bay blankets there and wraps her up tight in the rocking chair like a caterpillar in a cocoon.

"There," he says, "You'll warm up quick now. Lily, I'm goin' down to my truck to radio you some more help here. To hell with the military. You need medical attention. I think you're just a little hypothermic and I don't like that you're not talkin' to me. I ain't been *that* much of a bother. Now listen to me and my language. See, I don't spend enough time with you. I've forgotten my good English."

Lily's head still hangs a bit to one side and her eyes remain closed, her body eerily still as if she's on the brink of deciding whether to stay or go.

"All right now, sweetheart. I'm headin' down. I'll be back as quick as I can." He stands at the door for a moment, torn between staying, seeing her through this as he had so many times before—sadder times, happier times, times on the lake in the Winslow's sail-rigged dinghy, ragged nights at the taproom, hauling ass back before Mack and Mabel or his dad caught them, summer days getting stoned by the pond, fishing the Ausable, the Cedar, the Upper Saranac. "Dammit. I just knew somethin' like this would happen someday."

Jim can't control his chin any more than his mouth. This isn't his territory, this one with all the feelings. It's not that he's unfamiliar with it, it's just that he doesn't belong here at this cabin, on this land, and he never did, and yet, who else does Lily have? He comes back and kneels. "Lily, I just want you to know . . . ah, shit. You are my first sweetheart. I mean that. I don't care about all that other stuff. You know what I mean. And, well, I've got some stuff of my own, like I told you. I'm goin' to get you through this. Just like we been through all that shit together when we were kids. You just wait. We'll be fishin' again in the spring. One last time, baby. April first, you hear? April first I'll be here with a whole bunch of new flies I'm tyin'. You'd better be here. You'd better be ready. I will. I promise. You have the word of Runnin' Deer. Remember that." And with that he rushes out of the cabin, kick-snaps his skis on and sails down the hillside toward the lodge a half-mile away.

Lily, the great blue whale, rising, painfully breaking through the ice buildup, realizes the intrusive noise has stopped. Did somebody call her sweetheart? Running Deer, after all these years?

Chapter Eight

"I know a rose-tree springing
Forth from an ancient root,
As men of old were singing,
From Jesse came the shoot
That bore a blossom bright
Amid the snows of winter,
When half-spent was the night."

"Rosa Mystica," #17, Episcopal Hymnal, 1940

Traditional melody, harmony by Michael Praetorius, 1609

Text: Speier Gebetbuch, 1599; Hymnal version, 1939

Nineteen forty-three: Charles and Robert were back on leave from England, Eleanor was a toddler. The Friends without Family gathered for
the first Christmas together at camp. As usual Joseph Wingate MacIntyre,
Esq., or "Padre," was the first to arrive, to discuss Charles's and Emily's
legal and business affairs. Padre had gone to Harvard with Charles and
was serving in the war as well, although not in the same unit. They were
both in England, but Padre was more of a paper pusher. He would see
no fighting, a fact that rankled him. At Harvard, he'd been full of himself—prospects of a successful career in law or business like his father.
Then the war came and he'd enlisted, thinking he'd do his duty and
come home in glory, but a childhood bout of polio and a slightly lame
leg disqualified him from active service. He sat out the war at Camp
Griffiss in Bushy Park, the Eighth Air Force HQ near London, where

he tied in again with Charles and met Robert Martindale for the first time. He sat behind a desk there and later in Paris. Padre was Charles and Emily's best man in London before the war in 1938. Later, after the liberation of Paris, Charles and Padre stood up for Robert on the day he married Mariette.

Padre had yet to marry, and doubted he would, because no one quite suited him. Of all the Friends, he was the quiet one. He laughed at the jokes, but was never one to lead off the conversation. His advice was as solid as his legal and business reputation, which followed in the footsteps of his deceased father's—both of his parents killed in a boating accident off Cape Cod. He was the dutiful heir, the solid friend, the confidant whom one could trust. Because he played such an intimate role, he knew more about all of them than any one of them knew about him, or even about each other. This, in addition to his lack of interest in women, had earned him his nickname "Padre." He was a man of faith, as a Padre should be, attending Episcopal services regularly. When the children came along, he was kind but had no real skills where children were concerned. Eleanor liked him because he talked to her as an adult. Lily remembered him, years later, as though he was a statue—something to be looked at and considered with awe, reverence and appreciation, to a point; he was fun to throw snowballs at, because he didn't retaliate. But even Lily knew when not to push her luck too far and incur his displeasure. He had a way of looking terribly, terribly serious and unhappy at times that made the girls apologize for their presence and wander off in the opposite direction.

Years after that first Christmas on The Hill came Christmas 1951, the year Eleanor was nine and Lily five, before the end of everything, a Christmas about as memorable a holiday as any child could want. That year the rest of the Friends tumbled into the camp in clumps of two and three or four—James, Irene and Padre flying in from New York, hiring a car, arriving with armfuls of presents—toys and books and records, caviar and good gin. James Wood was Charles Winslow's chum from St. Paul's School. A rising politician in Boston, and also of good family, he had fallen in love with Irene Duvall, a divorcée. The scandal that ensued ruined his prospects for state government; it didn't seem to bother him much, but it drove his proper Bostonian Catholic family to distraction. They disowned him. For his own part, he was having too much fun to care. The girls could engage James Wood in all manner of pranks and malarkey—like short-sheeting the beds of incoming guests and booby-trapping bathrooms with paper cups of water placed precariously atop the doors. Irene's greatest attraction was letting the girls try on her jewelry, as well as her talent for makeup, dress-up, film star gossip, staging little plays, folding hundred-dollar bills into rings and knowing a vast array of knock-knock jokes.

Later came Irene's best friend, the actress Julietta Pima, who had recently made the move from New York to Beverly Hills. She was a great sloe-eyed Italian beauty and was single, although rumored in "Tell it to Louella" and "Under Hetta's Hat" to be dating every more-or-less-available leading man. She never brought any of these gentlemen with her, much to the girls' dismay, but told wonderful stories and often brought reels of hilarious outtakes that friends in the cutting rooms had put together. One of these friends was a director/screenwriter named Jack Bannister who had found himself caught up in Senator McCarthy's web and blacklisted in Hollywood. Because her association with an alleged communist would ruin Julietta's career, they traveled independently of each other. This distant retreat in the Adirondacks was one of the few places left in America where Jack could meet and socialize without attracting unfriendly attention. The blacklist had left him financially strapped, and Julietta, and Charles and Emily Winslow had stepped in with funds until he found a job working for *The Nation* in Washington, D.C. James Wood also frequently contributed articles to *The Nation,* but was best known for his humorous pieces in *The New Yorker* and *The Saturday Evening Post.*

Both Julietta and Irene sent costumes to The Hill, leftovers from balls and openings across the continent, until the cedar closet and collection of steamer trunks in the attic of Doxology Lodge were chock-full. The attic was a favorite center of activity for the casting and dressing of amateur theatricals, tableaux and group photos. Even Padre could be inveigled into participating and never ceased to amaze the Friends with his ability to remember the words to all the Cole Porter songs, sing them passably well, and even tap dance a little.

One addition in the 1951 Christmas costume shipment was a Santa Claus outfit for Mack and a Mrs. Claus for Mabel, which was made good use of on Christmas morning. The girls were enthralled, even though it was no secret who was behind the wigs, beard and glasses, at least not to Eleanor, the Wise. Lily said to Charles, "Geez, I knew you know a bunch of people, but the Clauses?"

The best present of 1951 was a film can of celluloid called "The Peace of the Onondaga." The whole group of Friends and all of the camp staff including those imported from Winslow Station had performed this elaborate silent script, which Julietta had written, the summer before. It had taken most of the month of August 1951 to put it all together with casting (everybody in camp) and costumes (again, having had to order everything or make it on the spot). Then there was the selecting of locations (canoes on the lake, cabins in the woods) and, finally, filming with a borrowed movie camera operated by the film's director, Jack Bannister.

The story of "The Peace of the Onondaga" was a simple one. In the woods one day, Lucy Bridge, a white settler's child (played by Lily and later by Eleanor in a school age scene) meets Running Deer, an Onondaga boy (played by Jim Porter, the local ranger's son). They form a bond of friendship, which is discouraged by both sets of parents. Padre and Julietta played the settlers, James and Irene the Onondaga natives; Charles Winslow and Emily were the white child's aging grandparents, who dispense sage advice from rocking chairs in front of the guest cabin called "Rosa Mystica," advice such as "No good never come of a friendship 'twixt white skin and red skin," which appeared on printed cards edited in after the filming. There is a tearful forced parting of the children (it was actually very difficult to separate Jim and Lily, so seriously did they take their roles).

Lucy Bridge is sent away to school in a distant state (a scene of Eleanor as Lucy toiling at a desk, a large pile of books teetering, her calico bonnet draped at her back, her bangs and over-rouged cheeks altering her face dramatically). Miss Doris, the schoolmarm, leans over her in the scene with a yardstick, which, when observed closely, can be seen to bear the printed words "Old Forge Hardware, Old Forge, New York." Running Deer (now played by one of Mack and Mabel's sons), on the other hand, is sent on an impossible quest by his elders—to find and tame a pure white deer, and bring it back to the tribe as proof of his manhood. If he fails, of course, he must never return. If he returns empty-handed, he'll be killed.

Running Deer spends many years in the woods (Robert takes over the role at this point), searching for the deer. Lucy Bridge (now played by Mariette) spends those years studying to be a cultured "lady." Running Deer returns in secret each spring to spy upon the settler's camp, hoping to catch a glimpse of Lucy Bridge. He sees her, now grown and dressed in a fine gown, and realizes he can never win her. One day (according to the script), Running Deer sees a beautiful white deer, but its face is the face of the beautiful Lucy, and he cannot bring himself to capture the creature. He realizes he must return to his tribe and face certain death, the only option preferable to life without the woman he loves.

Plucky Lucy, however, sneaks away from home on one of her visits. She enters the Onondaga meeting hall, making the sign of peace that Running Deer taught her years ago. Just as she enters, she sees Running Deer, bound and telling the tribal elders and medicine men of his vision. Around him are the trophies he has brought as tribute—many bearskins, deer hides and antlers (the walls of the dining hall and lodge were denuded of their trophies for this). The elders are moved by his devotion to Lucy when suddenly they turn and see her. She drops her hooded cloak, and they see she is dressed in white buckskin and beads—her hair braided with white feathers. The couple, reunited, are blessed by the tribe and sent off into the woods (riding Butch and Daisy covered in Hudson Bay blankets). There is a hot pursuit by the settlers on foot carrying shovels, pitchforks and peaveys (in these scenes Indians and settlers alike were played by anyone else who happened to be in camp, including guides and waitstaff hired for the summer). When her parents see Lucy and Running Deer waving to them from a distant hill (The Hill Next), they realize they have lost their daughter. In the final scene, the settler parents find a sledge of skins on their porch on Christmas day with a note on birchbark reading: "Love from Lucy and Running Deer." The Onondaga parents join together with their tribe and the settlers in a communal banquet feast, which leads to the film's closing words: "Peace on Earth, good will towards all men."

Cecil B. DeMille would have been proud, Jack Bannister said, as they celebrated after the camera stopped rolling and the feast continued. It had taken a week of filming to get everyone in on it, plus enough film of the surrounding woods, lake and hillsides. Even after judicious cutting, it ran about an hour.

The film had its premiere on Christmas Day 1951 in the lodge with all the friends and townsfolk in attendance. Julietta and Irene had put together a soundtrack from player piano rolls, and created dialogue cards bearing sentiments such as "Their bond of love was stronger than the bond of blood."

The girls watched the movie over and over. Robert would run parts of it backward for them, which they loved. Often, for months afterward, Lily and Ellie could be found trying on the costumes again, reviewing the scenes, improving their performances (with Ellie directing), and advancing through the later parts of the script. Often, Jim was around to reprise his role as the young Running Deer. He played the role seriously and with great flair, adding wonderful bits of woodland lore that he'd picked up from his granddad, a guide and trapper. Jim became a regular at the camp, when he could get away from chores at home. His fidelity to the girls lasted through all manner of quarrels and disagreements. And it seemed that, even though they were only five years old, he was always sweet on Lily.

The annual Friends' Christmas and summer photos—and many stills from the movie—were hung on the walls of the butler's pantry in the lodge, each edition of the last reunion solemnly acknowledged in the next. They were kept carefully dusted and lined up straight over the years by Mabel as long as she lived at the camp and by Eleanor and Lily after that. They never altered the spacing of the photographs to make them fill the empty space created by the abruptly ended halt in the series. It was Mabel who, the spring after the tragedy, finally sent Padre the Hasselblad plates that Charles had snapped that last night before they flew to Montreal. Padre returned the best of the lot to her in frames and with copies enough for their friends. After that night, there were no more photographs, though. The empty space on the wainscoting was left unfilled, as a tribute to the passing of all that, the boundary between joy and grief defined by the edge of the last frame like a knife that cut off any vision of a future, any further Christmas worth remembering.

There were many days in her residency as caretaker when Lily walked back to Flatulence Pond. The pond was so named by Eleanor, who as a young girl couldn't abide the smell of algae on a hot day and was fascinated by the deep mats of pond bottom that produced the bubbles of gas that broke the surface. (This was the same kettle pond where, years before, they'd made a skating rink for the Christmas that never happened, and where, years later, Lily was to have her confrontation with the A-10s.) The pond was Lily's official place of mourning. She liked to go there of a warm spring or summer day and sit quietly. There, in years past, the Friends had their picnics and campfires and skating parties. And it had been the scene of the Peace Banquet in the film.

Before Lily was born, a lean-to had been built close to the pond shore and in front of it a large circle where logs had been set as seats around a massive campfire. Only pieces of the site were left after a blow-down. Lily had a mind to clear that all away and rebuild it, when she could find the time. She had gone so far as to stack and cover some of the reusable planking and logs, but the job would require more than one person, and this particular spot on the property was not a place where she would readily consent to having company, even for a worthy project. The memories here were too dense and troubling, much like a swarm of black flies.

Thinking about rebuilding the lean-to would lead to thinking how much she missed her father, her mother, the Winslows, Mack and Mabel, Tom and Doris, Butch and Daisy, Padre. In those long-gone days the rebuilding of the lean-to would have been a late summer project like the filming of the home movie, involving anyone and everyone who was in camp. The task would have been accomplished in a few days, maybe a week, depending on the amount of partying in between tasks. The girls would have been assigned the chore of gathering balsam boughs to line the cedar-planked floor. There would have been a feast of biblical proportions to celebrate the completion. Someone would have come from town with a fiddle, someone else with a guitar or mandolin or concertina, and the children would have fallen asleep in the arms of their parents to the musical notes of "Assez mon Moine, vous voulez danser?," "Un Canadien Errant," "V'la le bon vent," or any number of show tunes—a blend of French Canadian, Adirondack logging camp and Broadway.

That way—remembering—Lily knew, lay madness, a madness where she had dwelt too long—the miserable land of Koodashuddawooda, as Colin would say.

On one particular spring day, in a depressed and reflective state, Lily was thinking of the old biblical maxim: that in life we are in death and in death, life. She was aware of her breathing and of its finality, knowing that she breathed but would not always. She was, as the Buddhists say, mindful. It was one of many such times when she was at peace of a sort. She had hoped the warming air, the birdsong, the early blooms of witch hazel and shadblow would lift her spirits. Schwartz was with her, circling overhead, calling, then finally alighting at the edge of the pond where he paraded, turning over stones, hoping for a slow frog.

As she approached, a blue heron took flight and soared across to the far side. It was early spring, late April, warmer than usual, as it had been for several days. At the pond there were two mated pairs of Canada geese—one couple had two goslings, the other six. She found a seat on a plank from the old lean-to and watched the geese swimming and feeding while always gauging their distance from her. She studied the shoreline—dragon and damselflies, starlings and blackbirds, frogs and an occasional bream or pumpkinseed swimming by placidly on the warm day. Lily marveled at the capriciousness of nature: what had been dead and frozen was now alive again.

Staring at the edge of the pond, she became aware of a face just below the surface of the water close to where she sat. The face was triangular and about the size of a large man's fist, yet Lily wasn't sure that it was real—perhaps a mask-like confluence of sticks and algae. Still, it was unnerving to see this face seeming to stare straight at her, not kindly but maliciously. She stared back at it for some minutes, not wishing to look away, not wanting to approach it. Finally after quite some time, the face slowly sank and vanished: an enormous snapping turtle.

She realized she had been holding her breath in a state of some small terror. She worried for the remaining goslings of the unlucky family, and guessed that the disparity in the number of goslings was because of that face—a mask of malignity in an otherwise sublime and serene spot full of birdsong and bloom. She was reminded that even she, Lily, in this small heap of garment at the top of the food chain, would battle such a weighty monster, perhaps tire in the spring chill of the water, perhaps sink like a stone in its jaws. No parent to fly to her side, and even if there were, no parent strong or capable enough to help or do anything more than turn away, noticing one more gone, sailing on.

She walked slowly around the entirety of the pond, stopping to watch a confrontation between Schwartz and the Great Blue. The heron had speared a pumpkinseed, and Schwartz, seizing the opportunity, had marched up and nipped at the long legs of the bigger bird, annoying it until it turned and dropped the fish. There was an open-beak squawking of one bird to the other, comic in their Mutt and Jeff difference. Schwartz kept well out of range of the larger bird, but would feint again toward his tail, or make a grab for his outstretched wings. Finally, seeing Lily approach, the heron took flight.

The fish was lying on the bank, speared several times through. Schwartz had triumphed in the battle of the panfish and was having a little late afternoon snack of it. Lily thought of death in the brief blink of life. She continued her walk, head down.

Back at the cabin, Lily made herself a stiff cup of tea and sat outside on the deck, with Schwartz on the railing, back from his snack by the pond. He had something blue in his beak, and she presumed it was something he planned to cache somewhere about the log structure of the cabin as he did with his "treasures," but instead he held it between his feet and turned it over and over with his beak.

All this she was barely noticing. The scene at the pond, the snapping turtle, the memories, had rattled her. She breathed deeply, trying to calm her rapid heartbeat. Nature was like that, she told herself, glory and gore. She had grown all too familiar with the grim, and not present enough in grace. Some day, she thought, she would have to find the balance between the two.

Lily directed her attention to what Schwartz was doing with this blue object. Over and over he turned it, taking it in his beak, then dropping it, rolling it over between his feet, picking it up again, looking around. There were not very many times when the old bird came close to Lily. He usually kept a distance of at least three to five feet, just in case, after all this time, she decided to lunge at him for some reason. But Lily just sat there in her chair watching him as he sidled closer, and with one airy leap, graceful in his way, he hopped to the back of the chair, stepped onto her shoulder, and dropped the object into her lap. He started to, as it were, speak to her, and even took gentle hold of her hair, preening her a bit. She picked up the blue stone—glass actually, cobalt blue.

"Why, thank you, dear," she said. She held it up in her hands and, as Schwartz had done, turned it over and over so he could see her admire it. She placed it on the back of her left hand over her fourth finger, as though a gem setting in a ring. She carefully lifted one finger to stroke Schwartz under his beak and then down his breast feathers. Schwartz shook himself, ruffed out his neck feathers, dipped in a kind of bowing motion, and continued his little conversation with her, a sort of "mmmm" sound, but continuing into a triumphant claiming croak.

How like Jim, sweet Jim, with his old offerings of love—hand-tied flies, a box of shells, a Ka-Bar knife. Here was Schwartz, scavenger, thief, bringing her a tribute of what he knew best. Yet Schwartz seemed to know her best, better than Jim. Bring her something shiny, something pretty and frivolous in this all too unfrivolous landscape. This was the best kind of, could it be, North Country courtship? She thought of Jim, his awkward, shuffling and rambling overtures when they were teenagers, virgins. How once they had, well, mated, he could not shut up, could not do enough for her, be with her long enough, get enough words out. He was the best of spring birdsong, but irritating like the phoebe, repeating over and over how in love with her he was; here try this new fly, there's a big trout under that log over there; look, by the spruce swamp, isn't that the biggest buck you ever saw? What a trophy he'll make, and he's all yours, Lily. Jim was full of natural gift giving, hunting prowess, tenderness in tents and on balsam boughs, on peaks, in ravines and by waterfalls. He hunted and fished with the Indian blessing on his lips, as though every act of cruelty came with the knowledge that life given and taken was the greatest gift. Sometimes Jim was a stupid jerk. Sometimes he was a genius of spirit.

Stroking Schwartz's glossy feathered chest, she found it sad that she had a stronger connection to this carrion-breathed, noble raven than she had to Jim or any other human. She had been very cruel to Jim. Stupid, cruel, unfair. Hiding away herself, hiding away the only other thing of love and value they could have shared—not guns and fishing lures and gear. Not that at all. There was, you see, a child.

Jim Porter, at one of the Christmases they celebrated at The Hill with Lily and Colin and Eleanor and other guests, had dragged out the old film and run it through the projector again. He could remember having seen it as a child, but he couldn't really remember having been a part of it. Eleanor took the film can back with her to New York and had copies transferred to videotape so that everyone could have one. She even tracked down the couple of remnants of the Old Friends. Jack Bannister, who'd loosely stayed in touch after the tragedy, the only one of the group to do so, sent a long letter and received in return an invitation to revisit the camp, which he later declined, citing poor health. Julietta, who, still beautiful and proud, sent a simple, somewhat curt thank you letter. Irene had died of some kind of cancer, years before. James, her longtime husband, now elderly and ailing, never responded to the receipt of the tape. Doris and Tom had passed away long ago in England, though throughout their life they had been good about sending Christmas cards to the girls. No. Like everything and everyone else since 1952—Mack, Mabel, the horses, good times—gone.

Eleanor sent Jim a copy, and returned the original film in its can to the lodge at The Hill. Jim showed the video at the Methodist Church during the Cabin Fever movie nights one February. He and Pastor Clara invited Lily to come, but she declined. The audience howled at the old black and white footage shot just across the lake. They recognized Jim as a child and some of the other really famous people, as well as local kids involved more than forty years before. There were gasps at the ending when Mariette appears dressed in white buckskin, with Robert Martindale, so handsome as Running Deer. And there, Charles and Emily Winslow dressed in pioneer costumes, but still as elegant as royalty. What a tragedy. A little more than a year later they'd be dead.

There was a lot of discussion afterward over coffee and brownies about Lily and her tenancy as caretaker of The Hill, and stories told and swapped again of how well she cared for the camp and seemed to either look after or terrorize local fishermen and hunters. It was meetings like this in town where the legends tended to grow and take on a life of mythic dimension—Lily as patron saint, Lily as crazy, loon-laughing mental case.

There was one story, though, that was not repeated that night, although it was in the back of everyone's mind. Three years before, a couple of guys, strangers, had tied one on at Aiken's Tap Room one spring night, not too long after the ice had melted off the lake. They had a muddled idea of taking off over to The Hill to find the little inlet cove there where this hermit lady was said to live in an old cabin and maybe pay her a visit. She must be lonely, they reckoned.

Tom Aiken watched, worried, when they left, and called Jim Porter and Joe Finn and Clara. The guys had a head start in a motorboat, which showed a certain low level of intelligence, because Lily could have heard them coming a mile away, and Jim knew she'd be armed and ready for them; it wasn't the first time something like this had happened, what with all the hikers and sportsmen around who did not respect boundaries.

Jim and Joe met at the marina and took Jim's boat to follow the guys out. They did find the boat some distance from where it would have been had they headed directly for The Hill. They found the boat, but the guys were not in it. It took days to find the bodies, and neither man had a mark on him—hypothermia was ruled the cause of death. No one could figure if they'd just jumped into the water, or had a fight, or one had stood and lost his balance and the other tried to save him, or the boat had tipped enough to throw them out and then righted itself. It was a mystery. But the water was cold enough, forty-five degrees, so that they would have died fairly quickly. Strange though, they hadn't been gone that long, hadn't even made it three-quarters of the way over to Lily's before Jim and Joe caught up with the boat. The whole event had happened in less than an hour after they left the taproom. When Jim and a state trooper talked to Lily, she said she never saw them and didn't remember hearing the motor. Their boat had never made it to shore, that much was clear. They wouldn't have had time to get that far.

"She's protected," Pastor Clara said, mysteriously. "Someone watches over her, and I don't mean Jim Porter."

Stories like that enhanced one other legend. It was said that hunters had seen a white deer, in a herd of regular deer with a big thirteen-point buck at its head, all following a great black raven. Maybe the old home movie got that one started, but stories like that, fabricated by hunters and fishermen? It was inevitable.

The raven, at least, was true. The raven came to Lily in the second year of her solitude on The Hill Next. She was fishing the inlet stream and shallows below the cabin early one June morning when she saw, tossing in the water, one wing of the large bird extended in a lazy wave, a salute to a passing life. She waded out and saw the messy tangle of monofilament fishing line caught around its wing and beak, and a small trout's tail protruding partially, the source of the bird's present misery and potential demise.

Lily lifted the raven and tugged at the tail of the fish with some difficulty until she managed to pull it out. She'd strapped her old bamboo rod down on her jacket, and was trying not to entangle the bird further in her own three-pound test line and tippet. Lily was wary of his large, broad beak and surprised at his heft, but the old dude was apparently too weak to struggle. He lay limply in her arms while she snipped the fishing line from around him with her nippers and unwound it all carefully. She carried her burden over to the shore, sat down, and unhooked the little trout from the lure—a little Mepps—and shifted the bird gently to a more upright position. He seemed to curl, she thought, a bit like a cat, with his tailfeathers fanned around. He croaked and opened his beak several times, snapping it shut as if to test his ability to work it. Then he sighed, blinked a couple of times looking at her, croaked once more and, again like a cat, rested his head on her left knee, and apparently went to sleep.

Lily held still, sitting with the raven awkwardly but content to admire his deep and radiant blackness. She tried to remember everything she could about ravens—from Poe to pictures of them on some long-ago nature program that showed one sliding down a snowbank and apparently enjoying himself. Lily sat cross-legged with the raven's head on her knee. Except for his regular breathing, she wondered if he might not just die right there. She wondered about bird lice and what if he woke in a panic and bit her or dug in with his, what? Talons? She wondered all the while, in bits and pieces of thoughts. Male? Female? How do you tell? Do they mate for life? How old is this one? She thought she'd heard they live for ages.

After a time, the creature rustled himself and stood up on her knee. She held the trout in front of him and he eyed it for some time and then took it gently in his beak. He stretched one wing, then the other, but Lily was in the way, so he stepped off her lap, flapped a couple of times and stood there with an air of uncertainty with the little trout still in his beak. He took a couple of steps, stretched his wings, tossed his head, and swallowed the fish.

Lily figured that was that and she'd leave him to his recuperative stretching and likely grooming, but she continued to sit there, resisting the temptation to reach out and touch his deep black feathers. He turned and looked at her and took a deep breath.

Lily stretched her legs slowly, and stood up stiffly. A breeze had come up, riffling the surface of the water, making it difficult to see anything of a trout nature floating near the inlet stream, but there was plenty of stuff coming down off The Hill Next and bubbling along. Nothing was rising to the stuff floating down from above, so she stuck with the wet fly and made a few roll casts to avoid the shoreline and get close to a sunken log. Nothing was biting. She reeled in the line and hooked the fly to the grip of the rod. She'd come back at dusk in the Hornbeck, go out a little farther, fish a little deeper.

As she climbed back up the path to the cabin, she looked around for the raven. He had flown up to a low branch of a dead hemlock just off the path and was watching her. She continued up the path and heard his wings behind her. When she got back to the cabin, she made herself a peanut butter sandwich and sat outside on the deck. The raven watched from his perch in the hemlock. She broke off a chunk of her sandwich and laid it on the railing for any passing squirrel or chipmunk, and was surprised when, with a fluster of wings, the raven settled himself on the railing, where she had propped her feet, eyed the sandwich, and took a peck at it. Deeming it suitable, he took the whole piece in his mouth and flew off to a neighboring white pine to feed. Thereafter, whenever Lily came out to the deck or wandered around, there also was her black companion. She carried chunks of bread for him. When he fished for himself on the lake, skimming a floater off the surface, or retrieved a bit of carrion from the main road, he would sometimes drag a stinking chunk of it back to the cabin, sit on the railing or on the big pine, while Lily attended to her feeders or sat with her notebook of the season. Over time, the raven cached bits of sticks, glass, small river stones, metal can tabs and food in the crevices of the cabin logs. Sometimes such treasures were forgotten, sometimes retrieved with passing interest, and sometimes provided more intense involvement. It seemed to Lily that he would drag something out of a seemingly forgotten trove, turn it over and over with his black toes, and then pause to look at Lily with a turn of his head and a bright shining eye. She thought sometimes he was judging her, asking her opinion of the find, waiting for her response, approval, anything.

Pastor Clara, on a rare visit, was reminded of the Prophet Elijah to whom God sent ravens bearing food. This, then, became the legend in the area, that this raven of Lily's was bringing her food to eat so she didn't need to hunt or fish for herself. When Jim Porter heard that, he snorted and said, "The day that girl can't provide for herself is the day we carry her out on a stretcher."

Chapter Nine

"Frail children of dust, and feeble as frail,
In thee do we trust, nor find thee to fail'
Thy mercies, how tender! How firm to the end!
Our Maker, Defender, Redeemer, and Friend!"

"Hanover," #288, Episcopal Hymnal, 1940

Tune: William Croft, 1708; Text: Robert Grant, 1833, based on Psalm
104

It had always been a great mystery to the Friends and to the folks of
Winslow Station what Jim Porter ever saw in Lily Martindale. When they
were kids she treated him sourly, teased him mercilessly, and used him
like a hanky. But Jim was impervious. Still, then as now, he behaved as
though she owned him, that she was just joshing when she told him to
shut up or be quiet or leave her alone. That was just a sign that she really,
truly liked him and totally depended on him for his friendship and love.

There was more than a little truth to the impression that Lily was
difficult to befriend. But Jim never seemed to notice. The more she
argued and criticized him, the softer his soft blue eyes became, the
meeker and more gently he behaved toward her. Everyone agreed he
was not so much dim as besotted. But there was no finer guide in the
northern Adirondacks. He knew more than many of the old-timers knew.
His grandfather, one of those brave early settlers at the beginnings of
the glorious and misery-ridden environment of the Adirondack Park,
had taught him much about trapping, logging, hunting and fishing. Jim's

father, the local ranger up there in the forties and fifties, had been one of the most respected voices for protecting the Adirondack wilderness, and had traveled many times to Albany to defend environmental legislation and even run for office. Jim came from good Adirondack stock, but like many of the full-time residents of the park, he could be a little rough around the edges in polite society. Unlike some mountain dwellers, he never got enough of conversation. His social graces got all tangled up between his old bootlaces and his flapping tongue.

For her own part, Lily never minded the roughness. In fact, they were alike in that way to some extent. Her education abroad in Switzerland hadn't polished her that much. She resisted discipline and enjoyed using her thorny tongue on the unwitting and stuffy. When she took on some of the more pompous city types, Jim thought she was hilarious. She was small and feisty to his tall and laid back. He was six foot two and maybe weighed 170, and his most notable features were his deep and dreamy eyes that seemed to take in everything around him as though all was right and perfect with the world. She was only five foot four and 110 pounds, and there was nothing deep and dreamy about her. She was small and tight in both body and mind. She also took in what she saw around her, and it seemed as though she didn't care for it too much. Noting their relative sizes and body structures, one Southern writer who visited the camp took a look at Lily and Jim when they were in their late teens and said, "Y'all ever make love, you'll be nose to nose and her toes'll be in it. Toes to toes and her nose'll be in it." They were quite a pair, were Jim and Lily.

But God knew he was just too talkative for Lily's temperament. He reminded her of the red-eyed vireo, asking and answering his own questions and keeping up the dialogue all by himself most of the time. "Do you think the fish'll be bitin' up to Tupper? Maybe not since it's been s'cold," or "Did you see the flyin' squirrels out last night? But sure you did; you never miss a trick." By the time they were young adults, Lily could silence him with one ferocious glance. There were only three situations when Jim would ever be quiet—when he was fishing or walking in the woods, when Lily gave him "that hush-up look," and when he was holding her, kissing her, making love to her.

This was the case until she moved back to The Hill. The time he visited her at her cabin after she first arrived was the beginning of the first seed of understanding in his brain. She really wasn't going to call him. She wasn't going to go to church or out on dates with him. She wasn't going to sleep with him ever again. He sort of understood that then, and for a time he was depressed, and for a time he was angry, and by the time she fired on the A-10s he'd given up. He was just going to be a long-distance friend, if even that, and maybe he ought to get out more, get another life, another woman. And that was exactly what he did. And Lily knew it.

Jim would have been surprised to learn that Lily really thought of him as her best friend, next to Eleanor. And he was her only lover, ever. She always knew he would look after her, albeit from a distance of some miles, and that was fine, she felt. That was exactly the way she wanted it in her life as a hermit, ornamental or not. Part of that was for his sake. When she returned to the camp, she was deeply ashamed of how she had treated him back then, and guilty at every transgression of trust and honesty. She'd buried so much, so deep, and it had fermented poisonously over the years. She knew that until all that acid drained out of her, she needed to be alone. Whoever crossed her path generally got in the way of a lot of old, sad history, of which Jim, poor soul, was an unwitting and sorry part. But alas, we are all as sick as our secrets—weighed down, corrupted, tainted, contaminated, polluted. The Adirondack Mountains, strong, ages old, were as vulnerable to the toxic prevailing winds bearing acids that would taint the lakes and stunt the growth of the forests with a deadlier force than all the logging of the nineteenth century. Lily was just a small tract of her own devastation.

Eleanor had experienced Lily's temper, so had Colin and many others, once even a former president of the United States of America. It was the stray hiker, someone who wasn't paying attention to the signs and wandered in while she was out splitting wood or fishing, who was caught unawares. Most of them she could ignore, but it was those who wanted to start a conversation, beg some water or even a beer, that she screamed at with her wild, wailing banshee scream. These days, however, she had come to learn that no one knew her anymore. These guys hiking through were younger by twenty years and most had never heard the old story, or never paid attention, never seen those photographs, newsreels and magazine spreads of her and Ellie when they were kids. Or they certainly didn't associate that story with this rough-looking woman with the sharp axe and the old Battenkill fly rod. She was just another crazy Adirondacker in the woods.

More and more, she had begun to relax. Perhaps not everyone was after her, maybe not even the Air Force. Maybe she didn't need to be a hermit any more.

⚜

It takes a little doing to get Lily, semiconscious on that late Sunday afternoon, down off The Hill Next and medevac'd to the hospital in Saranac Lake. It takes three men and a long length of rope attached to a rescue sled, with Lily strapped in and all bundled up, sliding over the snow and ice. Lily has slowly risen from the depths, slowly focused. There is suddenly warmth again, movement, jostling, voices, then the cold air on her face. She opens her eyes on the way down to the lakeshore to meet the helicopter. Jim is there by her side. She isn't surprised. She's still just tired and in pain.

"Hi, there, kiddo," he says. "Welcome back. You had me worried there for a minute, but I knew you wouldn't let me down."

"Am I going to jail?" she asks.

"Nope. Not yet. Not if I have anythin' to say about it. You're goin' to the hospital in Saranac Lake," he says. "You were pretty cold, but I think you'll be okay. These guys'll take care of you. I'll stay here and get things warmed up for Eleanor and Colin."

"They're coming?"

"Yeah."

"Shit."

"You're all right. Don't worry. I'll come see you as quick as I can. You're goin' with these guys here."

"What guys?"

"Medics. EMTs."

"Not the other?"

"The what?"

"The guys in the planes, the jets."

"No. They don't care about you. You're not the Unabomber. Me and Eleanor will take care of them."

"Shit."

"It'll be all right, Lily."

Overhead the raven calls. Lily looks up and tries to wave. "Hey, Schwartz," she calls weakly, then she moans.

"What's a matter, Lily?" Jim asks.

"I hurt, Jim. I hurt all over. Dammit, Jim. I hurt so much."

"Where does it hurt?"

"All over, dammit all to hell."

"She's in pain, guys," he says to the medevac crew. "Take it easy with her."

He watches the helicopter thrum off across Winslow Lake toward Saranac Lake. Schwartz has flown away somewhere to avoid the noise and commotion. Jim trudges back to camp, where he switches on the generator, opens up Doxology Lodge and Rockingham, and makes sure the lights are working and the water is on. At the lodge, he starts removing dustcovers from the chairs and couches, and does the same upstairs in the master bedroom. He notices that the canvases and screens have been ripped down on the sleeping porch and the snow has come in pretty bad. Now that Lily's laid up, he'll have to come up and deal with that when he has a free day. The old porch has trouble supporting that weight any more. He'll bring Joe Finn along. They might need to do some work on the supporting timbers.

In Eleanor's childhood room, he smoothes down the pillows with one lean stroke of his hand and a tenderness of memory. Here they'd play card games and board games when they were little. Chutes and Ladders he remembers, Sorry, Monopoly. Dumb games, but it might be storming outside so they were stranded upstairs or down in the library or in the attic with the costume trunk, making believe, fooling around like kids do. He walks downstairs to the butler's pantry and stands a moment looking at the old framed pictures of all of them.

"Well, folks," he speaks aloud, "nothin' more to do here but plow out the rest of the way. The old place is startin' to warm up. They sure knew how to build these beauties back then. And don't you worry. I'll take care of Lily."

He skis back down to his pickup with the blade on the front, plows the rest of the way around the camp and then drives back to his house in Winslow Station. He washes up, grabs a bite, calls in to report, gets back in the pickup and drives to Saranac Lake to sit with Lily. He'll call his fiancée later.

Eleanor drives the Subaru wagon as though it's the *Queen Mary*—stately, speedy and against towering waves of traffic. Colin rides shotgun with his hands clutching the door grip. She remembers the old days of summer when they nearly always flew in on a pontoon plane, her father or Robert piloting. They would joke about letting the girls parachute into the lake to get in the first swim of the season.

Heading north from Manhattan to the Thomas E. Dewey Thruway, to the Northway, the traffic beyond the exits for Glens Falls and Lake George slims down to a bare trickle of pickups, front-wheel, four-wheel drives, Canadian eighteen-wheelers and rust heaps. It's late afternoon. The cars with skis and poles are traveling south after the weekend at Whiteface. The Subaru pulls off at Exit 30 heading toward Lake Placid and Saranac Lake. The eighteen-wheelers drone on toward Montreal with the other traffic.

Eleanor has been humming snatches of a hymn from the morning service, the one about "frail children of dust and feeble as frail." Colin recognizes the signs. "You're happy aren't you? You don't mind this at all."

"I'm glad you understand, Colin, dear. It's as though I just woke up from all the jet lag. I can't wait to get there. I can't wait to see Lily. I can't wait to see The Hill."

"I love The Hill, too, you know, but it's such a sad place to love."

"To me it's not a sad place. I think Lily sees it that way, too. I hope she's all right. I hope Jim is there."

"We both hope she lets him anywhere near the place."

"Right," Eleanor says and returns to her humming.

"I've always been terrified she's going to shoot him some day."

"Oh Lily loves Jim. And Jim loves Lily."

"Yes, but I no longer think we can vouch for her state of mind regarding any intruders, whether military or old boyfriends. And Jim has moved on. That's a very good thing."

But Eleanor just shakes her head.

Five hours and twenty minutes after leaving Manhattan, the Subaru cruises through the town of Lake Placid, where Eleanor finally has to slow down. Colin releases his hold on the door long enough to massage his fingers, and begs for a break and a drink. She obliges by heading into town, pausing frequently for shoppers and pedestrians. She pulls into the main parking lot of the Mirror Lake Inn.

"Will the coolers be all right?" she asks.

"They have enough ice to reconstitute the snow cover over Greenland."

"Well, only another hour or so and we'll be home."

"How bucolic. I can't wait to see the headline in *Town and Country*. 'Historic Adirondack Great Camp hosts MPs at uniform-only event. Former socialite held for questioning.'"

"Oh stop."

"Not 'til we get there, darling. Not until we see her sunny little face."

Eleanor calls Jim from the Mirror Lake Inn where they stop for a break, but he doesn't answer at his house, and no one answers at Doxology Lodge. That phone has not been as busy since the old days, and there's not a human soul around the camp to care.

Lily manages to doze most of the way to the hospital in the helicopter. She thinks this is her first helicopter ride, and she's a little sorry she can't sit up to watch the scenery. The medics attempt to engage her in conversation, but she ignores them. She isn't worried; why should *they* be? One of them is monitoring her heart rate and tries to place an oxygen mask on her face. She pushes him away with surprising strength, then moans. She's just so bloody tired and she hurts everywhere, every joint, every nerve ending. No spit left in her for a fight. So for all of fifteen minutes, she tries to sleep, until they land on the pad behind the hospital, and suddenly her whole world is an explosion of lights and noise. She keeps her eyes tightly closed and turns her head, panic rising, her body starts shaking again and she's moaning in fear and pain. When they try to ask her questions, she pretends she's unconscious, except she flinches at the needle when they hook her up to the IV. She tries to concentrate on tuning it all out, keeping her eyes squeezed shut.

One voice penetrates—one with a lovely accent saying he is doctor something. She likes listening to that voice. "Miss Martindale," he says, "Miss Martindale, I'm Doctor . . ." but she tunes out the words and just listens to the sound of his voice which is soothing. It reminds her of someone she used to know, also a doctor, years ago in New York. He existed for a brief time in her heart—a sweet man.

He was one of the doctors she met when visiting the children's ward at New York Hospital. He was dark and multilingual . . . spoke Arabic, Turkish and French as well as English. He was great with the kids and they adored him. He had the right ability to kid around, help them relax. He never talked down or was too loud. This doctor and Lily became friendly in a chums kind of way, and she was surprised when he asked her out to dinner.

He took her to a nice place in Chelsea—French. He bought an expensive bottle of wine and ordered for her as well, which she thought was a bit cheeky, but she let it ride. She was flustered and deranged about things, like the potential areas where the evening might lead. She liked this guy. He was the first in many years to show an interest, asking the right questions, posing the right topics to discuss—her disabled kids, her activities on their behalf, life in the city, good food, good wine, good movies—just like a normal person. He never asked personal questions. She assumed he was unaware, which added to the excitement. God, how she loved that! A man who was unaware of her past—ambrosia to her soul.

She invited him home, but he stopped short at the doorway with heavy breath and trembling. He kissed Lily goodnight in the most awkward fashion, whispered something about impossible situations, how much he had enjoyed the evening, and then he walked away. She never knew what the whole story was, but he didn't continue the friendship as before. Cold and cordial—that was it. She never pressed him, wondering what she might have said or done to put him off, but maybe it was just the old story. How, then, could he know? She later heard that he was married. That may have had something to do with it.

Sometimes she had been tempted to track him down, call and apologize for, well, tempting him, perhaps. Maybe he and his wife had had a spat. Perhaps he was practicing Western ways while he was still new and fresh to the country. Perhaps his wife had threatened to leave and return home to, was it Dubai? Maybe it was just all that old Lily baggage catching up with her again. She never knew, but Lily missed her dark multilingual friend, and should have called to tell him so. It would have been nice to draw off the darkness of him to warm her loneliness and isolation. It was not so much an issue of sex as it was of a certain communion of spirit she thought they'd had. Clearly, she had been mistaken.

It was in remembering such moments as those that Lily sometimes thought of returning to the real world. Then she would remember that there are now things called jet skis, and if that were not enough insult to the fragility of her peace of mind, someone had the kindness to send her a picture of little African children with their hands hacked off by machetes. There was a note stuck on the side saying "pray for us all." In the hammock she had strung for herself between the polar opposites— her solitude in the mountains and her love of the city, she despaired of her ability to pray either for herself or for the world. She was utterly defeated in this. Her life was like a high-speed crash. Nothing about it was tidy, discrete or even sanitary, and here she is in the hospital at last—glaring white lights and walls, shouting, needles. She is utterly broken, in pain and scared to death.

She thinks of the cabin, of Schwartz, the raven, and of the wind chimes that soothe her when the breezes blow through her life, the mysterious melody she's heard played for her by unseen hands. She wonders if she'll ever hear them again.

Jim drives to the hospital, and by the time he gets there all hell has broken loose. There are police cars, a local news van, and a couple of military vehicles.

"Aw, shit," says Jim.

He remembers the only time he ever visited Lily and Eleanor in New York City, oh, probably twenty years ago. How they went out to dinner and when they came out of the restaurant, there were all these photographers, maybe a dozen of them, shouting and taking their pictures. Lily had said then, "Well, Jim, welcome to the circus that is our life."

For some months afterward, Jim found, he lived in fear that he'd step outside his house in Winslow Station to find somebody sticking a microphone in his face asking him, "Isn't it true you were Lily Martindale's sweetheart? Were you with the girls at the camp here when the plane went down? Were you?"

Jim thought he could handle just about anything in life—a High Peaks rescue, a charging sow bear, a drunk with a knife in the taproom—but he would never, ever, be able to handle those jerks with the cameras and the questions. Yet Lily had faced them all her life. No wonder she was crazy.

Jim approaches the highest-ranking officer he can spot. Captain Jeff Andrews, the public affairs officer.

"My name is Jim Porter. I'm the ranger you spoke to. I'm a friend of the, uh, of Miss Martindale's."

"A friend, huh? You the one who got the transport for her?"

"Yes sir."

"Thanks for the call. Saved us all a lot of time. Let's get us a cup of coffee and some answers to some questions here. Your 'friend' shouldn't be running around with a rifle, trying to shoot jets."

Jim shook the captain's hand. "Yes sir. I believe I can help clear this all up, if you'll let me. But first I want to check on Lily."

"Well, actually . . . I have to ask you to come with me first. Miss Martindale is under care and under guard. So let's just have that cup of coffee."

Jim shook his head. "Yes, sir, but you all are makin' one helluva big mistake."

"It's a new world, my friend. It's a whole new world. And I suspect you've got quite a story to tell me."

Chapter Ten

Eleanor walked most always with her nose in a book, or sat or lay down the same way, oblivious to much of what was happening around her. Her father often commented that she would have read through the London blitz. But now she noticed the silence. For all its remoteness and solitude, The Hill was almost always active with some kind of daily urgency at any hour of the day before midnight, but not now. On this Friday before the Christmas holiday week, which would normally herald an extraordinary amount of household industry, there was not a sound except a soft *pit, pit* on the copper roof of the porch outside. No banging of pots from the kitchen away off in Rockingham Hall, no shouts to the horses, no phones ringing, no motors running, no running water anywhere. Lily had fallen asleep on the settee in the library. Her small round face was perfectly peaceful and there was no sound from her either. She was quite still, quite deeply asleep.

Eleanor started to read again, then stopped. "Expect us back by suppertime on Friday," her mother had said. "But don't be worried if we're a little late."

She looked around. She was cold, but not because the room was cold. She put the book down and quietly left the library so as not to disturb Lily. It was quite dark outside. Eleanor realized she might have been reading for hours and had no concept of the time. She ran upstairs just to check, just to make sure. There were no suitcases, no boxes, no coats. She ran back down. Her parents' boots were still missing. She looked outside, but the big car was nowhere to be seen and there were no tracks in the now glistening snow, glistening, she thought, oddly, with rain. She quickly got into her jacket and boots, gloves and hat. Outside, she realized it was wet and very slick with ice, not rain. Ice was falling. She turned up her face and little pellets of frozen rain pelted and stung slightly. She held onto the railing of the stairs, but it was just as slick as the steps. She stamped hard going down, to break the glaze.

Well okay, she thought. The weather is terrible; her parents aren't home yet. They're late because of the weather. Perhaps they decided to stay one more night. But all the same, her heart had a queer, unpleasant little flutter.

She wanted to run, but couldn't because of the ice. She stomped through the thick crust forming on top of the snow, moving as quickly as she could toward the only lights in camp besides the lodge, those at the caretaker's cottage, Hyfrydol, and the barn close by. Mack was in the barn tinkering with the tractor sledge. She tried him first. Mack lifted his head from the engine block and glanced at his timepiece.

"Oh my. Looky at that. It's past five. Nobody home yet? Hmm. Let's go ask Mabel."

Mack and Eleanor walked outside, where Mack slipped and nearly went down. Eleanor could not see his face, but recognized she now had a companion in her knowledge, in her fear. Things were not right. It wasn't just the storm.

"Got so involved in what I was doin'. Holy Crikes! Look at this here," he said, taking in the icy shine on the snow.

Mabel was in her own kitchen in the cottage, pulling a pie out of the oven. She had started supper with an extra bit of beef stew. "No I haven't heard a word. Nobody's called. I wondered if the lines are down. Here, let me check . . . well, that's why. Phone's out."

"Where's Lily?" Mack asked Eleanor.

"Asleep in the library. We both fell asleep I think. I've been reading and I must have . . ."

Mack reached above the fireplace in the cottage and pulled down a couple of ski poles. Out in the hall, he strapped on his studded snowshoes. "I'll go roust Lily. I need to check the generator, too. Ellie, will you head down to Miss Doris and Mister Tom's? Tell them we're eating here if they want to join us. You got enough for supper, Mabel?"

Mabel asked him to stop by Rockingham for milk, butter and bread.

"We'll be glad of Tom's radio with the phones out. I hope the folks are still in Montreal. Or stopped in Malone. Naught we can do but just sit tight," he said.

Outside, Eleanor and Mack headed in different directions, Mack on snowshoes, with poles, Eleanor stamping her way with the aid of two ski poles she'd taken from the hall in the cottage. The ice was still coming down in little stinging pellets. She had to brace herself with the poles as she went down the hill toward Miss Doris's cabin, and found it easier walking off to the side where the snow was deeper and she could crunch through. She made the cabin without incident. The light inside gave off a false cheer to the evening. Eleanor knocked on the door and gave her report.

"Oh my!" said Doris, "I don't think I shall be going out in this. How did you make it down the hill? How should we make it up? Tom? Tom? Look at the ice outside, Tom! Oh dear, I hope they stayed in Montreal. This is no weather to be out in, especially in an aeroplane. Oh, Ellie, you must be worried sick."

Tom came up behind her. "Dear Lord, a sloping skating rink. Not for me. We'd need crampons to get up the hill. Tell Mack I've been trying to save up the juice in the batteries for the radio, but I think I should get on now and see what's up. Maybe I can get a rise out of someone."

"I was hoping you could," said Eleanor. "It would help."

"So, tell Mabel we won't be joining you for dinner. I'll heat up a tin of something for us here."

"All right."

"And Ellie . . . don't be afraid. Your father and Robert are excellent pilots. They would never do anything foolish."

Eleanor nodded, but she did not feel at all comforted by her tutor. Slowly and carefully, she made her way back up the hill to wait. "Naught we can do," she remembered Mack's words, words she'd heard before when the tractor broke down, or the boat needed parts, or a cow took sick. "Naught we can do," he would say, and they'd wait patiently for the part, the medicine, or the knacker man.

After fetching Lily, milk, butter and bread and delivering them into Mabel's care, and when he'd checked the generator, Mack headed down Hill Road in the old Linn tractor with the heated truck cab. There were downed branches everywhere, and it took him an hour to clear the first three miles of the six-mile run; but he kept going, kept hoping he would see the Packard's lights at the other end. Maybe, if they did get this far, they'd turned back to Malone. Maybe, curse the thought, they'd spun off somewhere.

He had his big spotlight with him on the roof of the cab. Every couple of feet, when he stopped to clear another set of deadwood and downed branches, he'd scan the slope off the side of the road to the lake. It would be a mess to clean all this up properly, and might better wait until morning if it weren't for thinking they might be out there somewhere. It was four more miles to the main road, which led to Paul Smiths one way, to St. Regis and Malone the other. Besides them, what he really wanted to see more than anything was Jerry Hammill's old state trooper car, or James Porter's—the state ranger's—Willys Jeep. But there was no one in sight. Occasionally he switched off the engine to see if he could hear anything. It was an awful feeling, watching branches snap off under the weight of the ice, skitter down the hill, hearing the lake groan with the shifting of its ice. If he wasn't careful, he'd get clobbered himself, like old Johnny Hoy at Sagamore, struck fatally by a falling tree as he took young Vanderbilt and a governess on a carriage ride around the lake there at Sagamore.

Three miles down the road there was a big old dead white pine, a good five feet of girth, smack dab across the road. They'd have had to turn around if they saw that. Holy Mother of God. Naught to do. Naught to do but . . . He had a chainsaw and a couple of garbage cans full of sand in the back. As long as he didn't slip, fall, and slice his leg off, he could cut the center out. It was going to take a while but he'd bust this beast up, push out the center with the front of the Linn and get it off to the side somehow. It couldn't roll as far as the lake; too many trees in the way. But at least it would slide right along on this ice.

Lily, Eleanor and Mabel sat quietly around the table. Mabel sopped up the last of her stew with a slice of bread and butter. Lily pushed her peas and carrots around in the gravy, mashed the potatoes with her fork, and took little nibbles. Eleanor slowly buttered another piece of bread and tried to talk about Christmas, but no one seemed to be picking up on the attempt at distraction, and once again the conversation dove off a cliff into cold water. It was now past eight-thirty, the girls' technical bedtime, but nobody was moving either to clear dishes or retire. Finally, around nine, Mack came in, looking as worn out as a ragged grey sock. "Well, I got to the road in the Linn." he said. "It's just one big mess out there—branches, trees. I got the worst of it. If they make it this far at all, they can get home. They've got chains for the Packard. I'm starvin' and I could smell that stew two miles away. God bless the Linn. I had to push a big ol' chunk of white pine half the way back to the road before there was room to move it to the side, and the Linn, she purred along just as nice and steady."

Mabel gave him a big portion of stew.

"Did you see anything?"

"Nothin'. Nothin's movin' out there. Even if I was a sharp-hoofed deer, I'd be bedded down for the duration in the deepest, darkest part of the spruce swamp. I wouldn't be movin' to forage for a coupla days. Now, don't you gals worry. Good news takes its time, but bad news comes on fast. Ice storm or no ice storm."

In fact, this news did come on fast, in spite of the storm. Mabel put the girls down, clothes and all, in the spare room upstairs in Hyfrydol, where they'd spent the nights since their parents had left four days before. It was then that Lily started to cry although she did not entirely comprehend why she should cry. Christmas was coming and *Maman* and Papa would be home soon with the presents and then Santa Claus would come, too and maybe, just maybe, he'd agreed to the puppy. Mabel suggested that they say their Now-I-Lay-Me's and put in a special word for all the road crews, rangers and state police out there working so hard to make sure everybody was safe. That gave Lily something to do.

Mabel understood what Lily didn't: that everyone's tone and the changes in routine from what was expected had rattled her to her little core. Nothing much varied in this camp from what was expected day to day. Something like this quite shakes a little person up, that and Christmas coming. Mabel could remember her own kids—two boys, both wound as tight as a Swiss watch for weeks before the holiday. They were barely any use at all, back then when Charles Winslow Senior had the place, and her waiting hand and foot, night and day on poor Mrs. Winslow. Mercy, it was bad. There was that time Mabel found her in the bathroom with her wrists cut. Now *that* was a day. That was the end of visits to The Hill for Mrs. Abigail Winslow. She was off to that home in Boston and Mabel never saw her again. If it hadn't been for Mabel's efforts to bind her and get help (the men were all off fishing), she would not have lived. It was just a fluke too that she'd happened to go check on the wood supply and had knocked to see if Mrs. W. wanted anything. And there she was in the tub full of water all red with her blood and looking like death had already taken her off.

Mabel turned her attention to Eleanor once Lily was calmed down. There was one you never had to worry about, Mabel thought. Ellie was solid as a chunk of granite, and no matter what happened Ellie would probably hold herself together and keep everyone else on an even keel as well.

"You all right?" she asked the ten-year old.

"Nothing yet to not be all right about," Eleanor answered. "Not yet."

"Well, likely there won't be."

"Mabel?"

"Yes, sweetie?"

"Will you wake me if they come back? Will you come wake me, if there's any news?"

Mabel rose and switched off the lamp. "I surely will. Now you try to sleep."

And she did. She really did try. Counted sheep and everything, because whatever happened, there would be a lot to do in the morning and she was so tired. Her mind ached with all the possibilities, good and bad. She needed her rest. If something had happened to her parents, she thought, she would be in charge of everything.

When Ellie woke again, her face was turned to the wall. It was pitch dark in the room, but she heard very soft voices downstairs. She looked out the window and could see the shape of a truck in the soft lights coming from the cottage. She got out of bed quietly so as not to rouse

Lily, and, carefully as she could, opened the door so she could hear. They were in the kitchen. She had to move closer to the stairs and it was then she could just make out, over the murmur of voices, the sound of Mabel weeping.

Chapter Eleven

"Drop thy still dews of quietness,
Till all our strivings cease:
Take from our souls the strain and stress,
And let our ordered lives confess
The beauty of thy peace."

"Rest," # 435, Episcopal Hymnal, 1940

Tune: Frederick C. Maker, 1887: Text: John Greenleaf Whittier, 1872

The first spring Lily was caretaker at The Hill, she called Frank Guilbeault Junior, from Guilbeault's Marina, when she needed someone to look at the old Dix Runabout, which had been out of the water and under a tarp for about three years. It was just such a beautiful thing, that boat from the nineteen-forties. It needed to get back in its natural habitat and gleam just like it had when Lily and Eleanor were girls and Mack used to take them across the shining lake to the marina. There, Frank's dad, Frank Senior, and his wife, Tillie, would let them pick out their own bait and lures and give them cold sodas out of the big ice cooler in the back of the store, where it smelled of damp cedar, gasoline and old boat manuals.

Frank came over to look at the boat early that spring, as soon as the road was passable after a mud season that lasted so long into May that year, and he looked around and saw how well everything had been taken care of and how Lily talked about the boats as if they were her old friends, each with a story, and how she remembered his dad. And

Frank remembered aloud when he used to come with his dad back then, when Charles Winslow was just a young man, to help out with restoring old guide boats and the runabouts like this one and even some grand old Rushton canoes from Canton.

Frank told everyone down at the store and at the marina how everything was all swept out at that boathouse and neatified and ready for him to look at. He said he pointed to the roof of the old boathouse at a big old black raven there that seemed to be watching them and Lily looked up and said, "Oh that's Schwartz, he's my buddy," and she tossed the bird some bread from her pocket and the raven bowed and ate it. He'd never seen the like, Frank said. And when she showed him to the dining hall, he said, the place just gleamed like she polished the floors and tables every day. Not only that, but she made a fine cup of coffee! He couldn't imagine why no one ever married that woman and straightened her out sooner.

And wasn't it the truth, he told them at the store, that time and moon tides will shape someone out to be so different than when you knew them before. No wonder Jim was crazy about her. They were two of a pair, Jim and Lily, crazy as hooty-owls in some ways and just as nice as they could be in others. He'd remembered aloud to Lily, he said, when his dad and Jim Porter's dad came back from the search up around Owl's Head that dreadful night with the ice so thick two of the state vehicles went off the road on the way and how they had to climb and slip and climb and slip and climb and only found the wreckage by following the smell. "And you know the rest," he said to Lily.

"No I don't actually. What smell? No one ever told me. I was so little. I don't really remember much. What smell?"

"Oh, I'm sorry. I shouldn't be bringing up old sorrows."

"What smell, Frank?"

"Oh Lily, the plane, every . . . thing burned so badly. They knew the location of the wreck pretty much by the last radio contact and the fire. But once the crews got out there in the woods downwind of the crash, the only way they could find it was by the smell of the burned . . . you know . . ."

Lily stared down at the table in the kitchen where they sat, where she had spent her last hours with Mariette making bread and scones for tea in December 1952, where she'd written her letter to Santa Claus.

"Was there a dog, Frank? Did anyone find a dog?"

"What?"

"I had asked for a puppy for Christmas. I wondered if anyone . . ."

"No, Lily. I don't think they had a dog with them. There wasn't much of anything left. And what was there crazy folk tore to pieces for souvenirs. Brought in acetylene torches even. Some of our folks went up when they heard that and they cleared it all away. Every bit of it. Be done with it. Disgusting. I hear even now there's bits of that plane at auctions. Just madness to be so disrespectful. What a tragedy."

"I know. Jim and I hiked up there once to see if we could find it. He knew where to look. I wanted, you know, to put some kind of marker there or something. But I never did."

"My dad took me up once much later. You could still see the impact back then. I was maybe sixteen. Dad said all they could find that wasn't burnt was one Christmas bow, you know, like you put on top of a present. Stuck up in a tree it was. My dad fotched it down and kept it for years. It's gone now. I don't know whatever happened to it. The woods took over the site by the time you were grown up enough to hike up there." Frank took a sip of coffee and stared hard at the old wood cookstove, as though he could remember Mariette there, stirring some great pot of venison stew for the hunters from town that came every year to trek out with Charles Winslow and Robert Martindale, get their own limit and fill the larder at The Hill. Those were some fine days—his first hunt with his dad was right here at The Hill. And Mariette made a fine stew. Man, that woman knew how to cook, her laughing and singing all the while.

He roused himself from his silent reverie and said, "I love the woods for that, for taking over. Man passes through, lives and dies, but the woods cover up all trails, given 'nough time. Beautiful spot, up there, Owl's Head."

"I remember. I haven't been back for years." Lily was quiet for a moment, and Frank sipped his coffee. "I don't know where I've been, Frank," she said, "but I'm home now."

Frank reported all this to Sue Ellen and Pastor Clara and they all nodded and knew that Lily was right. "She's home now. That's for sure," Pastor Clara said.

Lily took herself to Owl's Head on a two-day hike not too long after Frank drove off with the Dix Runabout loaded on his trailer. The hike was sixteen miles as the crow flies, but it took a lot longer than that to maneuver around the ponds and streams and marshy areas. She didn't tell anybody she was going, which was stupid but she had to make the trip by herself. She didn't want Jim along, talking all the while; she didn't want anybody. She wasn't sure where to look, but she knew Frank was right. She climbed all over the flank and shoulders of Owl's Head, bushwhacking like a maniac, but after nearly forty years the woods had reclaimed the site and she couldn't find it.

She camped in a spot looking down over Upper Chateaugay. She lay awake all night listening to the barred owls, and a fox yipped just outside the campfire's circle of light, but the voices she truly hoped to hear did not speak to her. It was a beautiful night full of stars and sounds, but the presence of her parents and the Winslows was not in that place. The site of their deaths did not hold them. The little that was left of them that had not been cremated by the crash and explosion was carried back to New York City and encrypted in a columbarium at St. Bartholomew's on Park Avenue. But that was just the trash and detritus of their mortality. *They* had, like Lily, gone back to camp where they belonged, the place they had most loved in all the world. The Hill was full of them, and not just in the photographs in the butler's pantry.

Jim, of course, would have led her right to where it happened, but that just didn't seem to be what mattered any more, the where and the awful how. It was what happened after that she needed to get down to the work of getting over. Getting over herself. And that, pretty much, was what she spent the next ten years doing—forgiving not the fates that took her family, but herself for making such a mess of her life afterward. To honor the shreds of memory she carried with her always, she built a cairn of stones, in the most likely spot she could find, before she headed back the next morning. She left a piece of paper beneath the stones with all their names on it and the words: "Rest. Peace. Love, Lily."

Peace and the heart. Lily's fretful muscle and the ruby fluid it pumps, now under examination at the hospital in Saranac Lake. It's a ruined heart. And here's another sweet-voiced doctor to cheer her up and then what? Hold her hand into the next world? She's lived more than ten years in the clean air, with the hard physical labor of shepherding the camp and the cabin through the four seasons, two of which are so arduous (winter and mud—she doesn't count black flies since they don't seem to bother her that much) that simply to move one's body about is a physical challenge.

And now this awkward heart, with valves that stumble open and closed, receives and dispenses damaged goods and services with some apprehension, as though anticipating a sudden work stoppage. It inflates or puffs itself up a bit, a matter of seconds' worth as a warning that whatever she's doing or thinking is wrongheaded. Her heart—the scold. Sometimes it swells to the point that it presses against her left lung, causing her to cough, and that hurts. Other times it lies dormant, quietly pumping away as it's supposed to, like a gentle, faithful, panting dog with its tail thumping on the hooked hearth rug. She thinks it was always this way with her heart—these intermittent periods of barking and calm.

It was most pronounced when she lived in the city and trying to do too much, keeping absurd hours and drinking astounding quantities of black tea and alcohol. She saw a cardiologist then at the hospital and he explained the trickiness of the mitral valve and pronounced it benign but worth listening to with regard when it stirred. She generally paid as much attention to it as she did to her hair. But lately it had been waking her in the night and not letting her sleep as it kept up its weird jazzy rhythm. Her heart is broken from loss, lots and lots of losses. Over time, that will take its toll.

Dr. Bhijan Habib recognizes Lily Martindale as soon as she comes into the emergency room at the hospital in Saranac Lake. How extraordinary, after all these years since Switzerland, where they'd been in school together. He was a couple of classes behind Eleanor and just ahead of Lily's, so they weren't friends at the time. He remembered hearing the story about the plane crash and the orphans clinging together and all the ballyhoo that ensued in the press and the courts of law. He remembered some of the children at the school calling Lily "Cinder-Lily" as the American papers had done, which brought Lily to such a rage that she threw some punches, gave a girl twice her size a black eye. He remembered how some of the students had rushed to be friends with Eleanor, but how Lily, at least at the beginning, was sullen and quiet, stayed by herself, with only Eleanor as a compatriot.

And here is that same Lily, on his watch. He has no idea what has happened to her since school. How odd are God's ways, to bring two such different and yet similar human beings together—both of them alone, loners. How often he has thought about this very person, what her life must have been like in the ensuing years, how she has fared, compared to him.

She presents with a rapid, irregular pulse, glistening skin. She's pale and feverish and pretending to be unconscious; probably the shock of the trip, the hospital. When they move her, even gently, she moans and cries out in pain, as if everything hurts. They say that she's been in the woods a long time, living up at the old Winslow Camp. He's hiked around there before, but never trespassed. Never imagined she would be there. At school, when she came out of her shell, at the odd times she did, she was so bright and funny. She was the class clown—wit with a sharp and bitterly honed edge. He remembered her toiling in the chapel (Bhijan had been an acolyte), cracking wise about the choir or the headmaster, sneaking the communion wine and getting caught. It seemed that Lily was always in trouble. And then he graduated and came to the states for college and medical school, and never heard more of Lily Martindale, until now.

"Miss Martindale? Lily? Do you remember Bhijan from school? It's Bhijan. I'm a doctor now, Doctor Habib. I'm the attending physician here at Saranac Lake. Oh, come on, you can talk to me. Don't be afraid. I remember you in the chapel, cutting up, stealing wine. We're old friends, aren't we? Or at least we knew each other. Don't you remember?"

The mention of school gets Lily's attention more than the name Bhijan, although she seems to have an image of a young boy, small, dark and shy, who helped her polish the chapel brass before the Christmas holidays and smiled at her jokes, before she and Eleanor would meet Padre to go skiing at Gstaad, where Lily would fume and complain that she only wanted to go home to Mack and Mabel, and why was everyone being so mean to her? God, she was such a pain in the ass. She hated everything and everyone. She probably hated little Bhijan, too. Was he the one, or one of the ones, that had to stay at school during the holiday because he had no home? Was he the one whose mother was hanged in Persia for being Baha'i? Father and son escaped or something, to France. She wonders if little Bhijan was one she had been mean to, made fun of when he couldn't get the altar candles to light. God what a mess. Why can't she just die? She closes her eyes tighter and turns her head away from the soft voice of the man who claims to be a boy acolyte and a doctor at the same time.

Dr. Bhijan Habib shakes his head. "You are going to be fine, Lily, Miss Martindale. I will take good care of you. You were so funny. So don't worry. Your friends will be coming here. The old school gang, say what? You will be well cared for, Lily Martindale. You will be treated tenderly, I will see to it personally. Meanwhile, I'm giving you something to ease the pain. I see that you are hurting, and we can't have that."

Dr. Habib turns to go, taking a crew of people with him, barking orders in a wholly different voice, shouting outside to the press, military, Jim Porter and law enforcement that no one is to bother his patient. "They can wait until morning, all of them. They can talk to me in the meantime."

Hah! Lily thinks. Since when has anyone given a rat's ass about me?

She cracks her eye open. It is now nighttime. The room is dim with a few sources of glowing light. She's hooked to a monitor and an IV drip. She would, under any other circumstances, rip them off and head out, but she's way too tired and she hurts too much. Where is that doctor, she thinks, trying to remember what terrible offenses she must have committed against little Bhijan. She thinks of him with cute little rabbit ears, a cute little brown rabbit, dancing. Yes, there had been dancing classes—ballroom dancing. She had danced with Bhijan, that little shy brown rabbit. She would like to dance with him again. They were both so uncomfortable—he with his permanently cast-down eyes, which would, if she made a joke, suddenly sparkle and light up. Maybe she hadn't been unkind to him because he was a rabbit. Didn't she used to call him "Rabbit," and it started all the students doing so?

She would like to sleep now. No dancing tonight. Dancing tomorrow. Dancing with Bhijan. She is loved. Beloved. Maman and Papa are with her, Mariette sitting in the chair by the wall, Robert leaning against the end of the hospital bed smiling at her. She's feeling better now, much better. She'll smile and joke around with the flyboys and their brass. She will show them around the camp, tell them about the fateful night when she and Eleanor were orphaned. She can be good with people when she wants to. She was good with all the trespassers that rang the old bell, disturbing her peace with questions and problems. She can charm the pants off them all. People, animals—they're all alike.

The raven known as Schwartz sits in the ruins of a dead white pine on the lake side of the cabin on The Hill Next. He has finished off the hare Lily snared for him. He had to spar at one point with the three-legged fox for the last bit of bone and rib. It is mid-evening and the ice fishermen, one of them Frank Guilbeault Junior from the marina, are down on the other side, the other end of the lake, in their huts. Schwartz will pay them a visit later on, but the sound of a car catches his attention first. He'd watched as Jim drove out hours earlier, after the helicopter left. Now someone is coming in. Schwartz flies down to the main camp to a perch on the boathouse to watch, preens a bit, and gives one croak as though in greeting.

Colin and Eleanor drive up in the Subaru, stop, get out and stretch, looking around. The raven flies to the rail of Doxology Lodge. Eleanor sees him first.

"Hello, Schwartz. Where's your sweetheart?"

"Meal ticket, you mean. Old beggar."

Schwartz watches as Colin carries the suitcases in and then reemerges to drive around to the dining hall to unload his coolers of food. Schwartz follows.

Colin sets the first of the coolers down just inside the kitchen entrance. The dining hall is cold. The thermostat reads forty-five degrees, so Colin turns it to sixty-six. He sees that the old wood cookstove in the kitchen is ready to light in case anyone wants supper. There's a supply of matches in a Mason jar by the stove. He extracts one, strikes it, and sets the flame to the base.

Things have not been attended to as of old, he notices. There are mouse droppings on the butcher block, dust on the surfaces and shelves, cobwebs in the rafters. Not awful, but it is obvious that Lily has not been present since the Christmas holiday. He's not surprised—it did not go well, and he wonders if that might have anything to do with Lily's present circumstance. Soon they would know.

Colin draws a large pail of water to heat. He plugs in the restaurant-grade refrigerator—something Jim had forgotten to do—and methodically, mechanically, begins to stock it with platters of dim sum, sauces, marinated flank steak, four still-frozen French racks of lamb, bags of crisp greens and chopped vegetables, six bottles of white wine and six of inexpensive Spanish sparkling wine (their house staple). From a large canvas tote he removes various cheeses and several loaves of homemade wholegrain and seeded bread, boxes of pastry, cookies and a *gateau* of pears and almonds—one of Lily's particular favorites. He assumes she's at the cabin awaiting their arrival. He mops down the counters and the old butcher block with Clorox from under the sink, and decides that the best thing to do, as always under every circumstance, is to cook something simple and fortifying. It is the most helpful thing he can do for himself, for Eleanor, for God knows who might show up in the next several hours. Cooking is what he is good at, what he loves and treasures. Cooking makes everything right. He ladles some water from the big pot into a smaller one, adds a beef bone he's retrieved from the cooler, washes out a stainless steel pan, and proceeds to sauté a few things, chop some herbs, open some cans of cannelloni, and make a brothy but substantially hearty Tuscan bean soup. It will be ready in an hour, come what may. Colin goes outside for a moment and notices that Schwartz is no longer there.

Jim Porter spends the better part of the evening talking to Captain Jeff, two representatives of the FBI, his own boss, and the local sheriff. As word gets around, they are joined by Pastor Clara, Sue Ellen Finn, and Tom and Mary Lou Aiken from the taproom, who make sure everybody knows they are welcome at Aiken's for a draught beer when they finish up here with Lily Martindale, who never harmed a soul in her life.

Dr. Bhijan Habib has cordoned off the entire floor, with one of the sheriff's men and one from the FBI standing guard outside Lily's room and no one allowed in except the head RN and himself and only if Lily rings or her monitor alarm goes off. He peeks in to make sure she is sleeping soundly. He has given her a decent sedative and she is connected to a heart monitor, which so far shows nothing more than a sinus tachycardia, probably intermittent or paroxysmal. He wants to schedule a stress test for later, and a psychiatric evaluation, and keep her for twenty-four to forty-eight hours depending on the findings, but he suspects she can be discharged in a few days and go home, whatever that means to Lily Martindale and, at this point, the FBI. He explains all of this to the authorities and to Jim Porter and the rest of the contingent from Winslow Station. When Pastor Clara insists on seeing her, he kindly suggests she wait until the morning and that everyone go have a good night's sleep because that is the only thing to do at this point.

Jim offers to relieve the officer sitting outside, but the sheriff and the feds, under the circumstances, decline his offer and stay hunkered down in place. The public affairs officer addresses the media and explains the situation, which "is still under investigation" but which involves no threat to anyone, least of all the United States of America, from Lily Martindale, who is currently under a doctor's care for a heart problem and will be undergoing a routine psychiatric evaluation in the next twenty-four hours. There has been considerable disagreement between the authorities and the good people of Winslow Station regarding both Lily Martindale's sanity (perfectly fine for the most part, like any other full-time Adirondacker) and her accuracy with a gun (reasonable but not sharpshooter) and intent to harm (absolutely none). The officials get a volley of angry complaints about the flyovers, which everyone understands the importance of in this new age of terrorism and a Unabomber, but which should not terrorize the good and honest, hardworking taxpayers of the Adirondacks.

Captain Jeff Andrews, one of the FBI officers, a squad of soldiers, and the sheriff head up to The Hill to talk to Eleanor Winslow Livingston. They leave in a convoy, with a wireless connection to Washington, D.C. Any slight excitement at the prospect of a manhunt, or the discovery of a nest of spies and bombers, seems to have settled down to the mere reality of a fifty-something woman with graying hair, heart trouble and attitude. The officials look exhausted and pissed off. Jim finds a chair and sits in the hall outside Lily's room for the night. The rest of the townsfolk head home to Winslow Station.

Chapter Twelve

"My God, thy table now is spread,
Thy cup with love doth overflow;
Be all thy children thither led,
And let them thy sweet mercies know."

"Rockingham," #203, Episcopal Hymnal, 1940

Melody adapted by Edward Miller, 1790; harmony by Samuel Webbe, 1820

Text: Phillip Doddridge, 1755

While Colin fusses over his Tuscan bean soup in the kitchen at Rockingham Hall, Eleanor pulls on boots and snowshoes, takes the largest flashlight she can find, and starts down the lane toward the cabins, testing the doors as she goes along out of habit, like Lily, almost mindlessly looking in the windows to see that everything is in order. She notices that, other than the plowed road, there are none of the usual tracks indicating that Lily or Jim has been present, until she gets to the base of the path that climbs to The Hill Next and rings the bell. Here, there are numerous tracks, skis mostly. She starts to climb. She is still a little jet-lagged and wants nothing more than to rest and have a drink by the fire, but she needs to find out what's going on, talk to Lily and Jim.

She stops to catch her breath a couple of times. Her lifestyle in the city and working for the United Nations is not conducive to strenuous exercise, though she tries to keep walking wherever she is and is known for her game readiness to explore whatever country she's visiting. The long airline flights are hard on her. Still, it's nice to be back at camp, breathing this crisp, cold air, feeling the ease of quiet peacefulness that envelops the woods and the lake. If only she could stave off the onslaught of the officials who are likely on their way.

When she gets within sight of the cabin, the sky is getting dark and there are no lights on inside. Now what about these tracks? She plays the flashlight beam over the deep ruts in the snow. She sees that the cabin door has been splintered. Frowning, she pushes it open, looks around. The old raccoon coat and the snowshoes are there, but otherwise there's no sign of Lily. The story plays out in Eleanor's mind as she follows the tracings left by snowshoes descending the switchback trail to the lake with a dragged weight in their midst, and there on the lake the place where the helicopter landed, snow blown in a frozen ring around the perimeter. Eleanor takes her time, thoughtfully, going back to Doxology Lodge. It's Lily that was carried out. Oh God, what if something terrible has happened to Lily? She tries not to think the worst. Maybe Jim has left a note or something. But he has not.

Eleanor gets on the phone at the lodge. There are a couple of possibilities—Saranac Lake, Burlington and Albany have helipads. She calls the hospital in Saranac Lake first, and gets stonewalled. She thinks to call back, does, and has Jim Porter paged. That works. When he gets to the phone, he tells her in detail as only Jim can do in his breathlessly animated voice, about how he found Lily and that she is under a doctor's care and everybody's saying she's finally lost it. But they won't let him in to talk to her and she has this foreign doctor that he's met once before and everybody says he's okay.

Ellie calms him down and assures him that he should stay there, that he's done all the right things, and there's nothing more she and Colin can do but wait here for the officials, who will likely want to talk to her. And they can damn well come to The Hill if they want, but she wishes they'd wait until morning. Jim informs her that they are already on their way.

Eleanor listens to Jim's explanations of all he has done to get The Hill ready for them, how there's some serious work that needs to be done on that sleeping porch, but she firmly tells him she has to go, and says goodbye. She drums her fingers on the arm of the Morris chair next to the phone. Looking out the window at Rockingham Hall, she sees the lights and the rise of smoke from both the fireplace and the kitchen

Colin will join her soon; he will make drinks. She thinks perhaps she should wait until these officials, whoever they are, have arrived at the camp before she drinks anything stronger than tea. Tea would be lovely right now.

Eleanor drags her own wheeled suitcase up the stairs of the lodge. The covers have been removed from the furniture and hastily dumped in the corner by Jim, but she notices that things are dusty and untended. Not like Lily. She wheels her bag to the far end, where the master suite looks over the lake. The sleeping porch off the side has about three feet of blown-in snow in it. She remembers speaking to Lily about that at Christmas. Until they can repair the struts and supports under the main deck, the sleeping porch is bearing too much weight. The canvas awnings have been replaced twice in her time, most recently about ten years ago, about when Lily took over. But one is now hanging ripped and useless and the screens are all pushed in as though a raccoon or something has foraged there, letting in the snow. The only possible reason is that Lily hasn't been here since Christmas. Eleanor sighs. Why always Christmas?

Eleanor sits on the bed, then slides around and falls back against the pillows, drawing her knees to her chest and pulling her fur coat around her. The room always makes her sleepy and sad—this bed where, two mattresses past, her mother and father had slept and embraced, the very bed, in fact, where Eleanor had been born. Mabel and Doctor Burton were in attendance on that day almost fifty-five years ago, in a scene that must have been like an old black and white movie; Charles Winslow and his buddy from the War Office in Washington Robert Martindale downstairs drinking and smoking Havana cigars and listening to the phonograph, turned up loud in case Emily was not as much of a trooper as they hoped. Eleanor wondered what music accompanied her birth. Charles and Robert had been such kidders; she imagined Beethoven, or Tchaikovsky's 1812 Overture. But no. They were jazz lovers and jazz would have been so soothing to them. Maybe Duke Ellington. Perhaps Billie Holliday.

It was late April when Eleanor was born. The daffodils that Mabel and Emily had planted were just coming up through the remaining snow around the lodge, and the whole world was full of full of anticipation and planning for America to join the war with Germany. Now, more than five decades later, all is silence and silently crumbling. The camp is almost one hundred years old and has held up better than she, Eleanor feels. But still, enough is enough.

She closes her eyes. It would be good to sleep, but she knows she hasn't time. Oh, how she wishes Lily and Jim had made a go of it. The child. There would have been others, too, possibly. Perhaps *she* should have tried again after the first miscarriage, but she'd thrown herself into her work. Now she was sorry she hadn't, now that she was staring at the future with time on her hands. It could have been something so wonderful, so alive, to have the place really lived in, children who loved the place as much as Lily and she—that infectious love of place. Eleanor is too stupidly sentimental and sad to be practical about The Hill, about Lily and now this coming invasion.

She hears the lodge door shut and Colin's tread on the stair and coming down the hall.

"They're here," he says simply. "The Hollow Men have arrived."

Eleanor says nothing.

"Shall I make a fire?" he asks.

"Yes, please," she replies. "Burn the whole place down."

Colin comes over to the bed, puts his arm around her and holds her while she cries.

"Lily, oh God, Lily. I can't do this anymore."

The morning after the ice storm was bright and sunny. Lake Winslow glistened like a white china dish. The rattle of the brittle branches and the cracks of breakage and ice shattered all around. These were the sounds that awakened Lily, age six, from a deep sleep. The sun was so bright coming in the window upstairs in Hyfrydol that it blasted the sleep from her eyes and with it any memory of the ice storm the night before. She looked across and saw that the other twin bed was empty and wondered if Ellie was up or had never slept there at all, but the sheets were pulled back.

Lily rubbed her eyes and realized she was still in her clothes—her Western-style shirt and dungarees that Ellie's mom had bought her last winter when they went to Arizona in January. The jeans were still a little big on her. She had to pull the beaded Indian belt tight and wrap the extra length back around and tuck it underneath so it wouldn't flop around. There were cowboy boots, too, red ones, but she couldn't wear them in winter because they weren't warm enough even with socks, and they were slippery. Ellie's mom had shown her how the heel was meant for saddle stirrups and desert walking. She said cowboys were often bowlegged from riding horses so much from boyhood.

Lily sat up in the bed. She thought she heard voices downstairs in the kitchen—Mack and Mabel. It was funny nobody had called her. She flopped back onto the pillow and closed her eyes, then opened them and chased the little floating eye gremlin that wandered around in her vision, the little pearlescence of a figure just out of sight. Presently she fell back into a kind of half-sleep with little fuzzy thoughts tiredly looming and receding.

Mabel let Lily sleep. She and Mack had stayed up late with Eleanor after word came on the wireless and Jerry Hammill, the state trooper, made it through to the camp in his truck. Then they put Ellie down on the couch where they could keep an eye on her after giving her a hot milk, honey and brandy. The girl understood, Mabel knew. She understood all too well.

Mack got in the truck with chains on the tires and drove in to the Station. They'd need all the help they could get, if they could get it. Everybody would have their hands full after such a heavy icing. Power lines, phone lines, burst pipes, dimwits who'd try to stay warm with a charcoal stove and die of carbon monoxide poisoning. He'd have to have the sheriff and rangers post a watch at the end of the camp road, because when word got out (and it was out), people were going to start making a commotion and the press, Lord, the newspapers would be all over them like leeches in a backwater.

And what about Christmas? What about the girls? What about all the people coming and no one to cook like Mariette and only Mack now to mind the livestock and the barn? The only good thing about this here, he thought, was that he'd be so busy, he wouldn't have time to think too much. This was when being an Adirondacker was a very good thing. Times got tough? People got tougher.

Mabel was in bad shape, but she knew she had to get the kitchen running, open the dining hall for the cops, the guides, the drivers, the searchers coming down from St. Regis, Malone and Owl's Head, and up from Placid and Saranac Lake. She'd need to make plenty of hot coffee, open up some guest cabins and rooms for people to get into hot showers and dry clothes. Hot water, hot coffee, sandwiches, doughnuts. She'd need help. She'd sent Mack to town with a list and knew he'd come back with plenty. She prayed Padre would get here fast. Tom had managed the wireless most of the night. Doris was prostrate, he'd told Mack. Mabel realized that Doris'd be precious little help. Good with the books, but not a crumb of help in the kitchen where she'd be needed.

Every time Mabel looked in on Lily she was sleeping. So little. Mabel kept shaking her head. She'd be sleeping like a sweet little dog, twitching a bit. Dear God in Heaven, this was just more than a body could bear. And she started to cry again.

Ellie woke up first. It was about nine a.m. She swung her legs over the edge of the sofa and blinked in the bright sunshine coming in the east window. She pulled on her sweater and slid her feet into a pair of socks, shivered, and picked up her shoes and went into the kitchen. Mabel was sitting at the table with a cup of coffee, her face red and puffy. She wrapped her arms around Ellie.

"Is Lily still asleep?" Ellie asked after awhile.

"Yes and I hope she stays that way. I need to pull myself together here. I need to get some help up here. Mack's gone to the Station to see what he can do."

"Does everybody know?"

"Everybody knows around here by now—Malone, Saranac Lake, Placid, Plattsburgh—all of them," Mabel paused. "They radioed out last night to Padre. I'll feel a whole lot better when he gets here."

"So will I. Padre will know what to do."

"You hungry?" Mabel asked.

"No. Yes. I can make myself some toast."

"I've left everything out. I've got to get over to the big kitchen. Can you keep an eye on Lily? When she gets up, you can both come over. I need you to be, oh Lord, just be with me, can you? I think if we all stay busy and organized, we'll get through this. Padre will be here soon."

"Sure."

"Let Lily sleep, though."

"I know." And Mabel knew she did.

Ellie fashioned herself a breakfast of toast, orange juice and Ovaltine and sat at the kitchen window looking out at the jeweled trees brightly lit by the sun, the white, shining hillside, the glistening iced lake, the smoke now rising from the kitchen flue in Rockingham Hall.

Ellie wondered how they were going to manage, and suddenly felt very new to herself. She would need to be different. She was ten. She thought of how important her father was and how now she had to be somehow like him, to make sure everything was okay. And her mother. Her mother was important, too. Both of them had been very important people—people who appeared in newspapers and magazines and even on the television. Every time Ellie thought she might feel like crying, she grabbed her hands behind her head and braced her neck back against them. She would cry later when it was dark, when no one could see. Lily would be there. That was important, too. She got out a piece of paper and made a list with a pencil. She listed all their names in order of importance, then redid it. First she had Padre as Most Important. When she redid it, she had herself as Most Important, then Lily, then Padre. Lily was like her sister. They had to be The Two Most Important, but Lily was only six, so that left Ellie to run the show.

Eleanor Winslow took her dishes to the sink and washed them carefully and put them in the drainer to the side. Then she went upstairs.

Lily was lying there in her clothes with the covers just over her feet. Ellie crawled quietly into the other bed. There was a stack of old comics on a shelf by the bed, left over from when Mack and Mabel's boys had lived there, before the war, before Ellie and Lily were born. There were Superman comics, The Phantom, Prince Valiant. She picked up one to read when Lily stirred.

"Hey."

"Hey."

Lily looked around to see what Ellie was doing. Then she looked out the window.

"Ooooh! Lookit," she said, "How cold is it? Can we go skating today?"

"Probably not. Probably not today."

"What are you reading?"

"Superman comics. Want one?"

"Sure."

Eleanor handed her one. "I'll make you breakfast if you're hungry. Mabel's gone over to Rockingham."

Lily crawled in next to Eleanor and looked at the covers of the comics. Eleanor flipped back to the beginning and started to read aloud. Lily stopped her frequently to ask questions. Who was Lex Luthor? Lois Lane? What was Kryptonite? The girls lay together like that for a little while, then Lily got up.

"C'mon. I'll make you breakfast," Ellie said.

"Where's *Maman*?"

"They're not back," Eleanor said, looking straight at her. "They didn't come back last night. Let's go down. I'll make cinnamon toast. Mabel's busy."

Lily leaned over to tie her shoes. She stood and they walked downstairs together.

"Why can Superman fly?" Lily asked on their way downstairs.

Ellie explained that he came from another planet. She explained about superpowers and hidden identities and bad guys. Lily listened carefully, while Ellie explained and made her breakfast. She listened and watched Ellie's face as she ate her toast. Ellie was her best friend. She didn't kid around much ever. She was pretty quiet and serious most of the time. But now she looked really, really sad.

"Lily. What if I was to tell you that they're not coming back?"

"That would be stupid."

"Yeah, I know. But what if it was true? What if they kept flying and flying and flying and flying until they were so far away they could never come back? What if they flew all the way to, you know, outer space or something? Another planet, maybe?" Ellie was crying. "What if they get all the way there, and it was just so beautiful, they decided to stay?"

"They'd come back."

"But they couldn't."

"Why?"

Ellie struggled for a bit. "No gas. Can't fly. Without it."

Lily looked out the window at the slick glaze on the snow, hard like boiled sugar candy, but so, so cold. She looked back at Ellie.

"I don't understand." She took another bite of toast and looked at Ellie's face. Lily was suddenly very afraid and very aware, like a dream, a bad dream was following her into the daytime.

"I get it. It was the ice. They crashed didn't they? They're not coming back because they crashed."

Eleanor looked around as if there might be someone to intervene for her, some angel, or ghost of a parent who might take Lily aside, comfort her once more, explain the truth.

"Are they dead?" Lily asked.

"Yeah." Eleanor was trying very hard not to cry, but it wasn't working. "Lily. What are we going to do?"

Lily put her last piece of toast down and got up and went over to Eleanor who was really, really crying now.

"I don't know, Ellie."

"Lily . . . what about Christmas?"

Lily looked up at her suddenly. "Christmas?"

Eleanor put her head in her hands. The Santa factor. She had completely forgotten about Santa. Lily was still a believer. It had been so easy to keep it that way, living up here in the woods so much. Christmas had gone down in the plane, too.

Lily, her hands still a little buttery from the toast, took Eleanor's hand. "It's just you and me, Ellie. And Mack and Mabel."

"And Padre's coming."

"We'll have Christmas, won't we?" Lily's eyes started to sting and her throat was closing up and it hurt a lot. She hated to cry and she knew she couldn't talk when she cried. She couldn't say what she needed to say, so they sat there, the two of them, sobbing and holding hands across an ocean of turbulent sorrow.

Chapter Thirteen

"Watchman, tell us of the night,
For the morning seems to dawn.
Trav'ler, darkness takes its flight
Doubt and terror are withdrawn."

"Aberystwyth," #440, Episcopal Hymnal, 1940

Tune: Joseph Parry, 1879; Text: John Bowring, 1825

For an hour following their arrival, the Hollow Men, as Colin called them, politely but firmly interrogate both Eleanor and her husband over Tuscan bean soup, wholegrain bread and a variety of sturdy cheeses in Rockingham Hall. After this they fan out into the chill of the night and pay particular and close attention to the layout of the camp, the number and type of boats in the boathouse, the contents of closets, cabinets, and especially the guns in the sturdy, locked gun case in the lodge. The deep silence of the camp is now filled with boots and the crackle of walkie-talkies.

Finally, they trek up to the cabin on The Hill Next and spend some time engrossed by the military trunk that once belonged to Lily's father, which contains a number of old composition notebooks with Lily's daily notes and sketches. Her old rifle is carefully handled and permission is requested to remove it from the premises for further examination. Eleanor agrees. She has not insisted on search warrants. What good would it do, even if she did? This is a federal matter. She stays wisely out of their way, and they are extremely polite and deferential. Even *they* are beginning to see that this is not a case of international terrorist activity or a mad bomber deep in the Adirondack Mountains. It is not in Eleanor's nature to interfere with such men (and they are all men). As cordial as they are, they are stern. Her years dealing with third world bureaucrats and government agencies are of inestimable value here, this night. Let them go through their specific, prescribed methodology. A simple glance at any of the notebooks reveals nothing more than Lily's repetitive daily routines about the camp, some thoughts on the weather, the nature of elusive happiness, and her better-than-average pencil drawings of the day's visitors to the cabin and its feeders. Outside in the such-as-it-is garden, the Blessed Mountain Woman in her bathtub elicits some puzzled looks and comments on the camouflage-painted robe and old guide hat. The privy, too, is examined with some comical thoroughness in the painful glare of their halogen flashlights. They even trek up the steep and slippery slope to explore the cistern and remark at the size of the enormous glacial erratic perched there at the top. Schwartz has not been seen since Eleanor and Colin arrived, and Eleanor does not see the importance of mentioning the presence of the creature in Lily's life. Eleanor watches the men silently and contains her growing irritation and exhaustion in smooth, glassy, ambassadorial calm.

Finally, they seem to be satisfied that they have found nothing more than what Eleanor had expected. There is no evidence of terrorist activity or sentiment in the solitary life of Lily Martindale. The cold is daunting to the men even more than Eleanor. They stumble back down toward the lodge and the warm fire waiting for them.

Eleanor sits in the Morris chair by the library fire, body forward, eyes bright and intent. She listens with impassioned interest and comments wisely. She explains once again that Lily Martindale is a dutiful caretaker, and it is extremely likely that she felt that either she or the property was somehow threatened by the military flyover. Remember, too, she notes, how isolated Lily is much of the time—without access to radio, phone or television in the life she has chosen for herself and in which, until recently, she has thrived. She is blissfully uninformed about the state of the world and the United States of America. She is politically and emotionally uninterested and unimpressed by anything outside the realm of the camp and her duties. Eleanor, being the good, international law–trained ambassador that she is, astutely parries all accusations and suggests that the FBI and the Air Force make sure that said A-10 Warthogs were flying above the regulation two hundred feet. (Everyone in the Adirondacks knows those pilots take flagrant advantage of the rules as they skim over treetops and housetops.) And surely there can be a compromise reached without resorting to legal harassment of a small, middle-aged woman like Lily. Right now, her health and well-being are paramount. Surely the officials and the government are satisfied there is no real threat or danger from such a person.

And Eleanor states what has only recently been on her mind, as if to reassure them. It is time, she says, that she had a different arrangement for The Hill. Lily has been a wonderful caretaker, but she is now ill. She's been ill since Christmas, it seems, when Eleanor and Colin last saw her. There have been years of emotional issues since the loss of their parents and the very stressful lives she and Lily have both led. Eleanor has been aware that Lily will have to retire someday and be replaced by someone younger and stronger. Perhaps this whole situation can be resolved if she retires sooner than later. Even Lily will realize that.

Colin huddles in the butler's pantry feeling out of sorts—not unusual for him. It's late. He's tired. He has plugged in the old coffeemaker in the pantry, ground his special blend, added a touch of cinnamon, and now stands there half listening, half wondering, half remembering. He is looking at the pictures on the wall just as Jim had done earlier that day— the long heritage of the Winslows, going back to Charles's parents and through to the last photograph. These photographs, aged and fading, still invite endless curiosity and speculation. But Colin now realizes there is a small, gritty bit of irritation brewing within him, standing there alongside the percolating coffeepot. He knows that neither his wedding to Eleanor, lo these many years ago, nor all their subsequent Christmases together on The Hill had constituted enough of an honor to be immortalized by a photograph on this particular wall. Sure, there are other photos up and down the stairs, in the bedrooms, in the hallways, pictures of their own sequence of notable friends visiting the camp. Those were Eleanor and Colin's celebrated moments with each other, with Lily and all the others. But not one of those photographs ever earned the honor of being placed here in the butler's pantry. He thinks he has not so much married a woman as an historical event, a tragedy, after which their own lives are a shadow play and himself, even he himself, an incidental character. They only seem to be a real couple in New York, where this separate life does not exist so strongly, so intensely. Up here at the camp, life is always about the camp, not about them, not ever; it's always about how to repair this, how to extend that, how to please Lily, whom to offer a coveted invitation. He, all along, has had only one important job, and that is to laugh, be jolly, and make sure that everyone is well fed. He once suggested to Eleanor that they turn the camp into an elite cooking school, and he would run it, he and Lily—Lily with her exceptional organizational skills and mind for budgets, hard-work ethic and love of the place. But no, Ellie couldn't see that. She couldn't see that at all.

How long has he, Colin, played the good husband, serving his wife's service to the country, the world, as ambassador of peace, aid to suffering indigent folk, succor to the poor? Eleanor, unstinting in her duties to her fellow citizens of the world. In New York it all makes sense. Here, it all unravels. New York is distraction and enjoyment of art, music and dance. Here is this bloody awful silence and remoteness. Lovely, yes, so lovely and quaint, rustic and peaceful and bloody awful. Colin wants to race to the horrible old Victrola, put on that scratchy old recording of Billie Holiday and wail along with the blues, driving the stuffed uniforms, the public servants, the Hollow Men, the defenders of the homeland far away with his wailing.

But the phone rings. Colin wipes his face, takes a quick breath, and answers.

"Hello? Yes? Oh, hello, Jim." Colin idly wipes down the counter as he listens. "That's a blessing. Well, we're a little tied up here now." He continues listening, shaking his head now and then. "Ellie's made some calls. We, she, hopes to resolve this tonight." He takes the tea towel he is holding and fusses with a spot at the corner of one of the photographs. "Tonight? Jim, it's so late. Can't it wait? We'll . . . sure Jim, we'll see you tomorrow then. Thanks so much. Kiss her for us. Oh . . . well. Oh, really!" He straightens his back, which has begun to stiffen a bit. His eyes examine the ceiling above seeking a means of escape from the endless conversation so typical of Jim. No wonder Lily had trouble with him. He was like a big wind-up toy, one of those that had a pull string and an ever repeating loop of chatter that never seems to stop in the hands of a mindless child. "Yes, Jim. That's very interesting. I'll tell Ellie. All right. Thanks again, Jim. Yes, Jim. Gotta go, Jim. Talk to you soon."

Colin hangs up the phone, takes another long slow breath. He leans over the sink, spits, and splashes his face with cold water, pats it dry with the Irish linen tea towel that he had been gripping, wiping, twisting and fussing with. It was one on which Mabel had demonstrated to the girls how to hem on a rainy summer day; the very tea towel, in fact, that had covered over the sandwiches served at high tea four nights before the plane went down. The spring before, the Winslows had made a trip to England and brought back yardage of fabrics from Harrods to make bath towels, tea towels and hand towels for the guest cottages and the kitchen. Colin doesn't know all this and would not want to know how this common item is as steeped in the very history which does not now and will never entirely include him. Instead, he mops his face with the tea towel, pours the coffee into a silver-plate pot on a silver-plate tray next to the cream, sugar, spoons, china cups and a tin of cookies from Fortnum and Mason. Then, nobly, as always, enters the library with his burden to serve.

When the phone rings again that night it is the governor, and a conference call transpires with the gentlemen of the FBI, the state trooper, the public affairs officer and the head ranger from Malone. While she talks on and off the phone, Eleanor pats the seat beside her and pours a cup of coffee for Colin.

"That was Jim, before," he tells her. "He wanted to come up tonight, but I told him it wasn't a good time. He said Lily's condition is stable, not life-threatening—some heart irregularity, possibly induced by stress, dehydration, generally not taking care of herself very well. So they're going to keep her under observation and have a psychiatric evaluation done. The doctor ran some other tests, too. Evidently she was in some pain. So at best a few days, possibly a week depending. She can refuse all the psychiatry stuff, of course, but then she's more at the mercy of the law—"

"I think this is going to work out," Eleanor interrupts. "I think they understand. This call should resolve it."

"But the psychiatric thing?"

"Well, yes. We'll wait for that. Lily will have to agree to that, for her own good. But we need to talk about The Hill. I think it's time to move on. I've been thinking."

Colin's eyes widen and he takes a very deep breath. "Oh, Eleanor. Yes. Yes! It's time."

"It's absolutely time for Lily. She's been here too long."

"Oh, Ellie, you did the best thing bringing her back to face her dreams and demons."

"We'll do right by Lily and The Hill. I think I have the answer."

Colin takes another sip of coffee. He is feeling much better by the moment. "I'm sure they will insist that she leave here, get treatment, retire, whatever. They don't hold all the cards. She did hit the jet."

"Not all of them. Lily and I still hold The Hill."

"Oh, before I forget," Colin helps himself to more coffee, "Jim mentioned the name of her doctor—Bhijan Habib. Says he went to school in Switzerland. Knew Lily there, and you."

"How interesting. Name rings a bell."

"Still, he's an ally, a possible godsend."

By the time the contingent of government, military and local law enforcement return from the phone in the living room, it is clear they are finally convinced that their fears were unmerited and there can be a very simple solution worked out regarding Lily Martindale. When the president of the United States calls and talks to Captain Jeff Andrews and his coterie, the evening's sortie in the Adirondacks comes to a formal end.

Lily had been at The Hill as caretaker for some years when she realized she had been away so long that she had lost touch with time. The seasons passed, that was clear enough; but she had no idea about the state of the world, what movies were hot, what was the price of a gallon of milk. She was isolated most days of the year without desiring access to television or radio, although there was a radio down in the lodge. After a period of time, such things did not mean anything to her—news, world affairs, politics. She could tell the weather well enough by looking out the window and watching the wind. Even in the frequent tempests that shook the mountains, and the presence of avalanches, blizzards and ice storms, she was never afraid. What had come to terrify her were Labor Day and New Year's.

Twice a year, on Labor Day and New Year's, Eleanor commanded Lily to come down from The Hill Next and meet people. Twice a year she dressed in one of her old India print cotton skirts and a peasant blouse and attended Eleanor's gatherings of people whose names and faces most people would recognize in a skip of the heart. Their faces were as unknown as Lily's had become with age and time, but she needed to walk among them, Eleanor insisted, just to keep her sociable. Sometimes those faces were strained, bored, sloshed. Sometimes the conversation soared so far above Lily's head with events and gossip of which she had no concept. Then she would retreat to the porch to sit and toss tidbits to Schwartz.

Although some of Eleanor's friends had met Lily over the years, she became an object of profound fascination during her long stint as Eleanor's resident hermit. She had become as out of touch as a Cistercian monk. The writers, politicians, artists, filmmakers, stars, whoever they might be, would ask Lily to tell them of her life. Their most common question was "What do you do in winter?" meaning that they would be off to sunnier, warmer places of the world or hunkered down over *important* jobs, while Lily, who once, they knew, had had an important job and loads of money, would be frittering her time away up here in the snow and cold. "Don't you miss civilization?" was the other, as if everything she could glean from their conversations would tempt her back to her life of medicated rage. Sometimes the more sensitive guests would express their simple envy (as if they truly understood) and desire to lead a life such as hers. They would invite her to switch with them for a day or a week (as if she were interested in being a tanned, tucked, massaged sybarite). Some thought Lily was depressed or a lunatic. Some eminent Park Avenue type would want to counsel her, suggesting that she had been suffering all along from an extended, protracted post-traumatic something or other. Some would want to film her, camp out with her, or worse, sit *darshan* as though she was a holy one. She told them all to fuck off. The new and uninitiated would be warned about this. Still, they persisted.

But sometimes, not often, there was one who truly seemed to understand, even through their confusion at times, about the life, the state Lily had chosen. One of these, she was later told in gasps of hilarity, was the president, who asked her to call him by his first name. One New Year's, Lily took this man and his wife on a cross-country ski around the property through the woods, with some other strange guys following behind. The quiet (which, along with the raven, the wind and the wind chimes, Lily took for granted and honored in her own life as anthropomorphic companions), this silence was as alien to the president as ignominy, and as uncomfortable. This chummy, first-name-basis, Leader of the Free World skied along remarking aloud at the silence, the landscape, the cold, and then, seconds later, remark at it again, and seconds later again, with a voice that grew louder and louder each time.

At one point, Lily turned to him and said, "You remind me of a child in church."

The president blinked and cocked his head and then frowned. He realized he was about to be scolded.

"You fill the space in an act of pure domination, hubris," Lily said matter-of-factly. "You are so foolish. You're like all the jerks who ever came in here with a chainsaw and a plan. You don't get it."

"I'm sorry. Get what?"

"That this is all there is—this solitude, this silence. Out here you can die from not listening attentively enough. You could die not paying attention. So shut the fuck up."

The ensuing seconds were awkward, but Lily would not have known it, for she had launched off on her skis down the trail. The man and his wife followed, stunned. From that moment on, he was silent. When they finished the short trek, he came to Lily and very gently embraced her with such tenderness and sadness that she knew he had heard the silence and had learned something. Indeed, they say that in some ways he was a changed man from that moment on. To a point, anyway.

Back in the days of the first Winslows, it was clear that the senior Mrs. Winslow, neurotic and depressed as she was, was driven further to dread, despair and misery by the silence and remoteness of the camp. For a while she tried to bring a maid with her from Boston, but her imperious manner made it difficult, even during the Great Depression, to keep someone in tow, and the maids, too, hated life away from the city. The earnest, devout Irish. The earnest, devout Negroes. The sturdy Romanian woman who massaged her twice daily, fed her fortifying broths, and force-marched her on long invigorating walks down to the lake. Only Mabel, then a much younger woman and yet with years in the Adirondacks, approached her with the stoic kindness, no-nonsense firmness and patience that life in the North Country produced like thick, tannic bark on the hemlock. She minded and bustled and Mrs. Winslow accepted her with what little graciousness her distraught temperament could muster. But Mrs. Winslow came less and less frequently to camp and never during hunting season, and finally never again, after the suicide attempt when Mabel found her in the bathtub.

The Winslow men loved the concept of the "random scoot," the wisdom of the old guides like Jim Porter's dad and Mack, too. They loved tramping endlessly to this peak or that stream, loved the still-hunt for the white-tailed deer, the attention paid to the hatches of mayflies. It was, would always be, a man's world full of manly tests. And as men, they always passed; but Mrs. Winslow, alas, failed. It was Charles and later Emily, Robert and Mariette, as in love with the landscape as they were with each other, who passed the devotion on to their daughters. The tramps through the woods, the paddles on the still lake waters and the carries upstream to the better, bigger trout, the swimming challenges, the climbing, the evenings by the campfire or in the library reading to the girls, listening to good jazz on the Victrola. This was love as big as the hearts of the mountains, as strong, as hard and as deep.

Lily was born of that love. Lily was tough. But everyone gets older, and no matter how strong the sinew and the nerve, Time's rasp files us down. All that stuff of the past piles up on top of you like the shifting crust on the deep snow that curls and lips over the rock shelf, needing only the merest sneeze to send it avalanching down. The mountains, the winter, can be deadly to those who are weak, careless and unprepared. The mountains can also bestow great vision and health. Lily's last climb would be the hardest of all.

Chapter Fourteen

"He who would valiant be
'Gainst all disaster,
Let him in constancy
Follow the Master."

"St. Dunstan's," Hymn #563, Episcopal Hymnal, 1940

Tune: Winfred Douglas, 1917; Text: John Bunyan, 1684

The news of the tragic deaths in December 1952 of Charles Winslow Junior and Emily Linstead Winslow wiped everything else off American and European headlines for weeks. The loss of the handsome couple, the end of the promise of a potentially great national leader, was awful enough. But it was a reporters' and photographers' free-for-all. Suddenly the very private life of a very interesting couple was made very public.

And there was the child. Every journalist angled to get close to, get a shot of the little Winslow heir: Eleanor. Dubbed "Little El" by the press, she became "America's Orphan Princess," beloved, prayed for, hunted. The Hill became an armed camp to keep out members of the press and the public. Mack and Mabel had their backs to the wall, pressed there as much by grief as by their efforts to protect The Hill's perimeter (with the help of not only every available state trooper and ranger, but also a small contingent of the National Guard). The state and the National Guard posted warnings that trespassers would be arrested and prosecuted to the full extent of the law, First Amendment notwithstanding. If it hadn't been for that and the harsh Adirondack winter, The Hill would have been overrun.

Mack and Mabel readied the camp as well as possible for Christmas without a particle of joy in the process. Food was laid in—much of it ordered weeks before for the expected guests. Mabel's cooking expertise was mainly pedestrian farm-style heartiness and her logging camp breakfasts were legendary, but Mariette was the one who knew what to do with duckling and grand cuts of beef, the kind that the Winslows' people liked cooked rare and bloody, a thing that made Mabel shudder.

"Naught to do," Mack would say. "Just soldier on here with your good stews, and their wine stores will take care of all else. I'll ask Joe Finn and the Aikens if they know what to do with a side of beef like that there. Ah, lookit here! A big haunch of pork. Cook that to death and no one will care with a mess of stewed apples on top. There you go, old girl. There you go. And you know how to do a turkey, don't you?"

The good people of Winslow Station, Doc Burton, the Finns and everyone pulled together to help out, every one of them, and never asked a nickel for their time or their services. It was a terrible time, but as Mack kept saying, "Naught to do. Naught we can do but keep a-goin' here."

Before he left New York after hearing the news, Padre called the friends to ask them not to come to The Hill for Christmas. He wanted to keep the tragic holiday as simple as possible while he decided what was best for The Hill, the help and Eleanor. This did not sit well with Julietta at all. She wanted to be in the thick of the tragedy, although she didn't say that, instead draping her enthusiasm for drama in the cloak of wanting to help. Padre was firm, even curt with her, and that became the beginning of the dissolution of the group of old friends: the women in petty bickering with Padre and/or each other, James and Jack in divisive support of Padre or of one of the women over the other, and Padre in the middle, unable and unwilling to exert the energy needed to hold the old friends together. It seemed that, for as long as the Winslows had been alive, there'd been a reason to be friends. Lacking them, the center collapsed, and no one could understand how they had ever been so close. In the end, it was like any family squabble, but like any family squabble, all the wrong reasons to differ were taken to heart, nursed with toxic emotions and bitter recriminations. The difference here was that most of this took place in the public forum of the press. That's not something anyone could ever succeed in foisting on Padre. Invoking the treasured love of privacy the Winslows had held inviolate, Padre shut the door in everyone's face. The former friends, and the press, loathed him for it. Thankfully, the simple people of the town, the camp, kept their wits about them and were of invaluable service to Padre. Mack and Mabel, of course, would stay on and protect the family's interests at the camp. Their two sons agreed to return home temporarily to help, too, but they had families and jobs in other states that they couldn't leave for long.

Doris and Tom, suddenly finding themselves at the center of a maelstrom of unwanted interest, begged to be let go to return to England. Padre asked them to stay on as Eleanor's tutors until some other schooling could be arranged for her. They reluctantly agreed, but only until the coming spring. Everyone assumed that Eleanor would be placed in school in New York, close to Padre.

Speculation ran rampant about Padre's closeness to any one, any woman who might be a prospective bride. He was, after all, Eleanor's godfather, and as such could be deemed not only her religious patron, but likely her guardian as well. In control of the legal affairs of the Winslows, Padre would be, as the press put it bluntly, "sitting pretty" on a vast pile of Winslow wealth, of which Charles Winslow had been the only steward. (In addition, there was a considerable amount of money from Emily Winslow's inheritance.) Then there were all of Charles Winslow's political connections and aspirations—a mantle to be assumed by someone well connected to his inner circle. Who could that possibly be, except his dearest friend and advisor, Joseph Wingate MacIntyre, Esq.? Some nasty words in the press alluded to Padre's possible complicity in bringing the plane down somehow, until the state and federal investigators scotched that evil rumor with their evidence that it had been the ice storm, pure and simple. They shouldn't have been flying that night. That was all there was to it. And no one would ever know why they took the chance, or if they were surprised, so close to landing at Malone, by the sudden buildup of ice on the wings of the plane and the awful recognition that they had made a fatal mistake.

At the other end of the spectrum of newsworthiness, Padre was deemed "Most Eligible Bachelor of the Year" by one of the society columns in New York.

And poor Eleanor. Padre worried that there would be, as there had in the thirties, the threat of kidnap, extortion, violence. Not since the dramas surrounding the Lindbergh baby, Gloria Vanderbilt, or Shirley Temple, had the public's fears and desires concerning a young child so maddeningly consumed a whole nation. "Little El" was big news. And about to get even bigger.

Meanwhile, the fate of another little girl seemed to have been entirely ignored, at least in those early days after the plane crash.

As Mabel had predicted, the camp became a harbor for all those who had participated in the search or manned the barricade into the camp, as well as the people of Winslow Station, who came to offer help and stayed to commiserate and mourn. They in turn reported to the outside world that The Hill would survive this terrible upheaval. They reported that Eleanor had seemingly taken it as her responsibility to be present with the visitors and helpers, accept their embraces, tears and condolences, show them where they could clean up if they'd been working up at Owl's Head.

The camp cleared out by nightfall the day after the accident, except for the shifts at the end of the camp road. The older Finns (Sue Ellen was not yet born and Joe was a toddler in diapers) stayed the longest to help Mabel with the cleanup. The pastor back then, Pastor Dan, wearing a crisp but too-small cook's apron that looked like a handkerchief on his stout frame, outdid himself in hard physical labor at the kitchen sink, washing endless dishes. His wife, Peggy, proved to be a master at baking and took over that chore from Mabel. It was the last time after Mariette's death that flour flew with such abandon in the Rockingham Hall kitchen until Colin appeared many years later. Eleanor and Lily took turns helping Mabel in the kitchen or serving coffee and doughnuts, sandwiches and macaroni salad in Rockingham Hall. In many ways, this frantic need to serve, to thank, to participate was far better for the girls than any private mourning. They fell into bed at Mack and Mabel's that first night exhausted and slept through until late the next morning.

That next day, St. Dunstan's, Padre's usual cabin, was readied for him. Mabel (with the girls again helping, to keep them busy) freshened the sheets and the air with newly cut balsam boughs in a jug, dusted the bureau and the fireplace mantel, and scoured the sink and tub. Most everyone else had gone home except for the pastor's wife, who took care of the kitchen while Mabel tended to the lodge and cabins. She secured the doors of the Winslows' and Martindales' rooms, until Padre could get there.

Doc Burton left, after giving Doris a sedative and instructions for bed rest until she felt stronger. She rose late on the second day, pale and haggard but determined to serve where she could. Tom kept by the wireless radio, fielding messages, offers of help, requests for interviews and expressions of deep mourning from around the United States and the world. The phones had come back on later the first day, and Mack and Tom finally succeeded in getting all calls routed to the Winslow office in New York City, where secretaries worked around the clock dealing with inquiries and requests, and handed out or dictated prepared statements to the press.

Mack, relieved that the phone had at last stopped ringing so much, loaded up the wagon with wood as Robert would have done and made his deliveries around the camp, making sure that everything was in good shape. Mack carried four loads of wood to St. Dunstan's, anticipating that Padre would be staying for some time in the cabin. Mack's mind was working overtime. He was exhausted and grieving and his knees and back were giving him trouble. He wasn't getting any younger, was Mack. He needed to look to the future and trust in the Almighty for strength. His sons would help out as much as they could. They'd be coming in that night, too—Ben from California where he'd worked in a navy yard since the war. Ben would wait for Samuel at the airport in Albany. Sam was working as a contractor in Columbus, Ohio. Good boys, but they had lives elsewhere now, like a lot of North Country boys who had served their country. The mountains had no special hold on them. Not many jobs. How'd the song go? "How you gonna keep 'em down on the farm, after they've seen Paree . . ."?

Mack carried in the last armful of split and seasoned ash and maple and stacked the logs against the wall by the fireplace. Padre was a good fellow, Mack thought. Quiet sort. Polite. You could tell a lot about a person by the way he treated the help, and Joe MacIntyre, Padre, had always been a gentleman in that respect. But you never quite got to know him. Unlike some of the others of the Winslow friends who came every Christmas and often during the summer as well, he stayed aloof from most of the frivolity that attended such occasions, another factor that raised his stature in Mack's esteem. No wonder they always called him Padre. He was the only one that hardly ever had a woman on his arm. He was the one that made sure the others got back to their cabins all right without falling down the hill or into the lake after a night of drinking—he and Robert and Charles. They were all such good men. Now only Padre was left to look after things. He wasn't a North Country man, however. He didn't hunt and fish. He didn't split wood, or at least Mack had never seen him do so. Not that he was a pantywaist, not at all, but he wasn't a North Country man. Even so, Mack would be relieved to have him. Maybe he'd give up his city lawyering and become an Adirondacker after all.

Once he got through the cordon of shivering state cops, reporters and photographers stationed at the end of the road, Padre made it up the freshly sanded lane without problems. After he checked in with Mack and Mabel, promising to have dinner with them and the girls, he dropped his bag at St. Dunstan's, lit the fire that had been laid for him, and sat down at the small hickory desk by the window. He pulled some papers out of his briefcase, lit a cigarette, and began to review what was in front of him—the last wills and testaments of Emily and Charles Winslow Junior and those of Robert and Mariette Martindale. The hand that held the cigarette massaged his brow as he read.

Charles had left his entire estate to Eleanor should he and his wife predecease their daughter, but he had also generously provided for Robert, Mariette and their offspring and for the retirement of Mack and Mabel. The girls' educations were handsomely taken care of. The question was: What to do with two young orphans? Emily's English relatives were elderly and infirm with the exception of a younger brother, well known for his gambling debts and affairs. Charles had no one left. Robert was an orphan himself, and Mariette likewise had no one in her family that she chose to associate with. They had all supported the Vichy government during the war, and she had broken with her parents long before she left with Robert Martindale for the States. Padre pondered the importance of finding someone, anyone, who would care for Lily. And there was always the question of dealing with whatever strange claimants might approach through the post or over the phone, demanding their share of the Winslow family fortune.

Flipping through the pages, Padre examined the disbursements of property to Robert and Mariette. Except for whatever they'd managed to put aside during their employment with the Winslows and his wartime service, and the twenty-acre parcel on The Hill Next, the only thing they had in the world was Lily. Under his guidance they had provided that, should they die before her, Lily was to remain with the Winslows in their care, something he vividly remembered them agreeing to shortly after Lily was born.

Padre stared into the crackling fire.

If worse came to worst, he would have to take Lily himself. He knew that even thinking of sending Lily to France and into unknown hands would be devastating for both girls. No. Somehow he had to keep Lily and Eleanor together, as long as they wanted. Somehow he had to manage that.

On Christmas morning, Mabel made pancakes for the girls, but they barely touched them. She had a few presents for them, as did Doris and Tom, but Lily seemed uninterested in even opening them to see what they were. Mabel had sent away for potholder looms and loops for both girls. And from Doris and Tom—books of course. There were project books for Eleanor to practice cursive (her handwriting was a mess). For Lily there were coloring books, as well as a picture book from England—one showing the young Prince Charles and Princess Anne, who, it appeared, were fortunate enough to have a *maman* and papa still alive. Lily was old enough to understand what death was, having seen this barn kitten carried off by a fox or that bird lying beneath the lodge windows with a broken neck. But she was unable to comprehend the enormity of people dying, especially the four most important to her. It seemed like some purposeful event, designed with cruel intention to make her cross and miserable. Even Santa Claus seemed to have it in for her. Not only had her parents died, but there were no puppies under the tree that morning. Not even one.

Padre had come empty-handed, since his usual Christmas gift was to give money to St. Bartholomew's Church and Anglican Charities in New York—one of Charles and Emily's favored charitable organizations. But he promised that he would take both girls on a long trip, maybe on the *Queen Mary* or the *France,* as soon as he could straighten things out.

One of the early calls that came in was from the bishop, offering help, if needed. Padre admitted he had no idea what to ask for, except that there be a memorial service at St. Bart's for the two couples, not just Emily and Charles. It seemed odd to have to explain that the co-pilot and the cook killed in the crash were close friends of the family, much more to the Winslows than servants. Much more. He also reminded the bishop that there were *two* small girls involved in the losses and that they were devoted to each other. That, he said, was what was complicating things insofar as future planning would go.

For her own part, Eleanor had only one concern far beyond any self-interest, and she maintained this through it all. She hardly let Lily out of her sight. Although she mourned, usually out of the hearing of those who tried to help her, each time she reappeared from their room, her eyes red and cheeks pale, she bore something of her mother's poise and her father's dignity. But whenever anything came up regarding her staying in New York with Padre and attending school there, she assumed a fury so fierce that many around her were shocked at this change in her No, she said. She would stay at The Hill to be with Lily. Lily, they must understand, was her only friend, and no one—no lawyer or banker—was going to ask her to leave anyone she loved, ever.

Padre watched all of this, as did Mack and Mabel and even Doc Burton, who thought he'd seen every treacherous event the mountains had to offer, from bear attacks to a calcified fetus. But this was one of the saddest things he'd ever witnessed—two little girls with all the money in the world and no one to care for them except a lawyer.

After Christmas, after Ben and Sam had returned to their homes, the girls decided themselves to share the room together at Mack and Mabel's. Together they cleared their belongings out of their previous rooms—Eleanor's at Doxology Lodge and Lily's in the suite of rooms her parents had occupied above the kitchen in Rockingham Hall. While the girls were doing that, Doris and Tom and Mabel helped clear clothing and personal effects from the remaining rooms. Doris, that is, sat on the bed, folded things, and wept. Padre sifted through drawers in the master bedroom to see if there was anything of value that should be itemized. There was much discussion about what to do with all such things. There was jewelry left by Emily—not much, since most of it remained in a safe in their

New York brownstone. There were hats and coats and walking sticks and Emily's Chanel gown for Christmas. Much of it, Doris thought, belonged in a museum. Padre offered to take it all back to New York with him, thinking that perhaps that was where the church could help. There must be someplace in the city capable of discreetly disposing of such high-quality clothing for the benefit of some charity or other, he thought.

Finally, with the girls settled in together at Hyfrydol, the semblance of a plan emerged. There would be memorial services in New York and likely Washington. All of this would be, Padre suggested, upsetting and strange, especially with the press involved. He wished to honor Charles Winslow's tradition of keeping his daughter out of the public eye as much as possible; he hoped the girls would help each other and him through it. When things cooled down, they'd talk about the next step.

"What next step?" Eleanor asked.

"I don't know, Ellie. I simply don't have a clue. But I don't think you can stay here at the camp indefinitely. We need to think about your schooling, your future."

Several days after Christmas, Padre, Mabel and the girls drove to New York City with the car full of Winslow belongings. The stately Winslow brownstone on the East Side of New York became their home for the spring, and would, years later, become Eleanor and Colin's home. Padre moved in, as did Mabel, Doris and Tom. It became immediately clear that perhaps he'd made the wrong choice. The press was constantly outside the door. Police cordoned off the area around the brownstone, but any activity outside the house was compromised by crowds and photographers. Eleanor and Lily were virtual prisoners.

Since school was out of the question for the time being, Doris and Tom continued to act as tutors, but they were counting the days until May, when their ship would sail for England. Doris, for one, enjoyed the notoriety conferred by the press's attentions, although she, in her proper British accent, declined to answer any of their questions.

The memorial service was held at St. Bart's on Park Avenue. Julietta Pima and Irene, and Jack Bannister and James Wood showed up. Irene wore a full-length black sable coat and fur-trimmed boots. She'd been crying. James and Julietta were directly behind her, all looking like they'd stepped out of *Vogue* and a mortician's office at the same time. The ladies embraced the girls emotionally while at the same time snubbing Padre. Eleanor and Lily stayed close to each other and Mabel, Doris and Tom.

Lily, uncomfortably dressed in her Liberty of London finest, followed closely along with Padre in the Book of Common Prayer and the hymnal. After the service, the bishop and one of the priests took them to visit the little columbarium area down in the crypt of the church where the remains of the Winslows and the Martindales would be interred, but Lily couldn't understand that her *maman* and papa could be in such a small place where she couldn't see them. She was puzzled and upset. Eleanor solemnly joined her hand with Lily's over the cold brass plaques. Ellie whispered, "Don't worry. It's not like they're really there. You and I know where they really are."

"Back at camp?" asked Lily.

"That's what I think," Ellie replied.

"That's what I think, too. Like ghosts?"

"Not scary ones. They'd just rather be there, don't you think?"

Lily nodded. "They'll be there when we get back, only we won't see them. But they'll be there."

"That's right."

For a brief moment, they were afforded this much privacy. But when they left the church, the ever-present cameras were there, upraised, flashbulbs exploding and the reporters shouting questions at the girls. One photographer won a Pulitzer for catching the now-famous picture of the girls clinging to each other, Lily screaming in rage at the cameras' flashbulbs, Eleanor trying to shield her from the madness Not visible in the picture is a frantic Padre, pushed aside by the crowd. It was only Mabel who, with her customary presence of mind and country aplomb, stared down the mob and told them they should be ashamed of themselves, frightening two young girls. Taking each youngster by the hand, she firmly marched them to the hired limousine, where, safely inside, they waited for Padre to extricate himself and join them, after nearly coming to blows with one reporter on the way.

America ate it all up with a spoon. Now they had not only "Little El" but "Cinder-Lily," daughter of the cook and "butler." Americans loved that picture as they had loved the picture of the sailor and girl kissing in Times Square at the end of the war. They wrote letters to the White House, to their congressmen, sent money by the bushel to set up a trust fund for Lily Martindale. Ministers, priests and rabbis praised the egalitarian spirit of spunky young Eleanor Winslow for being so concerned for her less favored friend. Invitations came from Hollywood; there was even one from the Queen of England, and there soon appeared on certain radio stations in the South a popular song called "Little El," reminiscent of "It Was Sad when the Great Ship Went Down"—the one written after the sinking of the *Titanic*.

One would have thought that on the night Charles Winslow's plane crashed in the Adirondacks, a nation's hopes and dreams had gone down as well. And all this transpired against the backdrop of the Korean War, the Cold War, and the new threat of nuclear annihilation. America sailed a storm-tossed ocean like a rudderless Ship of State.

The children understood only some of this. What was most treacherous to them was the sudden dissolution of all that had been familiar—the parents gone, the friends, the camp life. The madness that Padre had hoped to contain escalated out of control. All he could think of was the years of psychoanalysis both children would be facing if any more emotional high tension wires were touched.

More than just the trauma of leaving the church, the memorial service and all that followed were a trial for this quiet, stern man. The press deliberated the appropriateness of Joseph MacIntyre's role in the care of the Winslow heir and family fortunes, and this enraged him. New York became a hotbed of gossip about him. His work in private practice came to a full stop for the most part as he shuttled back and forth to The Hill, returning Eleanor and Lily there as soon after the memorial service as possible. Padre was always relieved to return, dump his bags at St. Dunstan's, light the fire, and have supper with Mack and Mabel and the girls.

Weeks passed into spring melt and mud season, and with it a semblance of healing and a return to some kind of calm. It was Padre's plan to return to the city with Eleanor in tow. That was the "next step" Padre had mentioned to Ellie. There was quite a scene when he told her this. The girls had been discussing their own future, looking on the bright side instead of moping, losing themselves in a kind of fantasy. Perhaps they would go together to Arizona or New Mexico, learn to ride rodeo and do tricks on horseback. Butch and Daisy had been most patient in their practice routines over the years, but were simply too large and ungainly for the high-speed maneuvers the girls had in mind. Ellie had said there was a schoolhouse at one of the dude ranches she and her mother had visited the year before, so they could go to school together while they were there. Lessons in the morning and ride all afternoon. It was the one thing that had kept Lily excited and happy since Christmas. So when Padre told Eleanor she was to come to New York, it was as if he'd stepped on a Western diamondback rattlesnake, such was her poisonous rage. He was flummoxed.

"It's for the best that you come with me. I can't leave you here. We can live in your parents' house. You'll go to a proper school. Tea at the Plaza Hotel. Broadway shows! You'll love it there."

The stare continued unwavering. She whispered low and seriously, "Not without Lily. I'm not going anywhere without Lily."

"I'll tell you what," he said. "Come with me to New York and when we get you settled we'll send for Lily to come." He heard himself making a promise that he wasn't sure he could keep. "El," he said, pleading with her, "I'm in a terrible position here. I have to do what's right according to your parents' wishes. No one could have foreseen it would end up this way. I'll do what's right for Lily, too, but I have to get back to New York. I have my practice there. I have work. I can't watch Lily. I need to take care of your needs first."

"What will I do?"

"You'll go to school, of course."

"Then why can't I just stay here, if that's all it is."

"Because I'm responsible!" He heard himself starting to shout. Eleanor had never heard Padre use that tone of voice, and then she noticed that he had tears in his eyes, and she also started to cry.

She threw her arms around him. "I'm sorry, Padre. I'm sorry."

He lit a cigarette, his hand trembling.

Spring came to New York with cherry trees and dogwood in bloom and flowers everywhere, while in the Adirondacks the snows melted slowly and the dull brown of mud plugged the back roads. Eleanor pined for, begged for her friend Lily to be delivered to her. At The Hill, Lily did the same. Left in the care of Mack and Mabel, she was only aware of a child's sensation of hollowness and sadness, from which, even in one so young, it was difficult to distract her. They tried to enroll her in the little one-room school in Winslow Station, but she cried so bitterly when they left her there that Mabel said, "It's just too soon—too soon." So Lily moped about, obeying Mabel and Mack and staying briefly with the tasks at hand, keeping her bed made, her few toys picked up, setting the table, gathering eggs. Mack let her saddle soap the harnesses for the Percherons, taught her how to sharpen skates, build birdhouses, tie flies, which she seemed to enjoy, chatting all the while to the animals in the barn. But soon she would be gone, and Mack or Mabel would find her in the library, face down, crying.

It was Easter when the girls were reunited. Once again, Lily made the trip with Mabel to New York. They attended Easter services at St. Bart's, and again the press and photographers waited outside. This time the police were there to keep the girls from the crush of the crowds waiting to see them. After a time, these excursions out on the streets of the city became a familiar routine, and the girls were seen sometimes with a slight smile on their faces, but more often the unhappy grimace under the pain and duress of the attention.

Stoic as ever, Padre became their buffer and their shield. He took charge of the girls in a very public, very messy battle with the friends. Both Irene and Julietta offered to adopt Eleanor, but seemed less interested in Lily, a fact which didn't take the girls long to figure out. Everyone wanted Eleanor Winslow. Lily was another matter entirely. Whenever any discussion came to a mention of the girls' future, Padre was the only one who could now see that they would not, could not be separated, that to do so would be to create a much larger mess than the one they already had.

"Are you our father now?" Lily asked one day soon after Easter, cloistered once again in the Winslow brownstone.

Padre just shook his head. "I'm a lawyer. I have two children but no wife, and now, it seems, no friends left."

Eleanor stood by the chair and put her hand on his shoulder. "I'm sorry."

"This isn't your fault, Eleanor, Lily. None of this. Nothing anyone could have done would have stopped them from flying that day. There's nothing I can do except what I promised Charles—that I would look after his affairs. As executor, I'm in charge. As a lawyer, I'm bound legally to do what is right for all of us. As an unmarried man, I haven't a clue what to do with two young girls in my care."

Then he started to tell them about a school he'd found in Switzerland. *L'école du Bon Berger*, it was called, and it was a very special place—more like a home than a boarding school. The bishop had told him about it, because it was an Anglican institution. It specialized in caring for children who had suffered great and public loss of home and family—children of all nationalities, faiths and colors, orphans of wars and assassinations. He thought it sounded perfect, something both the progressive Winslows would have thought ideal. And both girls would go. They would be together. All this publicity was making it impossible for them to stay in New York or be protected at The Hill with just Mack and Mabel.

"So you're sending us away?" Eleanor asked with her uncanny ability to sum things up.

"Don't put it like that. Do you want to stay at the camp or New York knowing your every move is going to be hounded by the press and photographers?"

"I hate them," said Lily.

"So do I," echoed Eleanor.

"In Switzerland, there are people there who know how to care for children in your position. I will take you there. I won't leave you there forever. I'll come get you at Christmas and holidays. We'll go skiing; we'll travel and see the world. Things will calm down eventually. You'll see."

"What about me?" Lily asked.

"You, too, Lily. We'll be the Three Musketeers."

"Can people cook there?" asked Lily.

"Oh yes. Switzerland, especially French Switzerland, has wonderful food—just like your maman made. And chocolate—all sorts of chocolate. And wonderful bread and fresh butter, cream and milk from the cows on the mountainsides. Switzerland is wonderful. I'll come visit you whenever I can. You'll have lots of friends and great teachers—much better than I can offer you. I can see you so little during the days and weeks, because of my work. I can't be like a mother and a father, too. I have to go ahead and just be a lawyer and try to protect you both. And you need to be in school. Doris and Tom are leaving soon."

Well, it wasn't Arizona with rodeos, but the girls managed to get excited about the prospect of skiing down mountains and hot chocolate like Mariette used to make, and when they weren't pretending to be princesses meeting European royalty, they were schussing down the stairs of the brownstone and, Padre thought, starting to look and behave a lot like normal little girls again.

Doris and Tom sailed on the *Queen Elizabeth* on the first of May. The girls and Padre saw them off with flowers and champagne and promises to write every week. They were all as good as their word, and over the years there were visits to England to see their old tutors whenever they could. Doris kept all their correspondence and snapshots of the camp and the girls in an elaborate album. With a generous gift from the Winslow estate, she and Tom were able to buy a small house in Godalming in Surrey. Tom sang in the local choir and played piano for community musicales; Doris taught English in the local school. They were quite happy, and still firmly refused any efforts by the press to interview them over the ensuing years.

Soon after Doris and Tom's departure, the girls returned to The Hill with Mabel. After a time, the publicity calmed down. Padre visited frequently and stayed in his St. Dunstan's room, and read to them like their fathers used to do in the evenings after dinner at Mack and Mabel's. No one visited. No one was invited, except for Jim, the ranger's son, and a few of the other town kids who came for special events, like the Fourth of July picnic before the town fireworks and the Labor Day regatta that raced from the marina in Winslow Station to the dock at Melita boathouse at The Hill. Other than that it was a very quiet, a very, very quiet summer. The Friends stayed away, alienated by their own rage and Padre's stoic insistence on caring for the girls himself. And then it was time to leave for Switzerland.

The old Hill station wagon was loaded. Padre was to drive the wagon, with Lily and Eleanor in the back seat. The rear was packed to the roof with their belongings, and he was concerned about being able to see. Mabel was loading the last of Eleanor's things while Eleanor and Lily sat on the porch of the lodge, not speaking, not doing much but watching.

"I want to go to the barn," Eleanor said. "Do you want to come?"

Lily nodded, sighing.

Eleanor hailed Mack. "We'll be right back," she said. Mack watched to see which direction they'd take and then nodded to his wife and followed the girls from behind at a distance. He gave them a hundred yards' lead and then cut around where they couldn't see him. He had his reasons; mostly to be sure they stayed safe and clear of the cows, which they did, but also to be a witness to their last minutes at the camp. Someday, somebody would be sure to ask him, and he wanted to know. He wanted to be able to represent them accurately. He knew this, but he also knew above this that just now nobody needed anything else to go wrong, and there was nobody left but him and Mabel and Padre to make sure it didn't. So he watched, although he knew what they intended.

Ellie headed for the oat bucket and so did Lily. Lily would remember years later that they did this every time they entered the barn, just as Catholics do with the font of holy water at the back of a church. They each grabbed a fistful of oats and marched to the stalls where the Percherons stood. Butch put his massive head over the bottom-latched gate made of rope. When he snuffled at their upturned, flattened hands, he blew most of Lily's oats on the ground. Daisy looked out next. Lily ran back to the oat bucket and got two fistfuls, one for Ellie. "Here," she said, spilling most on the floor, which she then scooped up and offered to Daisy.

"Mister and Missus Percheron," Lily said, "You will, by our solemn orders, look after this place for us. And also to keep our parents' ghosts—"

"Not ghosts, Lily. Spirits."

"—spirits company and guard them and take them for rides when they want—"

"Their last name is not Percheron," Ellie told her.

"What is it then?" Lily asked in mock exasperation.

"I think it's Winslow, just like us."

"Like us?"

"Like us."

"Am I a Winslow too?"

"Yes. You are. You are adopted."

"But don't you have to have parents?"

"Nope. What I say goes."

"Okay," Lily looked at her with her eyes as wide open as a camera lens, taking it all in for future reference. "Thanks."

And with this, Mack saw the girls shake hands. Then they walked out of the barn with their arms around each other, as solemn as sisters who have sworn a great oath.

Chapter Fifteen

"Forty days and forty nights
Thou was fasting in the wild . . ."

"Heinlein," #55, Episcopal Hymnal, 1940

Tune: M. H. in Nürnbergisches Gesangbuch, 1676; Text: George Hunt
Smyttan, 1856

Jim Porter sits outside the door of Lily's hospital room through the night
and into the early morning hours following her medevac from The Hill
Next. That foreign doctor says she's pretty sick. He suspects there are
other problems, too. They have to wait for the tests to come back. Right
now, she's in pain, she's emotionally overwrought, strung out, exhausted,
and malnourished. The combination of all these is causing multiple problems. She's still in pain; she's off her head much of the time, so they're
keeping her sedated. Jim goes in when he's allowed, but often she's so
out of it, she can't talk or respond, or won't. Jim feels he's not helping
much in the process and there are probably better ways he could be
spending his time, but damn it, it's Lily here. Lily, his first real sweetheart. And Running Deer doesn't run away from his duties to the one
he has always loved.

Switzerland. Those were miserable years. Not just miserable for these
two girls who had lost so much, but miserable for all unhappy children

165

everywhere who ever went away to school. Those years of school remembered and loathed: the close quarters with new and unrelated people, the bitter ends to friendships, the games lost and tests failed. All these have much to do with this story and all to do with the damaged heart of Lily Martindale. The school was a refuge at the time, especially from the press and the well-meaning American public, although Lily could not see it that way. To Lily, school was privation. It was *not* The Hill. There was now the loss of every connection that had ever meant anything to her, anything, that is, that was left to her: Mack, Mabel, Tom and Doris, Butch and Daisy and every other creature from the white-tailed deer to the smallest barn kitten, deer mouse. She missed the big, black ravens that called as they passed over the camp from hillside to hillside across the lake. She mourned the chickadees and nuthatches, and lined the margins of her notebooks with sketches of little birds and great horses. She wept for the Wee Lassie canoe that had been promised her and which she had yet to master. She mourned along with every roll of the tires, every thrum of the giant ship's engines and churn of the train on the tracks all the way to Switzerland. With every new friendly, warm, and attentive face that Lily Martindale encountered, there was, for one so young, only the questioning puzzlement of why none of them were any of those she particularly loved. So she chose to hate them all, as if by retreating to anger she might dwell somewhere apart in her own mind, walled off from anything expected of her, anyone trying to make contact. Everyone but Eleanor; and that would prove a problem for Eleanor, who faced the identical sorrows and losses as Lily. The world in which they had been set adrift, guided only by Padre and this new place in Switzerland, would try to befriend them, help them. Only Eleanor would accept the offer. Lily feared and resented everyone.

The girls were not to see The Hill for several years. *L'école du Bon Berger* became their home as well as their school. But they saw a great deal of Padre. As in so much else, he never lied about this. He did visit often, and traveled with them during the summers and the holidays. On his own, back in New York City, his practice recovered from the trauma of the press coverage after the accident. He worked tirelessly along with bankers and investment professionals to preserve and prosper the Winslow estate and form the Winslow-Martindale Foundation for charitable causes. Padre, as always, lived simply and on his own. No matter how hard the press tried, they could never dish any dirt on this man who proved to be as honorable as his word to both his duty and his charges. He fended off the anticipated queries from hundreds of claimants to the fortune, especially those who wanted their dear Lily back. It did not take much to dispel the claims from France. Mariette's family, it seemed, had all either died or disappeared in the aftermath of the war. Those people that offered proof of claim to Lily and a portion of the fortune could never prove a true family connection. Claim after claim of any sort was carefully researched by Padre, his staff, and the Winslow-Martindale Foundation. None of them stood up to scrutiny. After about a year, he was finally able to relax. He came to love his connection to Eleanor and Lily and his thrice-yearly visits to Switzerland to take them on outings. Lily, however, would prove the greater trial.

The girls made friends—at least Ellie did. Lily, so much younger and so dependent on Eleanor, watched and envied, with painful jealously and fear that Eleanor would abandon her. Eleanor thrived through those years, and she loved the school. Much of what she needed in terms of healing and grieving the loss of her parents took a few years. Here at the school she was given what she most needed—privacy, support when she needed it, and time. She grew from a child of remarkable resilience and strength to a student of great capability and finally, at eighteen, a young, handsome woman of considerable promise. When she had finished her A-levels (performing with great distinction), she returned to the states and entered Wellesley College. Eleanor's departure from the school was much celebrated by everyone except her young companion. The much-anticipated graduation was attended by Padre and even Mabel, who had been flown over for the occasion—her first plane ride ever. Tom and Doris were invited, but were now fully engaged in their new lives in England. They sent Ellie *The Book of Common Prayer* and the *1940 Hymnal* and *Hymnal Companion,* which she treasured for years. Lily sulked in her room. Only Mabel could get her to come out in time for the commencement ceremony.

After Eleanor left for the States, Lily retreated into the black cocoon of her own troubles. The school counselors fretted and fussed over her and yet she remained quiet and often sullen. Those remarkable moments when she smiled or joked around were cause for hope among the staff of the school. At an awkward fourteen years, she had not gained much ground since her arrival. Her behavior over the years swung wildly from puerile and fawning to stonily quiet. She barely passed any of her subjects, failing catastrophically in math and science, and she was often in trouble.

Her test scores, contrarily, were high. It wasn't that she was dull-witted; in fact she was quite intelligent, loved to read, and had an extensive vocabulary owing to an exceptionally absorbent brain. She was a hard worker on all things outside the classroom. She had a knack for looking after the very youngest children who entered the school. She truly cared for them and watched over them when she was able and allowed to. And she liked serving in the chapel. Although in those days, acolytes were boys only, Lily did everything else. She took care of polishing things and making sure the vestments of the attending priest were clean and pressed. The staff was pleased with this display of devotion and obedience, until they noticed that the locked cabinet housing the communion wine was not inviolate. And she had a tendency toward irreverence. As Dr. Bhijan Habib would later remember, she could be very funny. He couldn't remember the Lenten dirge they sang except for the verse Lily had invented that began "Forty days and forty nights, we will sing lugubrious hymns."

All that was not so bad, but when Eleanor flew back to the States with Padre and Mabel after school, Lily was left behind, partly as punishment for the communion wine infraction and partly because Padre could employ Eleanor in his office over the summer and keep an eye on her, but Lily would have been a problem. She needed more, much more, supervision. As it turned out, he would have done better to take Lily along as well. The first thing she did that summer was to go AWOL from the school, tramp two towns away, and take the train to Paris. Until she was spotted by a gendarme who thought he recognized her, she managed to have herself a high old time wandering the streets, cadging coins, and stealing fruit from an open-air market. A representative of the school was dispatched to collect her, and she went quietly back to Switzerland. This happened two more times. The second time, she stole a car.

By her seventeenth year, Lily had calmed down only slightly. In fact, she was somewhat tractable, and Padre felt comfortable welcoming her back to the States to spend the summer at The Hill. Eleanor was on break briefly from law school at Columbia. It was the first time that the girls had been back to the Adirondacks together since saying goodbye to the horses. The horses, in fact, were gone. Mack had sold them off, as he had nearly all of the livestock except for a half-dozen chickens and a steer. Mack was ailing. The camp was ailing as well.

It was during that summer that something switched on in Lily's brain, something subtle and reasonable and so unlike her. She figured out just how much of a charity case she really was. One night over dinner it occurred to her to ask the question of Padre, and, with Eleanor present, she got the answer.

"Where has the money come from to pay for school, for me to go to school in Switzerland and to come here?"

"From the Winslow-Martindale estate," Padre answered.

"So this is all Winslow money. I really am Cinder-Lily."

"Lily, no—"

"Look, I'm just asking. Nobody ever talks to me about this stuff. I have no idea what I'm supposed to do when I leave school."

"First of all you have to pass your O-Levels."

Lily got quiet again.

"Can I come back here to live? Can I work here?"

"Lily. Ideally you'll pass your A-Levels and go to college in the states and get a job, like Eleanor."

Lily forcefully pushed the food around her plate, but did not speak, did not look at them.

Eleanor entered the fray, "We'll help you find work, Lily, no matter what. You should teach or work with kids somehow."

"I thought I could work here with Mack and Mabel. You know. Like my mother. I could go to cooking school. We could make this a resort hotel or something. It could make money for you. I could pay you back. Every nickel."

Eleanor carefully circled her mouth with the cloth napkin, in Rockingham Hall. The food was indifferent. It was so hard to find capable help, and the Aikens' niece was hardly capable, although she tried. She'd even been sent away to take cooking classes. But making this camp a public place was not what Eleanor and, she was sure, Padre had in mind. It had become an altar to the memory of her parents for both her and her lawyer. In fact, it had occurred to her that she should ask Padre to marry her, when she was professionally settled as a lawyer, of course. Eleanor during those years was practical in all things relating to the camp and its preservation and had not an inkling of what it was to think of anything else—men, for one. She'd never had the experience. Padre was not a love interest; he was a means to an end. At any rate, nothing would be resolved, on that or any subsequent night.

Lily and Eleanor spent a relatively quiet summer. Lily took a stab at studying for her O-Levels. Eleanor spent much time in New York at Padre's law firm and the Winslow Foundation learning her trade. Jim Porter, the ranger's son, started hanging around the camp, for the first time since he and Lily were children. Jim, tall and lanky, chattering away like a squirrel to his old friend, became a frequent visitor to The Hill that summer. Before long, he and Lily became the talk of the hamlet; they were inseparable. Eleanor watched and worried. When she and Padre traveled back to New York for work, Lily refused to come with them, and stayed at Hyfrydol with Mack and Mabel.

Chapter Sixteen

"With thy living fire of judgment
Purge this land of bitter things;
Solace all its wide dominion
With the healing of thy wings."

"St. Leonard," #518, Episcopal Hymnal, 1940

Tune: Johann Christoph Bach, 1693; Text: Henry Scott Holland, 1902

The hospital in Saranac Lake is an ocean of noise—waves of wheeled carts, IV stands, squealing gurneys, beepings of phones, voices, loud-speakers—inundating, receding, then inundating. There are men's voices, women's voices, and then, piercing high above any other, the sound of a baby crying, shrieking. Lily's monitor goes off, heart rate spiking into some seismic region. The RN on duty runs in to find the patient once again wild-eyed, struggling with her straps and tapes and tubes. Behind the nurse is Jim who has been startled out of a sound sleep as he sat upright in the hall. Behind Jim is the state trooper, determined that there will be no bushwhacking around his assigned duty to guard the patient.

The nurse orders the men out of the room, but Jim, EMT-trained, stays. Lily's heart rate is skyrocketing, she is thrashing about while the nurse tries to restrain her on one side and Jim on the other.

"Lily, sweetheart! Come on now."

But the sound of his voice makes Lily's struggles even more violent.

"No, no! Get out. Leave me alone," Lily shouts. "Get away from me, you stupid bastard! You idiot," Lily shouts.

Finally, as a host of attendants and then Dr. Habib come in, Jim rides the flood of people out of the room and moves down the hall. He pulls a knit wool cap out of his pocket and smashes it onto his head. The trooper tries to ask him something as he follows behind, but Jim keeps walking fast. He takes the stairs down, stopping at the landing to press his head against the cool wall. The trooper is standing silently above, having watched and followed.

Jim sees him and shakes his head. "I can't take no more of this shit." He drags his forearm across his face. "Tell them I've gone home to shower and then, then I don't know. But I'm done here."

When he gets outside, dawn is just breaking. It is Monday, February third. It seems as if he's been in that hospital for weeks and weeks, when it has just been one night. The sky is clear. It feels like twenty below. He gets in his truck. If he times it right, she might give him breakfast and coffee before she leaves for her first class at the college. June, that's her name. She is thirty-five years old and she's all right, and even with two kids and a drunk for an ex-husband, she's a damn sight less complicated than this nonsense right here. This here is just too damn much and it's time he stood up and figured that out for himself.

Jim pumps the accelerator and starts the truck. He pulls out on the road headed with haste for Paul Smiths. At some point, he thinks, he's going to have to call Jenny.

Somewhere between adolescent rebellion and self-realization, Lily discovered that she was attractive to men. Most specifically, she was astoundingly attractive to Jim Porter. She and Jim lost their virginity together that summer when she was home from school, and ever after that he assumed they were a couple. She had other ideas. But in October of Lily's last year in Switzerland, when she had just turned eighteen, she was very clearly, to herself and others, pregnant.

Padre got the call from the school. Once again he packed his bags and flew to Geneva. He took Lily to dinner at the inn near the school, where she desultorily dipped her spoon in the leek soup but never managed to get any to her mouth. She remained, as always, maddeningly silent and sullen. But her face, instead of hardened and tight, he thought, looked as though she had seen the future—that thousand-mile stare he'd seen on soldiers in hospital who'd given up hope of ever getting home. Padre remembered Lily as a child and could see without a map to guide him that almost every step he had taken on her behalf had been the wrong one—wrong ones everywhere at every turning. He should have let her stay with Mack and Mabel at The Hill. She could have gone to school there after a while. Mabel would have taken her to church. She could have been a North Country child, brought up strong and stable in that place.

"How can I make things right between us, Lily?" he asked lighting a cigarette and offering her one.

"No thanks," she said. "Thanks anyway. Not good for the health of the fetus. And I think you know, don't you? I don't belong here. I belong with Mack and Mabel. I want to go home."

"Lily, there's nothing there—"

"There is everything there. Everything I have ever loved."

"Jim?"

"*No*. Not Jim." Her face once more saw the future, and for all purposes there wasn't a future, the way she was thinking. "You're right. I can't go back. I won't marry Jim. I don't even want him to know this is happening."

"Ah. I wish you'd rethink that."

"No. No rethinking. I didn't think very well this summer did I? Well, it's my choice here. Jim's not around. I get five letters from him a week." She took another bite of bread and seemed to be warming to the soup. "He writes even more than he talks."

"Do you write him back?"

"Yes. No. Not very much."

Padre stared out the window at the surrounding Alpine valley. "Well, as you can imagine, *L'École* has had to deal with these kinds of situations before. There's a clinic near here and place where you can work, have the child and it will be adopted. Immediately. They have a waiting list. All very professional and respectable. How's your French?"

"Fine."

"How's your Schweizerdeutsch?"

"Passable."

"If you came to the city," Padre's face was trying to envision that situation, the press hounding him and Lily and Eleanor again.

"No. I'll stay."

"You might be alone. I can't be here always."

"I'm always alone, Padre. I don't ever remember being anything but alone, except for Ellie and at the camp in the old days. I have no friends here."

"Do you want Ellie to come be with you?"

"No."

"Mabel can't do it. Mack is not well at all. Who then?"

"No one."

"You have no friends here at all? No one at all?"

"Well there's Rabbit. He's a nice guy. He's Persian. Very shy. He and I get along okay. But he doesn't know. He wouldn't be any help anyway."

"Do you have a roommate this year?"

"I haven't had a roommate since I came here. They know better than to stick me with someone."

"Well," Padre shook his head, "finish up your soup. Let's go back and gather your things. We'll go over and have a look-see at this, um, this place. It's not far."

In the ensuing days, Padre settled Lily in a town not far from the school, where she stayed in a *pension,* worked for a nearby ski resort through the winter as an office clerk, and awaited, alone, the birth of her child. She was terrified—hospitals terrified her, the unknown process of birth, the rumors of pain and complications. The doctor she saw for exams did little to prepare her. She hated going to see him and avoided it most months, even though she felt ill a good deal of the time. Then spring came, and she was so very large that she had trouble moving enough to come to work, though work for the ski season was almost over. Eleanor was in her last year at law school and couldn't make the trip, but sent flowers and wired money. Come May, the child was born after thirty-six hours of difficult labor. Lily learned that it was a girl. She learned that an American couple were waiting gratefully to take the baby back to the States, but no one told her who they were or where they took the child.

The nurses and attendants were all brisk and matter-of-fact, and Lily, weak and exhausted from the effort and some blood loss, shut her eyes as if to close off the world. They had given her something to help her sleep, but it was not enough, never enough to wipe away the image of the white and blue back of the nurse as she carried a small bundle away and out the door of the delivery room, the sound of the infant crying, shrieking, and the companion ache in Lily's young breasts as they filled with milk for the baby that was never to be hers.

She stayed at the hospital for three days, and they wanted her to stay for at least one more, but she was determined to get out of there. Several teachers from the school visited her, expressing the hope that she would come back next year and finish.

Since she faced a summer of no work, and saw no sense in attempting to go back to New York or The Hill, she went to *L'École* to see about her chances of coming back in the fall or taking classes over the summer. The staff seemed glad to see her, though somewhat reserved. They worried for her behavior. They worried for her studies. What, if any, plans did she have for the summer? She told them that Padre was coming for her (he wasn't). They would travel together around Europe (there was no such plan—Padre assumed she was back at school and had only called once while she was in the hospital). She'd be back for the fall term.

There were still about six weeks till the end of the school year, during which she had nothing to do, so she took her meager savings from work, added it to the sum Ellie had wired, and traveled by train to Italy on her own. She told no one where she was going, and something about that was wildly thrilling, as if she could be free at last of all that history, be someone new and different. She made up names for herself: Liberty Martin was the one she liked best. But she met few people who asked. She was not one to invite idle conversation then or ever. Often engrossed in a book (she loved Georges Simenon) or staring out the window of the train, she was left alone by even the keenest fellow traveler. No one in all her travels seemed to be the slightest bit interested in her. She wandered in and out of museums, duomos and shrines. No one pointed or stared. Perhaps, she thought, she was always just Ellie's shadow and without Ellie, her life could be peaceful like this, anonymous.

"Nonnie Maus," she thought. She liked that name, too. From youth hostel to small inn, she traveled as Liberty or Nonnie. Only one border crossing customs official raised his eyebrows when he saw the name "Lily Martindale" on her passport, but he looked at her only fleetingly, a hesitant question on his lips which he decided was better not asked. She was traveling alone like any other young school person on summer holiday in Europe. She wasn't six years old anymore.

When the money ran low, she parceled out enough to get back to Switzerland, thinking that if she ran out, she could always hitchhike, but she was careful for once. She returned to school, made up her classes with a sense of renewed interest and finished her last year, passing her O-Levels; after all she'd been through, the achievement was remarkable. She did not pursue the A-levels. Padre managed to get her taken off the waiting list and into a small junior college in Connecticut. She had, unlike Eleanor, asked to take on Padre's name, so that she would not be hounded in college. Every Christmas, the press asked the question, "What ever happened to . . . ," and there would be this unnerving time of looking over her shoulder to see if anyone had figured it out. Every Christmas, there would be letters and appeals from the newspapers and magazines to interview the girls. They were always politely declined, usually by Mabel, who had now taken on the role of secretary in addition to the rest of her responsibilities at the camp, with the help of folks from town and occasionally one of her sons and his family, who took turns helping out, especially now that Mack was ailing.

Lily took up residence in New York after graduating from the junior college, living in the old Winslow brownstone temporarily. She did not try to go to The Hill. To see Jim again, Jim who knew nothing about the birth of the child, was impossible. Padre gave her a choice: get a job or go back to school in Europe. As Lillian MacIntyre, she ended up at Katharine Gibbs for a year-long course and then got the job with the Anglican Charities and started, belatedly, to settle down, at least to all outward appearances.

But the press found out who she was. She thought to appease them with interviews, but someone talked about her arrest record in Europe. Anglican Charities was kind enough to keep her on, as she was a diligent worker and seemed to have a head for organization and pulling off events. Reassuming the name Lily Martindale, she worked for them for three years, traveling to Africa frequently—a sort of glorified personal assistant, often attaché to a traveling bishop here or there. Once she met the Archbishop of Canterbury. He was the only one ever to ask her if she was related to the Lily Martindale from America who lost her parents in a plane crash. "No," she said. "That was some other Lily Martindale." But he looked at her strangely all the same, trying, as so many others had done, to see the face of the six-year-old child in the newspaper photograph present in the serious face of the young woman before him.

But then Ellie wrote to her to come home for the holidays at The Hill. Ellie had gone back to help Mabel manage things. Padre, too, but Padre was ill, she said. And Mack had had a stroke. Mack was gone.

Chapter Seventeen

"Time, like an ever-rolling stream,
Bears all its sons away;
They fly, forgotten, as a dream
Dies at the opening day."

"St. Anne," #289, Episcopal Hymnal, 1940

Tune: William Croft, 1708; Text: Isaac Watts, 1719, based on Psalm 90

When Frank Guilbeault Junior said to Lily that he loved the woods for their ability to cover all traces of man's passing, he did not know how indelible were the sorrows accumulated in the heart of someone like Lily. There was a stoic bearing that both girls adopted over the years that became solidified into a statuesque formality—a "quartz contentment," as Emily Dickinson once wrote. Eleanor's face held a practiced solemnity. Tall now like her father, and handsome, she had presided over the Winslow-Martindale Foundation for three years after her graduation from law school, shuttling between The Hill and New York. The same capabilities she'd exhibited as a serious and disciplined child grew as she became an adult. She could always move on, maintain perspective, focus on the present need. And she had found Colin, met him at a charity ball in the city. He was her rudder now, not Padre. He was a brick—fun-loving, bright, rich—her perfect foil. Within a year after Mack's death, they married.

Lily, on the other hand, had no one. She had, like Eleanor, a certain tensile strength of internal will, but was not as strong as her friend. She could be brittle, caustic and untrusting, especially with men. Lily as a child had always been up for a game, a dance, a hike or a laugh. She grew less so. Every ensuing crisis caused her to fester more and more inside. Her sadness had swollen like an abscess and with it the need to narcotize the pain. Eleanor never went that far, never took Valium, or anything stronger than a slow glass of wine or an occasional sleeping pill. It was always Eleanor who held Lily together—talking long into the night, bucking her up, coaching her, always promising better things to come once they got through this latest crisis. In the depths of Eleanor's care for Lily were the beginnings of Lily's heart strain—a sisterly and loving codependency that was bent to filigree—complicated and lovely in terms of Ellie's devotion, but never quite allowing Lily to heal all by herself, gain strength by herself. Then there was Mack's loss and the worry for the future of the camp, for Mabel, and now for Padre.

Padre had put off going to the doctor for too long. The phlegmy cough, the strain to breathe after minor exertion, and lately the bouts of chronic bronchitis worsened. He gave up cigarettes, but it was too late. He heard his death sentence in New York, and refused any except palliative treatment. He didn't see the point in prolonging things. No cajoling or reasoning from the girls could sway him. Mack's funeral was to be Padre's last visit to The Hill, his last Christmas there with the girls.

There had been morose dinners in Rockingham Hall since 1952. This one, nearly twenty years after the plane crash, was one of the worst. The Aikens' niece was still presiding over the kitchen, and once again overcooked the lamb, although the roast potatoes were fine and the mint sauce helped the meat. Lily, now twenty-five, had returned from an interfaith meeting in Nairobi, which hadn't gone particularly well for a number of reasons. The main reason was the distrust between the native Kenyans and the Sikhs who seemed to run all the local banks and businesses. Besides being jet-lagged, Lily was more than a little depressed and anxious, and once again facing a funeral service for someone she loved. Padre looked almost greyishly pale, and he hardly ate. He had lost a great deal of weight for a man who was never stout to begin with. Eleanor was vainly trying to keep a bright face on the situation. They had all spent an exhausting afternoon making funeral arrangements with Mabel, her sons and Pastor Dan. Mabel's sons were having dinner with her at Hyfrydol, making do with leftovers. The boys, Lily and Eleanor assumed, were trying to talk Mabel into moving away from The Hill, moving in with one of them. This, too, added to the solemn tone around the table.

"We could take Mabel back to New York with us," Lily suggested, "if she wants to, that is. You know, like a holiday for her. She hasn't had many of those."

Eleanor, the only one who was helping herself to seconds on the roasted potatoes, said, "We'll ask. But I think Ben and Sam get first dibs on their mother."

"How will we keep The Hill?"

"That is the question of the hour. We'll have to find someone."

Another silence draped itself around the table, until Padre spoke.

"I think this passing and its discussion brings up the necessity of discussing plans of my own."

Lily helped herself to more wine.

"I think you know," he continued, "that I'd like to be buried near your parents at Saint Bartholomew's. I do not, however, want a public funeral. There's a small chapel there. If we can restrain our natural, jolly inclination to include the press and the throngs of the American public rejoicing to see me gone at last, that would make my final days slightly more joyous."

His two charges tried to reassure him.

"One thing that encourages me is that the two of you are settled in jobs suitable for women in this new climate of women's liberation. I'm happy about that. Long overdue." He coughed into his napkin, and the cough seemed to shake his newly frail body like a rattle. "The only other thing that comforts me is the prospect, however theologically challenged, of seeing both of your parents again."

"But they're here, Padre. I don't think they ever really left here," Lily said, her eyes glistening and her face flushed.

"I know you believe that. I know how much you miss them, that wraithlike they still hang about the camp watching over us all, God help us. But it is the nature of the dying to cling to a vision of pearly gates and streets of gold and angels with harps—all that terribly corny stuff now seems attainable to me. It's the only thing I can imagine. Your parents, we, all of us were so good, so true to duty, so brave and forthright and patriotic." He started to cough again and took a sip of water when he could. "And now Mack. Mack at the forefront. Mack the guide. He's the only one, I think, who would be miserable without his woods and trails, barns and horses."

"I wish I could believe all that," Lily said.

"Oh, Lily," Padre said, "You're sorting things out, doing good work. You'll be all right. I know it. Remember the post-Communion prayer: 'And do all such good works as thou hast prepared for us to walk in'?"

"Sure."

"Well that's all you can do. Ask what the works are. Ask where you need to be walking. You don't have to believe, my darlings. You only have to ask. None of this Holy Roller stuff from my girls, just solid, intelligent little Anglicans in the end. That's all I ever hoped and prayed for. Please remember me when you go to church. Please go to church. The music is so lovely. Your fathers loved to sing those grand old hymns."

He finished his water, took a sip of wine.

"Walk me to Saint Dunstan's," he said.

Lily and Eleanor each took an arm and walked rather grandly (although Lily wobbled slightly), singing the hymn "No foes shall stay his might, Though he with giants fight . . . ." After they saw him through the door of his cabin, Lily and Eleanor went to the lodge and talked in front of the fire until it died down. They heard the Aikens' niece drive out of camp before they retired for the night. The lights were still burning at the caretaker's cottage.

Winslow Station that December was one long, white, broad street flanked with six-foot piles of plowed snow that would grow steadily through the coming months. The night before Mack's funeral it snowed another six inches. It looked as though the town was disappearing, drifting down in a soft bleached comforter. John Aiken, Tom Aiken's uncle (who so enjoyed the Stihl saw calendar girls that he displayed above the bar at Aiken's Tap Room), plowed the church's parking lot and had to use a front loader to scoop out enough space for the crowd.

The old Methodist church was packed tight, and Mack, who only showed his face there every Christmas and Easter, but otherwise "worshiped in the woods," lay in his coffin, his rugged old face still and pale, his thick white hair neatly combed for once and his bristle mustache clean of tobacco juice. He looked odd, all spiffy and dressed in a suit. He looked foreign, like an immigrant from some old country in Europe, lacking only a battered suitcase and a fedora.

Padre insisted on sitting at the back, in case he started coughing. The girls left him there to go sit with Mabel and the boys and their families. It had been wonderful, the last few days between Christmas and New Year's, to have children at the camp again, grands and great-grands of Mack and Mabel. Ben and Sam had two sons each and those children now had children of their own. The great-grandkids loved Lily, and the youngest sat on her lap during the funeral service. They all stood to sing "I walk in the garden with him" and "As pants the hart for cooling springs," which, Mabel had told Pastor Dan, were Mack's favorite hymns. Mabel seemed to be in pretty good shape throughout, but after the committal (North Country winter burials go on, now that machines can break the frozen soil) she said she was tired and asked everyone to excuse her from the wake in the church hall. Padre and Sam took her back to camp, along with Pastor Dan's wife, who busied herself in the kitchen and prepared three rolls of refrigerator cookies for the younger kids to bake later. Doc Burton came out to see if Mabel needed anything, but she was asleep, worn out between the holidays, the great-grandchildren, and the prospect of life at the camp and in her home without her husband.

Jim Porter was the only one missing that day. No one had seen him. Doc told Eleanor that he was worried about Jim. "He's been drinking," he said. "I've been talking to him, and he knows he's going to lose his job if he keeps it up. I don't know how he's managed so far, but I'll stay after him. It's a shame."

Lily and Eleanor helped Mabel's great-grandkids settle in their rooms in the lodge. They had food left over from the wake at the church, and they nibbled on roast chicken and the refrigerator cookies Lily and kids baked in the kitchen at Rockingham Hall, letting Mabel sleep. They had a good fire going and the older children wanted to tell ghost stories, but Eleanor said, in view of their grandfather's passing, those stories might upset the younger ones, so she read them the opening of the Mowgli stories from Kipling's *Jungle Book*. Eleanor's deep, resonant voice, which would later wield such power during the formation of the Adirondack Protection Agency, and later still, in international circles during the AIDS crisis and against nuclear proliferation, now entranced five young children with a story they only knew from a Disney movie.

Lily listened too, twirling her hair, agitating the rug with the toe of her shoe, scratching at a rough place on her thumb. She had dressed down after the wake and would have loved to go to the taproom for a drink, but the bar was closed in honor of Mack's passing (although he'd never set foot inside the place unless he had business to do there for the camp). She helped get the kids into bed after their parents came to say goodnight. Then she walked out with Ben and Sam and their wives into the frigid night air, crunching down the lane through the snow. She said goodnight to them outside Hyfrydol and headed to the kitchen, where a light was burning. She thought she'd make some tea there, sit for moment and gather her wits. She found that the Aikens' niece had had the foresight to leave the big coffee maker on. There was quite a bit left and it was still hot. She poured herself a cup and retrieved some cream from the refrigerator. She took a sip. She added some sugar, took another sip.

She didn't like coffee, really. Eleanor's mom and Doris had always made tea for her. Her own mother, she recalled suddenly, drank espresso after dinner with a little curl of lemon peel, and a snifter of good brandy off to the side and a cigarette. Mack and Mabel were coffee drinkers, but Mabel always made hot cocoa for the girls. Marlette made the best cocoa. Lily remembered her mother in this kitchen whipping up heavy cream with a balloon whisk, spooning large dollops into mugs of hot thick chocolate and sprinkling a little cinnamon and sugar over the top. Lily would stick out her tongue and lick the first sugary grains and a little of the whipped cream dissolving together. Heaven, she thought. There was no other. It was all right here in this kitchen, just out of her grasp. She felt she should be crying, but there were no tears, not for anybody, not even for herself.

Headlights outside startled her. She walked to the door. Jim had pulled up outside the kitchen, having seen the lights on. He unfolded his long, lanky frame from the cab of his pickup and stood a moment looking at Lily, before he took a step. Lily held the door for him as he listed a bit.

"Is that coffee?" he asked, looking at the mug in her hand.

"Yes, and you look like you could use some."

"Now don't you start."

"Okay, I won't. But you're going to have some coffee and a lot of it before you get back in that truck."

He sat at the table. Lily pulled up another chair. She poured him a cup with cream and sugar as she remembered. He took a swallow and grimaced. "Not as good as your mom's."

"Molly Aiken made it. I was just thinking about that. My mother always made us cocoa. How come you got coffee?"

"My dad still talks about Mariette's coffee and venison dinners during huntin' season. Once I asked her for some coffee and she gave me some, better'n this here by a long shot, I tell you. Half cream probably and a lot of sugar. I remember her standin' at the stove stirrin' somethin'. She'd bring somethin' out of the oven, some kind of biscuit or somethin'—"

"Scones. She made great scones."

"Yeah, scones. They were great all hot with some kind of thick stuff—"

"Clotted cream."

"Yeah. Clotted cream. That stuff was great. And wild strawberry jam. She called them somethin' else though."

"*Fraises des bois.*"

"That's it! You remember! *Fraises des bois.* French for wild strawberries or somethin'. I can't imagine pickin' those little buggers enough to make any jam with 'em. But I guess she did. She was a great cook. You cook, too, now? But sure you don't. You're a busy, workin' girl. That's right. You're workin' in the big city now. I hear you're a'travelin', too. Places like England and Africa and such. I ain't—haven't—ever been out of New York State. Not me. I like my place here. Me'n dad, just two guys in the woods."

Lily nodded. Jim forged on.

"And he's gettin' on. He gets on my case about the drinkin', him and Doc and Pastor Dan are all after me. But, I'm quittin' I tell you. Beat it, 'fore it beats me. This ain't me. I just need to settle down. My dad's gettin' on, you know. We'll be havin' that funeral one of these days. I hate to think about it. All these old guys, everything they know about the woods and the game, all disappearin'. Like Mack. Mack was one of the best. I've done my best to learn it all, but still. Will you marry me?"

Lily got up to get more coffee for both of them, even though she knew it would keep her from sleeping that night. "No."

"Why not?" he said, holding out his cup to her.

"Well, Jim. I'm trying to imagine you living in New York City."

"Don't you want to live here with me?"

"No. Jim, give it up."

"I can't, Lily. I'm all torn up inside over you. How's come you never call me no more, never write me? Have you got someone else?"

"I don't have anybody, Jim. Not you, not anybody." She paused to take another sip of coffee. "In fact, Jim, you're the only man I've ever slept with."

"Really? Whoa. Really? Well, then what's wrong?"

Lily just shook her head.

"I'm givin' up drinkin'. I told Doc."

"Good."

"And, looky, I ain't—I'm *not*—talkin' s'much. Did you notice?"

"Yes, I noticed. I think the alcohol slows you down a little."

"I'm a good man, Lily. I would be good for you. We had good times, Lily. I would be a good husband. Put food on the table. Work hard. We'd have kids. I've always wanted kids. Just think, Lily. We could run this place—you and me, and Mabel, too, if she wants to stay. I could keep my ranger job and do guidin' on the side, just like Mack used to do. I'm handy like him. We could get horses again and a couple of milk cows. This is a fine place. I've always loved The Hill. You know that, Lily." He wrapped his big hands around the coffee cup. "And I've always loved you."

"I know."

"So what's the problem, Lily?"

"Jim. I just don't love you," she said, looking straight into his eyes. "I don't love anybody. That's the problem, Jim. That's the big problem. I don't want to marry you. I'm sorry."

Jim hung his head over his coffee cup as if somewhere between the warm blanket folds of coffee, cream, sugar and the chill of the winter night, he could find the answer that was eluding him, that wasn't the hard one he had just heard. He took a last sip, stood as straight as he could for a tall man overly conscious of his tallness. He put his guide hat back on and his heavy jacket and walked to the door. Once there he paused and turned around. He smiled at Lily and said, "I think, Lily, I think someday you'll change your mind. I hope you will."

Chapter Eighteen

"Immortal Love, for ever full,
For ever flowing free,
For ever shared, for ever whole,
A never ebbing sea!"

"Bishopthorpe," #360, Episcopal Hymnal, 1940

Tune: Jeremiah Clark, 1700; Text: John Greenleaf Whittier, 1856

It took several years after Lily's return to The Hill as caretaker for Jim to finally realize she was never going to allow him into her life again. He had clung to hope like a rock climber to an overhang, tenuously dangling from little metal clips, fingertips and long cables. He had thought of her as his sweetheart since they were kids, and though he had fooled around a couple of times, he was faithful in his soul to Lily. No other woman had crossed his mind, until he met June at a singles contra dance at Paul Smith's College last summer. She was a forestry instructor there. She was the ex-wife of a guy he'd helped haul in for drunk driving, and he knew she had a restraining order. He may have saved her life, because the man had an illegal firearm and a couple of knives in the back of his truck, had gotten himself tanked up, and talked about heading out to visit his ex. The guy was drunk and obstreperous, and started a fight with Jim and the cops. He was now resting comfortably at Green Meadow Correctional Facility. It seemed natural that Jim would be concerned for the woman involved. They got friendly and she discovered that Jim liked to dance and Jim absolutely loved children. She had two, ten and eight. They liked Jim and he loved to take them out fishing and hiking, "traipsing," as he called it.

Sometimes, for fun, as a volunteer Jim guided for the Adirondack Mountain Club, and sometimes, for some extra cash, he guided for local resorts. He was leading a hike for the Mirror Lake Inn in Placid when he fell into conversation with a young woman from New York named Jenny. They were hiking up Pitchoff, a steep but short hike that on one side presented an impressive collection of balancing rocks and views of the High Peaks and Cascade Lake below. But Jenny wanted conversation more than views. She'd brought a little plastic water bottle and some nuts. It was a hot day in August, and she sat down next to Jim when the group took a break for lunch. She said she'd come up alone from the city for her two-week summer holiday. She was finishing med school. She wanted to know about the big families around the area. She wanted particularly to know about the Winslows and the accident that had taken their lives. Jim allowed as she was awfully young to have knowledge of that time. She said that she thought she might be related to the Martindales.

"Well, that's interesting, because, unless you come off of the French side, where Mariette Martindale hailed from, I don't know of any other way to be related."

And that's when she told her story.

She'd been born in Switzerland, twenty-seven years ago. She was adopted. In the last couple of years, as a student intern, she'd traveled back and forth to the little clinic where she was born. She was able, after some convincing of the officials, to see her records. Her mother was Lily Martindale, a fact that had long been suspected by her parents, who had followed the Martindale-Winslow story back in the day.

"When did you say you were born?" he asked.

She told him.

Jim was sitting with her behind one of the rocks out of the wind. The view from the balancing rocks spanned the High Peaks and it was a beautiful day for the view, not too much haze. He massaged his temple.

"Holy Christ."

"Why?"

"Well, the only person that Lily Martindale was goin' out with in those days, leastwise the only person I knew of . . ."

Jenny tilted her head to the left, looking at him like a curious dog who wonders what little tidbit he might be holding behind his back.

". . . was me."

They looked at each other studiously. For one rare moment, Jim Porter was speechless.

"Whoa," Jenny said.

Whenever she could get away in the ensuing months, Jenny and Jim spent a cautious time together, neither quite comprehending the truth, the good fortune, the coincidence that had brought them together. Jim was initially suspicious. Those years hearing stories about the press, the intrusions into Lily's life, the "accidental" strayings to The Hill by outsiders up to no good, had put him on high alert. Jenny, on the other hand, was delighted with Jim. She was, unlike many, content in a dreamy way to listen to him ramble on about life in the North Country, about his forays in the woods as a ranger and a guide, and especially about the old days at The Hill with the Martindales and the Winslows. She loved looking at old pictures in his house, which had belonged to his parents, and especially those of Lily and Ellie and him as kids making the movie or at a picnic at the pond, or on the deck at The Hill Next looking out over the lake, when they were teenagers.

"It's funny, lookin' back, how they were such close friends," Jim said, "yet the Martindales were technically servants, if you think about it, if you listen to the press. But then everybody was kind of family with the Winslows. They was just so friendly and good to everybody. They was so happy. Even when he didn't get elected state senator, they had a big merry, un-election party for their friends and the townspeople and everybody came, even some that didn't go along with his politics. Sometimes I still think about it. I still get sad. We all do. Hell, I was just a kid and didn't know from nothin', but boy, I understood for sure what had happened, what Lily and Ellie had lost. What we all lost. And then Padre sort of took over."

"Padre?" Jenny asked.

"Joe MacIntyre. He was the lawyer for the Winslows and he was the executor of their estate, so he was the one that made the decisions for the girls and pissed everybody—I'm sorry, I don't talk so good when I'm in polite society, but he ticked everybody off and sent the girls away, and Lily was never the same after that. She'd come back on vacations and she was just kind of weird—drinkin', drugs, actin' angry all the time. She got me so messed up it took a long time for me to get straight again. I still love her, deep in my heart, I do. I admit it. But even now that she's, you know, come back and doin' all right, it's a sure thing I don't go callin' on her. Nobody does except for Pastor Clara."

"Who's Pastor Clara?"

"She's the local Methodist pastor and a real good woman. If anybody is close to Lily, it's Clara, Clara and Joe. Lily's been, I don't know, a kind of good listener or something. Clara doesn't go up there often, but when she does, she comes back all relaxed and happy. I think if anythin' ever happened to Lily, she'd give that land up there to the church for Clara and Joe as a retreat or somethin'."

"What happened to Padre?"

"Lung cancer. The girls were pretty attached to him. Oh there was Mack and Mabel too, but Mack died and Mabel left the camp to go live with her son in California. Padre was all they had and he was a good man, I think, at heart. Just not, you know, warm and fuzzy. He was all business. Never married himself, no kids. Just them two and they were a handful, especially Lily. I asked her to marry me, but she said no. We were never again, you know, um . . ."

"She didn't have other children?"

"Not that I know of, but I doubt it. But she sure loved the kids she worked for in New York raisin' all that money for, millions and millions of dollars. Why, they say that Lily is worth a fortune if she ever went back to New York to claim what she's got. It's too bad. She was good with kids, and she could be real charmin' when she wanted to be. Just not, you know, real happy to socialize when she didn't have to. So . . ."

"So?"

"I suppose you want to meet her."

"Does she know I'm around? Does she even know I exist?"

"I haven't said a word. You're a grownup lady. I'm not good at these kinds of, you know, personal things. I'm to the point now where, much history as there is between us, I've found my peace with it all. If she needs me, I'll be there. But I'm not so twisted up about it no more. She made me crazy. I loved every minute of it, too. She's a pistol. But, what do you think?"

"Maybe I should talk to Pastor Clara. Would you come with me?"

The next day was Sunday, and Jim and Jenny attended services at the Winslow Station Methodist Church. After the congregation left, Jim and Jenny walked to the back room. Clara was taking off her polyester white robe with the needlepoint stole that Sue Ellen Finn and her mom had stitched for the time that Clara came to take over the church. The stole was beige, brown and forest green, with a deer, a bear, a moose, lots of simple pine trees and here and there a bright yellow sunflower blossom (Clara's favorite flower), and at the base of each side a cross. Stitched on the forest green felt backing was her name and the date of Clara's first sermon at the church.

She was in the back room off the choir stalls where she hung the robe and stole after each Sunday. A cup of cold coffee from Mom and Pop's was still sitting on the old pine table by a stained glass window of the Good Shepherd. Jim came in with Jenny. Clara had seen him sitting there in the back with this young woman and wondered if this could be his new girlfriend, but she seemed awful young. She was tall like him and had the same color hair, but she was dressed like a flatlander with nice slacks and an Oxford cloth shirt and a pretty jacket and those ballet slipper flats. A funny feeling came over the pastor just as Jim said, "Clara, there's somebody I'd like you to meet."

Clara extended her hand and then as suddenly pulled Jenny to her. "I think by golly that I know who you are. You look too much alike to be anybody other than a child of Jim's. Where have you been all these years?"

"Clara? Did you know?" Jim asked.

"I do now, God bless you both. I do now. You're Jim and Lily's kid from way back."

Jenny looked at Jim and said, "Well *that* was easy enough."

Frank Guilbeault Junior came in with the collection, all twenty-four dollars and sixty-two cents of it, about a buck and change equaling the number of parishioners in the congregation that day.

"Thank you, Frank," she said, "Jim, why don't you and . . . ?"

"Jenny. Jennifer Noonan."

"Why don't you and Jenny come over to the parsonage for a hot cup of coffee with me and we'll have a confab. Frank? Can you take Marla home?"

"Yes, ma'am," he replied and lifted an eyebrow at Clara's guests. Clara lifted another right back at him. He bowed out of the room, taking the collection money in a grey cash bag with him to deposit the next day at the bank in Malone.

Jim and Jenny sat down at the kitchen table at the parsonage, a simple three-bedroom, two-bath, double-wide at the end of the street that ran perpendicular to the church. The original Victorian parsonage, where Pastor Dan and his wife had lived for forty-six years, had burned down just before Clara came to take over the church. The kitchen in this new parsonage had a table with an oilcloth covering, red and white checked. The walls of the kitchen were robin's egg blue. There was an old white enamel refrigerator, sink and stove, and a collection of kitsch-y salt and pepper shakers on knickknack shelves around the walls. Over the sink was a window overlooking the back yard, where a tattered basketball net hung attached to a back shed. Above the window was the picture of Jesus praying at Gethsemane. Jenny was intently examining the salt and pepper shakers while Clara boiled water. Jenny, it seemed, was a tea drinker like Lily. Clara had a pot of coffee going, and one of the poppyseed cakes that she'd baked that morning still warm in the oven, in case anyone wanted to come over. She pulled a cold roast chicken and a container of slaw from the fridge, and some plates from the cupboard.

"Try that chicken, Jim. That's from McCalanaugh's boy over to Meacham Lake. He's in the chicken and egg business now and is doing real well."

Jim pulled off a leg and took a bite and smiled. "That's real good, Clara. They keep you supplied?"

"Well. They ought better come to church more often, but the chicken and eggs helps."

"You and Joe did a lot for them after McCalanaugh ran up against that barbed wire fence. Jenny, that's the man that Lily replaced. Skimobile accident. He still ain't quite right."

Clara refilled her coffee cup and added hot water to Jenny's cup. Jim was quiet, looking at Jenny, her face, her hands, noting the color of her eyes. She was attractive, even pretty like Lily, but had his height and hair and bone structure. And she was nice. That was the most important thing of all. And she was smart. Going to be a doctor.

Clara was watching, "So you got yourself a daughter, all of a sudden, huh, Jim?"

"I can't hardly believe it, but I'm startin' to, and it's very nice."

"And you got yourself a new woman and her with kids, too, I hear."

"June has two boys, and we get along real good. You both should know that I'm thinkin' of askin' her to marry me."

"Holy smokes," Clara said.

"Oh Jim, that's wonderful."

"Now all we have to do is tell Lily about this here. Now how in God's name are we going to do that?"

"My problem is that I have to get back to New York. I'm starting my residency soon."

"How would you feel if Jim and I went up to talk to her? Kind of break the news"

"I have no problem with that."

Jim took another hunk of chicken and a spoonful of slaw and added, "I think it's up to Lily whether she wants to meet Jenny. She's a funny one. Part of me thinks she'd be thrilled to know you were here and wanted to see her. Then again, I don't know half the time what she's goin' to say or do."

"She must've wondered all these years what happened to you," Clara said. "Any woman would wonder, even Lily. She's all business all the time when it comes to the camp, but I don't know what she thinks when it's the dead of night and the past sits there at the end of your bed and stares at you. I just know when I go up there she doesn't talk at all about the past. She talks about the camp, the raven and her other animals . . ."

"She has a raven?" Jenny gasped.

"She does. Schwartz is the name. She goes to work around the lodge, Schwartz is there. She's up at the cabin, he sits on the railing or on the roof. She goes fishing, he follows the boat and sits on the bow sometimes."

"Well, she feeds the damn thing. She's tamed it." Jim helped himself to more coffee.

"I don't know," Clara continued, "That bird kind of spooks me. Sometimes she talks to it and you'd think, looking at its eyes, that it understands what she's saying and if it could it would say something back. And all the other critters up there. They don't mind her at all."

"Here we go. We're going to make up another story for the Lily Legends," said Jim.

"No. I mean it. I'm not fooling. Someday I'm going to go up there and she'll be serving tea to a sow bear and her cubs."

"Clara," Jim said, "I think you need a vacation."

"From your lips to God's ears, sweetie." Clara pushed the plate of chicken toward Jenny. "How're you getting back to the city, Miss Jenny?"

"I have a car at Jim's." She carefully carved a bite-size piece of chicken breast after removing the skin. "I should probably head back soon. This is good chicken."

Jim was smiling.

"What are you so smug about?" Clara asked.

"Oh, nothin'. I'm just thinkin' how amazin' that I have a kid in medical school who bought her own car."

"Well, my parents, my adopted parents, put me through med school."

"What are they like, your parents, Jenny?" Clara asked through a mouthful of slaw.

"Very nice. Very down to earth. Dad is a surgeon. Mom is a market researcher for an advertising company."

"Other kids?"

"Yes. I have two adopted brothers. One is from Korea and one is from Salvador. I'm the oldest. David is in his last year of college and John is starting in the fall."

"When do you think you'll be back, Jenny?" Jim asked.

"Maybe close to the holidays in December. Depends on my schedule at the hospital."

"Well," Clara said, "we'll talk to Lily and see how she feels about all this. I'm sure it will be a bit of a shock. This time we have between now and when you get back up here may be just the ticket for her to get used to the idea. Or not. Who knows?"

"Sounds like a plan," Jim said wiping his mouth with a paper napkin.

"Jim?" Jenny asked. "Are you angry that she never told you about me?"

"Oh hell. I could be angry about so many things, Jenny. On the whole, I think it's just a complete waste of my time and energy. Sure it bothers me. I would like to have had a say in it, but I know what her answer would have been. She didn't want to marry me. She couldn't have taken care of you at eighteen. She was just too messed up. We both were. You're all right. You've got nice folks who could put you through med school and dress you nice and make sure you know how to behave. You even cut your chicken up with a knife and fork. You wouldn't have learned that from me. Maybe Lily, but not me."

"Well, it would have been nice to learn how to hunt and fish, too. I would love to live up here some day. I'm sure they need internists up here."

Clara poured herself more coffee and sat down to eat her own lunch. "Oh they do, sweetie, they do. And we would just love to have you."

"Long as you come to church," Jim said.

"Well, now," Clara said, "that'd be nice, but I don't pressure nobody no more. The Lord comes to each of us in time."

After Jenny drove off headed south, Clara turned to Jim. "You okay?"

"I guess."

"What?"

"I was kind of hopin' she'd drop the 'Jim,'" he said, putting his hands in his back pockets and staring off down the road after the disappearing car.

"Well, that might take a little more time. What I find so incredibly interesting is that you finally found a woman besides Lily that can shut you up. You are so all fired quiet around this new daughter of yours. And not only that but it seems like the minute you gave up on Lily, you found not only new love and children but you found Jenny. That's pretty cool, Jim."

"Yeah, I suppose you're right." He rubbed his nose and sighed.

"You want to head up to The Hill now?"

"I guess. No time like the present and waitin' isn't goin' to make it any easier."

Clara and Jim took Jim's truck up to The Hill. They came across Lily walking toward the boathouse with a couple of canoe paddles over her shoulder. She looked happy, and waved to them. Schwartz was just landing and folding his wings on top of the boathouse.

"Hey!"

"Hello, there, girl." Clara gave her a hug. "Can we go somewhere to talk?"

"Uh oh," Lily said, looking at Jim. "What's up? You eaten yet?"

Jim said. "We just had lunch down to Clara's," and he proceeded to run on about how good McCalanaugh's kid's chicken was and how Clara makes wonderful slaw and how nice her house looks since they painted the kitchen, that there was some weather coming in it said on the radio and he had a full week coming up. Then Lily shot him the look. Clara was amused.

At the Melita boathouse there were six bright green Adirondack chairs. Lily laid the paddles on the racks inside and took a seat with Clara and Jim. Jim told the story of the hike he took with this young woman from New York. He rambled a bit talking about the issues of guiding for resorts, but eventually he got back to the subject at hand. Lily stared off at the lake, her face a plain sheet of paper. Clara could hear her breathing, but it was as though Lily had taken leave of her body for a moment. When Jim finished, Clara told her about them coming to church that morning and then to the house for lunch. Then there was silence, broken after a time by a deep breath from Lily, who was still looking off to the lake, as if something huge might rise there and carry her away.

"Her name is Jenny," Jim told her.

Lily winced. "Jenny. Like a mule."

"Well, Jennifer then. And there's nothin' mulish about her. She's quite a nice, sweet person."

"Good. None of my doing would have turned out a child named Jenny who was a nice, sweet person."

"She'd like to meet you."

"Oh, God." Lily grabbed the sides of her head with her hands, then pounded her temples as if trying to shake out the memory. "The kid at the benefit. She was just a kid at a party with her parents. I wasn't sure at the time. Nobody said anything, but still. She wanted to take our picture. But that was the name. Jenny."

"Well, she didn't mention that. She'd just like to meet you."

Another great sigh from Lily, "What in the name of God for, after all this time?"

Jim reached down for a blade of grass. "Wouldn't you like to see *your* mother again? Even just once? Just supposin' you could, wouldn't you?"

Lily stood up. Jim could see her jaw working and knew the danger sign in that.

"Do what you want," she said. "I don't care. I'm not suddenly a 'mother' because this young woman shows up." Lily looked up at the sky beyond the boathouse roof where Schwartz was preening. "Shit," she continued, shaking her head. "Fifteen minutes ago I was happy. Not a fucking care in the world. It's a beautiful damn day. I've got my work done and an afternoon of careless enjoyment ahead of me, when you two nice, sweet people show up. You wonder why I live alone? You wonder why I struggle through the long winters up here instead of all that creature comfort down in New York City making big money and living in an apartment? It's days like this. Not a thing to worry about, and then you come along with this story. I don't understand. You know she could be anyone spinning a tale. Yes I had a child. I was what? Seventeen, eighteen years old? That's some years ago, Jim, and some serious water under the bridge. Since when are you the arbiter of truth versus legend? What if she's just someone who heard the story when she was visiting Switzerland and thinks she can cash in somehow or just step into what I hoped was finally the fading limelight of my life? Who does she think she is?" Lily had a habit of patting her chest when she was upset, as if to calm down her breathing and her heart. When she spoke again, her voice was softer. "When does it happen that I can stop saying I'm sorry to everyone. I'm sorry I'm such a bitch. I'm sorry I don't like company. I'm sorry I've hidden things from people. I'm sorry. I'm sorry. I'm sorry. *Please* go away and leave me alone."

"Well, Lily," Jim said, his voice rising. "I'm the one that's met her now, and I believe her. Jeez, all you got to do is look at her to know she's our child. Now I've got a daughter I didn't know I had, and I like her a whole lot. She's got her family and that's okay. I don't own her. She don't call me 'dad.' She's interested in the life up here, in her own, you know, history. She's just a curious young woman. Smart, pretty. We made a smart, pretty kid, Lily. I'm very happy about that. She wants to know me, and she wants to know you. You'd like her. You really would." Jim kicked at a pine cone. "Just give it a shot. She'll be back around the holidays if she can. You can think about it right along and if not, if you don't want no part of it, fine. She can stay with me, or at June's. Oh, and another thing," he said, looking away off toward his truck, wanting to be in it, to be driving away. "I've been seein' this woman down to Paul Smiths."

"So?"

"So, I'm goin' to ask her to marry me."

Lily nodded. She shrugged her shoulders. "Good," she said. " 'Bout time." Jim could see that jaw working again, impatience building behind Lily's eyes. It was remarkable, he thought, that it was so easy to read her. "Well, is that it then? All the news from town? Thanks so fucking much for dropping by." She started to walk away, then turned back. "Congratulations, Jim." Then she turned and walked up the hill toward the lodge.

Clara looked at Jim. Jim looked at Clara, but didn't speak. Together they walked to the truck, got in, and drove away.

Lily sat that afternoon on the deck at the cabin thinking deeply about how not caring was not the same as coming to terms with something, letting something go. Not caring was the antithesis of that, she knew. She had never wept over that particular loss since the child was born. She'd never shed one further tear for the baby, for Jim. She had just plowed on through life like those great V-blade road crew trucks in a winter storm plow down the state roads. But she wasn't healed at all. In spite of the wonderful summer day at the camp, doing what she was best at, smiling and whistling the tunes for each of the buildings she tended, she realized she wasn't genuinely happy. Nothing was resolved at all.

The birds at the bird feeder—chickadees, nuthatches mostly—continued with their midday meal. Lily chewed on herself, her thumb bloody, her heart going into its jazzy routine. It was time to give this all up, she thought. It's just getting to be too much. Soon it would be winter again and she'd have to face this particular demon in addition to all the others. Why Christmas? Why always Christmas?

Schwartz arrived in a black-winged fluster and settled on the deck railing. He huffed once, ruffled and preened in a fashion indicating he'd feasted somewhere while Lily was busy feeling sorry for herself. He'd had a lovely bit of rank carrion. She could just gnaw on herself all she wanted. And she did, until she stood suddenly, grabbed her fly rod and went down to put the Hornbeck in the water, patrol the shoreline, and continue with what was her current mission in life. Taking care of if not caring. Taking very good care.

$$\text{\large{☙}}$$

The next time Jim saw Jenny was at Christmas, when she drove up to visit him and, ostensibly, to meet her biological mother. He put her up at June's, over near Paul Smiths so there'd be no curiosity in Winslow Station, although, truth be told, everyone in Winslow Station knew that Jim Porter had a daughter and it was likely by Lily Martindale. He celebrated Christmas in two phases—morning at June's with her kids and Jenny, and then later he and Jenny drove to The Hill. Jenny picked at her green wool skirt as Jim chatted on, pointing out the various landmarks of his and Lily's childhood. There was very little snow on the ground for December. The sky was cloudy and it looked as though there was a good chance there would be more snow by morning. First the barn and sheds came into view, then the caretaker's cottage and Rockingham Hall and Doxology Lodge with its grand porches above and below. Smoke rose from the chimneys. Colin came out of the kitchen with a cooler and a tray. Jim parked nearby and offered to take the load.

"This is Jenny," he said, taking the tray. "Jenny this is Colin."

"We've met, I think. You're the, uh . . ."

"Noonans', Dorothy and Frederick Noonan adopted me," Jenny said, extending her hand. "I met you and Missus Livingston years ago at a fund raiser at the Natural History Museum. I was just a teenager volunteering for the Institute. It's nice to meet you again."

"My goodness, there is a likeness," Colin remarked, "especially between you two, but you have Lily's eyes and mouth I think." Colin turned to Jim and shook hands. "A doctor for a daughter! Jim you are a remarkable man!"

"I was sayin' to Clara that if we can get her to come up here, we could set her up in practice right off the bat when she's ready. This area's needed a doctor so's we don't have to truck down to Saranac Lake or up to Malone to get help. All's we got 'round here are EMTs and there's a bunch of us, but a country MD is what we really need, like ol' Doc Burton? Now Clara says—"

Colin interrupted, "Clara says that you stopped talking so much once you met your daughter, but I see that's another of her fabrications. Let's get this stuff and ourselves inside. NCPR says there's a storm coming. We thought, in view of the circumstances, we'd keep it simple tonight and so it's just usn's. Lily's not here yet. At least, not the last time I looked."

They climbed the steep stairs to the front doors of the lodge. The windows were all glowing in the misty grey gloom. There were the big wreaths on the door with their sprayed teasel and winterberry sprigs, and inside a roaring fire in the main room and a smaller one behind in the library. Eleanor was coming out of the butler's pantry with a tray of chilled champagne glasses and a glass of ice and can of soda for Jim. She put the tray down on the low table and walked over with her arms extended to Jenny.

"It's so nice to see you again. You're the Noonans' child. I remember. They were close friends of the bishop."

"Yes," Jenny said, reminding Eleanor of the night at the Museum of Natural History. "I brought a picture to show you. I've kept it all these years."

Colin put his Scotch cooler down on the floor and withdrew from it a bottle of Dom Perignon. Eleanor offered Jenny a soda, if she wasn't inclined to champagne, but Jenny replied, "I think champagne would help, under the circumstances."

"Lily should be here soon. She's always prompt about coming down. She usually stays upstairs over the holidays, like we used to. I can't understand why she wants to live in the cabin during the winter. It's too harsh, and she's not getting any younger. I worry about her. Usually she gets a big tree in here for Christmas, but she didn't manage it this year. Don't know why. Come on in, let me show you around."

Colin poured the champagne and the four of them wandered through the library and up the stairs, past the pictures of this and that dignitary and celebrity with Eleanor, Colin, Lily, sometimes Jim. They toured the bedrooms upstairs and the nursery on the third floor. Jenny, her eyes wide, taking it all in, ignoring the champagne flute in her hand for the most part.

"We'll show you the rest of the camp tomorrow. Jim? Can you stay the night?"

"Well, I thought I'd be gettin' back to Paul Smiths to see June. You see, I popped the question on Thanksgivin', and we've got plans to make."

There was a round of congratulations and the foursome settled downstairs in the main room by the fireplace.

"Jim! You must bring June up. Would you like to get married here? Have the reception here at the camp? Oh please say yes, Jim. It would be such an honor to do that for you."

"Well, thank you kindly. I'll mention it to June, but that's very nice of you."

Jenny was standing close by, and Jim reached out and put his arm around her. Just as suddenly he pulled her to him.

"I've got my whole true family together almost. Almost everyone I've ever loved, 'cept my mom and dad. Just add Lily and June and her kids and I'm a whole new man now—a family man." Jim Porter in full gush was the same impetuous little boy that Eleanor had known so many years ago. "Jenny, you are the best thing that ever happened to me. I'm so glad you've come. I don't remember bein' so happy in my whole life since I was a kid."

"I'll drink to that." Lily was standing in the entry way. She stood back as though not sure she'd come in. She was slouching with her back against the doorjamb. She was dressed in her old ratty jeans and a turtleneck with holes, underneath Charles Winslow's old raccoon coat. She hadn't bothered to take off her snow-caked Gokey boots. Her old guide's hat was smashed damply down over her head, and it looked as though she needed a bath and shampoo. Eleanor took a step toward her, but Lily held up her hand. "I'm not staying, I'm sorry. There. I said it again. Sorry I'm not dressed for the occasion but I had a little work to do today and, uh, haven't had time to, uh . . . clean up."

Lily looked at Jenny, who was still standing next to Jim with their arms around each other. Jim looked perturbed. Colin seemed to be the only one with an idea of what to do. He poured a glass of champagne and held it out for Lily, walking over to her. She took it and took a sip, then downed the whole thing. Colin winced. "And sorry I don't respect your Dom Perignon this year, Colin, and sorry I've come in at an awkward time, and sorry this is all such a weird theater set piece out of some Restoration drama. Welcome to The Hill, Jenny. You look as though twenty-seven years without us all has done you quite well.

We're an insular little family of oddities and kooks. Me especially. But we get along, at least when I'm left alone. I came up here to be alone, talk to the ghosts, find peace. Unfortunately I keep getting interrupted in my personal conversations with myself, my friends the animals, my memories. I won't bore you any longer. Good night."

Jenny stood, frozen. Lily turned to leave, pulling her coat close about her. Jim tried to follow. "No, Jim," she spoke firmly. "Thanks for the champagne, Colin."

"Wait, Lily," Jenny said, and she strode over to the woman in the bedraggled hat and squared off with her as though, mano à mano, she intended to take her on. "You're not going. You're not going anywhere. You're staying right here and talking to me. Me. My name is Jenny. How do you do?" And Jenny extended her hand. She wasn't smiling, she wasn't jolly, she was just taking the old girl on.

Lily slowly extended her hand. Eleanor and Colin and Jim stood perfectly still, half expecting and fearing that this very tall, solid young woman might flip Lily to the ground and press a knee to her chest, for all the power that surged in that moment. But there was just a simple, silent handshake.

"I'm sorry," Lily whispered.

"Lily, you have nothing to be sorry for. Nothing at all."

"Lily," Colin said, "Have another glass of champagne with us. C'mon."

Lily was still standing, hand still clasped in Jenny's. She stared hard at Jenny's face, searching for some reflection of her own, seeing only Jim, finding only the uncaring lost years. Then Lily turned and walked out and back up to the cabin, with Schwartz, ever vigilant, leading the way.

Chapter Nineteen

In the hospital, Lily stumbles through days of a sometimes drugged and foggy, sometimes lucid and active brain. Bhijan and Eleanor have had numerous discussions about her care, some with her, when she's alert. Working with the staff psychiatrist, they come up with a plan. The psychiatrist wants to send her to Burlington to the university hospital there where she can get more intensive psychiatric attention for a time. Bhijan is in a quandary. He thinks she's better off in Saranac Lake. He wishes to reduce her dosages sufficiently to the point where she will be calm, tractable but still more alert and receptive to treatment. He hates to see her restrained like a beast—this woman who has been free to roam the woods and hills for so many years. Even when he's off duty, he sometimes sits with her, quietly, wondering about the years of depression, social isolation, and their obvious effects on her physical imbalances—electrolytes, nutrition—especially since Christmas. The pain and the cardiac/atrial excitability have been a sidebar complicating all else.

The pain aggravates everything and has probably kept her from sleeping for many of the recent months. Her color is coming back nicely, but she is logy and sometimes unresponsive, as though hiding. Then there are the times when she is right out of her head, thrashing, screaming, trying to get free of the sheets. Then the restraints are used yet again.

This morning, Bhijan comes in humming. It is now early March and though it is still very cold in Saranac Lake, there is warmth to the sunlight in these somewhat longer days, and a little elusive thaw is underway. It's just enough of a hint of spring that there's a palpable sense of cheer in the halls of the hospital, on the streets of Saranac Lake, and deep in the woods where the chickadees and titmice have started calling in earnest for their mates.

Lily has been in the hospital for three weeks. The last few days she has exhausted herself. She is weak and washed-out. Dr. Habib checks her pulse, places his hand on her brow, and smoothes her dark hair, recently washed, brushed, and draped over her left shoulder by a nurses' aide. Lily is still a handsome woman, with strong features now drawn and rigid, with a terrible tension in her neck and jaw. He marvels at how her body fights the restraints even in repose. He places his hand beneath her neck so gently—the way an old girlfriend had showed him once when they talked about healing, how the lightest touch can soothe someone in distress. He leaves his hand there beneath Lily's neck and continues to hum.

Lily is underwater for the most part. Sometimes she wants to fly, sometimes she just wants to sink to the bottom like whale bones, shark teeth and shards of broken, brittle coral. Faces appear to her and recede. Sometimes she's aware of who they are—such as Eleanor, or the love-ly-voiced doctor. Sometimes she sees her father or mother, but is not sure that's who they are. Then there's her old friend Susan, free of her wheel-chair, hospitals and helmet at last, who flies past, her body now flowing and languid in the currents of air or water. Susan beckons, eggs her on. She thinks, "How lovely Susan has become. She's healed so beautifully." Somewhere above the waves or below them, she hears humming and feels the touch of a warm hand beneath her neck. She seems to know the song. No, not a song, a hymn. There were so many. Which one? Which cabin is named for it? She walks in her mind through the camp checking on the buildings, trying each door, plumping each cushion, checking the live traps, calling to Schwartz, humming along with the hymn. What hymn? Curiosity seems to make her buoyant.

Bhijan continues his little experiment. After a minute or two, Lily's face softens and her mouth begins to move. She seems to want to speak, but in fact, what emerges from the small, precise mouth is a bit of melodic hum in response to his. She even captures a phrase of the tune he has misremembered. It is a tune from chapel in Switzerland, and Lily, too, remembers—a good old English hymn and yes, the cabin, Drumclog, with the deer pictures.

"Lily," he says, "what were the words? Do you remember? Lily?"

Although the nurses have been getting her up, moving her around, Lily has remained listless, uncommunicative, often keeping her eyes closed, even when she has tried to fight them. Now she opens one eye a crack, then closes it again. She seems to drift back to that dark fluid place for a time. Dr. Bhijan Habib stays with her, his hand behind her neck or on her forehead. He continues humming, although she is silent for a long time.

Finally, "Rabbit," she says.

Bhijan gasps. He has not heard that name since schooldays.

"Yes. It's me. How did you guess?"

"Rabbit. Get me out of here."

"I'm working on it, but you keep fighting me."

"I don't fight with rabbits." Lily struggled with speech. The words came haltingly and slurred. "I like rabbits. Will you dance with me again?"

"Yes," he whispers.

She opens her eye, just one, and soon thereafter the other.

"You grew, Rabbit."

"You didn't, Lily."

"Are they after me?"

"No. They gave up."

"Will you?"

"Give up? No. I do not give up on old friends and dancing partners."

Lily sighs. "I need a friend."

"I am your friend, your doctor, and I'm here like a rock, like a mountain."

Lily yawned and tried to stretch against the restraints. "Do you like the mountains?" she asks.

"I love the mountains. I love to hike in the mountains. You remember, we used to hike at school. I loved it then. I love it now."

"Will you take me?"

"You, the hermit? You want company?"

"I told you. I like rabbits. Rabbits are okay. One rabbit is perfect. Where do you live?"

"I have a house a little south of here. High peaks. Trailheads everywhere. You'd like it. Tell you what. You get better, we'll go hiking. But you need to get serious here. You need to let us help you. Stop fighting."

"I have a raven. Do you like ravens? They eat rabbits, but only dead ones, so you're okay. Sing that song again."

And he begins again but stumbles on the words. Lily picks up the phrase: ". . . 'so longs my *soul* my *God* for thee' . . . no—it goes up there, remember? The melody goes up. 'Martyrdom' it was called, and there was another name, like of a martyr or something. But we like 'Drumclog,' I think because it sounds like a Scottish march with bagpipes, so we call one of the cabins 'Drumclog' because, I think, the Winslows thought 'Martyrdom' was too depressing for a camp cabin's name." She took a deep breath as though this exercise seemed to exhaust her.

"How do you know these things, Lily?"

"I read books, Rabbit. Lots and lots of books. Sing it again."

A couple of nurses and aides look in, hearing the singing. Pastor Clara and Joe are coming down the hall bringing warm poppyseed cake for Lily's breakfast, thinking the smell of something she loves will snap her out of this malaise. Clara is upset because there was no way she could keep the cake warm on the drive over in the cold morning. She argued all the way from Winslow Station about how they need one of those hot packs you can heat in the microwave, but the thermal lunch bag is all they have, and that's no *damn* good. Joe Finn looked at Clara as if a snake had just crawled out of her mouth.

"Well excuse me," she said. "I said damn, dammit." And now, coming down the hall shedding her down coat, she hears the soft sounds and says that word again, more softly. "Damn!"

She trails in behind the nurses, who make room for her, and there she sees Lily, drained and exhausted, looking up with something approaching happiness around the edges of her eyes as she and her doctor sing the old hymn. And Clara begins to sing along as well, and one of the aides who also recognizes the tune . . .

"As pants the hart for cooling streams,
When heated in the chase,
So longs my soul, my God, for Thee
And Thy refreshing grace . . ."

Dr. Bhijan Habib, who has been a doctor for more than twenty years, struggles a bit with his own connection to this patient. Lily had appeared at the hospital very ill, very agitated. Now she is getting better, partly because of something they shared so long ago when they were children, teenagers. They had been friends, but never close friends. Still, in some ways this puts him in a difficult position. He is having some mixed emotions, tangled up between his responsibility as a doctor with other patients, other responsibilities, and this suddenly renewed connection in his otherwise private life. He feels uncomfortable, and is unsure why.

He looks at the schedule, talks to the staff and the director, and asks to have some time off—just a day or two.

Bhijan's house near Lake Placid is a retreat invaded only by one other person—a retired widow who comes in regularly to cook, clean, and daily to walk the dogs when he's working at the hospital. This arrangement works particularly well for him, since his relationships with women have not been so successful. Bhijan has never married. He is known among colleagues and a few friends as an introspective, very reserved and somewhat lonely man. He loves skiing and hiking, and the Adirondacks provide ample opportunity for both. Bhijan, like Jim Porter, is a 46'er six or seven times over, including winter and night climbs. There is a local, very social crew of doctors and athletes who often get together for a run down Whiteface and out afterward for beers, and sometimes he joins them, but there is a rowdiness that makes him feel uncomfortable. He is not one to lose control.

And the women—some of them are very attractive, some of them he has dated, and one or two he has lived with for a time. Some are winter athletes, staff, local schoolteachers; they want either to settle down and have kids or travel the world skiing, skating or rock climbing. They seem to lack a core thing. He isn't sure what it is and has never probed too deeply for it, but it is something that needs to be filled in him as well; something that he avoids articulating whenever a relationship gets serious, though it seems to drape like a dense weaving between himself and the woman of the hour and even the sex becomes unsatisfying, incomplete.

Bhijan drives a nice car—one of the perks of being a doctor all these years. The four-wheel-drive BMW 328i SUV, bright, rosebud red is comforting, but only a symbol, he knows. Still, he drives it with plea-sure through North Elba and down Route 73 to his home. Philomena, the cleaning lady, is there, and the dogs, a yellow Lab and a golden retirever, are happily panting on the rug after a nice run out back with her. Philomena was an Iron Man athlete in days past and at sixty is still in peak form and loves to run in any weather. Sushi and Sashimi adore her. He wonders what they might think of Lily. Philomena is talking about going to live part-time nearer her kids and grandkids, near San Diego. That will make it difficult for Bhijan. Not insurmountable, but difficult. He wonders if Lily likes dogs.

When he was a child in what was still then called Persia, he had a mother and a father. His father was a well-to-do tradesman, selling elegant fabrics to the wealthy members of the Shah's Peacock Court. His mother was an educated and determined woman of the Baha'i faith. But in the mid-1950s there were persecutions and government-sanctioned (or ignored) mob attacks on Baha'is and their places of worship. Bhijan's mother was taken away. He remembers her last feverish kiss on his brow, her expression of love in Farsi, and her imploring his father to leave, get out of the country.

He was eight. He never saw his mother again, and his father never spoke of her. They fled with few possessions apart from the clothes on their backs and a trunk full of fabrics. His father, like all smart men in a troubled country, had saved money and had a plan. He and Bhijan fled to Pakistan, then India, then to France.

While his father reestablished himself in one country or another, Bhijan remembers struggling to connect with anyone. He would stare at children in parks with two parents or watch babies with their mothers. His father taught him to pray, using generic phrases patched from Islam, Hindi, Anglican. Bhijan loved his father, but his father was distracted, almost crazed by his losses. By the time they reached France, Bhijan remembers, the sadness was too great. Someone told his father about a school in Switzerland for children who had fled from political and religious persecution. Bhijan was put on a train with a few clothes and a book of the poetry of Hafez. At *L'École du Bon Berger,* Bhijan became a quiet and successful student. In his mind, he held onto the face of his mother as a talisman. He would be the perfect son, in case there was a heaven somewhere and she was watching. He learned later that his father had committed suicide not long after bidding his son goodbye and putting him on the train.

And now he finds himself in a world where he might, if he were not the long-established doctor in a small community, be a person of interest because of his cinnamon skin and his name and background. He sees this in the eyes of some of his patients. He saw it in the eyes of the FBI agents who questioned him when Lily first came to the hospital. They probably ran a background check on him. He is relieved that he never took an interest in weapons, in case they chose to search him, his house.

Suddenly, all the peace and love that had surrounded him at school in Switzerland, all the old Anglican hymns, the attention and praise that he'd received there in the absence of his parents, all that comes back as a dim memory of comfort in a world gone mad. Lily Martindale is a large part of that old, safe, comforting feeling. In remembering all of this, he thinks of Lily and her own losses as well as his. Perhaps it was the touch of his hand beneath her small and tender neck, so strained and rigid with years and years of grief. He places his own hand beneath his own neck as he lies on the floor with his two dogs. He wonders what it would feel like again to have someone, anyone, touch him with that sort of tenderness, with love.

He lies on the floor with the dogs after Philomena leaves. He has a lot to think about.

With the beginning of Lily's healing, the legend ends, such as it is, in all its forms and fantasy. Lily Martindale is taken to Burlington for a two-week-long period of observation among people who do not know her. There is not much of legend that stands up to the scrutiny of a university mental health unit staff. They have the reports from Dr. Bhijan Habib of Saranac Lake, from the FBI, from interviews with Eleanor Winslow Livingston (the well-known philanthropist and peace advocate of the United Nations), from Jim Porter, and from the Methodist pastor,

Clara Finn. They have Lily, who does not talk much. She spends much of her time writing. She ignores the doctors' questions, but likes to chat with the young medical students who come in on rounds. She is quiet and tractable and mostly cooperative, but firm in her insistence that she does not need pills. It was pills that got her crazy enough to go to the mountains in the first place. She gave them up then; she wasn't about to start them again. Then she has to talk, the doctors say. You can talk or you'll have to take the meds. So she agrees to talk.

Mike, the MD, PhD who's been assigned her case, comes in to introduce himself. Lily is staring out the window at the streets and buildings below. There is still snow on the ground, gray and dismally smashed in ragged plow piles. Off to one corner of the building, however, the one that each morning catches the sun, now rising earlier and somewhat warmer than the days and weeks before—just beside that corner in a flower bed something green is showing where the snow has melted. She's been keeping her eye on it as though it is an illusion—the daffodils beginning to emerge. Soon it will be Eleanor's birthday, she thinks. She thinks of her own birthday, which has gone uncelebrated for so many years. She is not even sure how old she is. She's not sure what the year is.

Before Mike has even spoken, she asks, "How do you live here?"

"Burlington? Burlington's a great town."

"I couldn't sleep last night."

"Why not? What kept you awake?"

Lily doesn't answer.

"Well . . . we can give you something for that."

"No. No pills."

" 'Kay. No pills, we talk. You talk first."

"No. You talk first."

"Hi, Lily, my name is Mike."

Lily does not turn from her view out the window to see his outstretched hand. He awkwardly retracts it and retrieves a pen from his jacket, pulls up a chair, and sits down. She turns and looks at him and smiles. She smiles partly because she wants to charm him, but also because he has a beard and moustache.

"What?" he asks.

"Oh, the beard and all. Is that a prerequisite for psychiatry?"

"No. I have a weak chin."

"I see. My old boyfriend, Jim, grew a beard and moustache when we were kids. Mostly to prove that he could. It looked ridiculous. Yours is all right. It's not bad on you."

"Good. Compared to looking ridiculous, I'll accept not bad."

Lily does not respond.

"So," Mike continues, "We've established that I'm Mike and you are Lily and the beard is not bad and you don't care for Burlington and can't sleep."

"I'm Lily and I don't have a beard at all. Quid pro quo."

Mike smiled. "So what have you got against Burlington, Lily?"

She sighs, and turns away from the window to face him. "I can't get out in it. I spent years in New York City and walked everywhere. I've lived in the Adirondacks for years and I hike and fish and swim in the lake. Now everyone thinks it's best to lock me up in a hospital, in a town I don't know."

"And so you're upset about that?"

"Not really. Scared. And curious."

"About . . . ?"

"Scared that you'll never let me out. Curious to know why people think I'm crazy."

"Do you think you're crazy?"

"Not at all. Just not entirely sociable."

"Well I can tell you that I can't imagine keeping anyone here indefinitely, and certainly not you. You are here for observation. You understand that."

"Observe for what?"

"Observe to make sure that you're no danger to yourself or anyone else."

"Like shooting at them with a rifle."

"Well, yes."

"Don't worry. I don't shoot at people. Only big, fast machines. No one in their right mind could accuse me of bringing down an A-10 with a little rifle. Couldn't even dent it, even if I hit it."

Mike is silent.

"I didn't hit the jet, did I?" Lily asks.

"As a matter of fact, yes," the young doctor replies.

"Really? No wonder. But, hell, look at me. A hundred and fifteen pounds dripping wet. Apparently we have a very edgy government in place."

Mike then has to explain to her that there was an attempt to bomb the World Trade Center in New York City a few years ago—a guy with a van full of explosives. They had to evacuate one of the towers. People died.

Lily is impressed. No one told her that.

Lily and Mike talk for a while. She finds he's congenial enough to laugh at her jokes, tolerate her silences when she's tired of talking. He's also serious enough not to fall for her smile. They meet regularly over the course of ten days. Eleanor comes to visit. Jim once, but she doesn't want to see him. He leaves her an invitation to his wedding. It's planned for August at The Hill.

One day, Mike asks her why she fired on the jets. She says they scared her. She'd fire on a bear, too, if she had to, if it was after her. That was the only reason she had a gun, for hunting and self-protection. They were loud, those jets. They scared the piss out of her. They were also flying lower than the law says they're allowed to. She's a caretaker. She was scared they were after her and the land. They seemed to be stalking her, surveying the property as if they were going to claim it, take it over for the military or something. She is sorry, but that's all to tell.

"I hear you have a daughter," Mike ventures.

"Oh, that. I'd rather talk about the jets."

"Why? What's wrong with talking about your daughter?"

"I'm not a mother. I would never be a mother. I seem to be lacking in maternal instincts."

"Well, it must have been odd to have, suddenly, this young woman show up . . ."

"Odd. I'll say odd." Lily chews on her thumb. Mike sees that it is bleeding and watches as Lily sucks the blood from the side. She tells him about the day Clara and Jim came out to tell her. How happy she had been that day before they showed up, how serene and content with the world, and then, suddenly, it's all haywire again.

"How do you mean, haywire?"

"Suddenly everyone's looking at me to exhibit some kind of *emotion.* All I can come up with is 'I'm sorry, but I don't really care.' No guilt. No regret."

"You gave birth to a daughter and made sure she had a good home and then lived with that knowledge the rest of your life."

"Again, I'm sorry. I don't care. I should feel guilty for not feeling like a mother. For not wanting to see her. For not caring about her, about Jim. About only caring for myself, my job."

"A caretaker."

"Ironic, no?"

"Do you want to see her again?"

Suddenly, Lily turns on him like a sow bear cornered. "No!" she shouts. "I don't *care* to see her again. She is not a baby. She is not *mine*. I don't know why she suddenly wants to show up again."

"Again?"

"She was at a party in New York once. She volunteered as a teenager for the institute where I worked. She asked to have her picture taken with me. There was this whispering thing going on with her parents. I was very suspicious of her. She was the right age, the right look about her. I just wanted to get the hell out of there. I wanted to . . ." Lily's voice trails off and she takes up the alternate destruction and nursing of her thumb again.

"Wanted to what, Lily?"

"I wanted to die."

Mike leans back in the chair. "Wow, Lily. That's big. That's really, really big."

Lily takes a deep breath. "But instead, I came to the woods. I came home. I gave up pills. I gave up alcohol. I got straight, strong and even found happiness alone. That's not sickness, Doctor Mike Whatever, that's not madness. That's health."

Mike asks, "Do you think you'll go back to the cabin, live alone again?"

"Not sure. I think I'm done with that. Eleanor and I have talked and she agrees that it is time for a change. I'd like to go somewhere warm, where my joints won't hurt as much, where the living is a bit easier, where I'm needed but not to do so much hard physical work. I'd join a convent if I was religious, but I'm not really. I like kids. I could be a teacher if I had a certificate of some kind, but I don't. I'd travel, and I have lots of money so I can do what I want, if the government and FBI will let me renew my old passport. I can pretty well do what I like, but I'm not sure what that is. I like the desert, but haven't thought much about which desert where. But I'm ready to retire from caretaking. That's a given. I just need to go back to the camp, pack up, say goodbye. A plan will come to me. Eleanor will help. That's all."

"No, that's not all," Mike says, "I'd like you to do one more thing."

"Oh God, what's that?"

"I'd like for you to meet with your daughter again."

"Why?" There is a pleading tone in Lily's voice.

"Because you haven't convinced me that all that emotional upheaval has been resolved. I think it's the last piece of the puzzle for you, for your health and happiness, that you establish some kind of rapport with this young woman who is your flesh and blood."

"Mike, you know there is much more to a relationship than flesh and blood. She may be mine biologically, but she is not mine emotionally."

"Well then, that poses the question about why you fell apart physically and emotionally after you saw her at Christmas. And I would suggest that you have, in effect, walled her out so that you *don't* feel the feelings, whatever they are, that are really there. That there is more to having a heart than just wearing it out with stressful beating."

Lily stares at him, her face hardening.

"Lily, I don't mean for you to take her into your life to have around like a piece of furniture or an article of clothing. You are right. She has parents. But she doesn't have *you*. You've blocked her out, and that's not right. You need to grant some access to this part of your life, make peace with it and her, let her know that she's welcome to visit, to talk about whatever."

"No. I don't. I won't."

"You're afraid?"

"Afraid of her? No. *You're* crazy." Lily, who has recently become so peaceful with her situation, now is getting angry.

Mike stands to leave. "I'll talk to you more about this tomorrow, maybe."

"Maybe? Mike! You've got to let me out of here. You can't keep me here any longer. I'm okay now. Jenny is fine. I'm fine. I just don't see the point. I'm *not* her mother. I never was."

Mike spins the chair around and sits leg-straddled with his arms over the back, "You are, at least biologically, her mother, and that counts for something. You need to honor that. You need to agree to feel, I don't know, at least agreeable about having brought a life into the world and being able to let her go. Many women could never do that."

"I was just eighteen, for God's sakes. I didn't know what I was doing. I was a complete idiot."

"You gave birth to a child and it was painful, and it was painful to let go and walk away. You just need to agree to acknowledge that and open up to, I don't know, opening up."

"You're not making any sense."

"Lily. Listen to me. A little memory work here. Describe *your* mother to me."

"Why?"

"Just tell me. What did your mother look like?"

"I . . . I . . ."

"Close your eyes. Whatever you remember."

"Apron. Flour on her hands. Flour in her hair. Her wedding band. Her hands."

"Describe her face to me."

Lily is breathing shallow and her mouth is slack and open slightly; she opens her eyes wide. Mike is struck by how like a little girl she appears at that moment, helpless, alone, scared witless.

"I can't. I don't remember. There are photographs at the camp. Lots of them. I can't see her face." And Lily begins to cry, not so much crying as keening and moaning as she bends over clutching her stomach. Mike reaches out and lightly touches her shoulder.

"Lily. Lily. A lot of this is just about love. Losing love, especially losing a mother and father's love, is the hardest thing we ever have to face. Losing all that love when you were little was just more than a kid like you could bear. You've suffered from that loss your whole life. It's made you angry and sour and lonely from the fear that you'll lose love again." Mike scratches at his beard and sighs. "And here I am asking you to open your heart to your own daughter. It's scary as hell. It won't be the same, but it will be something, Lily, something to bring the love back, allowing you to feel for another person, even just a little bit. If you can do that, you are a just a step away from a truly happy life, not just an intermittently happy one." Mike stands up, stretches and rubs the back of his head. "You need to cry for a long time, Lily. Cry and cry and cry. Then we'll talk again, okay?"

Lily does cry, and cry, and cry. Then she sits on the bed and practices remembering. It is a long and powerful meditation on the memories of her mother's and father's faces. It takes hours. The exercise frustrates her. She draws what she can remember in her journal. She writes pages and pages of descriptions. She writes about going through the drawers and closets in their old rooms above Rockingham Hall after the accident, of finding her father's work shirts and jackets and burying her face in the deep flannel softness; finding her mother's lace handkerchief from Paris, and inhaling deeply the scent of Chanel she wore before that Christmas. But the overpowering, lingering memory of scent she remembers most is flour, things baking in the oven at camp, breads, rolls, scones, cakes, cookies. And things roasting—rosemary and roasted lamb impregnated with slivers of garlic, standing rib roasts with Yorkshire pudding, roasted potatoes and roasted root vegetables with celeriac and fennel. Then suddenly she remembers aioli and bouillabaisse, artichokes and melted butter, chocolate and rum vanilla melting in the top of a double boiler and her mother's arms about her, as she licked the dark brown happiness from a wooden spoon or the heavy cream from the whisk of the Hobart mixer still there in the kitchen at the camp.

How can she say goodbye? How can she have eaten from cans all these years and not returned to that kitchen to cook? If she could bring Jenny there and show her what it means to be in that kitchen with all those wonderful smells, *Maman* at the stove, sitting exhausted with a glass of brandy and a cigarette at the table after a dinner for twenty or thirty, holding Lily in her lap and singing to her. Her mouth a lovely round "O" of red lipstick, her pageboy of brown hair, brown like Lily's, like Jenny's, her peach cheeks, round eyes brown with long lashes like Lily's, like Jenny's. And Papa in his scratchy tweed jacket, brown wool overcoat and red tie—tall, handsome, smiling at her, picking her up in his arms to kiss her goodbye before he gets in the Packard with the others and drives away down the long road out of camp. They are going to Montreal to bring presents back for everyone. It is a wonderful thing to be so loved and so happy. It's going to be a wonderful Christmas with everyone there and lots of presents and *Maman* singing to her in the kitchen, the *buche de Noël* fresh and dark from the oven, waiting to be rolled and decorated, waiting for Lily to help. Oh those wonderful smells—the kitchen and her mother's perfume of flour, rosemary and Chanel. It is good to be alive, to be filled with love and happiness.

It takes a few days and a few more conversations with Mike. Mike wants to make sure that this feeling is real, not something she has manufactured in order to please him, to get out of the hospital. More and more in their conversations together, Mike senses that she is more curious about the prospect of reestablishing a connection with her past, with

Jenny. Lily finally asks for permission to make some calls. First she calls Jim to get the number of Jenny's apartment in New York, and patiently listens to him telling her about the wedding plans. Then she calls Jenny. There is an answering machine with Jenny's businesslike voice. "Please leave a message."

"Hello. This is Lily. I wanted to talk to you. I wanted to tell you," she says, "about your grandmother, Mariette, and your grandfather, Robert. I was just thinking how much you look like your grandmother, my . . . my mother. I think you would have liked to have known them, and I think they would have been delighted with you." Lily pauses. "I *would* like to get to know you better, so if you want to talk, or write, or visit, let me know."

"There," she thinks when she hangs up. And the feeling is there, some real feeling, a little tenuous and uneasy, but made real by just hearing that voice, that voice and Jim's, too. The feeling is that everything might just be all right. Might just be okay. Finally. At last.

If she just had a plan.

The plan, or at least the beginnings of a plan, comes from Bhijan. He asks if he can come visit her in Burlington. Not as a physician, but as a friend, an old school chum. She shows the letter to Mike. He agrees. Bhijan drives to Burlington and spends part of a day talking to Mike and then to Lily.

"You are much better," he says.

"Yes."

"What next?"

"They say I can leave soon. I have to stay in touch with somebody over in Placid. I have her name."

"Where will you go?"

"Not back to the cabin. But I need to go get a few things. Say goodbye to . . . to all of it."

"To New York with the Livingstons?"

"No, not New York. Well, I have things in storage there. I need to get that all squared away."

"Where, then?"

"I don't know. God knows I can do whatever I want, but I don't want to do it alone anymore. I can't. It worked when I had the structure of the daily routine of the camp. Then, last Christmas, it all started to fall apart. I lost control."

"So . . ."

"So, what about you? How are you?" she asked.

"I don't know. I've been stuck for awhile. This is a great area, but I'm not sure I'm doing the best for me, for my career. I'm not getting any younger. What do I really want to accomplish in the years before I retire? What if I left my job, found someplace else to practice, something more challenging or more, I don't know, more of a social or humanitarian service? It's scary as hell."

"So, not leaving medicine, but leaving the area? Why do you have to leave? It's not like you've done anything except help people."

"I like it here. I would hate to leave."

"Where, then?"

"I don't know. Things are different now, lately."

Lily gives him a look. Her eyes narrow a bit, as if in considering what he has just said, she is alarmed. Then those eyes widen, not so subtly, so much as to say, "Oh."

She is to stay at the university hospital for another week, during which time Eleanor and Mike meet once more. Although Lily has said nothing to Eleanor about her conversation with Bhijan, the change in Lily since Bhijan visited is as obvious as the change of season going from the past winter into the current spring. Eleanor, sensing that something might be afoot, has a long conversation with Bhijan and finds nothing at all to raise concerns and everything to give her the great satisfaction that Lily might have found someone worthy of her and even able to handle her. Even if it never elevates beyond the status of old friends, they seem like two halves of an old seashell, rejoined comfortably and seamlessly.

Lily is allowed "off campus" to walk outside with Eleanor or Bhijan when they visit. With Eleanor she is quiet, even solemn, but with Bhijan she seems happy—something Ellie cannot remember since Lily was a little girl. Much of the stress and worry has drained away from her face. Her heart rate has returned to normal. Except for some lingering discomfort, she is doing well physically.

For her own part, Lily is content whether in her room or at meals with the community of sad people in the hospital, many of whom she speaks to. Many are students in crisis—drug and alcohol related, exacerbated by exams and papers. None of them, not one, knows or cares about the story or the legend of Lily Martindale and the great American tragedy of 1952 and all that followed. But when they hear that she's been living on her own in the woods for more than ten years, hunting and fishing, eating out of cans and whatever she could catch or grow, they are thrilled by this older woman. That someone could leave the city, a high-paying job and career, and live all alone; that is really something. And not only that, but to take on an A-10 with only a rifle! That, in the words of one liberal-minded student, is awesome! And this becomes an important part of her sense of self again. Somehow, in screwing up one last time, she has become a bit of a real live heroine, like someone in a movie, protecting the sacred land that she loves against all odds. In the movie, she would die trying. In the legend, she'd be turned into a raven or a bear—something substantial like that. In the real world of a university mental health ward, she is a living, breathing inspiration.

The discharge papers are signed. Lily says goodbye to the crew on the ward. Mike embraces her and wishes her well. There's a bouquet of daffodils from Bhijan. She walks out of the hospital at UVM very conscious of the difference between the April day and the day in February when this all began. Ted Kaczynski is in custody, ending the Unabomber search. Easter will be coming soon.

Colin drives her and Eleanor to Lake Placid. Lily plans to take a train to New York City, stay at Colin and Eleanor's brownstone, and start dealing with her belongings in storage. This will take a couple of weeks. In the end, she will get rid of all of it, right down to the last plaque and slotted spoon. The only thing she'll keep is a cookbook that belonged to her mother.

When Lily returns to Lake Placid, she checks in with everyone, including Bhijan. He invites her to dinner at the Mirror Lake Inn. Spring is still struggling to assert itself in April.

"You have spent a great deal more than forty days within your own circle," Bhijan says. He has ordered a nice glass of wine for himself. Lily sticks with water and lemon.

"What?"

"Hafez, do you know Hafez?"

"No," Lily replies.

"Poet. Persian. The greatest poet ever, to all Persians. He was born about two hundred years before Shakespeare and is as revered in Iran and Afghanistan as Shakespeare is in the West. No. More." He lifts his glass of the fine claret. Bhijan's eyes, Lily notices, have the very same glint and glitter that they had back at school when he got excited about some small thing he'd read or that someone had said. "It is said that Hafez drew a circle, sat within this circle for forty days. He was sixty years old or so."

The waitress arrives with Lily's salad and Bhijan's crab bisque.

"Was this his, um, the forty days and forty nights that would have us singing lugubrious hymns?" Lily smiled.

"Yeah. Kind of. Except there was a woman involved."

"Really? That's different."

"Well, he'd seen this beautiful, rich woman many years before when he was a poor young man delivering bread around the city of Shiraz in Persia. He knew he was never going to win her, so he devoted his life to the search for something more, something . . ."

". . . more spiritual?" asked Lily.

"Yeah. Not so much God, or Allah, but something like the connective tissue between that sort of passion for spiritual love and human emotion. Anyway, he comes out of his circle after forty days and runs into this beautiful woman from his past. He has a glass of wine, like this," he said, turning the glass this way and that and sipping again, with some relish, "and at that point, he achieves something like, I don't know, oneness, enlightenment."

"Did he get all shiny, like Jesus on the mountaintop? Are you going to get all holy on me?"

"Oh Lily, no" Bhijan said laughing. "You are so funny. I have missed you so much. Missed that irreverence. I tend to take myself way too seriously. That's something else you've reminded me."

"Really?" She waves away the proffered taste of his wine and clinks her glass of ice water to his. "Bhijan, you don't know me so well. A lot of years gone by. As you have probably gathered, I am not known for my social skills."

"But you have been through some pretty tough changes in the last year. It's as though you have been tested in the wilderness . . ."

"Oh please. Let's not get all philosophical when I'm not sure I even believe in God anymore, in any religious sense. I don't know what I believe. My time in the wilderness, as you say, was not a test. The real test was New York. I had to make a name for myself other than that nauseating Cinder-Lily that everyone romanticized. I had to become something, anything but cute and sweet. I was one angry, cranky, whining bitch. The problem, Bhijan, is that I still am. On The Hill I was happy, or at least I thought I was. I could be just as pissed off as I wanted and not offend anyone."

"You were happy until you realized what? That you couldn't escape completely? That everything that haunted you followed you?"

"Ghosts and secrets have a way of doing that, don't they?" Lily buttered another piece of warm roll.

"I have my own ghosts and secrets, too, Lily. In that way we are also alike. Uncannily so. When you came into the hospital, something changed in me, seeing you again. Not just that I had known you in school, but that you were, like me, a loner—solitary by circumstances, by duty, by personality. I felt a connection. And I was so happy when you remembered me. That was a wonderful moment for me. Someone remembered me from my lonesome childhood, someone who had made me laugh even though we had both lost everything we had loved." Bhijan takes a sip of the bisque. "This is wonderful. Taste this." He holds a spoon out to her. She takes the offering and closes her eyes. It is wonderful. There's a little hint of sherry, something her mother always used in cream soups like this.

"Would you like some salad?" she asks, and holds the plate up. He picks a piece of spring lettuce, with some vinaigrette.

"You know," he continues, "I feel so presumptuous here, but I feel that perhaps that you will understand me. Hafez says something about the jewels you get when you meet the Beloved. The jewels go on multiplying themselves. They take root everywhere. When we were singing that hymn in the hospital about the thirsty hart and the cooling springs, it's not just about yearning for love, whatever kind of love—spiritual, whatever—it's about searching for the Beloved. Here's the presumptuous part: I feel that when I am with you, and every time I am with you it grows. Not as a doctor for a patient he is caring for and not necessarily for a lover either, but for an old and dear friend."

"Perhaps you and Hafez mean the one who plays the tune on the wind chimes."

"The tune?"

"At the cabin. There is someone who plays a tune on the wind chimes. Not often, not always, but sometimes, and it is the Beloved. That's what I called it. I believed it was someone who was coming for me. I thought at the time it was a real person. But it could be something bigger—spirit, God, or even death. I thought I was dying. I thought that would be the only way to meet this Beloved."

"So you know what I'm talking about?"

"I think so. Everyone is searching for the Beloved. It is the only search there is, really, especially for those like us who lost so much so young."

Bhijan lets out a deep breath, and he takes another one in again.

"Lily Martindale, would you like to stay with me?"

"What?"

"I have plenty of room at my house. I'm often at the hospital. I have a housekeeper who comes in a couple times a week, walks the dogs and generally takes care of things, but she is leaving to go out west. You could stay, you as my friend, for a time, until you know what to do. We can share responsibilities around the house. I don't expect you to be my caretaker. You can ramble all you want in the area. The High Peaks—"

"Dogs?"

"Do you like dogs?"

"Yes! I love dogs. I've never had a dog. I've always wanted a dog. How many dogs?"

"Two. Sushi and Sashimi. They are rescue dogs from the shelter. Those two are a handful, but I think they would like to have someone to be with them more. Take them hiking. Calm them down. Then I have my own life to figure out. This change I'm thinking of. The winters are harder on me, too, Lily. I feel it in my back and knees. It has been hard for me living alone, too. It would have been harder to have had someone else in my life. It's the key reason no one has ever stayed with me, with my schedule so frantic at times. I'm not Mister Party Person, as you well know. Not so social like some of the guys up here. I'm always at the hospital. I'm thinking that has to change, too. I think I need to move on. I don't know. What do you think?"

"So you really mean it. You're going away."

"That's why I wanted to talk to you some more. This change. This story about Hafez. You and your Beloved. Me and mine. Like that."

"Like that. You and me. Do you mean we are each other's . : . ?"

"What do you think?"

"A soul mate? Someone you share a soul with. I've never thought of such a thing. Do you mean you want to be with me?"

"Well, a lot depends on how you feel. What you think at this point in your recovery and after so many years alone, without anyone. What do you think?"

"I don't know. All I know is that I think I like dogs."

"So, come meet my dogs? As a trial. See if you like it, if you feel safe and comfortable there."

"Live with you."

"Maybe not right away. It's likely you need more time, and I want you to have all the time you want. Then we'll see. There are obviously some things I have to think about, but I think it will be all right. Will you come, if I can work it all out?"

"Can I have another taste of that soup?"

"Sure, here."

"Thanks. I'm not sure, but I feel . . ." Lily pauses; she ponders that at that moment she has used such a word, and the use of it is beginning to soften something that had grown rough, like a callus inside her. For a moment, she thinks she is afraid, and that bit melts slightly, too.

"What do you feel, Lily?"

"I'm worried that I'm going to fuck up again. I'm not, never have been, a reliable sort of happy-go-lucky, what-the-hell person. What if it didn't work out? What if you walked out on me, and it was the whole stupid mess again? What if I went crazy again?"

"I realize it may take time," Bhijan says.

"It may indeed," Lily replies.

"It may not work, after all," he continues. "We may both be disappointed."

"It's a risk."

He holds up his glass of wine toward her. She reaches out, not to drink, but to clasp her hands around his, around the glass.

Chapter Twenty

"For the Joy of human love,
Brother, sister, parent, child
Friends on earth, and friends above,
For all gentle thoughts and mild . . ."

"Dix," #296 (alt. tune), Episcopal Hymnal, 1940

Tune: Conrad Kocher, 1838; Text: Folliott Sandford Pierpoint, 1864

A few weeks later, Bhijan and Lily make the drive to his house carrying one suitcase full of the clothes that Eleanor and Lily had purchased in Burlington. Most of what Ellie has gleaned at the cabin is in such an advanced state of wear and disrepair that it isn't even fit for rags. But Lily's boots are still in pretty good shape, and Ellie has found a couple of sweaters she gave Lily years ago, still in plastic bags and untouched by the mice, although the boxes they were in had been chewed clear through. Lily is dressed in jeans and sneakers, her hair trimmed by a friend of Jim's fiancée. Eleanor offered to take her for a facial and manicure, but Lily said that was going too far, too fast. It was enough to be peeled clean of her old clothes, her old role, cared for instead of caretaker. It is still a little odd, but she is learning to deal with that the way she has dealt with everything since she returned to the woods—in silence, paying attention, listening, and being present. Right now she is very, very present to Dr. Bhijan Habib. It is a sunny April day, but the mountains are still snow-covered and the melt steadily drips, forming ice in the shady parts, huge blue-white ice falls extruding from rocky ledges near the road.

Bhijan glances over at Lily during the drive, trying to get a reading from her face, but she looks so serene—a little smile, her eyes alert and watching the landscape. He, too, remains silent and pays attention mostly to the road. As they drive along, Lily reaches over and lightly squeezes his hand. He looks to his left at the walls of grey rock, white ice and a bristle of birches and pines rising straight up the sheer rock face of Cascade above the still icy coating of Cascade Lake. Just as quickly, Lily releases his hand. They drive on. Bhijan turns left onto a long road to the low lands that lie amid the Adirondack High Peaks.

After another mile or two, they pull into a driveway. Bhijan's house is a one-story contemporary log and stone structure with high windows set in large gables. Her father would have built such a place—spacious, lots of room to sit and admire the view. She imagines it would be the same inside, with a large stone fireplace when the view turns inward to the heart after dark.

As he pulls into the garage, she hears the dogs.

"Now, Lily," he says, "be careful. They are, um, exuberant."

"Dogs. Not one but two." Her eyes are shining. The dogs are barking and scratching on the inside of the door. What explodes from the house are two beautiful animals—one a golden retriever and the other a yellow Lab. They are all over Bhijan and Lily, almost knocking her down in their excitement. She sits on the concrete floor of the garage and hugs them and scratches their ears, allowing them to crash into her until Bhijan calls them to order and reaches a hand to Lily to hoist her up. The dogs follow them into the house where Lily, again, sits on the floor and lets them mob her. Bhijan returns to the car to retrieve a couple of bags of groceries.

Inside, Bhijan's house is wide open. Lily can see the living room from the kitchen. There are large picture windows and decks surrounding three sides in the rear, with a view of the High Peaks and a back yard, actually more like a field, that rolls down to a larger field. He has filled the interior very simply with comfortable furniture, the kind you can order from catalogs, and wall hangings made of fabric, collected by his father in Persia at the time of the shahs and the Peacock Throne. There is a large woodstove in a spacious kitchen and a huge stone fireplace in the living room. Lily puts down her bags and walks around the living room touching the fabrics and running her hands over the books in the large bookcase at one end, feeling the texture of the stone fireplace and hearth. She returns to the kitchen to help with the groceries, but soon wanders back to the living room to stare at the peaks outside the windows. There is a wind coming up and a soft tuneful sound coming from the deck. Wind chimes.

"What do you think?" he asks.

She just smiles.

Lily's chimes had been a gift from Colin and Eleanor one Christmas early in Lily's tenancy at the cabin. Colin had specified that the chimes be in a major chord scheme. A minor chord would sound lugubriously Asian or, worse, Gregorian, he thought. The major chord notes seemed positive, even enthusiastic, hopeful as though the winds and breezes brought good news, change, relief. In violent weather, the hysterical concatenation was almost unbearably urgent. Lily would sometimes take the noisemakers down until the winds eased. In winter, the ice would form in a great cascade off the roof and paralyze the chimes, and Lily would have to use a hammer to free them. But how pleasant was a morning in any season when a light breeze rose and the chimes awakened her, washed her brain clear of the terrible song into which she had written herself. Colin hadn't realized how important they would become in her solitary life.

Once, in early September, Pastor Clara paid a visit, after Labor Day, when the guests of the camp had left to go back to their cities. Lily had eased into her new role as caretaker and moved beyond being a mere oddity to someone like Clara Finn. The weather was still quite warm and sunny that September. Clara wore her swimsuit under a shift. She and Lily went down to the lake on the trail, Schwartz in his usual attendance. Lily did not have a swimsuit but stripped off her work shirt, jeans and boots to join the pastor in the water.

"I don't know how you can go buck-naked with that old bird watching."

"He doesn't know from clothes or no clothes."

"Well, still. He gives me the willies sometimes. I think he'd talk if he could." Clara shimmied out of her dress and dipped a toe in the water. "Lily girl, you've been up here some time now. Have you, you know, figured out what you came here to figure out?"

"I'm still waiting."

"For what?" Clara asked, splashing her face with lake water.

"For the answer to come walking through the door."

"Well, you never know up here in these hills. The damndest things happen."

When they'd finished their swim, they climbed back to the cabin and sat on the porch. Lily dried off and dressed inside while Pastor Clara sat on the deck, in an old wicker chair that had an ottoman and a seat cushion that covered a hole in the woven bottom. She loved that chair. She sat contentedly looking out over the lake. Lily came out with a poppyseed cake that Clara had brought and two mugs of tea on a tray. There was a little breeze, and the chimes rang happily at the side of the deck. Schwartz sat on the railing near Clara and Lily, in case they wished to offer him some of their cake. Clara remarked how lovely the chimes sounded, how peaceful.

"Someone visited me recently," Lily said. "You know what I was saying before about waiting for the answer to come through the door?"

"Who?"

"I don't know who, but he plays the chimes in a melody for me. It happened last month and again last week. I got up to look but no one was there. I went down to look for a sign—you know, footprints. Nothing. Isn't that strange?"

"I don't wonder. Jim maybe?"

"No. Jim would think twice about coming up here. I don't know who it is. At first I was a little scared, like someone might be trespassing and fooling around. But no. I couldn't find anything. It kind of had me on high alert there for awhile. But now I wait for the next time."

"You know what I think?" Pastor Clara said. "I don't think it's strange at all. Someone's looking after you."

"You mean like spirits?"

"Well, I like to think of angels. I have had more angel experiences than all those shows on television."

"They have angel shows on TV?"

"Yes, ma'am. But they've got nothing on my life. Why, I can't tell you the number of times somebody has just appeared out of nowhere to help me with something or someone, and then I never see them again."

"Usually in August?" Lily said smiling.

"Well yes. No! Lily, you rat. You know what I mean. Once I was trying to help Marla. You don't know Marla. She lives up over the ridge over there, way back, and she likes to come to church, but she can't drive and she's big, you know, real big. So I go up to fetch her of a Sunday when I can get up the road there in the pickup and bring her down. Once last winter she met me down at the road so I wouldn't have to drive up. I don't know how she made it all the way down without falling; but don't you know *then* she slipped and fell getting into the truck, and I couldn't lift her. Here we were in the middle of nowhere between here and Malone, and what was I gonna do with a three-hundred-pound woman down in the dirt and ice? Well along comes this big black GMC pickup, and this guy gets out, and he comes over and lifts Marla like she weren't anything much and helps her into the truck, and I thank him and we drove off. I says to Marla, 'Marla? Did you get a good look at him?' And she says, 'Oh, my Lord, yes!' And I says, 'He was gorgeous!' And she says, 'Oh, my Lord Jesus, he *was*!' He must have been about six foot four and a face to die for."

"So the man in the black pickup was an angel?"

"Well, I defy you to find a man with a face and a body like *that* anywhere in the State Park. Not an ounce of fat on him. He was something really special. I asked around, but nobody knew who it was."

"New York plates?"

"Yes, ma'am."

"I think I would agree it must have been an angel."

"Yes, ma'am. Out of nowhere he shows up. And I never saw him again."

"Amazing."

"So I bet that's who's ringing your chimes there."

And Lily laughed until tears came to her eyes. Clara smiled, quite sure, as she told others in the hamlet of Winslow Station, that not only did Lily have a raven, but it was quite clear that she was being attended by angels as well.

Chapter Twenty-One

"Rock of Ages, cleft for me.
Let me hide myself in thee."

"Toplady," #471, Episcopal Hymnal, 1940

Tune: Thomas Hastings, 1830; Text: Augustus Montague Toplady, 1776

At the very top of The Hill Next stood a glacial erratic of enormous size, pushed and tumbled smooth by half a continent of slow-moving ice and left perched like an archeological relic on the lip of the escarpment. It was named "Toplady" by the first generation of Winslows. Toplady became a key picnic spot, safe-home in hide-and-seek games, and Gettysburg's Little Round Top to be claimed in war, or an ambush point for Cowboys and Indians. From Toplady's position on the escarpment, the whole of The Hill Next was visible in a 360-degree view, which spanned the area from the lake, to the back of the last guest cabin (Picardy) at the main camp, and off to the west over the field, the apple orchard and the kettle pond in the distance. It was a noble spot for sitting and watching, favored not only by people but by fox, coyote and Schwartz. From this vantage, anyone could survey both the roughly twenty acres that belonged to Lily Martindale and the countryside beyond.

Lily and Eleanor, like their predecessors, had a great fondness for Toplady. It was approximately the size of a couple of pickup trucks, with the ends rounded down and enough grab-holds and cracks to give access to the summit—a spacious area to sit and admire the view. Over the years, improvements to the view were afforded by axe and chainsaw. Occasional pruning was needed to keep it clear enough to see the lake. Once the cabin was built in the late forties, the rock picnics and games were more easily supplied, and were augmented by retreat space at naptime for the little girls. The stream was near enough to keep a bag of beer or soda bottles chilled in the rushing freshet, which tumbled down the hill and along one side of Toplady at an approximate sixty-degree angle. The water ran into the cistern, fed the outdoor shower, and streamed through the pipes to the stove and under the stone floor to provide ambient heat in winter.

Robert Martindale was a clever engineer, but he could not have foreseen the events of that spring. It was probably in late April, as Lily was beginning her new life after her hospitalization, that an amazing thing happened. No one was sure exactly when, after the snow of snows that winter and more snow on top of an already significant base, but the melting and freezing and rivulets of water inundated the foundation of Toplady and saturated her compacted-but-permeable soil base. The overrun from the stream sped up the process, and with the help of gravity the land underneath the great rock shifted, there on the edge of The Hill Next. The greater-than-average rains of that early spring swelled the stream, which quickly became a flume of sizeable proportions, which increased the erosion and the flow of silt and granular matter down the hillside below the great rock.

Farther up the stream, above the field and past the kettle pond, was a neatly constructed beaver dam, against which a significant buildup of snow and ice, and now flood water, pushed. First in a trickle, then a rush, then a cascading torrent, the dammed-up water burst through, flooding the field where Lily had stood only a couple of months before in the snow with her rifle. The accumulated water tore along the stream bed and smacked old Toplady on her backside. With the sand and soil around her prodigious bottom already loosened and then removed by the swollen freshet, Toplady started to shift for the first time since the Ice Age. At first it was a slow, almost imperceptible movement, then, as more of the sandy soil eroded away and a muddy slick formed on the downward slope, gravity took firmer control and the slurry of silty mud lubricated the path of her descent until she slid like a giant child on a snow tube down the hill. She wiped out, flattened, and erased the old privy, the wood pile, the such-as-it-was garden with the BMW in her bathtub. It rammed so hard into the rear wall of Robert Martindale's exquisitely constructed cabin that it caved in the back of the stove before it came to rest more or less in the middle of the room, taking out three of the four walls, a chunk of the entry, and the side porch. Had the slope been steeper or the cabin less sturdily built, without such a deep stone base and rock foundation, Toplady would have slid all the way down into Winslow Lake, startling the trout and sending a little tsunami sloshing up against the docks at the marina in Winslow Station.

Pastor Clara liked, of an afternoon, to wander up to The Hill Next in Lily's absence and sit on the deck. Before the ice went out, she and Joe would sometimes take the skimobile across the lake to check on things at the cabin, make sure it was undisturbed. They even talked of buying or renting the place when Lily decided she wanted more time away. When the road reopened (Joe also ran the town plow and grader, doing this favor for Mrs. Livingston and the fire department, in case they needed to get in to the main camp), Clara would call Jim to let him know she was going up, but it was getting so he was never around much any more.

So one day after Easter, she drives up on her own, just to sit and be with her thoughts and the Lord.

It isn't a particularly warm spring day in the Adirondacks—maybe forty-five degrees—but the radiance of the sun's higher angle is cranking up the BTUs, and Clara feels the warmth on her back as she trudges uphill through the mud and melting snow. She notices first how deeply the path is guttered, as if the spring rains and the snowmelt runoff have excavated two or three gullies in addition to and including the old worn path itself. Even the bell is listing under its own weight. As if to warn the angels she is coming, she rings it gently before proceeding.

It is slow going, and her boots are covered in mud up to the ankles when she reaches the top of the path. And there she sees the demolished cabin, the splintered walls, and that old gigantic boulder squatting placidly like a mother toad in the middle of it all.

Her breath gone, she stands in shock, not sure what to do, witness to a death almost, a murder, a terrible loss on top of all the other losses. She feels like a refugee, returning after the wars and battles to find the remains of the old homestead. At the base of the mudslide, just beyond the reach of destruction, she recogizes the stone fireplace, the lakeside wall, and the deck, the precious deck where Clara loves to sit. Still there is her favorite chair, surrounded by shards of wood and glass. Clara stumbles toward the deck and what is left of the steps. She clambers up carefully and surveys the wreckage. It is all but complete. She gazes, stunned, at the great rock, which sank into the crawl space after smashing through the stone floor and rests on a tangle of twisted pipes, splintered logs and a jackdaw's nest of pillow down and mattress ticking, blankets, clothing, books and cardboard, which the critters had been borrowing for their spring nests. The old raccoon coat, which had once hung from a forged iron hook beside the door, lies in the wreckage like sodden roadkill, partially visible under one corner of old Toplady.

Clara bows her head. At the end, that is all she can think of, all she can ever think of. When she's finished praying, she dares to enter the cabin to see if there is something, anything, to salvage. There isn't much. On the inside of the lakeside wall is Lily's little desk where she sat recording the days' events—who was at the feeder, what needed to be done, or what had been done, in the camp. Clara had always been curious about the journals—black, blue, or green composition books filled with Lily's fat boarding school scrawl and little sketches of birds or animals. The desk is one thing that has survived out of reach of the destruction, and beside the desk the old military trunk that had belonged to Lily's father, still with his name and unit information stenciled on the outside. On top of the trunk is an old ratty copy of Dickens's A Christmas Carol.

Stepping gingerly and fearfully inside, Clara checks the desk. Eleanor or Jim must have come when Lily was in the hospital and taken the last bills. She'd seen them there before, in the clamp of a clothespin on a piece of fishing line that Lily strung over the desk for just such a purpose. There are no bills or envelopes there now. In the clasp of another clothespin is a photograph, something Clara has never seen in the cabin before. It is a group photo of Lily, and, yes, that must be a much younger Jenny, and Eleanor, all dressed up for a party or something. The photograph is bent and cracked. Lily is the only one not smiling. Clara jiggles open the desk drawer. Inside are a half-filled notebook, and a variety of pens, pencils and artist's gum erasers. Clara removes the notebook. She tries the trunk. It is latched but not locked and is full of old notebooks. This should be worth preserving, she thinks. She drops the last notebook on top, shuts the trunk and relatches it. She'll have Joe come up and drag it out of here to store someplace safe from rust and rot. It is a measure of her dignity and pride that she, against overwhelming desire, does no more than glance at the journal before she drops it into the trunk. She turns to go, and hears a distinct voice at the back of her mind whisper, "Who are you kidding?" It is then but a small step back to unlatch the trunk and release all earthborn pride and dignity, to step into whatever portion of heaven or hell Lily Martindale had created for herself on earth here in the Adirondack Mountains. Pastor Clara, two voices raging inside her, stoops once more to unlatch the trunk. She retrieves the journal that she has just relinquished. She takes the book outside to the deck, and in front of the Lord and the lake she opens it to the first page, dated August the previous year.

Do you remember when you were first in love, really in love? That frisson through your whole body, every fiber, every nerve? I woke up that way this morning when the chimes rang. The barred owls were singing "Who cooks for you?" which must have awakened me just before dawn and usually their calling makes me despair. Then I heard the chimes. Someone was ringing the chimes, and I don't believe it was the wind. The notes were too purposeful. I ran to the window, but once again no one was there. Just the idle swinging of the clapper, although the air was quite still. Someone was out there, and I know I am loved, and I love in return. This happened back in June sometime—the first time. There were storms then too that blew away the muggy dark air and left a blue sky with a few full, white clouds like Wedgwood. I could feel my dreams lightening. There was the merest breeze when I woke between five and six as usual. I was lying half awake, half asleep, floating. The birds had just started when suddenly the wind chimes began, eerily as though someone was standing there picking out the loveliest little tune. I heard nothing else, but as the music played, I felt all the muscles of my body relaxing and softening.

Later on as I worked outside on the woodpile, the breeze would come up over the lake and the chimes would ring, but they would ring a 2-note ding, dong—very uninspired, unenthusiastic, like a dull student in a boring music lesson. I went over to the steps several times looking for some sign of another person's passing—a print, a bent twig, grass pressed down in a way I would notice. I was prepared to be as astonished as Robinson Crusoe finding a footprint, but I was disappointed. What I heard this morning was a tune, played as though for me to waken and be cheerful. My heart is so moved that anyone would care to serenade me, and troubled to wonder who.

It's gorgeous, this feeling, perfect. The late night thunderstorm from the south blew the heat and humidity away and left these tatters of white clouds in a deep blue sky. On the mountains and ridges surrounding me, the white pines tower above all else—ragged fingers but graceful like an old dancer's hands with long fine nails and yet some swelling and rigidity about the joints. I am so in love. I am living my dream. I have found peace at last. I peek out at the world from my cocoon, my cabin, and find myself elastically drawn to it. In sharing my voice, my words with others, I am guided to some larger vision of myself, my natural environment and the people I must, I'm sure, return to serve again. I cannot avoid humanity entirely; I can only withdraw significantly to reflect on what I need to assimilate. At some future time, a time I can feel is not far off, I will rejoin with some semblance of good humor, however painful. The chimes have taught me that, have brought me hope and love.

But who is ringing the wind chimes?

And this entry in October:

The little area behind the barn, between the barn and Mabel's old Victory Garden, is where, over the generations, Winslow pets were buried. Cats mostly, but the occasional deer mouse or found bird.

On a dry summer morning it is peaceful to go there. Ellie and I were always big on funerals as a result of our twisted childhood. When she once found one of the barn cats dead, chewed by a fox, she took the remains and made a little bier of a cardboard box and a fire between two cinderblocks upon which the cardboard box rested with the cat's remains (and I do mean remains) on top. I was the priest using Charles Winslow's Book of Common Prayer for the Rite of Burial.

I imagined a scene out of Disney, where birds and rabbits would hop up and deer would stand by shyly at the edge of the Great Forest all solemn and reverential as they did for the glass casket of Snow White. Here we were, age 7 and 11, dressed in black and holding candles in broad daylight.

I think back on that now, the crackling wood fire, the bloody furry body scorching and smelling, our feet shuffling back away from the smoke and cinders. Finally hours later coming back to stir the ashes of wood and cat and little split sticks of bone—a little bit that we could box up and trickle over the lake. But, knowing us, we never got around to that last part. Besides, we probably remembered that cats don't like water. The burning was enough. We would end up distracted with another game of the day, teasing the horses, harassing Mabel to make cookies with us, hammering and sawing on some fort building project with Jim. We were like all kids who knew how to be kids, even after reliving the funerals over and over and over.

And this a few days later:

In the streets of New York City, I became adept at the empty face and purposeful walk, the stance that's supposed to save you should you be marked for a mugger's random attention. The ambling, head-bobbing tourists, gear all wrong for the streets, were most visible and vulnerable. Staring up at the towers of St. Patrick's or the Empire State Building or Rockefeller Center, they'd never see or feel the sneak-reach in the old pocket or purse and the grab for the goodies. I've seen it done.

There were great and good days in the city when my heart sang—the weather and all else in my life weighing in close to perfect on a scale of one to ten. Still I was always wary and alert, conscious of my surroundings and the proximity and bearing of all those around me. My radar was turning constantly, my heart under wraps.

Even moving up here to the mountains was tricky because the tendency on a good day is to let fly against the silence with all that old, pent-up emotion, the great songs from the best shows. Who would hear? But somehow I'm concerned that in drawing any attention to myself, the hunter's rifle would point my way, the moose or bear I can't see would charge. The tree would fall precisely where I'm standing—or the avalanche.

So I remain pretty quiet these days, not tempting fate. In there, in that space, is the sense of control over exactly when and how I might exit this life to the degree that it is possible. I think about it all the time and when I do there's this faint, nearly imperceptible flutter in my otherwise troubled heart—an intimation of joy.

Clara notices that there are no entries recording the time when she and Jim came up to tell Lily about Jenny. And there are no entries for a long time afterward. For someone as methodical as Lily, this is remarkable. Clara doesn't wonder that the news was a shock to Lily's entire routine. Then there is an entry dated in early December:

This morning there is a terrible sadness upon me like snow upon a hemlock bough. Like Nature herself, I am ancient enough to realize that if I am too stiff and resistant, I will break under the weight of it. But if I let the feeling settle over me at its own pace and without any resistance, it will cover me for a time, but I will not be broken. At the first rays of sun, or breath of wind, the burden drops away. The old ceremony takes on a new meaning this year. I wish I could let the day pass like any other day, but Ellie and I share it and since she is coming, we acknowledge it again, supposing that the speaking of it can command the sun and the wind that frees us. It never does. And now there is this new, younger person wanting to join us in this burden. I don't understand, and I don't condone it.

In the past we would light the candles near the picture of our families, Mack, Mabel and Padre and say a sort of prayer for peace in our hearts—especially mine. Even without children, Eleanor has found her heart's peace. I simply could never imagine a storybook ending for me and Jim—I don't care how the gods could have managed to rearrange the events of our lives, there was just no way I would marry him and bring that child up in a life of such unbearable sadness. Of course, Jim would have refused to see it that way. That's why everybody but me seems to attain happiness. Once again I'm resisting and this old branch is getting more and more tired and sore.

One Christmas before our parents died, we were taken up to Wilmington to meet Santa Claus at that Christmas place there—a tourist trap by most accounts, but a lot of fun for young children. And the Santa was a very special Santa, although I didn't know it until much later in my life. He was the well known, genu-wine, Adirondack hermit, Noah John Rondeau, who had fallen on hard times, lost his camp at Cold River in the blow down of 1950 and took odd jobs like this for employment.

I was shy and didn't want to ask Santa questions, but Eleanor did. To me, to be famous meant like being Roy Rogers or Gene Autry and being on television or in Hollywood, but this guy, with his real, soft white beard and sad eyes was Santa to me, and therefore as close to famous as I might ever get. We had our pictures taken with him. Quite a crowd had gathered, as I recall. Not so much for Santa, but for Charles Winslow, who was about to run for State Senate, and might be United States President someday and his pretty wife, who might just be First Lady. Funny, I never thought of Charles as being famous back then, but he surely was. And Emily. Emily was a natural. She was gorgeous.

Noah John Santa Claus asked me what I wanted for Christmas and I said that the turkey was enough because I like to eat it so much. He said he knew where to go to find them, and he'd shoot me one big wild one with his gun. Would I like a partridge, too? I said, no, I didn't care for partridge, but I had some quail once and thought they were tasty if you picked out the shot. He said that quail didn't grow up here. He asked me if I liked venison and I said yes, especially the way my momma cooked it with the currant sauce she made over the stove at the camp. He told me about his venison stew that he made at his little place at the North Pole just outside of Saranac Lake.

Then it was time for Eleanor. She asked him if she could hire him as a guide, which he thought was funny, but she was serious. She said she'd asked her dad for a Remington over-and-under and a Battenkill bamboo rod from Orvis, and she wanted "Santa" to take her hunting and fishing and teach her how to use them since everybody was talking about how he was the best mountain man there was. Noah John laughed and laughed until the tears ran down into his big white beard. I don't know if anybody had told him who Eleanor was or who her daddy was, but I'm sure he heard about it later when they died.

Ellie never got her gun and her rod, being so little, and that last Christmas, everything was destroyed including years of Christmases to come.

I never saw Noah John Rondeau again, and yet I remember him so well. The books I've read about him make him sound sort of odd and cranky and strange and sometimes violent. I even hiked down to Cold River once with Jim to see if I could find his Town Hall, but very little is left. His little hut was dismantled and reassembled at the Adirondack Museum. Noah himself is buried in North Elba. I've even been to his grave once. It's a nice little cemetery and a nice little grave, but he wanted to be cremated and dusted around the river where he lived and fished and trapped and hunted.

I have left my instructions very firm on this account. I'm bound for Mabel's old Victory Garden on the hillside behind the barn that catches the southern light. I wish to be reunited with years of cow, chicken and Percheron muck. That garden grew in the shortest of seasons the most sustaining bounty for my mother's famous cooking—the element of the life I loved so much for so short a time before it was irretrievably lost. I can't think of a more complete way to be reunited with my loved ones. My heartbeat is so weirdly irregular these days, and I am in so much pain in my back and legs, I can only think that it won't be long.

And finally, this last entry dated just after Christmas.

One would think that connecting with one's own flesh and blood, one's child, would be like touching the face of God, that final missing link to immortality and peace, but instead it has smashed me to pieces. I had, by the touch of her hand (she wanted to shake hands with me!), every last vestige of serenity utterly destroyed forever. I walk about shuddering and trembling and it is not from the cold. My heart is a mess. I ache all over and tingle and hurt. I feel like nothing more than sitting the days away in the rocking chair by the stove or the fire place. I have no enthusiasm for my chores, for living. Once again I thought of wandering out in the night and lying down in the last darkness. I cannot bear the thought that she is accessible, that we know where she is and seemingly wants to be a part of my such-as-it-is-life. Jim has so readily embraced her and accepted her as if she is the most normal thing in the world, as if she had never existed apart from us. It's as though I had never condemned her to exile from the fold, The Hill. I don't understand all of this. I haven't a clue and it's driving me crazy. Who is she, this standing miracle, this proof that I am nothing more than a common tyrant, a coward?

Clara snaps the book shut, goes inside, and finally allows the journal to drop back into the trunk. She walks out to the deck and sees, still hanging off the wall, the snow shovel and the push broom she'd seen Lily use to sweep the leaves and pine needles and snow beyond the railing. Clara uses them now to clear the glass and splintered wood, chunks of ice and snow, and other debris. She pushes it all in a pile over to the edge of the deck. The old wind chimes have fallen there, too, and she feels she does not have the right to resurrect those, as they would add too much life, too much of Lily's spirit, back into the broken dead mess of the cabin. Only Schwartz lingers, and he seems to keep his distance, making noises that sound like little croaky whines. She cannot tell if he is angry at her presence or Lily's absence or the destruction of the cabin.

When she has finished her little chore, she sits for one last time in her favorite chair and looks out over the lake, thinking nothing in particular but with one grand sweep of thought about all that has passed and taken with it her sorrows and Lily's. She thinks of her own coming to Winslow Station, her early days dating Joe Finn, her son, still serving in the military, her odd friendship with Lily and her losses, the trips to the hospital after she fired on those A-10s. Gazing into the nearly cloudless blue sky of a quiet spring afternoon, Pastor Clara knows that ineffable peace that comes when there is nothing that really matters any more except this view and the promise of warmer weather to come, the return of the geese already gathering on the receding ice of the lake. It is the old story of redemption and rebirth. Losing herself in these mountains, Lily found the sound of the wind chimes, ringing out the hope that someone would come for her—a lover, a daughter, a friend.

Charles and Emily Winslow spent part of their honeymoon at The Hill, having sailed back from England after their wedding. One of the first things they did was walk to the old rock and climb it to see the view. They had spent the day talking with Mack and Mabel about their plans to use the camp as a primary home, even raise their children there, out of the public eye, away from the circus of society life in either London or New York. Charles had asked his co-pilot, Robert Martindale, to join them with his new wife, Mariette. Together, Charles hoped, they'd get the old camp humming again, fix things up a bit, bring in some more livestock, invite guests (but not too many) for summers and Christmases.

Emily was in love with the plan. The only thing she might miss was riding, but Charles pointed out the proximity of Saratoga. He'd keep a plane at the airstrip in Malone and they could fly off to the races, or to the city or Boston or Montreal whenever she wanted a change of scenery.

What about schooling for the children? The new bride was curious to know how such a rural community as Winslow Station supported a school. Charles said they would visit the one-room schoolhouse, which served kindergarten through eighth grade, and they'd augment lessons with a governess, one of Emily's choosing. Then the little 'scapers would be off to one of the better boarding schools, if they liked—one that emphasized community service, perhaps even a Quaker school. These children would be strictly brought up to know the value of work and strength from living out of doors. There on the top of Toplady, he quoted Rousseau on education to her and she rolled her eyes, shook her head, and leaned into him. He coiled his arm about her waist and pulled her to him and kissed her. Charles Winslow enjoyed kissing this woman more than anything else, with the possible exception of flying. Life was wonderful, wasn't it? He asked her. Life couldn't get any better than this.

Pastor Clara officiates at the wedding of Jim Porter and June in mid-August. June's two boys are the co-best men and also give her away. Jenny is maid of honor. June wears a pretty blue cocktail dress and carries a bouquet of Queen Ann's lace. Jim has on his dad's 1940s ranger uniform, complete with creased, broad-brimmed hat and spit-shined, old-fashioned, lace-up leather boots. It is a Saturday afternoon about three o'clock at The Hill and it is bright and cool enough outside to have the service down at the lakeside. Most of Winslow Station is there and a contingent of uniformed rangers from around the state who have worked with Jim over the years. All together, there are about one hundred guests. The Noonans, Jenny's adopted parents, are there, too. Sue Ellen Finn has engaged a caterer from Lake Placid. There is champagne, compliments of Colin. Eleanor, in the full bloom of retirement, greets the incoming guests, poses for pictures with the bride and groom, and leads the toasting. Two Pembroke corgis and Bhijan's two dogs have exhausted themselves fetching Frisbees and tennis balls—an assignment given to June's two boys before the wedding. The dogs lie quietly during the ceremony.

Lily and Bhijan have driven up from his house, where Lily has been in residence for two months. Bhijan has left his job at the hospital, put his house on the market, and started putting stuff in storage. Lily and the dogs officiated at a very successful garage sale. The press came, which rattled her for a time, but they seemed more intent on reporting her departure from the camp after ten years than dragging up the past and the nonsense with the A-10s. She gave them the bare minimum of information, which they seemed to accept. The plan, she told them, is to drive across the country to New Mexico or Arizona with the two dogs and a few clothes and some gear. Bhijan has a lead on a couple of jobs. She intends to work with children again. No, she's not on any medication. She's fine. Just the hard work and worry about The Hill had gotten to her after ten years or so. Stay tuned. Life is good and getting a whole lot better. Thanks so much to everyone for their care and concern.

Throughout the ceremony and the reception, Lily and Bhijan hang back, quietly watching the proceedings. It is only when the music begins that Bhijan takes Lily in his arms and they step forward and begin to dance. It is a stunning moment for the people at the reception. Lily and Bhijan have apparently been practicing. With some artful, thought-out moves, she spins and twirls in a very un-hermitlike way. If not as elegant as Rogers and Astaire, they are precise and graceful in their movement together. The music is Cole Porter. The dance floor is theirs. Lily and Bhijan glide together under the great white pines and tamaracks.

Jim, June, and the kids and June's mom take off in the limo with the usual rattle of tin cans tied on behind. Jim and June are headed to the St. Lawrence Seaway for a boat cruise honeymoon. The boys will stay with June's mom in Malone.

Jenny and the Noonans, who were seated with Lily and Bhijan at dinner, have exhausted all lines of conversation and watch the remaining events quietly together. Jenny's parents retire early to their cabin—Picardy—and Jenny to St. Dunstan's. The high point of the evening for Jenny came when Lily led her parents and Bhijan through the house showing them the photographs, especially the photographs in the old butler's pantry. Both Eleanor and Lily have agreed that the photograph taken of them all tonight at Jim's wedding—Eleanor, Colin, Jenny and the Noonans, Jim, June and the boys, Lily and Bhijan and all the dogs—will grace the pantry wall, finally closing the nearly fifty years' gap that has loomed there since the tragedy. The last photograph will mark the beginning of the new heritage of The Hill.

The trio has finished playing, the caterers are clearing away their equipment, the guests have all left, and the last photographs have been taken. Bhijan, his arm around Lily, stands outside on the porch of Doxology Lodge and waves goodbye to Pastor Clara and Joe Finn, the last to leave. Even Eleanor and Colin have retired.

Bhijan asks, "When can I see your cabin, or what's left of it?"

Lily turns her head away.

"Come on. Let's get flashlights. I'm with you."

They walk arm in arm past the cabins. The old bell has been taken down by someone. The trail is overgrown, and there is a little barrier there and a "keep out" sign. Lily is quiet, and Bhijan leaves her alone with her thoughts. They maneuver around the sign and up the slope.

When they reach the cabin, Lily stands off to the side taking it all in, her arms wrapped around her own shoulders as though she is cold. The path carved by the big rock is still clearly visible as a brown scar deep in the side of the hill. The shed, the outhouse, the garden and its resident Blessed Mountain Woman shrine have all been obliterated. Toplady squats amid the wreckage of the cabin. Nothing has been moved except what could be reclaimed of her few belongings. Jim and Joe Finn retrieved her father's trunk with her journals and notebooks. There is a literary agent in New York who is keen to look at them, so Lily sent a few. Now there is talk of publishing them, but Lily is not eager to start that. She is not eager for anything except to get away, away with Bhijan. It will be a while before she comes back again to the North County. She will come back, but right now she is ready to go.

She looks around for Schwartz, realizing that he did not make an appearance at the wedding in spite of the number of guests and available food. She climbs up onto the only accessible portion of the deck, cups her hands around her mouth, and cries out in the deep croaking locution of the raven's call. Then she waits. After a minute, she tries again. Bhijan has clambered up onto the deck to join her.

"Wonder where he is," he says.

"Dunno. Maybe he sees you. Maybe he knows."

"What do you mean?"

"That he doesn't need to look out for me any more."

"Is that what you think?"

"Why? Is that crazy hermit talk?"

"Well. It's not exactly what you would call reality-based, but it's very, I don't know, kind of romantic and charming, like a fairy tale. The legend of Lily Martindale and Schwartz."

"There was no legend. He was like a dog, you know. Good company, good old chum of a boy."

"Sounds like Jim."

"Yeah, Jim's like that, too," Lily says. "But Schwartz knows me better." She cups her hands around her mouth and calls again. The lake is still; there is no breeze at all. The moon is just rising to their left. They stay and watch for a bit and then wander back down to the lodge.

The raven has been sitting all the time in a big pine off to the right, in the shadows. He watches them leave, then flies off in the opposite direction toward the marina.

Epilogue

It's autumn now. Quiet settles over the camp—a quiet that will remain for a few months more. But come next summer, the woods, the inlet, the town of Winslow will come alive with visitors to The Hill, the historic Hill.

It has been settled. Sold. Not as a private camp to some precious rich people from Texas, Connecticut or California. Not to be developed into lakeside condominiums. Here there will be environmental conferences, orienteering classes, college groups, no-octane regattas, elder hostels, weddings, workshops, fly-fishing weekends, bird walks, family reunions. The Hill Next has been acquired as well, annexed back to the camp as it had been in the early Winslow days. Now it is all a part of a vast historical landmark, a not-for-profit outpost for environmental and historic preservation, forestry education, and the tradition of old-style Adirondack logging. A place to stay and wander with colleagues, kids and grandparents learning about the woods, the Adirondacks, the history of the buildings, the first families, the rich folks who "camped" here.

Jim has offered to teach and guide here now. June is a volunteer. Joe Finn has his hands full with reconstruction needs around the camp. Eleanor is a major fundraiser. Lily and Bhijan are patrons. Frank Guilbeault Junior is back and forth all the time with boats and boat repair and newly purchased craft—mostly no-octane. Sue Ellen Finn is thinking of going into the catering business for the special events and benefits held at the camp. Her daughter is keen on helping, so between the two of them and the store, business is hopping. Jenny and her parents come to the benefit and support the fundraising efforts in New York City. There is new work for local artists, musicians, rustic builders and craftsmen of all kinds. The Hill is now more hive than hermitage.

The new caretaker and his wife are a young couple from Canada. They have come to have a look at the buildings and grounds. The loss of the cabin on The Hill Next is particularly saddening; it would have been a perfect place for them. They discuss various ways to try to reclaim, perhaps rebuild, at the top of the hill, if they are allowed to by the state historical preservation society. But it is clear that the water damage, erosion and destruction the glacial erratic created is potentially a hazard for guests visiting the camp. The new caretaker's top priority will be to bury Toplady, tearing down what's left of the cabin, perhaps making from the timbers a marker or monument to honor Robert Martindale's construction and Lily Martindale's time there as caretaker.

As they walk around the wreckage, a raven lands on a tree branch nearby and then glides down to the remnants of the deck. The new caretaker's wife watches as it strides purposefully over to a pile of leaves, pine needles and broken glass in one corner and begins to peck at something there underneath the junk. The caretaker's wife approaches slowly to see better and her eye catches the glint of something round and metallic. The raven, she thinks, is attracted to the shiny metal, so she investigates. The raven hops to the railing as she brushes away the leaves and moves aside some bits of what had once been an Adirondack chair and an old, much mended pair of snowshoes. She finds a cluster of metal tubes connected by nylon fishing line and she recognizes, as she carefully extracts it, the still strung-together components of a wind chime. Lifting it, she untwists the chimes from the tangle of line. The wooden paddle and clabber are missing, so she digs through the junk pile until she finds them, and manages to reattach them to the line. She mutes their clanging by gripping the chimes under her arm. The raven watches her patiently, as he had watched Lily so many times before.

The caretaker's wife searches the side of the standing wall and discovers a railroad spike driven into the wall over the balcony railing. Here she rehangs the chimes. Both she and the raven stare awhile at their dangling and quiet, pretty ding-donging. The caretaker's wife reaches into her pocket and pulls out a packaged granola bar. She unwraps it, breaks it in two, and places half on the railing close to the chimes. She eats the other half. The raven strides over to the offering, but bypasses it to examine the wind chimes. The new caretaker himself has now come around the corner and is watching the events on the deck.

"Ho, ho!" he whispers. "That must be the legendary raven we heard about from Missus Livingston. There's also supposed to be—" and he starts to speak of the bathtub shrine, but his wife hushes him.

The raven approaches the wind chimes and with his beak gently tests one and then another of the old pipes. Then, with seeming purpose, he knocks one, hops around, and knocks another, then another, and finally, grabbing the paddle carefully in his beak, makes the tones ring softly, gently in a lyrical little melody—dreamlike, full of legend and fairytale and even a slight hint of a love song.

Author's Note

The snippets of hymns that appear at the beginning of each chapter refer loosely either to the action or tone of the chapter or the location of the action, inasmuch as some of the buildings at this fictional camp are named after the tunes of hymns. Each hymn quote is followed by its number, its composer, the lyricist, and their dates, in that order.

In most hymnals, the title of a hymn refers to the subject of the hymn (as in "Ora Labora" or "Come Labor On") or the location of its composition (as "Geneva" for Geneva, New York) or the name of its composer or author ("Toplady" for Augustus Montague Toplady, who wrote the words, "Rock of ages, cleft for me"). The hymns quoted in this novel are chosen from the 1940 Episcopal Hymnal because the Winslows and, by extension, Lily—in her upbringing if not her later years—were practicing Anglicans. Hymns tend to repeat, overlap, and change depending on the service and denomination.

Often, hymn tunes and lyrics are swapped around, but the hymn can always be identified by the name of its tune. "Hyfrydol," for instance, has two different sets of lyrics, and the set used herein ("Love divine all loves excelling . . .") has three different tunes: "Hyfrydol," composed by Rowland Hugh Prichard, 1830; "Beecher" by John Zundel, 1870; and "Love Divine" by George F. Lejeune, 1872.

"Doxology," the name of the lodge building at The Hill, is the only name of a tune *not* listed in the index of the Episcopal Hymnal. The term *doxology* means words of praise and is generic to any Christian faith recognizing the Trinity. The actual tune most churchgoers are familiar with is called "Old One Hundredth," referring to Psalm 100 ("All creatures that on earth do dwell"), and was composed by Louis Bourgeois. The words "Praise God from whom all blessings flow," etc. are listed as hymn

#139 in the Episcopal Hymnal among the hymns for Thanksgiving Day. The words were written by Thomas Ken (1637–1722), who (for any fly fishermen out there) was brought up by his brother-in-law Izaak Walton, author of *The Compleat Angler*. In the Episcopal churches this author has attended, the Doxology is not used as part of the regular service. It was, however, used every Sunday in the Presbyterian Church I attended as a child, and was known simply as "The Doxology."

The compendium of information on hymns, composers, and their history used is *The Hymnal 1940 Companion*, Third Revised Edition, prepared by the Joint Commission on the Revision of the Hymnal of the Protestant Episcopal Church, USA, and published by the Church Pension Fund, New York (1949, 1951). www.hymnary.org was a viable source of information, which I found very useful.

Acknowledgments

This book is presented with special thanks to Beverly Bridger and Dr. Michael Wilson, Barbara Glaser and Paul Zachos of Great Camps Sagamore* and Uncas (some of the earliest W. W. Durant camps, which were an inspiration but are not represented in this novel). Also, thanks to the "WMDS" (Nancy White, Marilyn McCabe, Kathie McCoy, Lâle Davidson, and Elaine Handley) for their continued support and cheering. Marilyn McCabe kindly granted permission for her poem "Hermit I" to be used as an epigraph for this book. The cover painting, "Whiteface Landing" was graciously allowed by Laura Von Rosk, a great Adirondack artist and friend. Thanks also to Joseph Bruchac Jr. for sending me his poem, "Mannigebeskwas," and to both Joe and the late Carol Bruchac for being such strong supporters of local poets and writers. Also to Robert Miner, Jay Rogoff, Doug Glover, Dr. Jeff Flagg, and Dan Berggren, who were early listeners. And to Father Paul Evans, Gordon Boyd, and Bob Bullock, friends from Bethesda Episcopal Church in Saratoga Springs, who loaned me books and chatted with me about hymns and A-10s; also Liz and Kernan Davis, who provided geological advice and information. Many thanks also to Bob Heinsler, the late Lillian Van Welenef (former park ranger), and Vitolds Arste, who shared their time and conversation with me, who have devoted years to the caretaking and service of Great Camps Sagamore and Uncas, and who have enriched the Adirondack Park by their presence, concern, and care for the landscape, architectural treasures, and the people there.

---

*Great Camp Sagamore, formerly the Alfred Gwynne Vanderbilt camp, designed and built by William West Durant in 1899, is a National Historic Landmark dedicated to Adirondack historic interpretation, preservation, and environmental education. It is a not-for-profit organization open to the public for tours and for residential programs such as Road Scholars, Grandparent/Grandchild camps, and program weekends at reasonable rates. Check out www.greatcampsagamore.org, to visit and support this worthy, un-hermit-like retreat.

My fearless early readers were Nancy Walker, Geneva Henderson, Dr. Gary Oberg, Jillian Leider, Eve Sorel, Lâle Davidson, Kathie McCoy, Elaine Handley, Maria Van Beuren, Rob Igoe, and my husband, Vernon Hinkle. Many, many thanks for your support and egging on.

Thanks to the Adirondack Mountain Club for getting me out in our huge and beautiful state park and to Jerold Pepper and the Adirondack Museum in Blue Mountain Lake—a wonderful place to wander with history on your mind and time on your hands. Thanks to the New York State Council on the Arts, a state agency, for funding this project and to the Saratoga Program for Arts Funding and Saratoga Arts for making all that possible. There were numerous Saratoga County and Adirondack libraries, reading groups, and historical societies who were kind enough to invite me to read from the book as a work in progress. Also, huge and heartfelt thanks to Nathalie Thill and the Adirondack Center for Writing for their recognition of so many struggling regional writers.